*We Are Pleased to Provide You With
This Advance Reading Copy.*

*Please Send Any Mention or Review to
Media@HardCaseCrime.com*

Title: **SUPERMAX**
Author: **Ken Bruen & Jason Starr**
Publication Date: **November 11, 2025**
Price: **$19.99 U.S./$26.99 CAN/£10.99**
ISBN: **978-1-83541-225-1**
Pages: **608**

PLEASE NOTE:
*This is an uncorrected proof
and not the final edition.*

Acclaim For the Work of KEN BRUEN and JASON STARR!

"Two of the crime fiction world's brightest talents, Ken Bruen and Jason Starr, join forces for one of the year's most darkly satisfying and electric *noir* novels…This is one of the top guilty pleasures of the year."
—*Chicago Sun-Times*

"This tense, witty, cold-blooded noir…reads seamlessly—and mercilessly…Funny [and] vividly fresh."
—*Entertainment Weekly*

"Adventurous crime-fiction fans who like their literary escapism totally unrestrained will find this brazenly violent and downright vulgar novel…as filthy as it is fun."
—*Chicago Tribune*

"A full-tilt, rocking homage to noir novels of the 1950s… Hard Case's latest release is smart, trashy fun."
—*Publishers Weekly, starred review*

"Fasten your seat belts, and enjoy the bumpy ride of double- and triple-crosses, blackmail, and murder. If Quentin Tarantino is looking for another movie project, this novel with its mix of shocking violence and black comedy would be the perfect candidate. Highly recommended as a terrific summer read."
—*Library Journal, starred review*

"Really good…very violent and very funny."
—*Jenny Davidson, Light Reading*

"Two of the century's best thriller writers have joined forces to bring a postmodern twist to the black heart of noir fiction. Grade: A."
    —*Rocky Mountain News*

"A really black comedy…I pretty much laughed my ass off."
    —*Sarah Weinman*

"Some of the funniest dialogue this side of Elmore Leonard."
    —*Otto Penzler, New York Sun*

"Crosses and double-crosses, miscalculations and blunders, and plenty of dead bodies…For those who like the bungling-criminal genre, this is good fun."
    —*Booklist*

"A fearsome and wondrous mix of vile characters [in] a caper novel worthy of Westlake or Leonard…exquisitely conceived and flawlessly written."
    —*Book Reporter*

"Downright hilarious and bloodthirsty in the best possible way. With all the dirt and more you could ask about Hollywood and the world of crime publishing."
    —*Maxim Jakubowski*

"This hilarious series and its hapless, deluded main characters is like no other in the entire contemporary crime fiction world."
    —*Bookgasm*

"The prose reads like a dream. Fast paced and bursting with energy…Hard Case Crime have released some of the best new novels of the past few years. They've given us some amazing reprints of classic crime. But this book…has just upped the ante once more."
    —*Crime Scene*

Room 1812 was long and narrow, with the bed against the wall at the far end. The light on the night table was on so Bobby had a clear view of the action, which was good because the light from the hallway didn't make it too far into the room. Bobby went about halfway over the threshold and gently let the door rest against his chair. Then he raised his camera with a towel over it, the lens peeking out underneath.

Mr. Brown must've heard the snapping camera or seen Bobby out of the corner of his eye because he looked up and said, "Hey, what the hell?"

Bobby let the corner of the towel drop over the camera's lens, scooted out the door and let it shut behind him.

Riding the elevator down, camera tucked in his bag, Bobby was smiling, proud of his performance. Maybe he should've listened to Isabella, gone on some auditions. Maybe it wasn't too late. There had to be roles for guys in wheelchairs, right?

Nah, he decided, acting was too fucking boring. He needed the buzz, the action.

Crime was where it was at...

SOME OTHER HARD CASE CRIME BOOKS YOU WILL ENJOY:

PIMP by Ken Bruen & Jason Starr
THE NEXT TIME I DIE by Jason Starr
JOYLAND by Stephen King
THE COCKTAIL WAITRESS by James M. Cain
THIEVES FALL OUT by Gore Vidal
SO NUDE, SO DEAD by Ed McBain
QUARRY'S BLOOD by Max Allan Collins
THE KNIFE SLIPPED by Erle Stanley Gardner
SNATCH by Gregory Mcdonald
THE LAST STAND by Mickey Spillane
UNDERSTUDY FOR DEATH by Charles Willeford
THE TRIUMPH OF THE SPIDER MONKEY
by Joyce Carol Oates
BLOOD SUGAR by Daniel Kraus
LEMONS NEVER LIE by Donald E. Westlake writing as Richard Stark
ARE SNAKES NECESSARY? by Brian De Palma and Susan Lehman
KILLER, COME BACK TO ME by Ray Bradbury
FIVE DECEMBERS by James Kestrel
LOWDOWN ROAD by Scott Von Doviak
SEED ON THE WIND by Rex Stout
FAST CHARLIE by Victor Gischler
NOBODY'S ANGEL by Jack Clark
DEATH COMES TOO LATE by Charles Ardai
INTO THE NIGHT by Cornell Woolrich and Lawrence Block
THE GET OFF by Christa Faust

SUPERMAX

THE MAX & ANGELA TRILOGY

by **Ken Bruen** *and* **Jason Starr**

A HARD CASE CRIME NOVEL

A HARD CASE CRIME BOOK
(HCC-S10)
First Hard Case Crime edition: November 2025

Published by
Titan Books
A division of Titan Publishing Group Ltd
144 Southwark Street
London SE1 0UP

in collaboration with Winterfall LLC

Introduction copyright © 2025 by Jason Starr
Bust copyright © 2006 by Ken Bruen and Jason Starr
Slide copyright © 2007 by Ken Bruen and Jason Starr
The Max copyright © 2008 by Ken Bruen and Jason Starr

Cover painting copyright © 2008 by Glen Orbik

All rights reserved. No part of this book may be reproduced or transmitted in any form or by any electronic or mechanical means, including photocopying, recording or by any information storage and retrieval system, except where permitted by law, or used to train generative artificial intelligence (AI) technologies, without the written permission of the publisher and the author.

This book is a work of fiction. Names, characters, places, and incidents either are the products of the author's imagination or are used fictitiously, and any resemblance to actual events or persons, living or dead, is entirely coincidental.

Print edition ISBN 978-1-83541-225-1
E-book ISBN 978-1-83541-226-8

Design direction by Max Phillips
www.signalfoundry.com

Typeset by Swordsmith Productions

The name "Hard Case Crime" and the Hard Case Crime logo are trademarks of Winterfall LLC. Hard Case Crime books are selected and edited by Charles Ardai.

Printed in the United States of America

Visit us on the web at www.HardCaseCrime.com

Contents

Introduction
11

Bust
15

Slide
259

The Max
445

Introduction by Jason Starr

"How did you and Ken write together?"

Whenever I'm asked this question, my first thought is always: *I have no fuckin' clue.*

It really shouldn't have worked at all. We lived on different continents, had no way to meet consistently—this was many years pre-Zoom—and our styles are completely different. While we're both "noir crime writers," Ken's novels are minimalistic, poetic, Samuel Beckett-esque, with a distinctive cadence, and—as I used to always joke with him—"I write in English."

Most partnerships, at some point, have conflict, but Ken and I never had a single creative disagreement. It seems like we wrote these first three novels—*Bust*, *Slide*, and *The Max*—in a surge of insane emotional energy.

Ken and I met at a pre-Edgar Awards party at the Partners & Crime bookshop in 2004 where Anthony Bourdain was serving hors d'oeuvres. We became instant friends. It was partly because we have a very similar sense of humor, but Ken also has an uncanny ability to endear people quickly. Once, we went outside for a smoke at a midtown restaurant and ten minutes later he returned arm-in-arm with the owner of the restaurant who was boasting, "*This* is a great man."

A few months later, Ken was back in New York, and we met for drinks at the former Mansfield Hotel in midtown where Ken always stayed—and which we later referenced in our books. I ordered a light beer and a glass of water and Ken—simultaneously commenting on my wimpy Americanness and his steadfast Irishness—quipped, "It's not light enough? You need water too?"

I can't remember who suggested the idea of cowriting, but at one point one of us blurted out: "We should write a book together."

As with most late-night, alcohol-fueled plans, the next day this seemed like a horrible idea. I was under contract for a new novel at Vintage Books and Ken was just starting to break out big with his Jack Taylor series. Collaborating made no sense at all for either of our careers, but Ken and I have one major thing in common—if something sounds like a bad idea, it just makes it that much more appealing.

We ran the idea by Charles Ardai who had recently founded Hard Case Crime. If Charles had said no the idea to cowrite would have almost certainly fizzled, but Charles—who may be as nutty as Ken and me—thought that cowriting was a brilliant idea. So, suddenly under a contract for a book with a due date, Ken and I leapt head-first into the madness.

There were obstacles—mainly we needed to figure out what the hell we were going to write about. We kicked around some ideas, then I emailed him that I have a book "in my drawer" that wasn't quite working—maybe we can add an Irish twist and turn it into something good? So we used the plot of this book and reworked it together. We pumped up Max, making him as outrageous as we could, made Angela part-Irish, added Irish gangsters, and created other characters and plot lines.

At first—no big surprise—it seemed like two very different writers were writing a disjointed book. So I suggested, "What if I try to write like you and you try to write like me?" I relaxed my style to write like Ken writes, and Ken leaned into clean, straight-ahead prose, more like me. Some readers may assume that I wrote the American characters and Ken wrote the Irish ones, but that's not true—we had an equal hand in both. The merging seemed to work, but mainly it worked because we had the same attitude and vision. Neither of us wanted to redeem any characters or write serious novels—we just wanted the books to be as dark, funny, and wild as possible. We had a no holds barred approach; we didn't censor ourselves or each other. If one of us had an insane idea, we went with it. Initially, we thought *Bust* would be a one-off, but like a heavyweight fighter who refuses to quit, we kept coming back for "just one more." The series grew to become a trilogy, and then a quartet when *Pimp* was published in 2015.

But how did we actually *do* it?

I've told people that I was the quarterback and Ken was the big playmaker, which I think is a great way of describing our process. I managed the plots and Ken took the books in usually insane new directions, then we riffed off each other's writing until it sounded like a unified voice. The time difference between Ireland and New York worked in our favor. I'd write a section, send it to Ken, and in the morning his pages were in my inbox. A typical Ken email: "Love it, couldn't stop laughing, here's mine." Then I'd laugh for a while at what he wrote—what a great way to start a day!—and then move stuff around, add to it, sometimes change it, and send it back to him with my additions. This was all usually before nine A.M., which was great for me because a day had just started and I already felt productive. If one of us slacked off or needed nudging the partnership never would have worked, but in writing four books together, neither of us missed a single day.

We wrote like we were painting a picture together—working on different sections simultaneously, a splatter here and a splatter there. Sometimes Ken would take things in unplanned directions, and I would rework the outline and keep things moving forward. We wrote without egos, understanding that it wasn't about Jason's line vs. Ken's line, it was about trying to create a new voice together. Somehow, we wrote each of these books in under two months, and one in just six weeks. I really don't know how we kept everything organized and on track, but we pulled it off—four times—without any interruption of our solo writing.

Collaborating with Ken, improbably, became one of the most enjoyable writing experiences of my career, and Max and Angela are, without a doubt, two of my favorite characters I've ever had a hand in creating. Occasionally, I open one of our books to a random page and immediately start smiling—not necessarily at a funny line, but because the writing reminds me of how it felt to be at a bar late at night with Ken, laughing non-stop.

You know—the kind of nights you hope will never end.

Jason Starr
New York City
April 2024

BUST

For Reed Farrel Coleman, La Weinman (Sarah), and Jon, Ruth, and Jennifer Jordan, ro-bust friends

One

People with opinions just go around bothering one another.
THE BUDDHA

In the back of Famiglia Pizza on Fiftieth and Broadway, Max Fisher was dabbing his plain slice with a napkin, trying to soak up as much grease as he could, when a man sat down diagonally across from him with a large cupful of ice. The guy looked nothing like the big, strong-looking hit man Max was expecting —he looked more like a starving greyhound. He couldn't have weighed more than 130 pounds, had a medium build, startling blue eyes, a thin scar down his right cheek, and a blur of long gray hair. And something was very weird about his mouth. It looked like someone had put broken glass in there and mangled his lips.

The guy smiled, said, "You're wondering what happened to me mouth."

Max knew the guy would be Irish, but he didn't think he'd be *so* Irish, that talking to him would be like talking to one of those Irish bartenders at that place uptown who could never understand a fucking word he was saying. He'd ask for a Bud Light and they'd stare back at him with a dumb look, like something was wrong with the way *he* was talking, and he'd think, Who's the potato eater just off the boat, pal? Me or you?

Max was about to answer then thought, Fuck that, I'm the boss, and asked, "Are you...?"

The man put a finger to his messed-up lips, made the sound "Sh...sh," then added, "No names." He sucked on the ice, made a big production out of it, pushing his lips out with the cube so Max had to see them. Then, finally, he stuck the cube in his cheek like a chipmunk and asked, "You'll be Max?"

Max wondered what had happened to no names. He was going to say something about it, but then figured this guy was just trying to play head games with him so he just nodded.

The guy leaned over, whispered, "You can call me Popeye."

Before Max could say, You mean like the cartoon character? the guy laughed, startling Max, and then said, "Fook, call me anything except early in the morning." Popeye smiled again, then said, "I need the money up front."

Max felt better—negotiating was *his* thing—and asked, "It's eight, right? I mean, isn't that what Angela…?"

The guy's eyes widened and Max thought, Fuck, the no-name rule, and was about to say sorry when Popeye shot out his hand and grabbed Max's wrist. For such a bone-thin guy he had a grip like steel.

"Ten, it's ten," he hissed.

Max was still scared shitless but he was angry about the money too. He tried to free his wrist, couldn't, but managed to say, "Hey, a deal's a deal, you can't just change the terms."

He liked that, putting the skinny little mick in his place.

Finally Popeye let go, sat back and stared at Max, sucking on the ice some more, then in a very low voice he said, "You want me to kill your wife, I can do whatever the fook I want, I own your arse you suited prick."

Max felt a jolt in his chest, thought, Shit, the heart attack his fucking cardiologist told him could "happen at any time." He took a sip of his Diet Pepsi, wiped his forehead, then said, "Yeah, okay, whatever, I guess we can renegotiate. Five before and five after. How's that?"

Bottom line, he wanted Deirdre gone. It wasn't like he could hold interviews for hit men, tell each candidate, *Thank you for coming in, we'll get back to you.*

Then Popeye reached into his leather jacket—it had a hole in the shoulder and Max wondered, Bullet hole?—and took out a funny-looking green packet of cigarettes, with "Major" on the front, and placed a brass Zippo on top. Max thought that the guy had to know he couldn't actually light up in a restaurant, even if it was just a shitty pizzeria. Popeye took out a cigarette; it was small and stumpy, and he ran it along his bottom lip, like he was putting on lipstick.

Man, this guy was weird.

"Listen closely yah bollix," he said, "I'm the best there is and that means I don't come cheap, it also means I get the whole shebang up front and that's, lemme see, tomorrow."

Max didn't like that idea, but he wanted to get the deal done so he just nodded. Popeye put the cigarette behind his ear, sighed, then said, "Righty ho, I want small bills and noon Thursday, you bring them to Modell's on Forty-second Street. I'll be the one trying on tennis sneakers."

"I have a question," Max said. "How will you do it? I mean, I don't want her to suffer. I mean, will it be quick?"

Popeye stood up, used both hands to massage his right leg, as if he was ironing a kink out of it, then said, "Tomorrow…I'll need the code for the alarm and all the instructions and the keys to the flat. You make sure you're with somebody at six, don't go home till eight. If you come home early I'm gonna pop you too." He paused then said, "You think you can follow that, fellah?"

Suddenly Popeye sounded familiar. Max racked his brain then it came to him—Robert Shaw in *The Sting*.

Then Popeye said, "And me mouth, a gobshite tried to ram a broken bottle in me face, his aim was a little off, happened on the Falls Road, not a place you'd like to visit."

Max never could remember if the Falls were the Protestants or the Catholics, but he didn't feel it was the time to ask. He looked again at the hole in Popeye's leather jacket.

Popeye touched the jacket with his finger, said, "Caught it on a hook on me wardrobe. You think I should get it fixed?"

Two

To be nobody but yourself in a world which is doing its best to make you like everybody else, means to fight the hardest human battle ever and to never stop fighting.
E. E. CUMMINGS

Bobby Rosa sat in his Quickie wheelchair in the middle of Central Park's Sheep Meadow, checking out all the beautiful young babes. He had his headphones on, Motley Crue's "Girls, Girls, Girls" leaking out, thinking that his own crew would love all these great shots he was taking. Man, these chicks must've been starving themselves, probably doing all those Pilates, to look this good. Finally, he saw what he was looking for—three thin babes in bikinis lying on their stomachs in a nice even line. They were about thirty yards away—perfect shooting distance—so Bobby took out his Nikon with the wide-angle lens and zoomed in.

He snapped about ten pictures—some whole-body shots and some good rear shots. Then he wheeled toward the other end of Sheep Meadow and spotted two blondes, lying on their backs. From about twenty yards away, he snapped a dozen boob shots, saying things to himself like, "Oh, yeah, I like that," "Yeah, that's right," "Yeah, right there baby." Then, right next to the blondes, he spotted a beautiful curvy black chick, lying alone on a blanket. She was on her stomach and the string on her bikini bottom was so thin it looked like she was naked. Bobby went in for a close-up, stopping about five yards behind her. He snapped the rest of the roll. He had another roll in the jacket of his windbreaker, but he was happy with the shots he'd gotten, so he pushed himself out of Sheep Meadow, on to the park's west drive.

A panhandler came up to Bobby, with that annoying sad-eyed yet pissed-off look that all homeless fucks had. The guy looked strung out and the smell of piss, sweat and booze made Bobby want to puke.

"Got a few bucks, buddy?"

With the headphones on, Bobby couldn't hear him, but he could read the guy's lips. He gave him a long stare, thinking there was no way in hell some scumbag like this would have had the balls to come up to him back in the day. Just then, the Crue went dead, right in the middle of "Bad Boy Boogie," as the cassette got mangled—cheap rip-off piece of shit he bought on the street in Chinatown, what, ten years ago? He tore the crap out of his Walkman, thinking he had to go current, get one of those iPods. Then he flung the messed-up tape at the guy, spat, and said, "Here's some Crue. Broaden your fuckin' horizons, jackass…and take a fuckin' shower while you're at it."

The guy stared at the tape, stammered, "The fuck am I gonna do with this?"

Bobby smiled, not giving a shit, and said, "Stick it up your ass, loser."

And then he continued up the block, cursing to himself and at the people he passed. Nine ways to Sunday, Bobby Rosa had attitude, or in the current buzz jargon, he had *issues*.

When he got back to his apartment on Eighty-ninth and Columbus, Bobby went right to the second bedroom, which he had turned into a darkroom, and started developing the film. The three chicks in a row came out great, but the pictures of the black babe were Bobby's favorites. Somehow the woman reminded him of his old girlfriend, Tanya.

Bobby added the tit shots to the collection in his bedroom. He had three walls covered with Central Park boobs, taken during the past two springs and summers. He had all shapes and sizes—implants, flat chests, sagging old ladies, training-bra teenagers—it didn't matter to him. Then he had an idea, and said out loud, *"The Hot Chicks of Manhattan."* It had a nice ring to it; he could see it as a coffee-table book. He could make a few bucks on the side and it was kind of classy too. Rich assholes would have it out right next to their champagne and caviar. Then, laughing to himself, he took the ass shots and added them to his collection in the bathroom. Next, he went to his shelf, grabbed another tape, *The Best of Poison*. Letting "Talk Dirty To Me" rip, he leaned back in his wheelchair, admiring his work. He bet, if he wanted to, he could sell his pictures to some classy art magazine, one of those big, thick mothers you have to hold with two hands.

After a few more minutes of staring at the walls, Bobby looked at his watch. It was 2:15. He realized it was past his usual time for his bowel routine. So he went into the bathroom and transferred himself onto the bowl. As he dug his index finger into the jar of Vaseline he laughed out loud, asked, "This suck or what?"

•

About twenty minutes later, Bobby called the lobby and asked the doorman to send a maintenance guy up to his apartment. When the little Jamaican guy arrived, Bobby asked him to take out a big box from the back of his hallway closet.

"I thought you had a problem with your shower?"

"Yeah, well I don't," Bobby said.

He was a strong little guy, but the box was so heavy it took all his strength to carry it a few feet. He was out of breath.

"What the fuck do you have in there?"

"Oh, just some old clothes," Bobby said, handing him a crisp twenty-dollar bill.

When the guy was gone, Bobby opened the box, tearing off the layers of masking tape. Finally, he got it open and removed the bubble wrap, getting a head rush when he saw his weapons. He had three sawed-off shotguns, a couple of rifles, a MAC-11 submachine pistol, two Uzis, some smaller guns, and a gym bag filled with boxes of ammo. No two ways about it—you got hardware, you got juice. Suddenly the world took on a whole other perspective: Now you called the fucking shots. Poison were into "Look What the Cat Dragged In" and he thought, Man, this is it, guns and rock 'n' roll.

He took one of his favorite handguns out of the box, a .40 millimeter Glock Model 27 compact pistol. The "pocket rocket" didn't pack the power of a shotgun or a Mag, but he loved the black finish. Holding a gun again gave Bobby the same buzz that it always did. The only thing better was firing one, feeling that explosion of power coming out of his body. He'd had a lot of women in his time, but given the choice between a woman and a gun he'd take the gun. It didn't talk back and it got the job done, plus, it made you feel like a player and you didn't have to reassure the motherfucker.

Aiming out the window, Bobby zeroed in on a pigeon that was sitting on the ledge of a building across the street. He felt the muscles in his index finger starting to twitch. He'd always been a great shot, practicing on the range down on Murray Street in between hold-ups. "Bang," he said out loud, imagining the bullet exploding through the bird's brain.

Bobby was sweating. He wheeled into the bathroom and splashed cold water against his face, then he stared at himself in the mirror. This was happening a lot lately—looking in the mirror, expecting to see a young guy, but seeing an old man instead.

He muttered, "How'd that happen?"

He used to have thick black hair, but lately his forehead seemed to be getting bigger and bigger, and he had more gray in his hair now than black. He'd grown a beard over the winter, hoping it would make him look younger, but no luck there—it had come in mostly gray too. He used to only get wrinkles around his mouth when he smiled, but now he had them all the time, and the circles under his eyes were getting so dark it looked like he was going around with two permanent shiners. Although his arms and shoulders had gotten big from pushing himself around, his legs had shriveled up to almost nothing and he had put on a gut. Fucking brews, man—they kept you trucking but blew you out.

"What're you gonna do?" he said.

Maybe forty-seven wasn't old for some people, but it was old for a guy who'd spent fourteen years in prison, one year in Iraq, and three years in a fucking wheelchair.

It was time to get back to work.

Three

*Bust: A sculptured representation of the upper part of
the body / to break or burst / to raid or arrest.*

Angela Petrakos was raised in Ireland till she was seven and then her father packed them up, took her and her mother to America, saying, "Enough of this scraping and scrimping, we're going to live the American dream."

Yeah, right.

They wound up in Weehawken, New Jersey, living in what they call *genteel poverty*. "They" must be rich because Angela had never heard a poor person use words like that. Angela's mother was a pure Irish woman—mean, bitter and stubborn as all hell. She called herself a *displaced Irishwoman*. When she said this, Angela's father would whisper, "She means she hates dis place." Her father was born in Dublin, but his family was Greek, from Xios. Angela's Mom was from Belfast and constantly bitched about the huge mistake of marrying a Southerner with Greek longings. When Angela was a teenager, her mother went on and on about the glories of Ireland. All types of Irish music—jigs and reels, hornpipes and bodhrans—were shoved down Angela's throat, and a huge green harp hung on the kitchen wall. Angela's father, meanwhile, wasn't allowed to play Theodrakis or any of the music he loved, and Angela never even heard *Zorba's Dance* until she was twenty. When the micks lay down the rules, they're laid in granite—it was no wonder they'd coined the phrase *No surrender*.

All the songs of rebellion, the history of the IRA, were drilled into Angela's psyche. She was programmed to love the Irish and her plan was to go to the country and have an affair with Gerry Adams. Yeah, he was happily married, but that didn't ruin her fantasy; actually, it fueled it. Despite her years in America, she had a slight Irish accent. She liked the way she spoke, was told she sounded "hot" by the older guys who tried to pick her up—they often succeeded—when she was in junior high and high school. She went to technical college and learned Excel and PowerPoint, but she knew her real talent was seduction. By the time she was twenty, she'd learned all about the power of sex.

She worked her way through the crappy jobs and a string of asshole boyfriends. Angela wasn't pretty in the conventional sense but she knew how to use what she had and, by Jesus, she used it. She was medium height with brown eyes and brown hair, but she changed all that—went blond, went blue eyed, went wild. She got a boob job, contacts for her eyes and already had the attitude. Then her mother died and they cremated her—her father said he wanted her burned, "lest she return." Angela got the ashes, kept them in an urn on her bookcase. When *Angela's Ashes* came out she rushed out and bought the book, thinking it had to be some kind of sign or something. She didn't bother reading it, but liked having it on her shelf. Other books she bought but never read included *'Tis* and *A Monk Swimming*. She also had some DVDs like *Angela's Ashes*, *Far and Away*, and *The Commitments*. When it came to music, only the Irish stuff really did it for her—Enya, Moya Brennan and, of course, U2. She would've stepped on Gerry Adams to get to Bono.

Most of her money went on clothes. The most basic lesson she learned was that if you wore a short skirt, killer heels and a tight top, guys went ape. Her legs were good and she knew how to hike a skirt to really get the heads turning. She saved her money and went online to book a week in Belfast, brought the urn with her—which caused some commotion with Homeland Security, but in the end she was allowed to bring her Mom if she stashed her in freight, which she did. She stayed at the Europa, the most bombed hotel in Europe—that's what Frommer said anyway—and the customers were pretty bombed themselves. The city was a shithole—drab, grey, depressing—and the Sterling, what was the deal with that? And people kept getting on her about Iraq, like she had any freakin' say about it. She did all the sightseeing crap—maybe seeing blown-up buildings did it for some people, but it bored the hell out of her. When she threw her Mom's ashes into the Foyle there was a wind, of course, and most of her mother flew back into her hair. When she told the old guy at the hotel desk what had happened he said, "Tis proof, darling, that the dead are always with us."

Evenings, she ate at the hotel and had drinks at the bar. She didn't want to go out, not because she was afraid but because she couldn't understand a goddamn word anyone was saying. The bartender hit on her and if his teeth hadn't been so yellow she might have been into it. For the first time in her life, she felt American and that Ireland was the foreign country. The blended accent that got her so far in New York seemed useless here.

Her second-to-last night, she was sitting at the bar and a drunk began to hassle her. The bartender, of course, didn't help. The drunk had a combat jacket, sewage breath, and was going, "Ah come on, you want to suck me dick, you know yah do."

It took her a while to actually figure out what he was saying because of the accent; it sounded like, "Orr...kom on...yer want to truck meh duck."

Finally, she put it all together. Before she could react, a man appeared out of nowhere, grabbed the guy by the front of the neck and had him out of there in no time. Shaking, she tried to put a Virginia Slim into her mouth, and the bartender raced over, flicked a bic, and said, "There you go."

She accepted the light as she wanted that hit of nicotine then blew a cloud of smoke in Yellow Teeth's face, said, "And there *you* go you spineless prick."

Unfazed, the bartender said, "I love it when you talk dirty."

The other man had returned and now stared at the bartender, and said, "Leg it shithead." Then he turned to her, asked, "You okay missus?"

She could understand him, because he was from the Irish Republic and had soft vowels, sounding kind of like her Dad. He had a scar on his face, long grey hair and was as thin as the guys on Christopher Street. His lips were mangled but, hey, he was the first guy in the whole damn province she saw with good teeth. And the lips were kind of sexy anyway. They'd be strange to kiss, but they'd be great for other things. Maybe it was the near violence but she felt a raw sexuality oozing off of him that was so freaking irresistible. One thing that got Angela hot was danger and this guy reeked of it.

She felt a burning rise up her neck, spread to her face, and said, "Wow, I'm so, like, grateful. Can I buy you a drink?"

He smiled then said, "Jameson." He said it like a Hollywood tough guy, no bullshit with *please* or *ice*. No, just the one word, with a slight hard edge, the implication being, bring me the drink *now* and don't even think about fucking with me.

She asked, "Are you, like, for real?"

He parked his ass on the stool next to her, said, "The heart wants what it cannot hold."

Jesus, she thought, poetry and violence, how could a girl

resist? The Irish might know shit about cool but they sure as hell knew how to talk.

And she loved his voice, deep, devilish, and, yeah, sexy.

With a little of the same flirty tone, she said, "You want that on the rocks?"

He gave her the look she would get to know and not always love, and said, "I take everything…neat."

He put his hand in his jacket, took out a slim book and she saw the title, *The Wisdom of Zen*. She was impressed that a guy like him was carrying around a deep book like that.

He asked her, "You like The Pogues?"

She thought, Screw them, I like you.

Four

*Never do evil, always do good, keep your mind pure —
thus all the Buddhas taught.*
THE DHAMMAPADA

Max screamed, "To hell with you, you crackpot!" and slammed the phone as hard as he could and banged the desk with his fist. A moment later, he felt a jolt in his chest. Thinking, *Fuck, I'm dying*, he searched his jacket pockets for his Mevacor. Then he remembered he'd already taken his pills today but now feared that the Mevacor was interacting with his Viagra, causing some kind of reaction.

He was about to call Dr. Cohen, that jerk-off, back but he decided, What's the point? So far nothing that schmuck suggested had worked. Max took all the goddamn drugs he was supposed to, had even hired an Indian named Kamal to come over to his house a few days a week to cook macrobiotic meals. But his HDL-to-LDL ratio was eight-to-one, up from seven-to-one at his last check-up, putting him in the super-high-risk group for heart disease. Right now, he could feel his heart working on overtime, the pump already on its last legs.

To help relax, Max did a yoga breathing exercise that Kamal had taught him, inhaling and exhaling through alternate nostrils, but it didn't do crap. He made a mental note—fire Kamal, that Indian bastard, as soon as he comes back from his vacation. *Taj Mahal that, you little prick.*

There was a knock on Max's door.

Max yelled, "What?"

The door opened slowly and Harold Lipman, Max's new Networking Salesman, came into the office.

Lipman said, "Esc—" and Max said, "Not now."

"I just wanted to ask—"

"I said not now!"

Lipman left and Max went right to his office bar and made a vodka tonic. Ah, Max loved his office, the only part of NetWorld that he'd remodeled. Besides the mahogany bar, he'd paneled the walls, installed brand-new carpeting, and bought the most expensive desk and swivel chair available in the Office Depot catalogue. He figured it made a statement, that here was a hip guy, not showy, but with refined taste and a serious edge. You saw the office, you saw a guy who probably had drinks with the Donald, though not often because Max was "too busy." The office had no view, but elegant beige curtains concealed the windows. Behind his desk hung a custom-made picture of a blonde with Pam Anderson-size breasts sitting on a red Porsche. Inscribed on the car was the company motto, NETWORLD OR BUST.

The booze soothed Max enough so that he was able to concentrate on the important stuff again, like money. Over the past two days, Max had put away ten grand in his private safe. He had made small withdrawals from all of his bank accounts—corporate and private—and from his brokerage accounts where he had cash balances. But the bulk of the money, about seven grand, had come from the office's petty cash. Max thought this was a great idea because if the police investigated there would be no withdrawal slips or any other way to prove he'd hired a hit man. And fuck that crazy mick's demand for small bills—the money was mostly fifties and hundreds. What was he going to do, turn it down? Yeah, like that was going to happen.

As Max poured his second vodka tonic, there was a soft knock on the door, a pause, followed by a louder knock.

Max recognized the signal and said in his sexiest voice, "Come in, baby."

As usual, Angela looked dynamite. She was wearing shiny black boots, a short red skirt tight enough to see her buttcheeks, and a lacy camisole. She had big blow-dried hair and was wearing the diamond stud earrings that Max had bought her at Tiffany's last Christmas.

"You had two messages while you were on the phone," Angela said, the soft Irish vowels driving him crazy.

"Fuck the messages. How about you put those magic little hands of yours to work?"

Angela locked the door and came up behind Max at his desk. Max breathed deeply, moaning, "Oh, yeah, that feels so good," as Angela worked the muscles in his neck and shoulders.

"You have a lot of knots today," Angela said.

"I bet my blood pressure's shooting through the roof too."

"Was that Dr. Cohen you were screaming at?"

"Who else? I swear, I don't know how that jerk-off got a license. You know what that asshole told me? That I should start eating brown rice. Like the bacon, the fried chicken, the shrimp, the pizza—that's not killing me. It's the fuckin' white rice."

"Calm down," Angela said. "You have to learn how to relax, not let the stress get to you. In Ireland we say, *Na bac leat.*"

The fuck was she talking about? He asked, "The fuck're you talking about?"

She said calmly, "In American...*No biggie.*"

Max exhaled, then took a long, steady breath. Angela was wearing some of that perfume called Joy he had bought her last month at Bloomingdale's. Max couldn't tell whether it smelled nice or not, but it had cost five hundred bucks an ounce so he figured it must be pretty good.

"You should be careful," Angela said, "screaming in the office like that. Everyone could hear you."

"So? If they don't like it they don't have to work here."

"Yeah, but I don't think it's a good idea to, like, yell like that. I mean people could remember. They'll tell the police 'Come to think of it, Max was kind of acting crazy lately.' "

"But I act crazy all the time, I'm a crazy kind of guy, it's part of my appeal."

"I'm just saying—it's probably not a good idea."

"Eh, you're probably right," Max said. "You know what else Cohen told me? He said I'm fat."

"I love your belly."

"Yeah, well, Cohen says it's unhealthy. He showed me some chart that said I'm obese for a man my height and age. Meanwhile, you should see the size of that asshole's gut."

"How does that feel?"

"Nice. Real nice."

Angela spun Max around in his chair, kissed him on the lips, then Max whispered, "I just want all this shit to be over with already. Last night I had a dream she was dead. The ambulances were there and they were carrying her out of our house, covered by a white sheet, and you know what? It was the best dream I've ever had."

"You shouldn't talk about her that way," Angela said. She had her hands behind Max's head, gently rubbing her fingers through his thinning hair. He was glad she was touching the back of his head, where he still had some hair left. "You know what they say—if you say things about your first wife you'll say them about your second wife too."

"You and Deirdre have nothing in common, sweetheart."

"That's what you say now, but in twenty years you might be paying to have me killed."

"I'd be lucky if I lived another twenty years."

"You're not denying it."

Holding her head steady and looking right into those fucking beautiful light blue eyes, Max said, "I love you. You think I ever went around telling Deirdre that I loved her?"

"You still didn't deny it."

"I deny it, I deny it," Max said. "Jesus Christ."

Angela smiled. Max kissed her then said, "You know, the only thing I'm worried about is this Popeye character."

"Why?" Angela asked.

"First of all, I don't like his name."

"What's wrong with his name?"

"Come on, it's a fucking cartoon character. It's like I'm hiring Donald Duck to kill my wife."

"You can't expect him to use his real name. I mean, he has to protect himself, doesn't he?"

"Yeah, but couldn't he come up with something better, more hitman-like. I don't know, like, Skull, or Bones, or something like that."

"You can't judge somebody by their name."

"Eh, I guess you're right. And I guess we've gotta assume he's good at what he does or your cousin wouldn't have recommended him, right? God knows the guy's crazy enough to kill somebody. You should've seen the way he grabbed my arm."

"So what're you worried about?"

"I don't know, it's just a vibe. I just got a feeling the guy's fucking around with me somehow. And I don't like the way he changed the terms. It was supposed to be eight, then he made it ten. That's no way to do business with somebody."

Angela held Max's hand, said, "Don't worry. I mean, it's only another two thousand. It's not like he asked for twenty thousand."

"Yet," Max said. "I got a feeling this guy thinks he's got me by the balls or something. That's how he comes off, like he thinks he's in control. You know what he called me? He called me a 'suited prick.' Asshole. And I couldn't stand looking at him, either. Those disgusting lips."

While he spoke, Max was massaging Angela's breasts. He loved her breasts—they were the main reason he'd hired her. He'd always been a breast man. Even Deirdre had big breasts, although they were starting to sag below her stomach.

"This is probably a bad idea," Max said as Angela started to kiss his neck. "Tonight has to be our last time for a while."

"I can't wait till we can be together all the time," Angela said.

"Ditto," Max said. "But until then, let's just try to keep things as quiet as possible around here."

For the rest of the day, Max and Angela went about their business. Amazingly, they'd managed to keep their affair a secret from everyone in the office. Around other people, Max was always very formal, asking Angela to send faxes, take messages, bring him coffee, order in lunch and other crap that presidents of companies ask their executive assistants to do. They never went out to lunch together or left the office together at night. If they were planning to meet for dinner, Angela would always leave first and then Max would meet her at a specified location. As for the times they fooled around in Max's office during business hours, it wasn't unusual for an executive assistant and her boss to be in the boss's office together with the door locked.

At eleven o'clock, Max had his weekly meeting with Alan Henderson, his CFO, and Diane Faustino, the Payroll Director. They went over the company's payroll and budget and talked about expanding the company website and the need to hire two more Senior Networking Technicians. Max also told Alan that he wanted to reward his employees with a ten-percent raise next year, and sent out a memo about this pronto, thinking at least no one could say he wasn't in a good mood a couple of days before his wife was murdered. Besides, he loved giving raises, the surge of power it gave him, that he could make or break these assholes.

That evening, when the last person had left for the day, Angela locked the front door, and came into Max's office. Max was already naked, lying on his back on his office couch, doing Kamal's breathing exercise. She turned down the lights. It was almost dark, the only light coming through the window curtains. She took off her clothes slowly, moving the way Max liked, like she was a dancer at Legz Diamond's, the strip club on Forty-seventh Street where he took his clients. Finally, she took off her bra, climbed on top of Max and gave him some nice warm kisses. Then she slid down and ran her tongue over his thick gray chest hair. As she dipped further, Max grinned, thinking, Who the fuck needs breathing exercises?

Afterwards, holding her tightly, feeling especially close, Max said, "Let's get married."

"We're going to get married."

"I mean right away."

"But we'll have to wait *some* time. I mean it would look suspicious if we did it too soon, wouldn't it?"

"What difference does it make? Just because my wife is murdered I have to spend my whole life in mourning?"

Angela thought about this for a moment, then said, "Yeah, I guess that's true."

"There's another thing I want to talk about—kids. I've always wanted a little Max Jr., just not with Deirdre. What do you think about being a full-time mommy?"

"I'd love it."

"Well, I want to do that right away too—while I still have some good seed inside me."

Later, while they were getting dressed, Max interrupted whatever the hell Angela was saying, said, "Ange, there's something I wanted to ask you. I don't really know how to say this. I mean I don't want you to get offended or anything. I don't think you will but—"

"What is it?"

"It's stupid, really, but..."

"What?"

"It's just...have you ever thought about adding another cup size to your tits?"

Looking down at her implants, she said, "Why? You think they're not big enough?"

Max said, "I didn't say that. I just asked you if you ever thought about it before, that's all."

"They're already thirty-eight D's. Why, you're serious? You really don't like them?"

"I didn't say *that*. I just didn't want you to think there was something you couldn't have if you wanted it."

"That's really nice of you...I guess."

"I'm not saying that bigger tits are something that you necessarily need." Max wound on his tie, trying to come up with perfect way to explain it. He came up with, "I mean, I want you to have everything you want in life, whether it's a gold necklace, a beautiful dress, a trip around the world, or great tits."

Strapping on her bra, Angela said, "You really think it would make me look better, huh?"

"Not necessarily *better*, but I don't think it could hurt. Anyway, sleep on it. Although I don't mean that literally." He laughed to himself, then said, "By the way, did you make that dinner appointment for me tomorrow night?"

"Yes. With Jack Haywood."

"Good. I'll have to take him out to some busy restaurant,

maybe some Italian place on the Upper East Side. They have all those little restaurants around Second Avenue."

"There're a lot of bars up there, too."

"I don't know, I'd look pretty stupid—an old guy like me in some singles bar."

"You're not old."

"I'm only not old when I'm with you."

When Max finished getting dressed, Angela came over to him and said, "So this is it. The last time we'll be together—for a while anyway."

Hugging Angela made Max think about breasts again. He said, "You know, I don't think a restaurant is public enough. We should be someplace more visible. I know, I'll take Jack to a strip club."

Five

If my grandmother had balls she'd be my grandfather.
YIDDISH SAYING

"So I'm riding on the bus, coming downtown, when this chick gets on," Bobby Rosa said. "I got Cinderella going, feeling nice and pumped, so I figure, Why not? She's like, I don't know, thirty years old, blonde hair, nice little shape. So I start staring at her, you know, trying to get her to look at me. Make the bitch's day, right? They always say how chicks are hot for guys in wheelchairs—I wanted to see if that was bullshit or not."

Victor Gianetti, sitting across from Bobby at a table in the back of Lindy's diner in the Hotel Pennsylvania, said, "So what happened next?" Trying to sound like he gave a fuck.

"The girl starts to smile," Bobby said. "But it wasn't just a smile, like 'Have a nice day.' This was the smile of a girl who wants to get laid. So I'm thinking, This is it, my lucky day, when, all of a sudden, my legs start to spasm. I mean it's like somebody stuck an electric prong up my ass. My legs are shaking, the chair's bouncing up and down, people're coming over trying to help me. Finally, I stop shaking and I look up at the chick and her mouth's hanging open, looking at me like I'm some kind of freak."

"You are a freak, buddy," Victor said straight-faced. Then he said, "I'm kidding, I'm kidding. Jesus, where's your sense of humor?"

"I think you're missing my whole point." Bobby wondered why Victor never seemed to understand what the fuck he was talking about. "It wasn't like I gave a shit what some chick thought of me—it's just the way it is when you're in a fucking wheelchair, you start buying into this whole being a cripple shit, know what I mean? I mean when it comes right down to it, what does anybody do with their lives? You eat, you shit, you go to sleep—I can still do all those things. I can even screw. They have medicine, all these devices. It probably would be a big pain in the ass, but I could do it. I ride the bus, I can go anywhere anybody else can go. There's a word for what I'm talking about but I don't know what it is."

"You feel like people are putting you down."

"I said a word, not a sentence." Bobby thought, Is this guy a freaking moron or what? "It sounds like erection. Perception. It's like everybody's got this *perception* of me right off the bat. They see a big guy, late forties, wheelchair—they either feel sorry for me or they think I'm a fuckin' freak. Kids, Jesus, they're the fucking worst. Last winter, I go out to get a bottle of Coke when these three little kids start throwing snowballs at me. Not snow—ice. You know, like we used to throw at buses in the old days, now they throw them at people—what's the fuckin' world coming to? I swear to God, I was ready to go get my shotgun and blow the little fucks away. What happened to getting a little respect? The old days I'd walk down the street nobody'd come near me, but now the *perception*'s changed. I'm the same guy—I can still beat the shit out of somebody if I had to—but nobody else sees it that way. You see what I'm saying?"

"I guess so," Victor said and took a sip of milk.

Man, Bobby couldn't get over how shitty Victor looked in that bellhop uniform. Was this really the same guy who used to dress in style, wearing snazzy pinstriped suits and shiny shoes? Yeah, he'd always had thin hair, but now he was completely bald and he looked like he might've lost twenty or thirty pounds since the last time Bobby had seen him, what, six years ago? There was something wrong with his voice too—it sounded hoarse and scratchy, like an old man. Bobby might not've even recognized him at all if he didn't still have his dark skin and his big bent-out-of-shape nose that he'd probably broken dozens of times as a kid. Bobby could understand how a guy could lose some pounds and pack on the years, but he couldn't see how anybody could go from armed robbery to carrying people's luggage. Bobby might have lost his legs, but this asswipe had lost his balls.

Bobby slurped his coffee, said, "Remember the Bowery jobs?"

Victor smiling, suddenly looking young again, going back in time, said, "Those were real beauts, huh?"

"You plan a job, just the way you want it all to work out, and then boom—it goes that way, without one fucking hitch."

"Except when that little Chink pulled the alarm and started shooting at us."

"That wasn't a hitch. You gotta expect shit to happen when you're stealing jewelry. I'm talking about everything else. Getting to the car, getting on the bridge, getting to Brooklyn, switching cars in Brooklyn, getting to Queens, switching cars in Queens, and then boom—we're on the Island, counting the fuckin' take. Like clockwork. We did it, what, three times? All that fucking gold. Man, that was it."

He felt a rush, just seeing it replay in his head. It was like he was there again—ten years younger, looking sharp and in shape. When he saw himself standing in the jewelry store, holding his Uzi, and then running out to the street, he could feel his legs, like in those dreams when it all seemed so real, then he'd wake up and still be a fucking cripple.

"I should never'a gone out on my own," Victor said.

"That's exactly what I was talking about," Bobby said, "you

can't second-guess your life. So you fucked up, you took a fall, you're still what, fifty, fifty-five?"

"Forty-four," Victor said.

Thinking, *Jeez, the fucking sad sack looks sixty*, Bobby said, "See? Forty-four is like what twenty-four used to be. With vitamins, all the new shit with doctors, everybody's gonna be living to a hundred soon."

Victor, looking at his watch, said, "Fuck, I gotta get back to work. So what brings you around here anyway? You just wanted to shoot the shit or what?"

"No, it's a little more important than that." Bobby leaned forward, making sure the young guy reading the *Daily News* at the next table wasn't listening. "I got a job to discuss."

"A job we did?"

"No, a job we're gonna do."

Victor stared at Bobby for a few seconds, like he was trying not to laugh, then said, "Come on, you're joking, right?"

"Does this face look like it's joking?"

"What's this, April fools? Come on, Bobby, give me a fuckin' break, all right?"

"I'm serious, man. I came to you first because I know you're good and I know I can trust you. But if you don't want to hear me out I'll go talk to somebody else."

Bobby wanted to reach across the table and slap him, get him focused.

"All right, so tell me," Victor said, trying not to crack up. "What's this *job*?"

"I wanna knock over a liquor store," Bobby said.

Now Victor couldn't hold back. He started laughing, but it quickly turned into a cigarette smoker's hack. Finally, he recovered enough to say, "A liquor store? Jesus, you're too much, Bobby."

Bobby still wasn't laughing, or even smiling.

"Come on, Bobby," Victor said in that scratchy voice. "A liquor store?"

"What's wrong with that?" Bobby said. "That time we were shooting pool downtown what, seven, eight years ago, you said you wanted to work together again someday, right? Well, this is fuckin' someday."

Victor was staring at Bobby like he felt sorry for him. Bobby had seen this look a lot from strangers on the street, usually old ladies. One time an old lady asked Bobby if she could help him carry his bags home from the supermarket. Bobby wanted to fuckin' belt her.

"You can't walk," Victor said. "You know that, right?"

The waitress came over with Bobby's cherry cheesecake. Bobby took four full bites of cake then said, "So? Are you with me or not?"

"Come on, man," Victor said. "Weren't you just listening to me?"

"You know," Bobby said, chewing, "the old days you would've jumped if I told you I had a job to pull."

"The old days was a long fuckin' time ago. You're in a wheelchair and the doctor took some cancer out of my throat last year. They found a couple of spots on my liver they're watching—they said if it spreads down there, that's it—I'm a goner."

Bobby stared right into Victor's yellowish eyes. The cancer didn't surprise him—he knew there was *something* wrong with the guy. He said, "You know what I do every day now? When I'm not watching the fucking line-up on TV, I'm out in Central Park, shooting pictures of the broads in bikinis. I've got hundreds of pictures of boobs and asses, lined up on my walls like a fucking porno museum. Now you know that's not me, right? You know that's not what I do."

Bobby realized that he was talking too loud. People at other tables were looking over at him like he was crazy. Then Victor, looking at Bobby like maybe he thought he was crazy, too, said, "What's this? You a photographer now or something?"

"Why? You want me to take some pictures of your girlfriend? I'll make her look so good they'll put her in *Penthouse*."

"You couldn't make *my* girlfriend look good," Victor said. "To make her look good you'd have to shoot her with the fuckin' lights out."

Bobby and Victor stared at each other seriously for a few seconds then they both started to laugh. After a while they stopped laughing, but when they looked at each other they started again. Finally, they got control of themselves. Bobby felt like it was old times again, like he and Victor were twenty-five years old, shooting the shit in some Hell's Kitchen diner.

Victor, still smiling, said, "If you want to see some good-looking ass you should check out the whores they got workin' in this hotel."

Bobby knew Victor was just trying to change the subject but played along anyway, saying, "What? They got some good-looking hookers here?"

"You kiddin' me? These chicks ain't the needle whores they got dancin' on the stages on Queens Boulevard, you know what I'm saying? These are some high-class models they bring in here for the insurance faggots. You know what I'm talking about —call girls, escorts."

"Escorts, huh?" Bobby was getting a new idea. "They come here a lot?"

"Every fucking night."

"Yeah? And you're the bellhop here, right? I guess that means you take people up to their rooms."

"Why?" Victor asked.

Bobby smiled, said, "Tell me something else. Can you get me some room keys?"

Six

*She's a looker, yeah, probably. Jimmy's not known to pass
on a piece. It's what got him into a fix more'n once, a looker.
If you're asking because you're interested, remember what
she's doing with you before you fall in love.*
CHARLIE STELLA, *Cheapskates*

Max was in the Modell's sneaker section, trying on a pair of Nike running shoes. He liked the way they fit, but there was no way he was buying them. They were on sale for seventy-nine bucks, but Max never paid discount for anything. Nah, he'd rather go to some classy store on Madison Avenue to get them, even if it cost him double.

As he was trying on another pair, Max sensed movement next to him. He noticed that the briefcase he had put down next to him—with the ten thousand dollars, the extra set of keys to the apartment, and the code to the alarm with instructions—was gone. Looking back over his shoulder, he saw Popeye, wearing the leather jacket with the hole in it, walking away down the aisle at a normal pace, heading toward the stairs.

Suddenly, Max realized that Deirdre was dead—there was no turning back. Even if he wanted to call off the murder, he couldn't. He still had the phone number where he'd reached Popeye, but there had been a lot of background noise, and he'd had a feeling Popeye was at a pay phone somewhere. No, it was definitely over. By six P.M. Deirdre would be gone forever.

Max doubted that he'd miss her very much, but this wasn't his fault. Deirdre was the one who'd changed, not him.

Max had met Deirdre in 1982 at a Jewish singles weekend

at the Concord hotel in the Catskill Mountains. Back then, Deirdre was an upbeat, outgoing, friendly, big-chested girl from Huntington, Long Island. Max was living alone in a studio apartment on the Upper West Side, working as a twenty-four-thousand-dollar-a-year mainframe computer technician, and he decided that Deirdre was the best thing that had ever happened to him. After a few months of dating, he took her out for drinks at the bar at the Mansfield Hotel on Forty-fourth Street. It was a classy place, lots of books in the lounge, made Max feel well-read. Paula, the little blond barmaid, brought him his third screwdriver. He could see Paula understood he was a guy of wealth and fame, like the Stones song, what the hell was the title? Then Max, feeling nice and lit, thought, What the fuck? and popped the question to Deirdre. Six months later he was kissing her under the *huppa* at a synagogue in Huntington. They had a few happy years together—reasonably happy, anyway— living in a one-bedroom walk-up on West Seventy-seventh Street. Then Max left his job to start his own company. As his business started to take off, their relationship went downhill. They moved out of the walk-up, into a doorman building on the Upper East Side, and Deirdre slowly turned into the wife from hell.

She was constantly critical, angry, and depressed, and spent his money faster than it came in. But it wasn't the money that bothered Max so much as her personality. So, okay, it was the money too but, hey, that wasn't the main thing. It got to the point where Max couldn't stand spending more than a few minutes with her at a time. She was always starting arguments, telling Max that he was the cause of all her misery, that if she hadn't married him she would have been happy. Yadda, yadda, yadda. Then she started having mental problems. Manic-depressive, they called it, but Max had a simpler name—nasty bitch. Sometimes she was depressed, staying in bed all day, which Max actually didn't mind so much. But other times she was hyper—on the phone all the time or out shopping with his credit cards or picking fights with him. Max paid thousands of dollars for her to see the best shrinks in the city. They put her on lithium, which helped, but sometimes she stopped taking her medication. Max was convinced that on some sick level Deirdre enjoyed the torture she was putting him through. She was actually happy when she made him feel like shit.

Max tried to work things out peacefully. He went with Deirdre to a marriage counselor, but spending an entire hour cursing at each other didn't exactly help.

Finally, Max suggested divorce, but Deirdre said, "You know I'll never divorce you. I'm religious."

Max nearly laughed out loud, thinking, Yeah, if religion means tormenting a good man for eternity—wasn't that a Catholic thing? Deirdre was raised Orthodox Jewish, but she never went to temple or celebrated holidays—she didn't even fast on Yom Kippur, for Christ's sake. She was more atheist than Jewish and, besides, Orthodox Jews got divorces all the time. This was obviously just more bullshit Deirdre was using to try to prolong his agony.

When things got so bad Max couldn't stand living in the same house with Deirdre anymore, he considered moving out, separating. But he didn't see why he had to be the one to go. It was his house, he'd busted his balls to pay for it. If anyone went it should be her.

The situation seemed hopeless. Max knew that even if he could convince her to get a divorce, he'd be fucked. They had no pre-nup and Deirdre would take him to town in a settlement. She'd never worked a day in her life and they didn't have kids; Max didn't see why she deserved a cent of his money. But he knew a judge, especially a female judge, wouldn't see it that way.

Deirdre would get away with the townhouse, the Porsche, and at least half the money, and Max was ready to stick out the rest of his life being miserable before he let that happen. He'd worked too hard for what he had and there was no way in hell he was gonna let some lazy cow steal it out from under him.

Then Max went on Viagra and everything changed.

Max had thought he was starting to lose interest in sex, maybe even becoming impotent, but then he took Viagra and it worked miracles. Like a horny teenager, he started thinking about sex constantly. Whenever he passed a good-looking woman on the street he found himself imagining what she looked like naked. He bought sex magazines and ripped out the centerfolds, taking them into the bathroom at work and at home. He rented porn videos and nights and weekends he locked himself in the den of his townhouse and watched them. It was like he couldn't get enough of breasts. It got so bad he never saw women's faces because he couldn't raise his eyes past their chests.

Around this time Angela interviewed for a job at the company. As soon as Max saw her, he knew he had to have her. She was young, she had that whole Irish accent thing going on, and holy shit, the tits on her.

What surprised him was, entirely apart from what her body did for him, he liked being with her. She'd come out with some Irish-ism like, *Where's me coffee*, and he felt something swell up inside him. They never fought. She always laughed at his jokes and never bitched at him about the way he dressed or whatever. Max couldn't help dreaming about how great it would be if Deirdre was gone and Angela took her place. He could listen to that lilt his whole goddamn life. Hell, things worked out right, he'd bring her on a honeymoon to Ireland, maybe take her to a U2 concert. She seemed to like that Bono.

Max was more into the classical-type stuff. He'd worked at it anyway, bought the whole package of *Teach Yourself the Classics*. He still didn't understand what the hell it was all about, didn't even know the difference between an alto and a concerto, but he could fake it. He loved to bore the losers at the office, going on about his favorite arias.

When the murder idea came up, it seemed like a big joke. At first anyway. But the more Max and Angela talked about it the more it seemed like the only logical solution. He had offered Deirdre ways out, but she didn't want to take them, so what was the alternative? He was proud of himself, actually, for holding out for so long. A lot of guys who went through all the bullshit that he'd gone through wouldn't have had half his patience—they would have hired someone to knock Deirdre off a long time ago.

Outside Modell's, Max decided to walk back to his office instead of taking a cab. It was a great day—sunny, about seventy—and Forty-second Street near Grand Central Station was jammed with shoppers and businesspeople on their lunch breaks. Max felt cool, strutting along Fifth Avenue with his suit jacket slung over his shoulder, calling clients on his Blackberry.

When he arrived back at the office, Angela was sitting at her desk outside Max's door, eating a salad out of a plastic container.

Like it was any other normal afternoon, Max said, "Any messages?" and Angela said, "Not a one. How'd your meeting go?"

"Hard to say," Max said. "You confirmed that appointment for me with Jack Haywood tonight, though, didn't you?"

"Sure did."

"Terrific."

He felt his voice had the right mix of boss and mellow. Like he'd once heard a young temp say about some guy, *He had it going on*.

Max went into his office and closed the door behind him. He had a stiff vodka and grapefruit juice, thinking, This shit is good. At two o'clock, he met with Alan Sorenson, his Senior Networking Manager. There had been an emergency at a client's Newark office in the morning and Max wanted to make sure the situation was under control and that the company's network didn't experience any downtime. At three, Max met with Harold Lipman to discuss a quote Lipman was preparing for a new branch of a Japanese bank that was opening on Park Avenue. Harold had used a graphics program to design a full-color picture of what the bank's new Local and Wide Area Networks would look like. Max told Harold that the designs for the three-server network looked pretty and all, but it wasn't going to get him the sale.

The vodka hitting his stomach, Max said, "Take Takahashi to a strip joint or, better yet, call one of the escort agencies in my rolodex and buy him a whore or two. Trust me—that's the only way you'll close this thing."

Harold smiled, like he was embarrassed or thought Max was joking. Harold was thirty-six, tall and pale with thinning, graying hair, and he always seemed to wear the same wrinkled blue suit. Now *there* was a cheapskate who bought discount even if he could afford better. Before working for Max, Harold had worked as a retail computer salesman. He lived in Hackensack, for Christ's sake, with his wife and six-year-old daughter.

"I think I'll just take him out to lunch," Harold said.

"Guys don't want lunch, they want tits," Max said seriously.

Harold started to smile and Max cut him off with, "Hey, I'm not joking. If you want to start closing sales you'll have to learn this sooner or later. You want to be a big kahuna, get some money to buy yourself some new goddamn suits?" He was going to add, *And not at Today's Man,* but it was hard enough to educate the guy about table dances, he wasn't going to start fashion policing the poor slob.

"I don't think he's that kind of guy," Harold said uncomfortably.

"Is he a fudgepacker? If he is, I know a couple of guys who'd love to screw him."

"No," Harold said. "I mean, he wears a wedding ring and he didn't seem gay."

"Then I don't know what the problem is—take him to a strip joint. Believe me, as soon as he has some tits bouncing in his face you'll close the sale." Max waited then said, "In this business, it's make or break, and you gotta go for bust."

He let the joke linger, waiting to see if the schmuck got it.

Finally, Harold laughed uncomfortably, said, "I'm going to go to his office and present the proposal in person and see what happens."

Max said, "Is it your wife?"

"Is what my wife?"

"The ball and chain, the guilt trips, because if it is, don't tell her about it, that's all. You think I tell my wife every time I go to a strip club? But your wife'll be happy when you start bringing home the big commission checks. Trust me, I know this stuff and I certainly know women."

"It's not my wife."

"Then what is it, your kid? You?"

Harold, his face turning pink, said, "No."

"Look, you don't have to enjoy it, I mean if that's what you're worried about. You're not there to get off, you're there for the *client* to get off. He's Japanese right? Jesus Christ, the Japs love table dances. Trust me on this one. It's a cultural thing. Maybe it's because Japanese women, as a whole, have very small breasts. Why're you smiling? I'm serious. But whatever you do, don't, do not, buy him a Japanese dancer. Even if she has the big old-style silicone knockers, they don't like that. It gets them angry because it reminds them of what they don't have at home."

Harold stood up, took a few steps back toward the door, said, "Well, thanks for the advice, but I think I'll just stick to my own sales techniques."

"Listen, you putz, I don't want to have to let you go. I mean, I think you're a smart guy. When you started here you knew more about hardware than you did about networking, but you're catching up on your technical knowledge and I think in a month or two you'll be right where you need to be. That said, I hope you understand, I can't keep paying you your draw if you're not making any commish. I just can't run my business that way. Now I'm giving you some good, solid advice here. When I hired you I told you I'd give you all the training you needed, well this is part of your training."

Max was happy with this speech, his rally-the-troops schpiel. He knew he was great at motivation—that's why he was the head honcho and everyone else wasn't.

"I came here to sell networks," Harold said, "not table dances."

"Then maybe this is the wrong product for you," Max said. "Maybe you should sell bibles or something. Now go take Takahashi to a strip joint and close this goddamn sale, or else."

Toward five o'clock, Angela paid a visit. She locked the door and gave Max a few wet kisses and a neck massage and wished him good luck. Max said, "The funny thing is, I'm not even nervous."

Max made sure there was no lipstick on his face. He knew he must've smelled like Joy, but this was all right because a few months ago he had bought Deirdre some of the same perfume, in the smaller one-ounce size, so she wouldn't be suspicious when he came home reeking of it. If the police asked, he could just say he picked up the odor from Deirdre. He was covering all the bases.

In the bathroom, Max put a coat of spray-on hair fibers over his bald spot. The fibers could only be detected on very close inspection or by touch. The only problems were when it rained or when he was nervous—sometimes the fibers melted and dark streaks dripped down his neck.

At 5:25, Max left the office, still feeling very relaxed. Janet, the receptionist who was temping this week, and Diane from Payroll were nearby so Max made sure he said "See you tomorrow" to Angela, loud enough so Janet and Diane could hear how casual and professional he was being.

"Good night, Max," Angela said, not even looking away from her computer monitor. If they'd been alone, she'd have added *God bless* in that crazy way the Irish did. Psychos blew up half the UK and added, *God bless*?

Max hailed a cab on Sixth Avenue and instructed the driver to take him to Fifty-fourth and Madison, the building where Jack Haywood worked. Out of habit, Max memorized the driver's name—Mohammed Siddique—and medallion number—679445. As he got out, he said, "Thanks, Mohammed. God bless."

Max told Mohammed to wait double-parked while he went into the building to call Jack from the concierge's desk. Back on the sidewalk, waiting for Jack to show up, Max couldn't help thinking about the break-in.

He'd told Deirdre that he wanted to take her out to dinner tonight and to be sure to be home at six. Deirdre was usually good about keeping her appointments, but now Max was worried that something might go wrong. Deirdre had said she would be going shopping this afternoon, but Max wondered what would happen if she came home early or had decided not to go at all.

A car horn honked. The sudden noise jolted Max, made his heart skip a beat. He took deep breaths, trying to relax. If he looked nervous tonight and Jack Haywood or someone else noticed, it could also lead to some big problems later. He had to just trust Popeye. After all, the guy was a pro and a pro would know how to handle any complications that might come up.

A few minutes later, Jack strolled out of the building, wearing the jeans and sports jacket he had changed into for his night on the town. As Director of Operations for Segal, Russell & Ross, a big law firm with over two hundred employees, Jack was one of Max's biggest clients. He was only a few years younger than Max, but he kept in shape so he looked thirty-five. He was married with two kids and he had a house on Long Island, but he liked getting away from his wife and drinking and seeing naked women. Since he had become a NetWorld client, Max bought him as many table and lap dances and trips to the private fantasy rooms as he wanted. Once in a while, Jack asked Max to fix him up with a call girl. Jack would tell his wife he was out of town on business for the night and Max would book a room for him at one of the big New York hotels. Jack liked Russian women and Max knew two Russian call girls—sisters with monster-size breasts—who charged two thousand bucks for a *menage a trois*. It was above the going rate, but the money was well worth it to keep Jack as a client. He had a two-hundred-and-fifty-user network with four file servers and Max had placed three consultants there on a full-time basis. Including hardware and software sales, Jack was a million-dollar-a-year client. Besides, you had to love a guy who knew how to relax. What was the point of working your ass off and having no fun?

As soon as Jack got into the cab, Max turned on his "business personality." Usually, he hated small talk and phony conversation, but when there was money involved, man, Max could turn on the bullshit as well as anyone. During the ride across town to Legz Diamond's, Max managed to hold a conversation on golf, wine, real estate and the upcoming mayoral election, and half the time he didn't know what the hell he was talking about. But, shit, he knew that he was selling it well.

Legz Diamond's was on Forty-seventh Street near Eleventh Avenue. It was an upscale strip club—dark and glitzy, like a cheesy, suburban wedding hall. Although it was still early, the place was at least half filled with businessmen trying to keep their male clients happy. That's how the big city worked. You had a problem with it, get the fuck back to Boise, pal.

The host, a Mafia-looking guy with slicked-back hair, was on stage introducing the girls one by one, holding their hands and kissing them on the lips or cheek after he said their names. Max sometimes wondered whether all the girls screwed around with the host, but he was positive that the ones who kissed him on the lips had. Max was a known regular at the club so he and Jack got the VIP seats, right in front of the stage. Immediately, Max bought Jack a rum and Coke and a table dance with the girl of his choice. Jack picked a Puerto Rican with a big smile and a nice set of 38 or 40 triple-Ds. Perfectomundo. That was the way to get 'em in the mood.

Max was watching Jack enjoy himself when he heard someone call out his name. It was Felicia, a black stripper with 46 triple-Ds whom Max had bought dances from many times before. She was on the stage, leaning forward so that her implants hung down off her bone-thin dancer's body.

"How are you?" Max said.

"Wait up, baby," Felicia said. "Let me come down there and talk to you personally."

She climbed down off the stage and sat on Max's lap. Max knew that she was just being nice to him because he had tipped her a lot of money in the past, but he couldn't help but let the special treatment go to his head. He felt like Hugh Hefner, sitting there with a gorgeous girl on his lap. He wondered if Hef listened to Mozart. Guy spent his life in silk pajamas, smoked a pipe, he must listen to real music.

"That's better," Felicia said, wiggling her ass as she settled in on his lap. "So how you been?"

"All right," Max said.

"Yeah? I ain't seen you around here too much lately."

"I've been busy. You know how it is."

Max remembered once telling Felicia about his business and how this had impressed her.

"That's right," Felicia said, "you got some kind of company —computers or something, right?"

"That's right," Max said.

"That's cool, baby. Hey, anybody ever tell you how cute you are?" That lifted him in every sense. Who needed Viagra?

"Nobody who looked like you," Max said.

Felicia kissed him on the forehead and Max felt her hard implants pressing against his chest.

"I got an idea," Felicia said. "Take down my number. You can give me a call some time when I'm not working. We'll go out and have a good time. Or I can just come over to your place and we'll party there."

Max scribbled Felicia's number on the back of one of his business cards, then leaned back as she gave a nice, slow table dance. First she crouched backwards with her butt high in the air. Then she turned and danced with her breasts in Max's face. The bags were so big they were stretching the skin around them, and her nipples were sticking out like pencil erasers. In the middle of the dance, Max looked at his watch and saw it was 6:08. If all had gone according to plan, Deirdre had been murdered eight minutes ago. Felicia saw him looking at his watch and said, "You got a date tonight, baby?"

"No, I'm just checking the time. It's a little after six," he added so she would remember if anyone asked.

"A little after sex?"

"*Six*," Max said.

"Oh. I musta heard you wrong, baby."

"Right side," Max said to Asir Aswad as the cab turned onto East Eightieth Street. In the middle of the block, Max said, "Right here," and the cab came to a stop.

The meter read $9.70. Max gave Asir a twenty and took back the entire ten dollars and thirty cents change. He never tipped cab drivers and wasn't going to start now. He didn't want the police to think he had been acting in any way unusual minutes before discovering his wife's body.

It was 10:27. Max had dropped Jack off at Penn Station twenty minutes ago. Jack had seen Max writing down Felicia's phone number and it had impressed him a great deal.

"You gonna call her?" Jack asked.

"When I get around to it," Max said.

"If I were you I wouldn't wait on that," Jack said. "I'm getting a little tired of that Russian coffee cake. I might be in the mood for some chocolate pudding one of these nights. If you don't use that number, why don't you hold onto it for me?"

Jack was drunk, but not so drunk that he wouldn't remember that Max was with him all night while Deirdre was being murdered.

Of course Max had no intention of calling Felicia. Seeing those big gazongas in his face had definitely got him thinking, but before he had sex with a cheap stripper he'd need to see some blood work. He was just egging Jack on, trying to maintain his swinger image since Jack seemed to like it. It was part of the sales technique that he had perfected—*never show the client that you are in any way above him.* In other words, if the client sleeps with cheap hookers, then you have to come off as a guy who sleeps with cheap hookers. Besides, Max had Angela and he'd probably be spending the rest of his life with her. Although, he had to admit, it would be nice if Angela had knockers as big as Felicia's.

Max headed up the stoop to his townhouse. Through the lace curtains in the front windows he could see that there were no lights on inside. As he put his key in the first lock, he remembered what Popeye had said to him when they'd met in the pizza place, about how he might kill Max, too, if Max came home while he was still in the house. Max looked at his watch—10:29. Popeye must have left more than four hours ago. There was no way in hell he could be inside there now.

Seven

"Can't we go someplace else?" Mickey said. "How about one of those Irish pubs up on Second Avenue?"
"Irish pub?" Chris said. "What do you want to do, fuck an old man?"
JASON STARR, *Tough Luck*

After Angela's mother died, her father suddenly started telling Angela she had to find her Greek roots so last summer, partly just to shut her father up, she figured, Why not? and found a package on the Internet and went for a visit.

Bad idea. Real bad.

She thought she'd chill on the beach, work on her tan, but it turned into the trip from hell. All everyone kept asking her was when she was going to get married. She was twenty-eight, for god's sake, she didn't even have a serious boyfriend. One of her aunts made her promise that when she got back to New York, she would call Spiros, the cousin of someone on the island who was supposed to be a very nice guy. Just to get her aunt and everyone else off her back, she took Spiros's number and promised to call him. Jeez, a Greek got on your case, you were going to agree to anything.

A few months later, when she was back in New York and had just broken up with the latest dick she'd met out clubbing, she found the piece of paper with the phone number in the bottom of her suitcase and figured, What the hell?

Spiros was weird on the phone. He asked all kinds of questions—who was she, why was she calling, why did she wait so long to call. Angela was about to hang up when he suggested that they go to dinner Friday night. It wasn't like her social diary was overflowing so Angela went to meet him after work, figuring she'd go for the free meal.

Spiros was short with bad skin, a crooked nose, and a bushy black mustache. He looked sort of like Saddam Hussein. Angela wanted to ditch him right then, but they were at a very expensive Greek restaurant in midtown so she figured he must be loaded. During dinner, he was very polite and kept telling her how pretty her smile was and how her eyes were the color of the Aegean Sea, but Angela was more interested when he started talking about his money. He said he was in "the restaurant business," but he wouldn't tell her the name of the restaurant or where it was located.

He tipped big and, like all New Yorkers, Angela watched for that—it was a good sign.

They went out a few more times and he kept spending a lot of money on her and buying her presents. Whenever she brought up his restaurant he'd say, "Don't worry, I'll take you there some time," but he never did. Then, one afternoon, walking along Sixth Avenue, she spotted Spiros working at a souvlaki cart on the corner of Fifty-third Street. When she confronted him, he confessed that his plan was to marry her and put her to work selling souvlaki while he moved back to Xios. Angela's Irish temper came out in full force as she roared at him, "You fooking bollix!" He'd muttered that was a nice way for a lady to speak and she'd exploded, "I'm not a lady, I'm Irish yah cunt!"

Angela decided that she'd had it with Greek men. A couple of weeks later, she and her friend Laura went to Hogs & Heifers, a biker bar in the meatpacking district. They were having a blast, getting ripped on beer and shots of Schnapps, playing old Aerosmith on the jukebox. She'd had a thing for Steven Tyler years ago and still would've humped him in a heartbeat. Hell, the mood she was in, she would've humped any guy with money and decent breath. A few college girls, egged on by the surly bikers, stood on the bar during "Walk This Way" and started dancing topless. It was an informal ritual at the bar for girls to dance topless and the bikers started chanting for Laura and Angela to get up and join them. So Laura and Angela stood on the bar and did slow stripteases as the guys cheered them on. Laura stopped at her stockings, but Angela went all the way, pulling off her stockings and tossing them into the crowd of cheering men.

After dancing for about a half an hour, Angela got down from the bar, suddenly exhausted and dizzy. A sweaty Puerto Rican guy came over, holding Angela's stockings, and said, "Yo, I'm Tony. I think you dropped somethin'."

Angela was drunk and everything else that happened that night was a blur. As she put on her stockings and bra and the rest of her clothes, Tony bought her a shot of tequila. Then he said, "I like the way you was dancin' up there—you got all the moves. I like that accent too. You sound like that bitch from *Braveheart*."

They started making out, touching each other all over, then Tony brought her back to his place in Spanish Harlem. She wound up spending the weekend.

It turned out Tony made good money, as a union plumber, and Angela thought, Sex, money, a big apartment—she had it made. Then, one night, they were hanging out, watching a DVD of 24 when Tony pressed pause and said, "Yo, I got a wife in San Juan." Just like that, like it suddenly occurred to him.

Angela looked at him, said, "So you can divorce her, can't you?"

"Naw, naw, it ain't like that," Tony said. "I got three kids too and they all comin' over to live with me next week. Sorry 'bout that, yo."

Angela couldn't believe it. She'd spent all this time with this prick and let him do all that shit—tying her up, giving her a golden shower—then he says he has a fucking wife and kids! She literally became her mother, going at him like the very best of Irish women—clawing at his eyes, kneeing him in the balls, tearing out clumps of his hair. After she tore a bracelet off his hairy wrist, she took off and left him crying in front of the paused scene of Keifer Sutherland screaming at somebody. A couple of days later, Angela had the bracelet appraised. She expected it to be a fake and was stunned to discover it was white gold from Tiffany's, worth a couple thousand bucks. It cost five dollars to have the clasp fixed and she wondered if maybe her luck was changing.

As it turned out, her luck was changing all right, but not necessarily for the better.

The first change was that Dillon arrived from Ireland and bought her a silver Claddagh ring and a bottle of Black Bushmills, "the cream of the barley," he said. Dillon had that sly smile and those gross yet irresistible lips and said, "Mo croi, I'm stony."

He had to translate, that she was "his very heart" and what girl could resist that shit? A few weeks later, after they decided to move in together, he said, "Trust me, allanna, and we'll be in the clover."

Then the second change came—she caught herpes. Dillon swore he didn't have it, so she figured Spiros or Tony must've given it to her.

Then the third change: A job came to her out of nowhere. She'd applied for the position weeks ago and sick of would-be employers focusing on her shitty typing skills (she could only do twenty-four words a minute *with* mistakes) and lack of experience (she'd never had an office job above receptionist), she decided, To hell with it, she'd get the job like she got men—with her body. She dressed for the interview in sheer black pantyhose, patent heels, and a killer short skirt.

Dillon, reading his Zen book, looked up at her, smiled, said, "That position for typing or fucking?"

She'd answered, "Either way, I'm good to go."

Her appointment with Max Fisher, CEO of NetWorld, was for two o'clock and Angela arrived at the office half an hour early. The receptionist kept her waiting on the couch in the lobby for over an hour, and Angela got so pissed off she was about to leave. Then Max came into the lobby. Angela watched his gaze shift from her face down to her legs, then slowly back up again. When his eyes fixated on her bust, she thought, *Gotcha*.

She had.

During the interview, Max continued to eye her with his jaw hanging partly open. Angela thought Max was probably the most disgusting and pathetic guy she'd ever met. He was like some overgrown thirteen year old, with that picture of the blonde on the Porsche on the wall and the way he kept staring at her tits, with the tip of his tongue showing between his teeth. Angela said to herself, There's no way in hell I'm working for this loser. Then Max offered her a salary of sixty-four thousand a year plus full health benefits and three weeks vacation.

On her first day, Angela could tell that Max was seriously into her. It was more than just staring at her all the time and flirting. A couple of times when they were alone in his office he put his hand on her leg and one time he said he had knots in his shoulders and asked her to give him a massage. She figured, What the hell? The man had money, money she wouldn't get by blowing him off. Also, she liked the attention. Dillon hadn't been around very much lately. He was always staying out late, saying, *I need to hook up with the boyos.* The boyos meant the guys from the *Ra*, Dillon's name for the IRA.

But after only a few weeks, Max started to disgust her again. She couldn't stand his old, flabby body, and she hated the way he never stopped complaining. If he wasn't talking about his wife, saying things like how he was "ready to trade her in for a newer model," then he was whining about his heart or some other medical problem. And what was with all that crap music? One day he'd told her he'd teach her to appreciate "the nuances of the composers." She'd had to look up nuances in the dictionary, then realized how full of shit he was.

Max was like somebody's grandfather. She didn't know why she'd ever gotten involved with him. After taxes, sixty-four thousand dollars wasn't as much as she'd thought it would be. Max had bucks, she knew that, but he was a real tightwad. Yeah, he had the townhouse and the Porsche, but he never took trips or bought nice clothes. And when it came to tips he had deep pockets, but short arms. If she was going to see any serious amount of money out of the relationship, it wasn't going to be by just sleeping with him.

Meanwhile, Dillon still hadn't gotten her an engagement ring or talked about setting a wedding date. One night, Angela brought it up while they were lying in bed in the dark and Dillon said, "Mo croi, I gave you a Claddagh ring, that's as married as it gets. We get some green together, I'll bring you down to Vegas, do a Britney special, okay?"

Angela didn't want a fancy wedding. She just wanted to go to City Hall, maybe invite her father, her friend Laura and a couple of cousins and that's it. But Dillon wouldn't hear of it till they were, as he always said, "loaded."

He said it *low-dead* and she wondered for the hundredth time, was he fucking with her mind? She was Irish, and she knew how that worked. They did it just because they could, it was the national pastime. It explained the national sport, hurling, that cross between hockey and murder, played with no helmets unless you were, like, "a fag" or something. Talk about head-fucking.

To get revenge, Angela went with Max for a weekend to Barbados, telling Dillon she was going to Greece for an aunt's funeral. She came back more confused than ever. She didn't like Max any better, but she was still pissed off at Dillon. She wanted things to work out with him, but she knew they never would, because of money. He was always talking about how he wanted to have expensive cars and to live on the beach and not have to worry about working.

One day, Max's wife Deirdre came into the office and had one of her fights with Max. Deirdre was a nasty spoiled rich hag who'd probably never worked a day in her life. She wore designer clothes and expensive jewelry and always seemed to be coming or going from a manicure or an appointment with her hairdresser. Angela didn't know what they were fighting about today, but it didn't matter because it was always about something stupid. Angela heard Deirdre cursing at Max, then Max called her a "fucking bitch" and then, finally, they were both quiet. Max had told Angela that Deirdre was manic-depressive and was on medication, but Angela thought Max was just as pathetic for fighting with her all the time. She was sick—what was his excuse?

On her way out of the office, Deirdre stopped by Angela's desk and ordered, "Call Orlando at Orlo and confirm my three o'clock appointment."

Deirdre was wearing the same perfume that Max had bought her, but she used so much of it that she stunk up the whole office. She was overweight, but confident, swinging her big butt, walking on her three-inch pumps, a push-up bra making her chest look like a freak cartoon. Her short hair was dyed a blond that seemed almost orange and she was wearing her usual full face of makeup, like someone had just hurled it at her, letting it stick wherever.

"Why don't you call him yourself?" Angela said, wanting to add "yah dumb cunt."

Deirdre stopped and looked back at Angela with her mouth open, like she was shocked. "What did you just say?"

"Call him yourself," Angela said. "I'm not your fookin' slave."

"I would suggest you not speak to me that way," Deirdre said, "if having a job is important to you. You girls, you come over here, think you have cousins in the NYPD, think that dumb accent is the ticket to the good life. Well let me tell you, Maureen O'Hara is no Halle Berry, if you get my drift."

Deirdre laughed snootily then marched out of the office.

"Fuck you," Angela whispered then, the mick blood boiling, added, "yah fecking hoor's ghost!"

Angela knew that Deirdre couldn't get her fired—Max would just laugh if Deirdre complained to him—but she still didn't like being put down by some uppity bitch. It just didn't seem fair that Deirdre and Max had all that money and lived in that great townhouse. Angela knew if the shoe were on the other foot, and she was the rich lady, she'd be gracious, treat her inferiors with respect, helping out the poor, giving her old Donna Karan or whatever to Goodwill. She'd do a lot of stuff straight from her heart like that.

It was so frustrating—if only Angela had Max's money, she knew her life with Dillon could be perfect. Then the thought came to her for the first time: why *couldn't* they have Max's money? All he had to do was divorce Deirdre—whom he hated anyway—and then he and Angela could get married. Max would eventually have a heart attack and die and Angela and Dillon would be set. But when Angela brought up the divorce idea to

Max the next day he said he'd never even consider it. He was so cheap he'd rather stay with a wife he hated than give half his money away in a divorce settlement.

What could you expect from a bollix who didn't tip?

That was when Angela came up with the murder idea. The way she saw it, it was the only way things could ever work out with Dillon. The key was, she had to explain it to Dillon the right way. She couldn't say, "I've been screwing my boss for three months, you want to help me kill his wife?" She'd have to bring it up another way, tell him, "I know a way to get all of my boss's money, you want to help me?" Naturally, he'd say yes, once he found out exactly how much money he stood to make. He'd drop that Zen book in a hurry, replace it with a gun in jig time, that was for sure. Then she'd say that it would mean she'd have to fool around with Max a little. She'd say "fool around with him a little" on purpose, make it sound like it wasn't something serious.

When Angela told Dillon, he said he thought it was a great idea. He didn't even have a problem when she got to the part about "fooling around a little." He said, "But you can't say I'm gonna do it. You gotta tell him it's a friend of yours or some shite like that."

"I'll say you're a friend of my cousin's, but I need a name."

"Tell him I'm Popeye."

"Why Popeye?"

" 'Cause he ate spinach and we should keep the deal green."

Angela laughed.

"What's so funny?"

"I'm just imagining my boss's face," Angela said, still laughing, "when he finds out a guy named Popeye is gonna kill his wife."

"It was dumb to ask for ten," Angela said to Dillon. "You should've just stayed at eight."

Angela and Dillon were sitting in the dining area of her

apartment eating Apple Jacks and milk. The place was maybe four hundred square feet and there was no separate kitchen or living area. There was just a small area against one wall for the kitchen appliances and a countertop and a larger area with barely enough room for a full-size bed, a dresser, a small table and folding chairs from Bed Bath & Beyond, and a fourteen-inch color TV.

"He said yes, didn't he?" Dillon said. "You should be thankin' me. I got us two thousand extra dollars. You know how many Protestants I'd have to kill for that? A lot."

"You could've blown everything," Angela said.

"Blowing stuff is what I do, it's me birthright. That stupid fooker is going to bring us all that money. You should have seen his face—how scared he was."

Dillon's mutilated lips looked even uglier when he said this, as if he relished putting the fear of be-jaysus into someone.

"He was scared?"

"Fook yeah." Dillon started laughing. "You know what I told him? I told him he better not be home when I was there 'cause if he was home I might pop him too." Dillon was laughing harder. "I don't know how I didn't start laughing my arse off right then. But I kept looking at him like this…" Dillon made a serious face, his ruined lips making his features even more horrific. "It was like I was feckin' Michael Collins when he was arranging to kill the Brit agents, you should see that fillum, it's mighty. It was like I could see him thinking, Uh-oh, this fellah wouldn't be codding. It's amazing how somebody so rich could be so feckin' stupid."

"He's stupid all right," Angela said, "but he's not as stupid as you think. I mean a guy doesn't make so much money, own a company like that, being stupid."

"That's not true," Dillon said. "Look around sometime. There are a lot of stupid people in this city, and a lot of feckin' rich people too."

Dillon took his last bite of Apple Jacks, slurped down the flesh-colored milk, then reached for the bottle of Jameson. He poured a shot, called it his eye opener, and drained it. He waited for the liquid to hit his stomach, then gave what he called his *delicious shudder*.

Angela had a minor scare when Max said, "The only thing I'm worried about is this Popeye character." Everything had been going well, but now she was afraid that he would find out about everything.

Later that day, Angela had another scare when Diane in accounting came up to her at the coffee machine and said in a hushed voice, "Can I ask you a personal question?"

Angela knew that when a woman asked another woman that, it was a given that some kind of bitchiness was on its way.

"Sure," Angela said.

Diane was always trying to lose weight—lately she was on The Cabbage Soup Diet. Maybe she was going to ask for some diet advice, get some crack in that Angela should try the diet too, not that she needed to lose weight or anything because she looked *so good*. Yeah, right.

But instead Diane said, "Is there something going on between you and Max?"

"Max?" Angela said.

"You know..." Diane said, "I mean you're always going into his office, locking the door..."

"Who told you that?"

"No one. I just noticed it myself and I was just wondering, that's all."

"There's *nothing* going between me and Max," Angela said as though the idea repulsed her. But, just for effect, she held her stomach like she was going to throw up and said, "That's really disgusting. I mean, how gross is that? Could you imagine going down on that flabby belly?"

"I knew it couldn't be true," Diane said. "I mean, it's bad enough working for him. Who would want to sleep with him?"

Angela hoped Diane would forget all about it, but she'd have to watch her closely just in case. Then, walking away, she thought, *And hon, the diet, it's like, not working.*

That night Angela said to Dillon, "You know what that asshole said to me today? That I should add a cup size to my breasts."

They were in bed, passing a joint back and forth. Dillon took his hit and passed the joint to Angela then said, "So?"

"So?" Angela said. "What do you mean, So?"

"I mean, So? Like so what so."

Jesus, he sure knew how to annoy the shite out of a person.

"What? You don't like my breasts either?"

"I didn't say that," Dillon said. "I happen to like your tits, but I like your arse better."

"Thanks a lot," Angela said.

"You're welcome."

Angela sat up, looking down at her breasts. "I don't care what anybody says—I like them just the way they are."

Dillon sat up and started rolling another joint under the lamp on the night table. Angela, leaning over, started kissing his back and stomach. He had the smell of peat, the smell of the bogs, but she liked it. She said, "You know what else he told me. He said he wants to marry me."

"So?" Dillon said. "You gotta marry him so we get his money, right? That's the plan, right?"

"Yeah," Angela said.

She'd been hoping Dillon was going to propose himself one of these days. Dream on.

Dillon licked the edge of the rolling paper and sealed the joint. He lit up and took a long hit, then passed it on to Angela. Dillon said, "Dunno why I smoke this shite, it hasn't had an effect on me since the eighties. Now you give me a double of Bushmills, I can whistle the whole of the Star Spangled Banner."

She'd always gotten a big kick out of this—Dillon claiming that pot had no effect on him. Meanwhile, he'd smoke a joint, then pick up a shot of Bushmills and try to put it in his ear.

His voice already getting really slow, he asked, "See…what… I…mean?"

The day of the murder Angela kissed Dillon goodbye before she went to work, knowing it would be the last time she'd see him before Deirdre Fisher was dead. Dillon was in the dining area, sitting on a chair reading his book.

He held up a finger, said, "Listen to this." Then in his richest, most gorgeous voice intoned, "This is from Shunryu Suzuki… What do you want enlightenment for?…You may not like it."

She didn't get it, said, "I don't get it."

He laughed, said, "Tis few do."

Dillon said he loved New York, called it his *twisted city,* and she wanted to add, "Yeah, matches your lips," but never did because she was afraid of his temper. Although Dillon had never hit her, she thought he was the type who could. Violence simmered in him. It was never turned off—just went dormant sometimes.

"I'm going to take this town by the balls," he said, and she said, "Good luck."

He stood, produced a green emerald brooch, and said, "Back home, on Paddy's day, we have the wearing of the green." He pinned it on her breast, hurting her a little, but she didn't even flinch. She figured, like all his countrymen, he was truly fucked up and wouldn't give a shit anyway.

He put on a pair of very snazzy shades and said, "One time I was in Lizzie Bordello's in Dublin. U2 were holding court and I nicked Bono's glasses, you think I look like him?"

He looked like a horse's ass but being a woman, she said, "You kidding? You make Bono look like Shrek."

Dillon smiled, said, "Hold that thought, allanna."

Eight

*I had to give the guy credit. He didn't back down easy.
I'd have to watch him closely. His type could sneak right up
and bite you in the ass.*
REED FARREL COLEMAN, *The James Deans*

Sixteen years ago, when he got back from Desert Storm, Bobby took an acting class at some place downtown on Broadway. He didn't want to be an actor—no, that pussy *Hamlet*, *Streetcar*, Death of a Whatever shit wasn't for him. He just wanted to learn how to play a role, make people know right away he was the type of guy who didn't take shit from nobody.

He knew he needed some acting lessons big time when he pulled his first bank job, out at a Chase in Astoria. He went up to the teller, slid the note under the window, and stood there, trying to look like a guy who didn't fuck around, like Ray Liotta in *Something Wild*. But the girl looked at him, just for a second, like, Are you for real? Bobby thought he even saw her start to smile for a second there, like she didn't believe a guy looked like him could pull a bank job. His crew got away with the cash, no problem, but the girl's reaction still annoyed the hell out of Bobby. He wanted instant respect.

Before the next job, Bobby watched *Scarface* like a dozen times, trying to get the whole Pacino badass shit down cold. He thought he had it, but when he went up to the window at the bank the same thing happened. He thought it must be nerves or something. When he pulled smaller jobs, at grocery stores and supermarkets, it was even worse. He'd whip out his piece, say, "This is a stick up," and his mouth would be dry and the words would come out sounding all wimpy.

So he figured enough was enough and he signed up for the acting class. He felt out of place around all of the artsy-fartsy types, like he was crashing a party or something. He would've bailed but the teacher was this hot-looking little thing named Isabella. She'd been in something on Broadway and was in some soap opera for a couple of years. She knew her shit about acting and she gave great head too. Bobby stopped going to the class and got private lessons from Isabella. When she wasn't going down on him, she was teaching him how to emote, use stuff from his past, shit like that. Sometimes they'd read lines from plays to each other. It took him a while, but he finally got good at it. Isabella said he should start auditioning and that's when he knew it was time to dump her. From then on, whenever he pulled a job all he had to do was look at the fuckers and they knew what was going down. He probably could've robbed anyplace he wanted without ever showing a weapon.

Since Bobby got paralyzed he hadn't tried to act at all. But he knew that for what he had planned with Victor at the hotel, he was gonna have to have his acting skills sharp as a fucking tack or the plan would have zero chance of working.

Bobby opened his old *Riverside Shakespeare* book to a random scene in *Macbeth*. He took a couple of minutes to memorize the line, then he looked in the mirror, trying to look tough, like DeNiro in *Taxi Driver,* and said, "Come to my woman's breast and take my milk for gall you murthering ministers, wherever in your sightless substance you seek peace…"

He tossed the book away, realizing this was a waste of his fucking time. He still had the magic.

The townhouse was a lot bigger than Dillon had expected. He knew it would be big, but he didn't know it would be like *big* big, like a feckin' palace. There were three floors and the whole place was filled with all kinds of rich, ugly shite—couches, tables, chairs, mirrors, God-ugly paintings on the wall. Dillon couldn't wait till he was livin' in this gaff—then he'd make some *serious* changes. First he was going throw out all this ugly shite. Then he was going to put in a Shebeen bar downstairs with one of them giant screen TVs—like the kind they had in the sports bars—and then he was going to have his own feckin' club—call it A Touch of the Green. Every night he'd be blasting the Pogues with his own private DJ, and he'd invite all his boyos to come down, and they'd rock the place with jigs and reels. He might even teach some bollix how to play the spoons. He already knew how to play the odds.

Dillon still couldn't believe that all this was going be his just for killing some rich old lady. Jesus, he'd offed fookers for the price of a pint.

It was funny—before all this started he was getting tired of Angela and was thinking about dumping her when she came to him with this great idea. At first he thought it must be some kind of joke—it all seemed too easy. She said all she'd have to do was "fool around" with the guy and get him to want to marry her. The funny thing was, he didn't care if she took him on and ten of his friends, just as long as he got the dosh.

Dillon didn't know why Angela thought that they were going to get married someday. Yeah, he had considered asking her to marry him, but what the hell did that mean? He'd asked lots of colleens to marry him—it was just something fellahs said to women to make them shut up. He'd a supply of silver Claddagh rings. Angela also wanted to have kids, buy a house in the country or some shite. Dillon had three kids already, that he knew about, and he had four separate wallets with snaps of them. And if he really wanted to have a wife and kids, he would've stayed with Siobhan, the girl he got pregnant in Ballymun. There was a woman, fiery and able to sink the jar like a good un and cook, she made black pudding to die for.

The only reason he was with Angela at all was because of the way she was in that pub that night. Usually, he liked dumb women, but Angela looked good there, giving mouth to the ugly bartender. He'd been planning to take off after a couple of weeks, but he couldn't afford rent yet, so he figured he'd live with her till he found a decent score.

He told Angela a lot of lies, afraid if she knew the truth she'd throw him out. He told her he was a scout for the RA, thinking sussing out schemes for the boyos was a patriotic ideal she'd understand. The truth was he was what is known in Ireland as a Prov-een. When the Irish want to diminish something, somebody, they add *een*, making it diminutive. You call a man a man-een, you're calling him a schmuck, a wanna-be. The Ra had many guys who hung on the fringes, did off jobs for The Boyos but were never seriously considered part of The Movement. They were mainly cannon fodder, used and discarded and if they managed a big score, no problem. Dillon had actually made some hits for the Boyos, but it didn't get him inside, not in the inner circles where it mattered. He knew where they hung out in New York but he didn't know what the level of operations was. They kept him on a strictly need-to-know basis and a loose demented cannon like Dillon, he needed to know precious little.

There were two other other things he lied to Angela about—one was big, the other small. The small thing was herpes. He said he'd caught it off her, but the truth was he'd caught that shite a long time ago, back in the eighties. The big lie was that he'd only killed a few people before. Actually, he'd killed at least seventeen people—some memorable, some not. Like all his race, Dillon was deeply superstitious. All that rain, it warped the mind, added to a mountain of church guilt. What you got was seriously fucked up head cases or as they called them in Dublin, "head-a-balls," which doesn't translate in any language yet discovered.

The one that gave Dillon pause was a tinker he'd killed, not that the guy didn't need killing; he did, but you didn't want to mess with a clan who knew a thing or two about curses. It was in Galway, a city of serious rain, it poured down with intent and it was personal. That town had swans and tinkers, and culling both seemed like a civic duty. There'd been a case in the place, swans and tinkers being killed, and the citizens were outraged about, yep, *the swans*. Dillon had been drenched, lashed with wet, the week of the Galway Races. Fookit, he'd lost a packet on a sure-fire favorite and then in Garavans the tinker had snuck up on him, doing the con, going, "How are ye, are ye winning, isn't it fierce weather?" Like that. The whole blarneyed nine and then lifted Dillon's wallet, headed out of the pub. Dillon caught him at the canal, rummaging through the wallet, so intent on his fecking larceny, he never heard Dillon coming. A quick look around, no one about, then Dillon gave him the bar treatment, a Galway specialty. You zing the guy's head off the metal bars lining the canal for as long as it takes to say a decade of the rosary, keeping the deal religious. Thing is, you murder a tinker, you're cursed—they have a way of finding out who did the deed and then damn you and all that belongs to you. Still gave Dillon a tremor when he thought about it.

Todd, that was the tinker's name. Dillon would like to have lots of things in his past changed, and knowing the tinker's name topped the list. Knowing the name made it, like, personal and shite. You didn't ever want murder to be personal, you might start to take it serious, think it meant something. He felt the karma would come down the pike and hit him when he least expected it. He never shared this hibby jibby with anyone, but Todd was engraved in whatever passed for his heart forever. Wasn't that curse enough?

Oh, yeah, and he'd committed one murder in New York. He cracked some guy's head open against a brick wall because the guy had that plummy Brit accent.

Dillon had only gotten busted for one of his murders—a guy he'd cut for looking at his woman—and did five hard years in Portlaoise, where they kept the Republican prisoners. His first day, he'd found the Zen book on his bunk, left by the previous inmate. He'd picked it up from boredom and got gradually hooked. Hooked up quickly too with the Provo guys and got his arse covered though again, he wasn't privy to any of their councils. They'd look out for him but didn't feel any great need to stretch it.

He continued to ransack the downstairs of the townhouse. It was fun turning things over, destroying shite. A rush like when he was in his teens and the Brits came at them with rubber bullets, those suckers bounced off you, you hurt like a pagan for a week. The first time they got an armored car on fire and got the soldiers to crawl out, crying for their mammies, with a sniper picking the fookers off, one by British one. Fook, it got him hard just remembering. Those Brit accents, sounding polite even as they roared. Dillon was convinced then that he was one of the real Boyos. In fact, there was hardly a kid in the city who hadn't been bounced by a rubber bullet—it came with the territory.

When everything on the ground floor looked good and wrecked, he went upstairs. He found the bedroom Max had told him about, which was filled with more ugly old shite that looked like rubbish his grandmother would buy. Everything was made of wood and they had some fierce gold-colored bed. Dillon imagined what the room was going to look like when he put mirrors on the ceiling, put down some reed mats, like home, get one of them waterbeds, and put a jacuzzi in the bathroom. He broke all the glass stuff from on top of the dresser and night table and dumped all the clothes out of the drawers. Then he found the old lady's jewelry box and stuck all the diamond- and gold-looking stuff into a plastic bag he found.

On the wall, there were some pictures of a fat old lady—he

guessed this was Mrs. Fisher. There was also a picture of Max Fisher standing on a beach somewhere. He looked the same as he did at the pizzeria and in Modell's, except he had a bit more hair. Dillon couldn't wait till he got to do Max too. He knew the plan was to wait for him to die but, fook, Dillon wanted to get on with his life. He hated that old bollix, the way he was sitting there in his posh suit. He reminded Dillon of Fr. Malachy, his principal in school. Dillon never understood what the priest was saying but nothing about school made much sense to Dillon. The only reason he went was to keep the Social Services away. But Fr. Malachy was always calling him down to his office for whatever, or suspending him. Malachy thought he was God almighty because he was the principal and could do whatever he wanted. Now Max Fisher was trying to pull that same deal, trying to call all the shots, but this time Dillon named the jig— now he was the man in charge and Max Fisher was the little Irish schoolkid sitting on the other side of the desk. When Dillon had heard that Malachy died in real agony from cancer Dillon had muttered, *hope he died roaring*.

Dillon heard voices and a noise—a key turning in a lock. He took out the .38 he'd gotten from the Boyos' place down off the Bowery. When he'd showed up there, they'd rolled their eyes, like, here's this mad annoying fook again. But he had money to pay for the piece and, what the hell, he'd brought some decent bottle of Jameson. They treated him like a younger brother who's always hanging on but is never, like ever, going to be in the gang.

Heading downstairs, he remembered what the Yanks said and used it now like a prayer, albeit a dark one, *Lock n load*.

Nine

Straight to Hell
THE CLASH

As Max was feeling for the light switch, he slipped and fell. The way he landed and the way the pain was shooting down his side, he thought he'd broken his hip. When he started to get up he realized he was okay, but wondered what the cold wet stuff on his hands was.

For some reason, this whole time he'd been planning the murder, Max hadn't thought about what the body would look like. He thought Deirdre would die like people in old westerns died. In those movies you never saw any blood—the cowboys and Indians just fell off their horses and lay there nice and still. In modern movies, they always showed the blood squirting out of people's heads, gushing from their mouths. Max always thought it was just Hollywood exaggerating things, but now he realized that those movies didn't show half of the real horror.

If it weren't for her short, blond hair, Max might not have recognized Deirdre at all. Blood had leaked from her head into a two- or three-foot-wide puddle around her body. Although she lay on her back, Max could barely make out the features of her face. He thought, This can't be fuckin' happening. It was part of a dream—soon the alarm clock would ring and he'd wake up. When a ringing actually started, Max thought he really *had* been sleeping. But then he realized that the noise wasn't an alarm clock, it was the burglar alarm. Shit, it nearly gave him a coronary and his heart was in bad enough shape.

After he shut off the alarm, he glanced back at the scene, shocked again by all the blood. When he realized that the wormy stuff on the wall was part of Deirdre's brain he started to throw up. No one told him it was going to be so...gross.

He went into the downstairs bathroom where he took off his blood-covered clothes and washed the blood off his hands. He still couldn't believe this was happening. What the hell had he been thinking, planning this murder like some kind of lunatic you read about in the tabloids? The *Daily News* today had two twins on the front page, the ones who'd murdered their parents, with the screaming headline, TWIN KILLING. Wait till they got hold of this.

He wondered if he was insane. He didn't think he was insane, but what the hell did that mean? Insane people never think they're insane so how did he know if he was insane or not? He certainly felt fevered and needed a drink—a whole bar of them.

He had to get a grip. He could worry if he was insane or not later—right now he had to do what he was supposed to do or he was going to spend the rest of his life in jail, possibly on death row.

Trying not to look at Deirdre's body, he walked back out toward the front of the house. He went upstairs to make sure it was ransacked like the downstairs was. He saw that most of Deirdre's jewelry was gone, then noticed that Popeye had broken the jar that held his kidney stones. Now he'd have to get on his knees later and look for the fucking things. In the center of the room was a turd. Max squinted at it, truly horrified. Somehow it even seemed worse than the murder, that the animal went to the toilet on his carpet. How fucked up was that? Murder was one thing but this, this was a goddamn liberty.

He went back downstairs, just to make sure everything

was right before he called the police. He was about to dial 911 when he saw something that made him freeze. Sticking out from the hallway into the living room was another pair of feet—a woman's feet in high heels. He thought, Jeez, it's just like *The Wizard of Oz*. Then nausea returned fast as he inched toward the hallway, shaking, covering his mouth. When he saw the second blood puddle he gagged, coughing up stomach acid. He couldn't recognize this woman's face either, but something about her body looked familiar. She was heavyset, wearing jeans and a light blue sweater. Her long curly brown hair looked familiar, too, like…

Fuck, it was Stacy Goldenberg—his niece, on Deirdre's side. She was living in New York, going to school at Columbia. Sometimes she and Deirdre went shopping together and, for some reason, she must have come home with her tonight.

Max fainted. When he regained consciousness both hips were killing him. He remembered the dead bodies and how he needed to call the police. He thought about confessing—getting a shrink to say he was nuts. They'd medicate him, lock him up for a while, and he'd eventually get out. Or he could pin the murders on Angela—say it was all her idea. It *was* all her idea, wasn't it?

He shouted, "Get me the fuck out of this!"

Max couldn't remember anything. Suddenly, his whole life was a fog. Then he heard Popeye saying how he would get to him if he ever went to the cops. This Popeye was a total psycho —there was no doubt about that—and Max had a feeling he meant everything he said.

Max went into the kitchen, chugged some vodka, the booze burning like a son of a bitch. Then he did some deep breathing, pulling himself back together, and dialed 911.

✻

Max was staring through the lace curtains at the red strobe lights outside the townhouse and he didn't hear the last question Detective Simmons had asked him.

"Sorry," Max said, "what was that?"

"The alarm," Simmons said. "Could you please tell me what happened with that again?"

Detective Simmons was a stocky black man, about forty years old. He was wearing a wrinkled white shirt, obviously discount, sweat stains on the armpits, with a tie wound on loosely. Max was wearing the navy sweat suit he'd changed into before the police came. He knew it was stylish and made him look slim and athletic.

Other officers, forensic workers and a crime-scene photographer were gathered in the hallway, creating a din of voices and confusion.

"Like I told that other officer," Max said. "I tripped it off by accident. I mean I forgot to disarm it."

"So the alarm definitely wasn't ringing when you got home?"

"No," Max said.

Now Simmons was looking in a small notepad, saying, "And what about the other victim—Stacy Goldenberg. Did you know that your wife was going shopping with her today?"

"No," Max said. He was starting to feel nauseous again, thinking about how he was going to have to face his brother-in-law and sister-in-law—Stacy's parents. The vodka in his stomach was shouting, *Yo, buddy, how 'bout some more down here?*

"When was the last time you spoke to your wife?"

"Like I told the first officer—this morning."

"You didn't talk to her at all during the course of the day?"

Max shook his head, trying for that devastated look.

"The past few days, had your wife told you about anything strange that happened around the house while you were gone?

For example, did she say any strangers came to the door or rang the bell or anything like that?"

Max, still shaking his head, said, "No. Nothing like that," acting weighed down with grief.

"So far we haven't found any sign of forced entry," Simmons said. "What about keys? Do you keep a spare set with any friends or neighbors?"

"No," Max said, letting his voice choke a little.

"What about the code to your alarm? Do you share that with anybody?"

"No one knew the code except me, Deirdre, and the alarm company." Damn, if he could just squeeze a few tears out. How did they do that shit?

"You see what I'm getting at, don't you, Mr. Fisher? There are only two likely possibilities for how the killer got inside the house. He either broke in before the women arrived, or he forced his way in with them. If he broke in, he would have tripped off the alarm, and if he forced his way in with the women, the alarm would still have gone off unless he forced your wife to disarm it. But even if he did that, it wouldn't explain how the alarm got set again when he left, and you're telling me that when you came home the alarm was set. So the only logical conclusion is that the killer—or killers—somehow knew the code to your alarm."

Simmons gave him a look that seemed to scream, *I know you did it and I'm gonna hang you for it, you schmuck*.

Trying to ignore the look, pretending he was imagining it, Max said, "You know, I'm really not feeling too well. Is it possible we could do this tomorrow?"

He wiped his dry eyes, as if he were on the verge of some hysterical weeping.

"I understand," Simmons said, "but it's true what they say,

you know—the first twenty-four hours after a crime is committed is when most criminals are apprehended. If we could just clarify a couple of other things, I think it could help us a great deal."

An officer came over and started talking to Detective Simmons. Max wasn't paying attention, staring blindly again toward the activity outside the house.

"This is just routine," Simmons continued, "but can we go over your whereabouts tonight one more time just to make sure we got everything down right?"

He had a little edge in his voice, making it clear that this wasn't really a request.

"I was at Legz Diamond's entertaining a client."

"And what time did you get there?"

"I don't know. Somewhere around six o'clock."

"And you were with a gentleman named Jack Haywood?"

"That's right."

"And where does Mr. Haywood work?"

Max told him. Simmons wrote the information down then asked, "And how long were you at Legz Diamond's?"

He stressed the *Legz*, leaning on it, letting it show what he thought of those kinds of places.

"Like I said, I got home around ten, ten-thirty, so I was probably there, I don't know, till about nine forty-five, ten o'clock."

"And you say you took a cab home?"

"First I dropped Jack off at Penn Station." Suddenly, Max felt lightheaded again, a little dizzy. "I really don't think I can handle any more of these questions right now. I'm sorry." He couldn't wait to get back to that vodka bottle.

"You want to see a doctor?"

"No. That's all right. I think I just need to be alone."

Alone with vodka.

"You might want to think about staying at a friend's house or at a hotel tonight. We'll have to be here for a while longer, working on the crime scene."

"That's all right," Max said. "I'd rather stay here."

Simmons gave him a look, like, *Why would you want to stay at the scene of a goddamn bloodbath?* Max wondered if he'd fucked up.

Trying to temper it, Max said, "I mean, of course it'll be difficult, but I'm gonna have to deal with it eventually, right?"

Shit, that didn't help. Work, brain, work.

"You sure about that?" Simmons said. "Those reporters are like goddamn vultures out there. This is going to be a big news story, you know."

"I know," Max said.

"Your number listed?"

Max shook his head.

"Well, that's one good thing anyway. If you want, I could have someone call Mr. and Mrs. Goldenberg, spare you that at least."

"It's okay," Max said. "I'll call them."

That was good, letting the cop know he was a standup guy. Yeah, it was going to be a difficult call but hey, that's what Max Fisher did, the difficult stuff.

Yeah, right.

Simmons stood, putting his pad away in his shirt pocket, and said, "I'll be in touch with you again, let you know how the investigation is going. You're not planning to leave town or anything, right?"

Max thought this over carefully then, as if his whole life had ended, said, "Where would I go?"

Calling Claire and Harold Goldenberg was a whole other nightmare. For Claire, Deirdre's sister, the murders were a double tragedy. After Max told her, she screamed, "No! No! No!" then broke down, crying hysterically. Jesus, Max should have had that drink first. What the hell was wrong with him? Did he think she'd take it well?

When Harold got on the line Max had to go through the whole rigmarole again. He felt worse for the Goldenbergs than he did for himself. He'd always liked Harold, who had his own practice as a chiropractor in Boston, and he had nothing against Claire either. He didn't want to hump her or anything, but she was inoffensive. They were both nice enough people, and they definitely didn't deserve to lose their only kid in a tragedy like this.

Stacy wasn't so bad either. He never saw her very much when she was growing up, but when she started at Columbia she got closer with Deirdre, her "rich aunt in the city." It was horrible that she had to die, especially like this. She hadn't ruined anybody's life, caused misery for anybody. She was just an innocent college girl who probably didn't have an enemy in the world. Christ, she was only twenty.

Max felt his entire body getting hot and starting to shake—he wanted to call Angela, remind himself why he went through with all this crap in the first place. But as he picked up the phone and started to dial he stopped himself. That was exactly what Detective Simmons was waiting for. Max knew that Simmons suspected him more than he'd made out—why else would he have asked him if he was planning to leave town? The police had probably tapped his phone lines, put a cop on surveillance to watch his every move. They probably already knew about Angela, and her cousin, and Popeye, and now they were just waiting for Max to give himself away.

That alarm business had done them in, Max decided. That cocky Irish prick obviously wasn't as much of a pro as he claimed to be. Max kicked himself for not doing some kind of background check on Popeye before agreeing to all of this. He'd been thinking with his dick and that was never a smart move.

Max finished the bottle of vodka, the alcohol doing wonders to relieve his panic. He decided he was just acting paranoid, which was probably normal after you've paid to have your wife killed. He decided he couldn't have handled the situation any better than he had and the only thing he could do now was get some rest.

Surprisingly, Max slept like a baby, dreaming about Felicia the lap dancer.

In the morning, feeling clear-headed and alert, he resolved to keep his mind focused. He showered, shaved, and got dressed. The bedroom was still a mess so he did a little straightening up—he was able to retrieve all of his kidney stones—and decided he would have his maid come in later, or sometime soon, to finish cleaning. He was hungry and went downstairs to make a pot of coffee and some oatmeal. With a glass of water he swallowed a Mevacor and one of his little blue Viagra pills. The police had gotten someone to clean up the blood late last night, although there was still a faint stain on the wall where Deirdre's brains had splattered. Max decided he would have to have the maid deal with that too. He'd also have to get someone to repair the two bullet holes in the walls. Or maybe he could just hang pictures over them.

As Max ate his breakfast, the doorbell rang several times. Looking through the peephole, he saw the reporters outside his door. Finally, when he finished his food, Max opened the door and made a brief statement to the TV cameras.

He said, "This is a tragedy that no one who hasn't experienced the violent death of a loved one, or loved ones, could possibly comprehend. I just hope the police find the bastard who did this and that he's punished to the fullest extent of the law."

He knew he'd achieved the right blend of outrage and deep sorrow and that his face would look great on the news. Hell, he'd probably get letters from women asking to marry him.

The reporters shouted questions, but Max apologized politely and shut the door. He was proud of himself for handling the situation so well. He sounded exactly the way he was supposed to sound and he'd even managed to force out some tears. He'd put drops in his eyes beforehand and those suckers always stung him.

Keeping with Jewish tradition, Deirdre's funeral would have to be as soon as possible. Max calmly took care of all the arrangements, scheduling the service for Monday morning at the Riverside Memorial Chapel on Amsterdam Avenue, where he had gone for his aunt's funeral last year. The whole deal cost him a pretty penny but, hey, he wasn't no cheap date. He spent the rest of the day on the phone with friends and relatives, accepting condolences and sharing sympathies.

No one from the police department called all day, but Max didn't know whether this was good or bad. Late in the afternoon, he wondered if he should call Simmons to find out what was going on. It seemed like the natural thing to do, right? On the other hand, would that be something an actual grieving husband would do? Finally, he decided not to call and just wait and see what happened. This was more like the old Max, making informed decisions.

At six o'clock, he watched the local newscasts. All the stations had the murders as their top story—after all, it wasn't every day that two affluent white women were murdered in New York City. He watched himself on TV, again proud of his performance.

According to the reports, there still weren't any suspects in the case, but police were conducting "a thorough investigation."

The next day Max woke up early to prepare for his guests. His brother Paul and Paul's wife Karen from Albany were coming down and so were Harold and Claire Goldenberg. The Goldenbergs were only going to stay for one night, and they were going to stay in a hotel. Tomorrow they would attend Deirdre's funeral in the morning and then fly back with Stacy's body to Boston for her funeral on Tuesday. Max was looking forward to seeing his brother and sister-in-law, but he was dreading having to face the Goldenbergs. He hated to admit it, with them grieving and all, but they were dull as hell.

The Goldenbergs arrived first, but fortunately they didn't want to stay long. Claire said she wanted to see the spot where her daughter had died, but when Max showed it to her she lost it and Harold had to take her back to the hotel. An hour or so later, Paul and Karen arrived. Max and Paul had never been very close, but Max always felt good about himself when he was around Paul. He had six years on his brother and, although their age difference didn't mean as much now that they were both in their fifties, Max felt that same superiority over his brother that he'd felt when he was sixteen and his brother was ten. Now Paul was an English professor at some college in Albany. He taught Shakespeare and Chaucer, or something like that, and he and Max had zero in common. Max loved watching Paul drool over the fine house, the expensive furnishings. Try pulling that down as a goddamn teacher.

The phone was ringing constantly through the day. Relatives and friends he hadn't heard from in years came to the house to pay their respects and to find out about the funeral arrangements. A couple of reporters rang the bell, too, but Max had Paul explain that the family needed to be alone. Karen went food shopping and came back and cooked a huge roast-beef-and-potatoes dinner. Max felt guilty about eating the meat, but he decided to hell with being health conscious—this was a special occasion. And, fuck it, he was hungry. All that sympathy gave you an appetite. He even had a slice of cherry cheesecake for dessert. It was delicious, too, worth every goddamn milligram of cholesterol.

Finally, Max was starting to feel some of the relief that he'd thought he'd feel after Deirdre was gone. With all these people around, Max imagined how aggravated he would have felt if Deirdre had been there, going on and on about herself and her problems or confronting people like some kind of maniac. Now, for the first time in years, Max felt like he could relax in his own house. The way he was handling his grief, his whole attitude, was having an impact too. Was it his imagination or was he standing a little more erect? Posture had always been a problem but, hey, murder your old lady, you didn't need a chiropractor. Radical therapy, maybe, but it worked.

Max was also starting to feel less guilty about Stacy's murder. Yeah, it was horrible that she had to die, and yeah, he was upset about it. But it wasn't as if *he* had killed anybody. Popeye was the crazy one—he'd pulled the trigger. Stacy's death was just an accident, no different than if she had been walking across a street and been run over by a bus. The fact that she was murdered in Max's house, by a hit man whom Max had employed, was an unfortunate coincidence that Max had had no way of preventing.

And, besides, she died with her dreams intact, no major disappointments yet. He'd kind of done her a favor, when you thought about it.

On the news that night, there were reports about a woman in Brooklyn who had strangled her two children and set them on fire and a janitor in a Bronx elementary school who was discovered having sex with a nine-year-old girl. It was a good thing New York was full of sickos, Max decided—it meant that the stories of Deirdre and Stacy's murders would be quickly overshadowed.

The next day, Monday, was the funeral. Max wore a Hugo Boss suit, one he knew made him look good. Harold and Claire were at the chapel, along with the rest of Deirdre's relatives and friends. Many of Max's relatives were there too. Some people from the office came, including NetWorld's CFO and Vice President. Although Max was hoping Angela would show up, he realized it was probably better that she hadn't. Probably no one would have noticed, but it might have seemed slightly unusual for someone who had been with the company less than a year to take such a strong interest in her boss's personal affairs. Besides, they wouldn't have had a chance to talk in private anyway.

Max was barely listening to the rabbi's eulogy, but when he realized that everyone was breaking down in tears, he knew he had to show *some* reaction. He couldn't force out any tears, so he just put on his sunglasses and just stared down at his lap. He tried to emit some loud sighs but feared it sounded like he was breaking wind. He decided to let it slide, let the shades do the talking, like rock stars did.

After the rabbi, Claire stood at the podium and made a long sad speech about how she had lost two of the most important people in her life. This actually made Max cry and he took off his sunglasses for everyone to see. He was going for that swollen eyelid look that women seemed to pull off naturally.

Deirdre was buried in her family plot on Long Island. Max was glad they hadn't bought plots together and that he would never have to be anywhere near Deirdre again. After Deirdre was lowered into the ground, each family member covered the coffin with a shovelful of dirt. Max felt another wave of relief when the dirt he dropped clattered on top of her coffin.

Then came his moment, the grand slam, the slam-dunk. He approached the grave, letting a slight tremor rack his body, then produced one white rose. He'd planned to let it flutter into the hole as he gave a perfect moan but, fuck, he missed and the flower landed on the side. He had to bend down, dirtying his new suit, then muttered *Fucksake*, and threw the goddamned thing in.

The *shiva* sitting was at Max's house. During the next few days, people dropped by the townhouse, bringing food, and sharing stories about Deirdre. As much as Max had enjoyed the mourning bit at first, it was getting old. Besides, it made his jaw hurt, having to wear that hangdog expression day after fucking day.

Paul and Karen stayed until Tuesday night and then drove back to Albany. On Wednesday, a condolence card arrived from the office, along with a bouquet of flowers. Although the card was signed by almost everyone, Max didn't read anyone's note except Angela's. It read:

> *With My Deepest Sympathy, Angela*
> *Gra go mor*

What the fuck was with that, Greek or something?

Seeing her handwriting made Max suddenly desperate to see her in person. Again, he wanted to call her—just to hear her voice, that accent he loved, and hang up—but he knew that would be stupidest thing he could do. But he was becoming restless. He couldn't wait to go back to work, to get back into the swing of things.

On Thursday, Berna, Max's West Indian maid, came and scrubbed the wall and the floor in the downstairs hallway. A repairman came to fill in the bullet holes and now it was impossible to tell that anything had happened. Kamal had come back from India and on Thursday he came by to prepare Max's macrobiotic meals for the next several days. He hadn't heard anything about the murders. When Max told him he broke down crying.

Max hadn't realized how close Kamal and Deirdre had become. Max had hired Kamal a couple of months ago, after he had been referred by the massage therapist at his health club. Kamal had often come to the house while Max was at work.

When Kamal was composed enough to speak he invited Max to come with him sometime to an ashram on the West Side to meditate. Max said he'd think about it, although he couldn't imagine himself sitting in a lotus position and chanting like some hippie.

"Remember, people don't die, because they aren't born," Kamal said. "Birth and death are merely illusions. All people and objects exist now and forever in the universal unconscious."

Max stared at him, thinking, *What a crock*.

Max liked Kamal's cooking and he thought he was a nice guy, but he decided that if kept forcing this religious crap on him the guy would be history.

On Friday, Max couldn't stand being cooped up any longer. He took a cab to his gym in the Claridge House on Eighty-seventh and Third. He swam his usual forty laps, then sat in the steam room, reading *The Wall Street Journal*. After he showered, he weighed himself and was thrilled to see that he'd lost four pounds.

He had a relaxing weekend at home—eating Kamal's food, taking short walks around the neighborhood. On Saturday—a gorgeous seventy-degree day—he walked to Central Park and sat for most of the afternoon on a bench in the shade, reading networking magazines, trying to keep up on new developments in the industry. There'd been nothing about the murder or the police investigation in the newspapers or on TV. Max remembered how

Detective Simmons had promised to "be in touch soon" and now more than a week had gone by since the murder. While Max was glad that the story seemed to be fading, he didn't like the way Detective Simmons was staying away from him. As he walked home from the park, Max had a funny feeling he was being watched.

Ten

*Better not to begin.
Once you begin, better to finish it.*
BUDDHIST SAYING

Bobby was watching the girl with the blond hair and the big rack check into her room at the reception desk of the Hotel Pennsylvania. The way she kept looking around, twirling her hair with her index finger, Bobby could tell she was uptight about something. She was wearing low-slung jeans and a tight tube top and high heels. Bobby tried to imagine what she looked like naked and, man, he liked the picture that popped into his head. He wished he could whip his camera out right there. She had a slutty look to her, but there was something innocent about her, too, like she was afraid of something. She didn't look like a hooker, but she definitely looked like a girl who was someplace she wasn't supposed to be.

As she walked past the table with the big arrangement of red flowers, Bobby wheeled across the lobby to the Bell Captain's desk and said to Victor, "The girl near the elevator. Find out if she's expecting anybody."

Victor looked beyond the flow of people and said, "You mean the skinny chick with the knockers and the big hair? I never seen her before in my life."

"I didn't ask you if you've seen her before. I said find out if she's expecting anybody."

Victor went to the reception desk. A minute or two later he came back to Bobby and said, "She's meeting her husband up there, they're staying the night."

"I'm going up," Bobby said.

"You hear what I said? The girl's married."

"Married my gimp ass. She wasn't wearing a rock—she had some other weird fucking ring on her finger."

"That doesn't mean she's not married."

"I'm telling you, there's something going on with her."

"Look, let's just wait for a real escort to come along."

Bobby, looking at Victor in that dorky bellhop uniform, wondering if something had really happened to the guy's balls, if they fell off in the chemo or something, said, "Just get me the key to that girl's room."

"Come on," Victor said. "I really don't think this is a good idea."

"Look, if this is gonna work you're gonna have to trust me. You know I wouldn't do anything stupid, right?"

"Hey, I'm not calling anybody stupid, but you said we were gonna go after pros."

"I'm telling you, I have a hunch about this girl. She looked scared, the way she kept playing with her hair. If she's not a pro, I bet she's cheating on her old man or the guy's cheating on his old lady. We could make a mint with one good picture. I know when something's off and this smells to hog heaven, they're cheating, on someone."

"Whatever," Victor said. "But I'm telling you—I think you're making a big mistake."

When Victor came back with a maid's plastic keycard Bobby said, "So what name did they register under?"

"Brown," Victor said.

"See? Now tell me that isn't a bullshit name. I'm telling you, stick with me and you're gonna go places."

Bobby got off the elevator on the eighteenth floor. He wheeled himself one direction, took a few towels from a maid's cart, then went back the other way to room 1812. He could hear Mr.

Brown's moaning from two doors away. Fuck, you could of heard him in Queens. After making sure the coast was clear, he slipped the keycard Victor had given him into the lock and slowly pushed the door open.

Room 1812 was long and narrow, with the bed against the wall at the far end. The light on the night table was on so Bobby had a clear view of the action, which was good because the light from the hallway didn't make it too far into the room. Bobby went about halfway over the threshold and gently let the door rest against his chair. Then he raised his camera with a towel over it, the lens peeking out underneath.

Mr. and Mrs. Brown were going at it, but all the noise was coming from Mr. Brown—Mrs. Brown wasn't making a peep. As Bobby snapped a few quick shots, he had a feeling that he knew Mr. Brown from somewhere. Then he remembered seeing him pass by in the lobby earlier in the night. But downstairs the guy had had curly blond hair and now he was nearly bald. He almost muttered, *The fuck happened to you?*

Mr. Brown must've heard the snapping camera or seen Bobby out of the corner of his eye because he looked up and after staring at Bobby for a couple of seconds said, "Hey, what the hell?"

Bobby let the corner of the towel drop over the camera's lens.

"Jeez, I'm sorry, mister," he said. "I'm really, really sorry. I just came to bring you your towels—"

"Get the fuck out of here!" Mr. Brown shouted.

Wheeling toward the bathroom, Bobby said, "It'll only take a minute, mister. I gotta put fresh towels in every room two times a day or they get really mad at me—"

"Just get the hell outta here!"

"You don't want your towels?"

"Get out, you fucking moron!"

"What about your soap?"

"Leave!"

"Please, Mister," Bobby said, wheeling back toward the door. "Don't get me fired. I need this job. I need it real bad." He took a last look at the blonde, who'd pulled the sheet up around her tits and turned her back to him. "I'm real sorry about bustin' in on you, I didn't see nothing..." He scooted out the door and let it shut behind him.

Riding the elevator down, camera tucked in his bag, Bobby was smiling, proud of his performance. He was better than fuckin' Dustin Hoffman in *Rain Man*. Maybe he should've listened to Isabella, gone on some auditions. Maybe it wasn't too late. There had to be roles for guys in wheelchairs, right?

Nah, he decided, acting was too fucking boring. He needed the buzz, the action. Crime was where it was at.

As he wheeled out into the lobby, he started thinking about Mrs. Brown.

She was a good-looking girl all right. She had to be a pro—why else would a girl like that spread her legs for some middle-aged bald guy looked like that?

In the lobby, Bobby met Victor near the Thirty-second Street exit, said, "So far, so good."

"Yeah, sure," Victor said, all panicked, like he didn't believe it for a second. "What the fuck happened?"

"Stop shitting your pants, will ya?" Bobby said. "I got some good pics. Now we just gotta get the payola."

Bobby took the Eighth Avenue bus uptown. When he got back to his apartment, he developed the film as fast as he could. Two of the shots had come out blurry and one had the towel in the way, but two were clear as fucking day. In the one he was going to use, you could see Mr. Brown with his mouth open, staring at the camera, while Mrs. Brown was just starting to cover those big knockers of hers. Bobby thought for a moment, trying to come up with a good name, then on the back of the picture he wrote a note telling Mr. Brown to leave ten thousand dollars at the hotel's front desk for "Tommy Lee." He stuck the photo inside a manila envelope and sealed it.

When he arrived back at the hotel, Victor said, "I got some bad news for you. The guy and the girl—they both took off."

"Fuck, when?"

"Half hour after you left. Why don't you keep your fuckin' phone on? Goddamn phones—everybody's got 'em, but nobody's got 'em turned on."

"I thought you said they were staying the night?"

"That's what they told the girl at the desk, but that doesn't mean they're gonna do it. It's not like they're *obligated* to."

"Shit."

"And that's not all—the cops were here."

"The cops?"

"There an echo in here?"

Wanting to smack Victor, Bobby said, "What the hell'd the cops want?"

"Got me. When I first found out I thought, That's it—I'm fired. F 'n' F. Fired and fucked."

Now Bobby remembered seeing a big black guy in a gray suit in the lobby earlier in the night, thinking the guy had a cop look to him. Bobby had always had great cop-dar.

"Was he asking about us?" Bobby asked.

"No, that's just it," Victor said. "It was the couple. He was asking all kinds of questions about them. Who are they, have they been here before, what's the girl's name—shit like that."

"The girl? Not the guy?"

"That's all I know," Victor said. "Then when the girl left the cop followed her. Look, Bobby. I mean I like working with you again and everything, but we can't do this shit no more. Now with the cops coming down here, this is getting crazy. I can't lose this job, Bobby. It has nothing to do with you—I just can't lose this fucking job, I've too much riding on my paycheck."

Bobby, starting to wheel away, said, "The whole thing was a dumb idea anyway. Forget about it."

"Hey, come on," Victor said. "Don't be like that. Wait up a second."

During the bus ride home, Bobby was thinking about the cop, wondering why he was asking questions about the girl. He also wondered why Mr. Brown arrived at the hotel wearing that blond wig. Then he thought, What the fuck difference did it make? Even if the guy had paid the money it wouldn't've changed anything. Right now Bobby had enough money. He owned his apartment outright and had some savings safe with loan sharks. What would an extra ten grand do for him? It wouldn't get him outta the goddamn chair, wouldn't let him get up and walk to the deli or whatever. He wasn't doing this for the money. The money was, like, a *bonus*. Just to show he wasn't completely fucking useless.

A few months after he was paralyzed a vocational counselor at Mount Sinai Hospital asked Bobby if he was planning to return to work and Bobby said, "Hell yeah."

The woman went on about the different services available to him, how he could learn how to use a computer and maybe get some bullshit office job, and Bobby said, "I don't wanna do *that* kind of work—I wanna do *my* work. Can you guys help me do that?"

"And what kind of work do you do, Mr. Rosa?" she'd asked.

Bobby had mumbled something like, *Never mind*, and hightailed it the fuck out of there.

Bobby was lost in thought and suddenly realized that the bus was passing the Eighty-ninth Street stop. He started screaming at the driver, "Hey, what the hell's wrong with you, asshole! Didn't you hear me ring the goddamn bell? Jesus Christ, what the fuck does a guy gotta do to get off a fucking bus these days?" If he'd been packing, he might have shot the fuck.

Bobby continued to curse as the driver lowered him on the wheelchair lift. He heard the driver shout after him, "You're welcome."

Yeah, Bobby would have shot him.

When he got home, Bobby tried to relax on a tub chair in the shower. Then he flipped around on the TV awhile, but nothing was on. He ate a couple packages of Cup-a-Soup and then hit the sack.

The next day Bobby took a bus uptown to visit his mother at the Jewish Home for the Aged, a nursing home on 106th Street. He'd moved his mother up there last year, from a nursing home in Brooklyn, because it was only seventeen blocks from his apartment and he wanted to visit her more often.

For a while, he went every day, bringing her ice cream and Chinese food and getting one of the orderlies to wheel her out to the garden so she could get some fresh air. But then his mother had another stroke, a bad one, and now she just slept most of the time. Bobby still visited her three or four times a week; he would've gone more often, but it was too depressing to see her so out of it. He was afraid that when her time came and she died that was how he'd remember her—with her eyes closed and her toothless mouth sagging open.

As usual, his mother was in bed asleep. Her body had shriveled, especially on her left side. She'd always been short, but under the blanket she looked like she was four feet tall. There were tubes connected to her arms, meaning she probably had another infection. Bobby was gonna raise hell, find out why nobody called to tell him, but he knew this wouldn't do any good. It would just get him all worked up and his mother would still be lying in bed like a vegetable. Sometimes Bobby thought his mother would be better off dead and he even thought about taking her home and shooting her.

More and more, he just wanted to shoot somebody, go postal, let them know how goddamn angry he was.

He might've done it too, offed his Mom, except she was Catholic and he knew she wouldn't want that. She was probably already pissed off at him for putting her in a Jewish nursing home. But, hey, she was past complaining.

Bobby shook his mother's arm until her eyes opened. She couldn't smile anymore, but Bobby could always tell she was happy to see him. The dribble from the corner of her mouth could be a sign of happiness, he figured. Like she was trying to smile.

After sitting next to her for a while, Bobby took the elevator down to the cafeteria and bought a little container of ice cream. Then he went back up to his mother's room and shook her awake. She turned toward him, but this time only one of her eyes opened.

"Look, Ma, I got your favorite—vanilla."

His mother turned away, like she was angry, but Bobby kept the little wooden stick with the glob of ice cream on it in front of her face until she turned back and started eating it. Some ice cream dripped down her chin and Bobby wiped it off with the sleeve of his shirt. He took a lick himself and that shit wasn't half bad.

When she finished eating, Bobby stayed with her a while longer, watching her sleep. Then he realized that it was past one o'clock and her soap operas were on. He turned on the TV in front of her bed to channel 7 and cranked the volume. He leaned over the bed, kissed her, and then left the room quietly.

When Bobby got back to his apartment he realized he had nothing to do. He would've gone to Central Park with his camera and scouted for some new prospects, but it was getting cloudy outside and the air felt like rain. Maybe he'd just go out to the video store, check out the new releases, pick up some food at the supermarket, and then come back home and call it a day.

Bobby came back from the supermarket and cooked himself dinner—baked beans, powdered potatoes, and two cans of Beefaroni. Even Def Leppard couldn't get him out of his funk. When the Def couldn't crank you, it was way past time to shoot someone.

While he ate he stared at the pictures of Mr. and Mrs. Brown, thinking that the guy was starting to look familiar again. He didn't know if he was imagining it—maybe it was just that he was staring at the pictures for so long, of course the guy was starting to look familiar. But, no, there was more to it than that. Bobby had seen that face before. Then, suddenly, it clicked. He wheeled out to the hallway, to the incinerator room, and when he didn't find what he was looking for there, he rode the elevator down to his building's basement. In one corner, the porters stacked the old newspapers they picked up from the recycling bins on every floor. Once a month they'd tie them up and cart them off, but recycling day must have been a couple of weeks off because the pile was pretty big. Bobby fished through the papers until he found the week-old *Daily News* he was thinking of. But he didn't really get excited until he turned to page three and saw the big picture of Mr. Brown, and the story of the two women who were murdered on the Upper East Side in this very expensive-looking townhouse. Max Fisher, the article said, was the founder and CEO of NetWorld...

Bobby took the paper with him back to his apartment. Suddenly, Leppard sounded okay again. Thanks to a millionaire named Max Fisher, Bobby was back in business.

Eleven

Sutter looked at him. "I prefer tough, rich and a pussy magnet."
"As a cop, you might get two of those three."
Sutter smiled and said, "You never know."
JAMES O. BORN, *Walking Money*

On May 12, 1989, Alexis Morgan, a thirty-six year-old former model, was walking her two pet chihuahuas through a secluded path near Belvedere Castle in Central Park when she was brutally stabbed to death by a mysterious assailant. The single wound to her throat had nearly decapitated her, and police believed she was grabbed from behind and cut with a large knife or machete. There were no witnesses to the attack but several people reported seeing "a suspicious white man" in the area minutes before the killing and hearing her chihuahuas barking moments afterwards.

Although he didn't fit the description of the "suspicious white man," Mrs. Morgan's husband Henry, a wealthy real estate mogul, was a prime suspect. The Morgans had had a stormy two-year marriage, marred by loud public fights and Mr. Morgan's accusations that his wife was having an affair. While Mrs. Morgan's pocketbook was stolen in the attack, police believed this may have been "a decoy," to make it appear as if robbery had been the motive.

Mr. Morgan had a rock solid alibi—he was playing tennis with a friend at the Wall Street Racket Club at the time of the murder, and the friend and workers of the club vouched for him. However, the police still didn't rule out Morgan completely. They believed he may have hired someone to kill his wife. They created a composite sketch of the suspect and began a citywide manhunt for the killer. A few weeks later, police tailed Morgan to a meeting at a diner in Chelsea with Vinny "The Blade" Silvera, a killer known to have connections to the mob. Later that night, Silvera was brought in for questioning, but wouldn't confess to anything. Morgan was arrested separately. Under heavy interrogation, Morgan—who had his own business links to organized crime—was told that Silvera had confessed and then Morgan, falling for the ploy, promptly gave a taped confession, implicating Silvera. Both Morgan and Silvera were tried and sentenced. A few months later, Morgan was found beaten to death in a bathroom on Riker's Island.

Of course there were many obvious differences between Alexis Morgan's murder and the recent murders of the two women in the East Seventy-fourth Street townhouse, but there were many similarities as well. In both cases, robbery was the apparent motive. In both cases, the victims had been killed brutally, as if murder was the sole intention. And in both cases the husbands had convenient airtight alibis.

Kenneth Simmons, Detective Investigator at the 19th Precinct, had had nothing to do with the Alexis Morgan case. He was only in his second year on the force in 1989 and he was still spending most of his time doing clerical work. But, like everyone else who lived in the city at that time, he had followed the details of the case closely in the news. Several years later, at a promotion ceremony at One Police Plaza, he met Lieutenant Anthony Santana, who had broken the case, and Santana filled him in on many of the details. In particular, Kenneth recalled how Santana had told him that he would have broken the case much sooner if it weren't for all the media hype. "It was like a zoo," Santana said. "The suspects always knew they were being watched twenty-four hours a day." He believed that if Morgan didn't know he was being watched, he would have led them to Silvera much sooner. Santana said, "You can't shoot a deer when he hears your footsteps, you gotta sneak up on the fuck, know what I'm saying?"

Kenneth knew.

While he wasn't going to rule out any possibility, Kenneth was ninety percent certain that the townhouse murders were Alexis Morgan all over again. Max Fisher had hired somebody to kill his wife and Stacy Goldenberg was just in the wrong place at the wrong time. When he interviewed Max at the house he had a feeling Max was holding out on him and Kenneth's detective instincts were rarely wrong. But he also knew that the important thing was not to press him. Like Santana said—you can't let them hear your footsteps.

Kenneth was hoping that the townhouse case would be his big case, the one that comes along once in a detective's life. Solving the murders of two white women would also be great P.R. and could lead to a promotion to Sergeant or Lieutenant in a couple of years. Kenneth had been married for eight years and five years ago had had a baby son with Down Syndrome. The baby's condition had near destroyed his wife. And people's comments like

> *Mongoloid*
> *Retard*
> *Damaged goods*
> *Handicapped*

had ignited a rage in Kenneth that simmered close to the surface every waking moment. He was searching for an outlet to vent and Max Fisher was going to be it. He hated the prick anyway, with his freaking designer suits, fake hair, smarmy attitude, and that collection of classical music. Kenneth was a closet opera buff—not a fact you advertised as a New York City cop—but when he saw Fisher's classical collection he knew right away that the man was full of shit. He had all the big names out, like he was trying to impress, but it was obvious he had no true respect for the music.

And what was up with that navy tracksuit he'd been wearing during the first interview, acting like he thought it made him look all that? Kenneth wanted to put the man in another kind of suit—an orange one.

Fisher was going to be Kenneth's ticket to a promotion all right. His goal when he came on the force was to make Lieutenant before he was forty and to start collecting his pension by the time he was forty-five. He was thirty-nine now, so time was running out. He already had a time-share at a condo on the Jersey shore, but he couldn't wait until he was retired, and could spend all his days on the golf course.

Two days after the murders, Kenneth and his partner, Detective Louis Ortiz, were in Kenneth's office. Louis said, "Gluckman from Ballistics just called. They ran the bullets and shells through Bulletproof and Brasscatcher and came up dry."

Kenneth finished a long sip of coffee, said, "But they still say it was a .38, right?"

"Yeah, but get this—they think it was a Cold Lady .38. Our killer wouldn't be too smart if he bought a broad's gun on the street."

"Unless the killer *is* a broad."

"You really think so?"

"I doubt it sincerely. But I think the guy might've fucked up on purpose—sets the alarm and buys the pussy gun because he wants to give us a lot to think about."

"You really think that's what happened?"

"You know what I think. The job was sloppy—the guy who

did it wasn't a pro. He was a friend or someone Fisher had met. We got any priors with this gun?"

"*Nada* so far."

"Any word on the street?"

"They've been debriefing everybody they bring in, all Manhattan precincts, but so far nothing. Nothing from Forensics either. They said the women died somewhere between five-thirty and seven-thirty—probably closer to five-thirty, and both right around the same time. Nothing to go on with the blood either—it all came from the victims. The coroner also said the perp liked what he did. Some of the wounds were unnecessary, the victims were already dead. He called it overkill."

"And Fisher's alibi?"

"Rock-fucking-solid. A stripper remembered him—said she was giving him a lap dance around that time. Gave me her business card, too, by the way. She said she likes giving freebies to cops. You should've seen his friend, the client he was 'entertaining.' The guy was shitting bricks, man. He was like, 'You gotta promise me—this won't go back to my wife, right? This won't go back to her, will it?' Man, and I thought *I* was p-whipped." Then, smiling, he added, "But maybe we'll get lucky and get some DNA off the turd the shooter left."

Kenneth got up from his desk and stretched. He'd helped his wife move some furniture last night and he'd thrown his damn back out. He said, "Let's give it a couple of days—see what happens. At least the media isn't jumping all over this case the way I thought they would. Gives us a little more room."

"Yeah," Louis said. "It's lucky that crazy bitch set her kids on fire in Brooklyn."

"Hey, I'll take a break anyplace I can get it." Then Kenneth, rocking his hips to keep his back loose, added, "We still got one big problem—motive. Why did Max Fisher want his wife dead?"

"Wild guess—she was fucking some other guy."

"That's the obvious answer, so where's the other guy? And how come none of her friends or relatives ever heard her talking about a lover? I'm telling you, there's something about this case that just doesn't fit. The answer's out there—we just gotta find it."

As he always did when he was distracted, or when he was angry or frustrated about something, Kenneth touched the gold pin in his lapel. It showed two hands reaching out to each other, never quite touching and looking like they never would. It was the symbol for Down Syndrome, and one night on CNN he was thrilled to see Bill Clinton on there wearing the pin. Kenneth had done a little Google search, and discovered the pin had been given to Clinton by some obscure mystery writer. When he told his wife all she could say was, "I don't read mysteries."

Kenneth looked up, saw Louis watching him playing with the pin.

"You really wanna nail this motherfucker, don't you?" Louis said.

"Yeah, I really do," Kenneth said.

The next few days brought a couple of new developments. It was discovered that Max Fisher had made several withdrawals from his bank accounts the few days before the murders, but it only added up to several thousand dollars—something worth thinking about, but it wasn't enough money to prove that he had hired a hit man. Ballistics' Brasscatcher database determined that the Lady Colt .38 may have been the same gun used in the unsolved homicide of the owner of a shoe store in Queens a year and a half ago. At first, Kenneth thought this could be the big break, then he found out that Brasscatcher couldn't be one hundred percent about the match. And, even if the same gun was used in both crimes, it didn't mean that the gun hadn't changed hands on the street one or more times since the Queens murder. It was suggested that the Boyos, who had a front in the Bowery, were selling these guns on the street but it was almost impossible to pin anything on them. Worse, people liked them, because everyone had seen *In The Name Of The Father* and thought that's the way it really was. Trying to arrest an IRA guy was like trying to arrest a Mafia guy, you were messing with the public's romantic notions.

Louis questioned people at Max's office and friends and family members of Deirdre Fisher and Stacy Goldenberg and came up with no new leads. Jeez, it was going cold already.

Kenneth and Louis were having lunch, sitting at one of the back tables in Pick-a-Bagel on Second Avenue, when Louis said, "We gotta start looking at other possibilities, man."

Kenneth swallowed a bite of bagel with tofu scallion cream cheese, then said, "Like what?"

"Like maybe it was just what it looked like at the beginning—a guy was robbing a townhouse, the women came home, he panicked and shot them."

"The alarm was reset," Kenneth said. He hadn't been able to sleep for the past two nights, his frustration with the case getting to him. "Fisher set the alarm off when he went into the house. Unless Fisher was lying—and I see no reason why he would lie about that because it just makes him look more guilty—then Fisher must've given the alarm code to whoever killed those two women."

He'd gone over this a hundred times till his wife had roared, "You're obsessed."

She was right.

"Hey, that makes sense to me," Louis said. "So why don't we just bring Max Fisher in?"

"If I thought that would help—believe me, I wouldn't be sitting here on my fat ass eating bagels. But we gotta make Fisher think he's safe, let him get complacent. Every day that goes by that he doesn't hear from me he gets a little more nervous. Right now he's probably thinking, 'Why isn't Detective Simmons calling? He said he'd call.' But pretty soon he's gonna think we forgot all about him and that's when his big shot side is gonna come out. He's gonna think he's above the law, king of the world, and that's when he's gonna slip up. And that's when I come in and go for my knockout punch. That's when he gets the new tracksuit."

"Tracksuit?" Louis asked.

"Trust me on this one," Kenneth said. "We keep up with the silent treatment a few more days and start tailing him. Who knows? Maybe it'll be like Alexis Morgan all over again. Maybe he'll dig his own grave."

Kenneth put a twenty-four hour surveillance on Max Fisher, but this didn't turn up any new leads. Fisher went to the park, the supermarket, his health club, and other normal places. Then, just when it seemed like the case was going nowhere, there was a breakthrough. Some of the jewelry that was stolen at Max Fisher's apartment turned up at a pawnshop in Chinatown. The owner of the shop, Mr. Chen Liang, didn't speak a word of English, but through a translator swore to Kenneth that he didn't know who the man was who'd sold him the jewelry, he'd never seen him before. The man had allegedly come into the shop on Saturday afternoon, the day after the murder. He dumped the jewelry on the counter and said "How much?" Liang said he offered the man five thousand dollars, even though the jewelry was worth ten or twenty times that much. The man must've not known jack about jewelry because he didn't complain, didn't even try to negotiate. He happily took the cash and left the store.

Liang gave a complete description of the man. He was about five-eight, one-thirty, dirty grey hair, funny-looking mouth, and was wearing a leather jacket with what looked like a bullet hole in it. He spoke English with some kind of accent. Liang was very cooperative and polite until he found out he'd have to give back the jewelry. Then he started screaming like a maniac in goddamn Chinese, carrying on so much Kenneth almost had to cuff him.

Kenneth put out a citywide alert for the man. He knew that this guy might not be the killer—he may have just been a fence the real killer or someone else had sold the jewelry to—but finding him would definitely be a good start. Also, Kenneth now knew for sure that this wasn't a professional job. A pro wouldn't be dumb enough to unload jewelry he'd stolen from the scene of a double murder. And a pro wouldn't be dumb enough to sell off jewelry for a fraction of its worth. The alarm business meant that it couldn't have been random either, so the only logical conclusion was that Fisher had hired a non-pro to bump off his wife—either an acquaintance or a small-time hood. Fisher had gone cheap and that would cost him.

Later in the day, Kenneth got word from his cop on surveillance that Fisher had gone into work. Kenneth drove down to Fortieth Street in his tan Coup-de-Ville and took over the stakeout himself, hoping that this might be the day Fisher slipped.

Finally, after seven o'clock, Fisher left his office. He looked nervous—like a man who's guilty as hell, Kenneth thought—looking in both directions as he headed toward Fifth Avenue. Kenneth drove around the corner, making a right on a red, and made it to the corner of Fifth and Fortieth in time to see Fisher getting into a cab. The cab continued downtown on Fifth, so at least it didn't look like Fisher was going directly home. At Thirty-third, the cab turned right. It continued, inching along two traffic-congested blocks, pulling over in front of the side entrance to the Hotel Pennsylvania.

Kenneth stopped and double-parked about four or five car-lengths behind the cab. It was getting dark and he couldn't see clearly into the back of the cab, so he was surprised when Fisher got out wearing a curly blond wig. He looked so ridiculous that Kenneth almost started to laugh, asked aloud, "The fuck's with that?"

He got out of his car and followed Fisher into the hotel.

Fisher was at the reception desk, checking into a room. There was a lot of activity in the lobby, but Kenneth stayed a safe distance away anyway. After Fisher headed toward the elevators, Kenneth waited to see what would happen next. He wondered if Fisher was planning to meet his hit man to make his final payoff, just like Henry Morgan. He was already imagining himself in front of the mikes and cameras, explaining to the reporters how he had cracked the case. Then he saw himself, *Lieutenant Kenneth Simmons,* on the podium at One Police Plaza, shaking the Mayor's hand. His gold pin matching the new gold shield.

After about fifteen minutes had passed, Kenneth decided to go to the desk, start asking questions. The short woman with thick glasses behind the desk seemed uncomfortable, like she might be hiding something. He asked her if the man with the curly blond hair was meeting anyone in his hotel room and the woman pointed toward a good-looking white woman with big, blow-dried hair who was about to get on the elevator. For some reason, she looked familiar to Kenneth and a couple of seconds later it clicked. Earlier in the evening he had seen her leaving Fisher's office building. So Max Fisher was the one having the affair, not the wife. This was definitely getting interesting.

Kenneth asked the woman at the reception desk whether the couple came to the hotel frequently. The woman shrugged, then said, "I don't think so. At least not during my shift."

The woman told Kenneth that the couple had registered at the hotel under the name Brown and that they were planning to stay overnight.

Kenneth thought, *Brown? Are they kidding?*

About forty-five minutes later, the white woman with the big hair came out of an elevator and headed toward the Seventh Avenue exit. Kenneth considered stopping her and speaking to her, but decided it might be more valuable to follow her, see where she was going. Who knows? Maybe Fisher had met her in the hotel room to give her the money, and now she was on her way to make a final payoff to the hit man. Or maybe *she* was the hit man, or hit woman.

On Seventh, the woman hailed a cab going downtown. Kenneth didn't have time to get his car so he hailed another cab, presented his badge, and ordered the driver to follow the other car. It went across town to First Avenue and stopped on the corner of East Twenty-fifth Street. The woman got out and walked quickly up the block, toward Second. Kenneth followed her on the opposite side of the street, jogging to keep up with her.

About midway down the block, the woman went up the stoop into the vestibule of a tenement. Out of breath, Kenneth hurried up the stoop and followed her into the building. The woman turned around, startled. Kenneth was used to this reaction from white women in vestibules and elevators.

She was reaching into her purse—maybe for pepper spray—when Kenneth said, "It's all right, I'm a Detective—NYPD." He showed his badge. He always got a rush out of that.

"Jesus Christ," the woman said. She was breathing heavily now too. "You just scared the bejaysus out of me."

Kenneth registered the brogue and had a fleeting thought about the murder weapon's possible connection to the Boyos.

Kenneth said, "You mind if I ask you a few questions?"

"Questions about what?"

"Do you live in this building?"

"Yeah. Why?"

"Can I have your name please?"

"What's this all about?"

"Can you tell me your name, please?"

The woman, still breathing heavily, said, "Angela. Angela Petrakos."

"I saw you at Hotel Pennsylvania before. You went into a room with Max Fisher, didn't you?"

"No."

"There's no use lying about it—I saw both of you. Is he your boss?"

Angela didn't answer so Kenneth asked the question again.

"Yeah, he's my boss."

"How long have you two been seeing each other?"

"We're not seeing each other."

"You realize his wife and niece were murdered last week. Now I'm not saying you had anything to do with that, but you're gonna have to answer these questions sooner or later. We could either do this here or down at the precinct. Take your pick. I could be wrong but a nice lady like you, I don't think you'd like the Precinct, it's a bit…rough."

Angela waited a few seconds, looking scared as hell, and Kenneth almost fell sorry for her. She was good looking, with that blond hair and that great rack, and Kenneth wondered how she got mixed up with Fisher, what she saw in that sleazebag.

"Can we go inside and talk?" she said. "I have to go to the bathroom."

"Actually, I wouldn't mind using your bathroom myself," Kenneth said. "If you don't mind."

Following her upstairs he was thinking, Love that brogue, but what's with the Greek name? Then, watching her swing her hips back and forth, he thought, And she has a fine ass, that's for damn sure. Kenneth was faithful to his wife, had never cheated on her in eight years of marriage, but that didn't stop him from looking. And he'd heard cops talk about Irish girls in the locker room at the precinct. Word was they were like banshees in the sack.

The building was a typical tenement—the paint on the walls was peeling, there was a faint ammonia odor. Two floors up she stopped in front of apartment 5. She opened the door, said, "I still don't understand what you think I have to do with those people getting killed, this is really crazy," and then went ahead into the kitchen area. The lights in the apartment were on. Kenneth stepped inside and took a look around. It was a small place—a studio.

Angela said, "Can I get you something to drink?" and Kenneth said, "No, that's all right."

Then Kenneth noticed the shut door at the end of the apartment and the crack of light underneath. He was about to ask Angela if she lived alone when the door sprung open and a thin, pasty guy with long gray hair came out firing a handgun. Kenneth recognized the man as fitting the description of the suspect who'd hocked Deirdre Fisher's jewelry in Chinatown. Falling backward, he tried to reach into his holster for his own piece, but it was too late. He was already down.

Twelve

Of course it all went to shit. I should have known better.
VICTOR GISCHLER, *Gun Monkeys*

Dillon was watching *The Flintstones* on the Cartoon Network. It was one of his favorite episodes, with the Great Gazoo, and he was laughing like he'd been on the weed for a week. He'd had a wee dram of Jameson too, nothing lethal, when he heard voices in the hallway. It sounded like Angela talking to some guy, but he didn't think she was stupid enough to bring someone back to the apartment with her.

Dillon turned off the TV, hearing Angela say, "I still don't understand what you think I have to do with those people getting killed, this is really crazy."

Shite, Dillon thought, she brought home a Guard.

Cursing to himself, he took his gun out of his dresser drawer and went into the bathroom. The apartment door opened and Angela said, "Can I get you something to drink?" The guy said, "That's all right," and Dillon swung open the door and shot the feckin' cop two times in the chest, watching the fat bollix fall back, hit his head on the refrigerator, and land on the kitchen floor. If he wasn't so angry at Angela for bringing the cop home—what was the feckin' cunt thinking?—Dillon might've thought it was funny.

Angela was covering her mouth, trying not to scream. Dillon told her not to make a fecking sound. He didn't want the neighbors coming over, banging on the door. But then a minute went by, and another, and no neighbors showed up. Maybe they thought the shots came from TV or something. Angela was sitting on the bed, crying. The cop was in the puddle of blood on the kitchen floor. Dillon noticed a shiny gold pin on the wanker's lapel. He reached down, removed it, and pinned it on his own self.

Dillon knew he had to do *something*—get rid of this bollix fast. He couldn't carry the body down himself without breaking his back. Besides, where would he take it? Then he had a great idea. He heard this shite on TV once, or read it or some fuck. A guy was fighting with his wife or something and he hit her so hard she died. He didn't want the police to find out so he put her in the bathtub and poured battery acid all over her—covered her with it. When she dissolved, he just washed her down the drain.

Dillon had never tried that shite himself, but he thought that putting battery acid on the cop would be a great way to get rid of him—keep the gig nice and clean anyway. The only feckin' problem was he didn't know where he was going to get battery acid. He thought about it for a little while longer, then wondered, If battery acid could dissolve people, could Drano do the trick too? He didn't see why not. But he'd probably need a lot of Drano to get the job done and he couldn't go to the store now. Somebody might've heard those shots and by the time he came back cops could be raiding the feckin' place.

Angela was still crying like a Brit. Dillon went in the bathroom to take a leak and think, admired the way the pin caught the light when he tousled his hair in the mirror. He asked his own self, "Do I look like I just killed a cop?" The tinker's curse crossed his mind, but he shook himself free of it and said, "You look a poet me man."

When he came out, Angela was staring down at the cop, her eyes getting wider. Dillon looked over and said, "Jaysus, fuck me."

The cop's eyes were open and blood was dripping out of his mouth. He was trying to talk.

Dillon went into the drawer in the kitchen cabinet and took out a big butcher knife. He came back and jabbed the knife into the cop's chest. The cop's shirt turned redder, and the blood puddle grew, but his eyes closed for good. Dillon nearly admired the way the fooker had clung on to life, had tried to hang in there. But a butcher's knife, it doesn't do argument.

Angela was still crying, making noise now. Dillon slapped her in the face and said, "Shut up, yah hoor's ghost," and then went into the bathroom and washed his hands.

Dillon didn't know how things had gotten so fucked. After he sold the jewelry he'd taken to that Chinaman, he was planning to leave Angela and New York City. He'd always heard Miami was nice. He saw himself chilling out down there, smoking dope, lying on the beach and writing poems all feckin' day. To hell with moving into that rich fellah's house uptown. It was a stupid plan anyway—never would have worked. He was just going to hang out with Angela a little longer, till things cooled down, then it was *slan, alanna.* But, now, the stupid woman had fucked everything up—bringing home a cop right into her kitchen. Now, all of a sudden, Miami was in jeopardy.

He came out of the bathroom, went to the closet and took out two bed sheets. He tucked one of the sheets under the cop's fat body and then rolled the body onto the rest of it. Then he put the second sheet around the same way and went to the phone and called Sean, one of the other Prov-eens that hung around the boyos. Luckily, Sean was home. Sean was second generation Irish—thus more Irish than the real thing, used to be in the FDNY—and now he drove a livery cab. He said he'd definitely come to the city from Queens to help Dillon out, saying with his stutter, "N-n-nothing to pray about."

"Is the trunk of yah cab empty, Sean?" Dillon asked.

"W-w-why?"

"You'll find out me man."

After Dillon hung up he got two blankets out of the closet and he took the blanket and the sheet off the bed. Blood was soaking through the sheets that were currently wrapping the cop. Grabbing the cop by the feet, he dragged the body into the bedroom area, out of the blood puddle. He wrapped the body up the best he could. It didn't look very neat, but at least the blood wasn't leaking through anymore. Next, he got the mop and started mopping, wringing out the red water into the kitchen sink. He could mop like the best of them, prison taught you that. He got rid of most of it, but there was still a big red stain on the floor.

Dillon had nothing to do except wait for Sean, so he watched more *Flintstones* and some *Bugs Bunny*—American cartoons were feckin' mighty—then had another wee dram of Jameson. Well, you would, wouldn't you, after killing a Guard? After *Bugs Bunny* he watched some of the Knicks. He was gradually teaching himself about American sport, mainly to fill in the hours. He had learned that when you lose a game *you choke*. Jaysus, he loved that, *you choke*. And even better, if you lost a game, they said, Y*ou got your arse handed to you*.

He glanced at the trussed body and said, "You got yer arse handed to yah, fellah."

Finally Angela stopped crying. She went into the bathroom and came out, wiping her face with a towel. She sat down next to Dillon, held his hand, and said, "I'm sorry—I really, really am. I didn't mean to do any of this. He followed me home—I had no choice. It'll be all right, won't it? I mean nobody's come to the door so maybe nobody heard the bloody shots. If they did, maybe they didn't know what it was. Maybe they just thought it was a car backfiring or firecrackers or some shite. I mean the plan's still gonna work, right? We'll still get married, won't we? And we'll still get all of my boss's money too. You'll see. It's just gonna take a few months, right?"

He vaguely wondered why, all of a sudden she was speaking like an Irish version of Tony Soprano's wife.

"Whatever," Dillon said. He knew none of this was going to happen, but he never saw the point in telling a woman what he was thinking.

During the Knicks post-game show, the buzzer rang. First Dillon made sure it was Sean, then he buzzed to let him up.

Sean was like a caricature mick, red hair, skinny as a rail and with that death-white skin and freckles. He spoke with a stammer, especially when he was drunk, which was most of the time. He drank Guinness like water and spiced it up with Jameson. In the bag, he'd pick the hottest woman in any pub, sidle up to her, and go, "I-I-I d-d-d-dr-drive a c-c-cab. W-w-will you g-g-go ou-ou-out wif me?" Then the left side of his face would begin to twitch, ensuring that any dim hope went right down the toilet. But he had a streak of ruthlessness that rivaled Dillon's own. It was rumored he'd killed a priest, the worst sin of them all, and said, "I'm going to hell, going to have me own self a time first. The priest will be waiting for me, keep the fire nice and toasty."

At the door Dillon said, "You leave your cab double-parked like I told you to?"

"Y-y-y-yes," Sean said. Then he noticed the body on the floor. He said, "Ih-ih-ih-is it a nun?"

"No, tis nothing," Dillon said. "Just a rent collector."

You want an Irish guy on yer side, kill a snitch or a rent collector, and you have their undying loyalty.

"G-g-good on yah," Sean said.

Angela was scrubbing the stains off the kitchen floor with a sponge and Mr. Clean. She said hello to Sean. Dillon said, "Sean, say hello to Angela."

Sean said, "I d-d-drive a c-c-cab. Will you g-g-g-go ou-ou-out wif me?"

Dillon shook his head, said to Angela, "We're just going to drive uptown, dump it somewhere, and that's it." And to Sean, "You'll be back home in like a half hour."

Then Dillon and Sean picked the body up—Dillon lifting from the head, Sean from the feet. The body wasn't as stiff or as heavy as Dillon expected.

"W-w-w-w-what if s-somebody sees us?" Sean asked.

"We have to be quiet, that's all," Dillon said. And then, remembering Lauren Bacall, he said, "You can be quiet, can't yah, you just put your lips together and shit the fook up."

Jesus, he loved that broad, Bacall, she was a real dame, a ball-buster and with serious edge. Dillon wondered if she had any Irish in her. If not, he'd have been glad to supply some.

Dillon opened the door and listened closely to make sure nobody was in the hallway or coming up or down the stairs. Then he said, "Let's go."

They went down the two flights of stairs like they were carrying a piece of furniture. At the bottom of the stairs Sean walked too fast and the cop's head banged into the wall.

"Jaysus, yah bollix," Dillon said. "Take it easy, will yeh?"

They opened the first door into the vestibule then Sean stopped suddenly—his eyes staring ahead. Dillon turned around and saw a man coming up the steps into the building. There was no time to go back upstairs. They just had to move to the side of the vestibule and let the man pass.

Dillon had seen the guy in the building before. He was a typical nancy white guy—wore a suit every morning, going to work. He'd never said a word to Dillon before, but this time he smiled and said, "Moving out?"

He looked drunk and he smelled like alcohol. He was wearing one of his suits, but the tie was on loose.

"No," Dillon said. "Just tossin' away me old rug."

"Cool," the man said.

He passed by Sean and disappeared up the stairs.

Sean said, "L-l-l-l-l-let's just g-g-g-g-g—"

"Just shut yer stammerin' mouth and start movin'," Dillon said.

They carried the body out to the street. There was no one passing by and no cars were coming. Moving fast, they stuffed the body into the trunk and got inside the car, a dark blue Chevy Caprice. As they were driving up First Avenue, Sean went, "W-w-w-what if that guy c-c-calls the c-c-c-c-cops?"

"No, he was fucked up and he's a pillow biter, they don't do cops, if you follow me drift?" Dillon said. "He saw fooking nuthin."

"Nobody's s-s-s-s-stupid enough to think that w-w-w-was a rug."

"Just move it along, yah arsehole," Dillon snapped.

Cursing to himself and shaking his head, Sean continued to drive uptown. Dillon couldn't stand the quiet anymore and turned the radio on to a good local Irish station and cranked the volume. When they got to Eighty-sixth Street, Sean said, "Where are we headed?"

"Harlem," Dillon said. "St. Nicholas Avenue."

Dillon had used his idle time to walk around Manhattan and he already knew the city as well as a native. At 125th, they cut over to St. Nicholas and continued uptown.

At 144th, he said, "All right, this looks about right. Slow down."

They turned on 144th and stopped in front of an empty lot of rubble. The streetlights were burnt out on the entire side of the street.

"Come on," Dillon said. "Let's do this fast as we can."

Sean opened the trunk and they lifted the body out. It was

so quiet they couldn't even hear the traffic noise from St. Nicholas Avenue. There were only the sounds of a dog barking and some kids screaming, maybe a block or two away.

Stepping over the garbage and rubble, they continued walking into the darkness. A few times Dillon, going *Fookin thing*, slipped and almost fell. Sean was beginning to whine, asked, "How m-m-much farther?"

"Shut yer trap," Dillon said. Then, when he thought they were far enough away from the street, he said, "All right, right here. Drop it."

They let the body fall, then they started covering it with whatever garbage was lying around. It was impossible to see anything, but Dillon picked up what felt like wood, paint cans, dirt, whatever. When it seemed like the body was covered he said, "That's all right. They'll never look for a dead Guard here anyway."

"A dead *w-w-w-what?*" Sean gasped. He was almost out of breath. "Are you d-d-d-d-demented?"

"What?" Dillon said.

"You s-s-s-said it was a r-r-r-rent collector."

Thinking, *Vive la différence*, Dillon said, "Yeah? So?"

"J-J-J-Jaysus," Sean said like he was going to go for Dillon. "I don't believe it, I c-c-c-could murder yah. The Boyos told us s-s-s-stay clear of the G-G-G-Guards."

"It doesn't matter now, does it?"

"B-b-but G-G-G-Guards. That's like b-b-b-blasphemy."

Dillon stepped back and felt a sudden piercing pain in his foot. He almost screamed, but stopped himself in time. He realized he must have stepped on a nail or something, but didn't want to look at it until he was back in the car. Then he said, "Let's just get the bejaysus out of here." He was thinking, *Just me fooking luck to get that tetanus thing*.

Back in the car, the pain in his foot was even worse. He turned on the car's overhead light and saw the head of a thick nail coming out of the bottom of his sneaker. He had no idea how deep it was wedged into his foot, but it felt like it was hitting bone.

Driving down St. Nicholas Avenue, Sean said, "There b-b-b-b-better not be b-b-b-blood in the b-b-b-boot of me v-v-v-vehicle."

Dillon yanked off his tennis sneaker—a three-inch-long rusty nail came off with it. He said, "Fook, and I just bought these shites at Modell's."

Thirteen

*He had made someone else's world a hell, and someone
had made his world a hell. Supply-chain management
for human suffering.*
JOSEPH FINDER, *Company Man*

In the back seat of the cab, Max Fisher put on his curly blond wig. He knew he looked ridiculous—like a goddamn clown—but he figured it was better than nothing. He was still paranoid about why Detective Simmons never came back to talk to him and the last thing he needed was to be seen checking into a hotel room with his executive assistant.

When he went to work this morning he had no idea he'd wind up where he was now. His plan was to have a normal day at the office, get back to work, keep his mind occupied. But he had no idea how fucking tempting it would be to see Angela sitting at her desk, wearing one of her skirts that barely covered her butt-cheeks. Usually, he'd find some way to get her into his office and they'd have a quickie, but he knew that anything like that would be impossible today, and probably for a long time. Everyone was talking about how a detective was here last week, asking everyone questions about him and Deirdre, and if anybody had any "theories" about what might have happened. This proved to Max that he wasn't being paranoid—Simmons was definitely on to him.

Trying to bang Angela now would be nuts, but Max couldn't help himself. Knowing she was so close by, wanting her so badly, was driving him wild. Before lunchtime, he called her into his office, but left the door open. As she went over Max's schedule for the rest of the day, Max winked at her. Angela saw him, immediately smiled as Max wrote, "I have to be with you" on a pad and slid it across the desk to her. She wrote back, "How?"

Like two students passing notes back and forth in a classroom, Max and Angela plotted out their strategy for meeting later on at the Hotel Pennsylvania. He figured it would be better to meet at a big hotel, where there was a lot of activity, than at a small hotel where they were more likely to be noticed. He often set his clients up with call girls at the Hotel Pennsylvania and they never had any problems. Besides, they were planning to take precautions. They'd arrive separately, check in under phony names, and he'd wear a wig. The wig was his idea. Angela wrote that she could go buy him a nice one during her lunch break. He tried it on in his office, knowing right away that it made him look like Harpo Marx, but deciding that it was worth it to be alone with Angela.

When he entered the hotel lobby, he looked around, made sure he wasn't being followed. Surprisingly, people passing by didn't give him funny looks—maybe the wig didn't look as ridiculous as he thought. He'd already called the hotel from work and found out there were plenty of vacancies tonight and there wouldn't be a problem booking a room at the last minute. He checked in under the name "Brown" and told the woman who was working at reception that his wife would be meeting him, when she arrived to please send her right up. Then he paid for the room in advance, with cash.

In room 1812, Max made himself comfortable—showering, and then lying in bed, relaxing, watching TV, his right hand slowly sliding under his boxers down to his crotch, touching what felt like a spot where the skin was irritated. He quickly took off his underwear to examine the area more closely. He discovered it wasn't really irritation—shit, it was more like a blister, and there were several smaller ones there as well. They itched and hurt like hell. How could he not have noticed them before?

He rushed into the bathroom, sat on the toilet bowl, and leaned over his lap, examining himself more carefully. The longer he looked at the blisters, the larger they seemed to grow. He tried to squeeze them, but this only made the itching and pain worse. Soon the discomfort was unbearable. As usual, he thought the worst first and imagined he had ebola, smallpox, that flesh-eating virus. It had to be something horrendous.

After a few more minutes of total panic he realized he wasn't dying, but the word "herpes" crept into the back of his mind.

When Angela came into the room, Max was still in the bathroom. He had started crying. Although he'd washed his face with cold water, when he came out of the bathroom Angela immediately knew something was wrong.

Max's lips quivered—he couldn't get the word out. Then he dropped his boxers and held out his penis for Angela to examine. He was trying to see if she seemed surprised, but she didn't show any particular reaction, saying, "What's wrong?" Then she said. "Oh, I get it. It's some kind of joke, right?"

"Look closer," Max said.

Angela got on her knees, said, "Is that all you're worried about?"

"It looks like…" Max still couldn't say the word.

"What?" Angela said.

His face turning red, starting to cry again, Max blurted out, "Herpes!"

"Herpes?" Angela said, like it was the most ridiculous idea possible. "That's just a little rash, that's all. Knowing you, you probably made it worse from all your feckin' scratching."

"They look like blisters to me."

Angela laughed, said, "Jaysus, listen to you. You should go back to worrying about your heart, a wee rash and you're blubbering like a big baby."

Continuing to examine himself, Max said, "It hurts."

"What do you expect, scratching yourself like a feckin' monkey?"

"What about you?" Max said. "I mean you haven't been having any symptoms, have you?"

Angela was sitting on the edge of the bed, taking off her shoes. She froze for a moment then said, "What do you mean?"

"I mean this," Max said. "I mean you've never had any pain or seen any blisters or—"

"Are you asking me if I have feckin' herpes?"

When Angela turned around Max was staring at her with a deadpan expression. She said, "You better stop this, yah bollix, before I really start getting upset."

Now her eyes had all the fire and rage of an angry Greek woman in them. Max didn't realize until now how lethal this Irish-Greek-combo thing could be. It was one dangerous mix.

Figuring he'd better soothe her, he sat down next to her on the bed and put an arm loosely around her back. He started kissing the back of her neck, under her hair, until she started to giggle.

"I'm sorry, sweetie," he said. "I really am glad you're here. You don't know how horrible it's been—being in that house all alone all week. A couple of times I almost gave in and called you. When I saw your name on that card the office sent me I couldn't stop staring at your handwriting. It just made me miss you even more."

Max turned Angela's head toward him, started kissing her lips. Then he moved his right hand down her back, over that great ass and said, "God, you don't know how much I missed this."

Angela freed herself. "I have to go pee."

"Yeah, can I watch?" Max asked.

"You're so funny," Angela said without smiling as she went into the bathroom. He wondered, *That was a joke?*

Still sitting on the bed, Max said, "Have you heard anything from Popeye?"

"Why would I hear anything?"

"I mean through your cousin."

"No. And I think it's better if we don't know anything, don't you?"

"I guess you're right," Max said. "But I was ready to send a hit man after him a few days ago."

"Really?" Angela sounded shocked or confused—Max couldn't tell which. "Why?"

"The lunatic killed my niece. I mean she was just a young kid. When I found her lying there I was almost going to call the police and confess everything."

"Well, thank God you didn't do *that*."

"You're telling me," Max said. "After the funeral, the whole picture started to come into focus for me. I mean it was a terrible thing that she had to die and everything, but it wasn't as if Popeye didn't warn me. What was the word he used? *Pop*. He said he was going to pop me if I got to the house early, so I guess he had to pop Stacy, God rest her soul. I mean if he didn't pop her then we all would've been arrested by now, right?"

"Right," Angela said.

"But the thing that still ticks me off is that whole alarm business. It was supposed to look like he was waiting for them outside, right? Like he forced them to disarm the alarm. But then what does that jerk-off do? He arms the alarm before he leaves. What was the guy thinking?"

"Maybe he was trying to make it look like nobody was there."

"With two dead bodies in the foyer? This way, the cops know somebody gave him the code. I don't even know why he bothered to steal that jewelry. Like the police were gonna believe it was a robbery?"

"Maybe they'll think he made your wife tell him the code, or he memorized the code when your wife disarmed the alarm."

Max thought about that, then said, "Eh, maybe, but it was still a boneheaded thing to do. And why, why did he have to take a crap in the house, on my Oriental rug? You know how much it cost to clean that thing?"

"Oh, stop with your worrying," Angela said. "You'll see. A few months from now, when we're married, you'll look back on all this and think how crazy you were acting. Oh, and about the shitting, I heard once that it's not because burglars are, like, being disrespectful—it's from adrenalin."

Max thought Angela was full of shit, said, "You're full of shit."

"No, I'm serious. I read it in a book once."

Max, who had never seen Angela read anything except magazines and the *New York Post*, said, "I thought you said you heard it?"

"No, I read it, in a book about burglars. It was the history of burglary in America and there was a whole chapter about shitting on the floor. Great book—you should borrow it sometime."

Now Max was positive that Angela was just being all Irish again, spinning one of her stories that got more and more exaggerated with each telling. He didn't think Greek women did that. He didn't know a whole lot about Greek women and he was beginning to think he didn't know a whole lot about women, period. Why couldn't they just do lap dances and shut the fuck up?

Angela came out of the bathroom naked. She climbed into bed and pushed Max back, pinning down his arms.

"This is your night," she said. "You can have anything you want." The word *want* had that whole Irish accent thing going on, and it was so fucking sexy.

"I *want* you," Max said, trying to mimic it.

"How?" Angela asked.

Max flipped her over and pinned her down hard. He said, "You know we won't be able to do this again for a long time. It was way too risky to come here."

"In that case," Angela said, "you'd better make it good."

Max started on top, then ordered her to turn over. His blisters—or whatever the hell they were—were hurting, but he decided to ignore the pain. Doggy-style was his favorite position. He liked grabbing onto Angela's hair or squeezing her butt cheeks and imagining she was anyone he wanted her to be. For a while, he imagined she was Felicia, the stripper from Legz Diamond's. That worked great, especially when he had his eyes closed. Then he heard something off to his right. He looked over and saw in the shadow near the door some guy in a wheelchair with what looked like an armful of towels.

"What the hell?" Max said.

"Jeez, I'm sorry, Mister," the guy said. "I'm really, really sorry..."

Jesus Christ, the guy wasn't just crippled, he sounded retarded, too.

Max told him to get the fuck out of the room and the guy started babbling about how he had to replace the towels and the soap and some other bullshit.

Max yelled, "Get out, you fucking moron!" and that got rid of him.

Max wanted to call downstairs and get that jerk fired but Angela said, "Oh, give him a break. He's handicapped."

"So?" Max said. "He should still know better."

"He's gone now. I'm sure he's not going to say anything. He's probably scared out of his wits."

"Eh, I guess you're right," Max said and let himself fall back onto the bed. "Where were we?"

Angela turned around. Max grabbed onto her shoulders and squeezed hard, picturing Felicia.

Fourteen

Fear much trouble in the fuselage, Frederick.
THE ODD COUPLE

"It's herpes all right," Dr. Alan Flemming said to Max the next morning. "Simplex Two."

Dr. Flemming was Max's General Practitioner and they were in Flemming's Park Avenue office. Although Dr. Flemming was probably only a few years older than Max, Max hoped he didn't look *that* bad. Flemming had white hair, a hunched-over posture and a thin, wrinkled face. As Max had heard Angela once say about her Irish grandfather, *his wrinkles had wrinkles*.

This morning, Max had made an emergency appointment with Flemming when he woke up and discovered that the blisters on his penis seemed to have grown larger.

"You're sure it's herpes?" Max said. "I mean don't you have to wait for the lab results before you can tell?"

"Of course I'll need to confirm it with a Pap smear," Flemming said, "but I'm ninety-nine percent certain of the diagnosis. But there's no reason to panic—herpes isn't exactly a life-threatening virus. All you have to do is keep the lesions dry and apply some alcohol or witch hazel. You also might want to wear loose clothes. If you wear jockeys, you might want to consider a switch over to boxers. It also might be a good idea to blow dry your genitals from now on rather than toweling dry. But whatever you do, don't feel like you're a bad person or something's wrong with you because you contracted this. You can rest assured—millions of people in the world are going through the same thing that you are and it's really not as bad as many people think. I've had patients who've gone for months, hell, years even, without experiencing any symptoms whatsoever. The outbreaks will usually only occur when you're under a high level of stress or anxiety. With the tragedy involving your wife and niece, I'm not at all surprised to see you having an outbreak now. By the way, have you…been with anyone recently?"

"What do you mean?"

He knew exactly what he meant but he knew he couldn't let on.

"The only reason I'm asking," Flemming said, smiling assuredly, "is that herpes, in almost all cases, is a sexually transmitted virus. In all likelihood, you contracted it from someone and if you did it might be a good idea to warn that person."

"Maybe my wife had it," Max said. "I mean maybe she had it, but didn't tell me."

"Well, the only way she could've gotten it would be if she had—well, I don't think that's really important now anyway. After I have Christine do a Pap smear—and we'll also do some blood work—I'm going to put you on a medication to help suppress the virus and a painkiller for your itching and discomfort. Within a few days you'll be as good as new."

Max doubted that, doubted it a whole lot.

Flemming picked up his clipboard and started to leave the examination room. At the door, he turned back, smiled and said, "By the way, just as a precautionary measure, if you've been having unprotected sex you might want to think about an HIV test."

"HIV?" Max could barely move his lips to say it, frightened to fucking hell. "Why? You think I have—"

"No, no, I'm not suggesting that at all. I'm just saying it's best to err on the side of caution. Many people who have herpes also tend to be HIV-positive. That isn't to say that you're likely to be

HIV-positive. But, given that you have already contracted one sexually transmitted disease, it might be a good idea to check for others."

"Yeah well, I think I'd like to hold off on an AIDS test," Max said.

"Are you sure?" Dr. Flemming said. "The sooner you know—"

"I'm not taking the goddamn test."

Later, riding in a cab to his office, Max could barely breathe. There was no way in hell he was ever going to take an AIDS test. It scared him enough to have to call for his blood work from his cardiologist—he couldn't imagine making a phone call to find out if he'd been sentenced to death.

Max had heard somewhere that the first sign of AIDS is sometimes lumps on the lymph nodes. Max wasn't sure where the lymph nodes were, but he thought they were somewhere on his throat. Feeling around, he was convinced that he had lumps.

He screamed silently, *Fucking lumps!*

When he arrived at his office he hadn't calmed down much. He marched past the receptionist's desk toward Angela and said loud enough for everyone nearby to hear, "Excuse me, could you come into my office with me, please? I need to dictate a letter."

When Angela came into the office Max asked her to close the door behind her. Then, after she sat down with her pad, he said in a low, but serious voice, "Thanks for giving me herpes, you stupid bitch."

Angela seemed surprised, but Max was pretty sure she was acting.

She said, "Herpes? What the hell?"

"You don't have to deny it anymore—I just came back from my doctor. Irritation my ass. You knew you had herpes and you didn't even tell me."

"You went to a *doctor*? When?"

"This morning. Come on, I don't have time for this bullshit. Just admit it."

"Are you sure he isn't making a mistake? I mean how can he tell without a blood test?"

"They don't take a blood test, they take a Pap smear, but it's herpes all right. He's treated tons of cases before."

"Well, I didn't…" Angela lowered her voice and continued, "I didn't give it to you."

"Then where did I get it, a fucking toilet seat?" Max noticed that the left side of her face looked slightly purple, said, "What the hell happened to you?"

"Oh, it was nothing," Angela said. "My roommate opened the bathroom door last night and it hit me. I'll live."

But Max, not paying attention, said, "Well, if I didn't catch it from you, you got it now, so you better go see a doctor and pretty damn soon."

"Maybe your feckin' whore of a wife gave it to you," Angela said.

Her temper was coming out and the fire in her eyes was ferocious.

"My wife?"

"Yeah. How do you know she wasn't doing it with some bollix behind your back?"

Max considered this for a moment. Deirdre having an affair? It seemed crazy. Then he imagined Kamal naked, on top of her, and a sick feeling started to build in his stomach. Kamal was the only other man he knew about who'd had any sort of contact with Deirdre and he remembered how unusually upset he'd been to hear about her death. But that was crazy. He'd never heard Kamal even *talk* about a woman before and, besides, he was almost positive the guy putted from the rough.

"That's crazy," Max said. "No guy would've been interested in Deirdre and besides—you have to have sex to get herpes and Deirdre and I didn't exactly have an active sex life."

"I'm telling you the truth," Angela said. "If you don't believe me it's your feckin' problem, not mine."

There was a quiet knock on the door. Max said, "What is it?"

The receptionist who was temping this week poked her head into the office. She said to Max, "There's a man here to see you."

"A man?" Max said, looking at Angela. "I don't have any appointments this morning, do I?"

Angela shook her head. Max said to the girl, "Did he say what his name was?"

"No. But he said it's very important that he speak to you."

"It's probably a fucking salesman. Tell him to leave his business card and we'll get back to him if we're interested."

"He said he's not a salesman."

"That's what they all say."

"I think he's telling the truth. He's in a wheelchair. He said he won't leave till he sees you."

"A wheelchair? Jesus H., he's probably working for some handicapped charity. He's—" *A wheelchair. Jesus fuck.* Max looked at Angela, then quickly looked away and said, "I'll go see him."

Max went toward the front of the office, rubbing the back of his neck to help ease his suddenly pounding headache. He managed not to scratch his groin but, Jesus Christ, he wanted to.

The man in the wheelchair was waiting near the reception desk. He had a thick black beard and dark, serious eyes. He was a big guy, stocky, looked Italian or maybe Spanish. Was it the same guy? Max wasn't sure. The retard at the hotel had been in shadow. But two guys in wheelchairs showing up in one week? What were the odds?

Max said, "Can I help you with something?"

The man extended his hand, said, "You certainly can. Name's Bobby Rosa."

"What the hell do you want?"

"I want to talk to you and I got a hunch you're gonna want to listen."

It was the same guy, all right. Wanting to break the bastard's teeth, Max said, "Look, I don't know why you're here, but you're lucky I don't get you fired for what you did. I would've but we felt sorry for you because you're retarded."

Bobby smiled proudly. "You really thought I was retarded, huh?"

Shit, Max thought. If the guy wasn't a retard maybe he wasn't a housekeeper either.

Looking around, Bobby said, "Nice place you got here. You must have, what, ten thousand square feet? What kind of rent you pay?"

Max looked over at the temp who seemed to be busy typing. Lowering his voice and stepping away from the reception desk, Max said, "Look, if you don't get the hell out of here right now, I'm going to get someone to take you out. Got that?"

Bobby said, "You got a good set of balls on you for a little guy. It's no wonder you're such a successful businessman."

Max said, "You want me to call the cops, I'll call the cops."

"You're not gonna call anybody." They were both talking in low mutters now, but the fucking temp was probably listening to every word. Still, it'd look worse if Max asked her to leave them alone, wouldn't it?

"Yeah?" Max said, leaning close to Bobby's ear. "And why won't I?"

"Because," Bobby said, "I have some pictures here that I doubt you're gonna want the cops to see."

Max noticed now, for the first time, the manila envelope on Bobby's lap.

"Why don't you come into my office?" he said.

Max went right to the bar and started making a stiff vodka tonic, his groin itching like hell. Bobby wheeled in behind him, stayed by the door.

Without looking at Bobby, Max said, "Now what the fuck are you talking about, pictures? Is this some bullshit joke 'cause if it is, I'm not laughing."

"Sit down," Bobby said.

Max, holding his drink at the bar, turned around slowly.

"What did you say?"

"I told you to sit down."

"Look, if you think I'm gonna let you get away with any more of this bullshit just because you're paralyzed, you're out of your mind."

Bobby took out a five-by-seven glossy and slid it across the desk. Max looked back and forth between Bobby and the photo several times, then walked slowly toward his swivel chair. Although he was scared out of his mind, he tried to keep his cool. But when he sat down his hands were already shaking. He looked up at Bobby, whose face was expressionless. Who was this guy, some detective? The only explanation Max could think of was that Harold and Claire Goldenberg had hired him to investigate the murders.

"So who the fuck are you?" Max asked.

"Under the circumstances I think I should be the one asking the questions, don't you?"

"Are you a detective?"

"No, I'm not a detective."

"Then who are you?"

"I'm the guy's got a picture of you fucking your secretary while your wife's not even cold in her fucking grave. Might get some people thinking, you know what I'm saying?"

"What do you want?"

"What do you think I want?"

Max stared at Bobby for a few seconds, wondering if the guy was crazy—he sure as hell looked crazy—then he got up and went back to the bar to make another drink. He said, "You like vodka?" thinking that maybe he could warm the guy up.

But Bobby said, "I don't drink."

"You have liver problems?"

"Excuse me?"

"You don't drink. Is it because you have a bum liver?"

"No, no, nothing like that. I just don't like what alcohol does to my brain." He touched his index finger to his head, said, "I like to stay sharp upstairs."

"I know what you mean," Max said, turning on the charm, starting to schmooze with the guy. "The only reason I drink is to keep my HDL up and my LDL down—doctor's orders." Max drank half the drink in one gulp. "What's your LDL?"

"My what?"

"Your bad cholesterol level."

"I don't pay attention to that shit. But yours...I figure yours is right off the goddamn chart. Am I right or am I right?"

Max, walking back to his desk with the drink, said, "I hope you're kidding, Bobby. I mean, you must be in your forties, right? I probably have about ten years on you, but you should still start thinking about HDL and LDL. Believe me, problems can sneak up on you, especially if you have a high-fat, low-fiber diet. And you especially need to watch yourself, I mean being crippled and all. You probably don't get your heart rate up a lot."

Bobby, glaring, said, "Thanks for the medical advice."

"No problem," Max said, resting the drink on the desk. "Now, Bobby, look. You can see I'm a nice guy, can't you? I mean I'm concerned about your health and everything. And you seem like a pretty nice guy to me. We're both older guys, been around the block a few times—we probably have a lot in common we don't even know about. So what I want to know is why can't you just be straight with me and tell me exactly who you are and why you took that picture."

"Why I took that picture? Because if I didn't have that picture you wouldn't pay me the quarter of a million dollars you're going to." He seemed like he was getting a big rush from this, fucking with a big shot businessman. Yeah, this was probably the highlight of this loser's life.

Max's hand was shaking, but he said, "Why the hell would I pay you one cent? So you have a picture of me screwing my executive assistant. Big shit. I could've hired someone to take that picture myself if I really wanted it."

Max forced a laugh, but Bobby stayed deadpan.

"You're going to pay me a quarter of a million dollars cash on Monday morning at nine o'clock," Bobby said. "If not, a copy of that picture's going to the NYPD."

Max stared at Bobby. Finally, he smiled, said, "That was a joke, right?"

"I'll be here at nine o'clock sharp," Bobby said. "I want the money in one suitcase, two at most. How you get it in there is your problem."

He started to back away from the desk.

Max said, "Whoa, whoa, hold up a second. This is all bullshit. I mean you're kidding, right?"

Bobby started wheeling away. Suddenly, Max was feeling light-headed and he wasn't sure whether it was drunkenness or panic. He said, "Hey, get back here."

Bobby stopped, turned around slowly.

In a hushed voice, Max said, "Look, usually I'd tell you to take a hike, but I really don't need this bullshit in my life right now, so here's what I'll do—the picture for a thousand bucks."

"My price is non-negotiable," Bobby said.

"Come on, a quarter of a million dollars? You have to be out of your fucking mind."

"I know a lot more about you than you think," Bobby said. "I read the papers, but I also use my head, I put two and two together. 'Grieving husband' my gimp ass."

Max said, "Look, even if I wanted to give you that kind of money, I don't have it."

"Monday—nine A.M. sharp. Oh, and you can keep that copy of the picture." Bobby looked up at the poster of the blonde on the Porsche. "Maybe you wanna hang it on the wall."

After Bobby left, Max poured himself another vodka tonic. His head was spinning and he had lost sensation in his face. Feeling dizzy, he opened his door and called for Angela to come into his office. When she came inside, Max was lying on the couch, holding his head.

"What's wrong?"

Max told her to lock the door, then motioned with his hand weakly toward the desk and the picture. Angela picked up the photo, stared at it for a few seconds, said, "That bollix." Then she started smiling, said, "I look pretty good, don't I?"

Max snatched the photo and said, "I can't believe this day is happening. First herpes, now this!"

"What did he ask for?"

"The bastard wants two-fifty K or he's going to the police."

"So?"

"So, did you hear what I just said? Are you an idiot or

something? Once the cops find out about me and you they'll be on our backs for good."

"That wasn't nice."

"What?"

"Calling me an idiot. You do that in Ireland, you better be holding more than a fookin drink."

"Jesus, I feel like I'm gonna throw up," Max said. "What the hell are we supposed to do now?"

"I'll get you some coffee."

"Fuck coffee! There's only one way out of this," Max said, and he covered his face with his hands. How the hell did it come to this? "Can you get in touch with your cousin today?"

"My cousin?"

"I think we have another job for his friend Popeye."

Fifteen

"What about your coffee?"
"Fuck the coffee."
"I would, but I don't fancy the blisters."
ALLAN GUTHRIE, *Two-Way Split*

The coffee burned Dillon's tongue. He was in the Starbucks beside Penn Station, and he spat out the scalding liquid, going, "Fookin thing."

A guy, yuppie-looking, gave him a long stare. Dillon was up for it, was he ever, glared at the guy, snarled, "The fook you looking at?" He was delighted how his New York accent was coming along, and the brogue still riding point. The guy quickly looked away. But Dillon was antsy, needed to wallop someone, some bastard needed a hiding and soon. When the compulsion hit him, as it did more and more, he had to have an explosive interlude, blow the cobwebs out.

He got out of there, an employee asking, "Everything okay, sir?"

Dillon paused, then said, "Hunky fucky dory yah wanker."

Translate that.

It was evening, the darkness bringing out the predators, skells in abundance. Even though Forty-second Street was now more a tourist attraction than a sleaze zone, it still had pockets of peril and Dillon had quickly found them. He stood in a doorway near Ninth Avenue, saw a lost Japanese tourist, camera hanging from his neck, a T-shirt with "Giuliani Rules" on it.

Dillon moved fast, hit the guy from behind, his knife out and the nip's throat sliced before he could mutter, "Banzai."

Dillon said, "Call it quits on Pearl Harbor a cara."

But, for fook's sake, all the guy had was plastic. Where were the bucks? He also had a packet of Menthol Lights and a Zippo, with the inscription *Small change*. No truer words. Dillon kicked him in the head for good measure and, as he headed up the block, he lit a menthol, enjoying the crank of the lighter, thinking, Johnny Cash and Zippos, it was a mighty country.

He began, like a mantra, the sports lingo he'd been learning, measuring out the phases like a new language. You grew up in Ireland and hurling was the sport of necessity, this American deal was a whole new territory. But he loved the sound of it, like praying but without the guilt or the bartering you had to do with god. He started, "Them Knicks need to take it to the next level, what to plug in and take out, they need a point guard, Isaiah Thomas better get his head outa his arse, the old days, Patrick Ewing, John Starks, they had a core, then the Bulls, ah they had it, the fookin Lakers, what was going on there, and the Sox, way to go boyos." Like that. No idea what he was saying but getting off on the melody.

No one paid him any heed, just one more crazy fuck, with a menthol cig and a bug up his ass.

New York, you gotta love it.

Walking down Fifth Avenue, all Angela could think about was the way Bobby Rosa had looked at her. On his way out of the office, he'd winked at her and smiled and said, "Goodbye, sweetheart." He wasn't really her type. She didn't mind the wheelchair, but guys with beards had always kind of disgusted her because they reminded her of her uncle Costas from Astoria who used to try to feel her up when she was thirteen. But Bobby didn't seem like a bad guy. She felt bad that they were gonna have to kill him.

Angela didn't know how everything had gotten so screwed up. It was bad enough that that innocent girl had to die, but then Dillon had to go and kill a cop. Getting Max's money was turning out to be a lot harder than she'd thought it would be. Besides, after hearing on the news about how brutal Dillon had been with the two women and then seeing him stick that knife into the cop's chest like he was getting off on it, she wasn't sure she wanted to marry him anymore anyway. You marry a whackjob like that, were you expecting white roses? Yeah, right. She didn't know where all that rage came from. One minute, he was talking about all that Buddhist peace shit or quoting the poetry of that Yeats guy, and the next thing he'd smack her across the face.

She'd go, "The fook did I do?"

Nothing, was the answer, but he'd laugh, go, "Just in case you were thinking of fooking me over, and there's more where that came from—call that a taster."

Then he'd take out a knife and start cleaning his nails with it, staring at her with that deadeye look.

But she couldn't break up with him now. She had to wait until this mess was over with and then decide what to do.

It started to rain as Angela continued along Fifth Avenue. She didn't feel like taking a bus or paying for a cab so she just kept walking, hardly realizing that she was getting soaked.

When she got home Dillon was sitting in his underwear on the bed watching music videos saying, "You brung me fookin dinner, I hope."

"I figured we'd just order in or something," Angela said.

"You said you were gonna pick it up, yah bleedin bitch."

"So I forgot. What's your problem?"

"I've been trapped here all day and guess what, I'm starving—

that's what my problem is, so get in the kitchen, get me some stew—you're Irish, stew is yer birthright. Put lots of cabbage and bacon in there, and don't forget the spuds, you got that, bitch?"

"I'm not your bitch," Angela said.

Now, his voice getting all gentle again, he asked, "What's that, mo croi?"

"Shut up."

He laughed. "That's funny," he said. "I really like that, mo croi."

Angela sat at the kitchen table and started taking off her wet shoes.

"Food, now!" he roared.

"You could've ordered in something yourself," she said.

"And have a delivery boy come up here and ID me? It's all on the news and shite. They're talking about how that cop *you* brought up here is missing and they got a cartoon of me in the paper, tis the spit of me too. That Chinese hoor informed on me arse, the one I dumped that jewelry on in Chinatown. What if the cop I did told other cops he was following you last night? I've been sitting here all day, waiting for the cops to show up—Jaysus, it's worse than the Falls Road, waiting for the Brit patrols."

"I told you you shouldn't sell that jewelry."

"Well, I did and get this right in yer dumb head, you don't *tell* me dick. You have two jobs, and both begin with f. One is food."

"Fuck you."

"Yeah, and that's the other one."

"If we wind up in jail now it's because you sold that jewelry."

He got up suddenly, a bad sign, and said, "I don't do jail, get that?"

There was something in his voice. "That's it," Angela said. "I've had it."

She marched past Dillon and went into the bathroom, slamming the door behind her. He banged on the door, demanding that she come out, going, "Where the hell's me dinner?" Angela covered her ears with her hands and sat down on the toilet seat, squeezing her eyes shut.

He was pounding on the door, now saying, "I'm too hungry for this shite. I'm going to ring for some takeout but you have to go to the door to pay for it. I'm not kiddin' yah."

Angela turned on the shower to drown him out, but it didn't work till she got in. As long as she kept her head under the water, his ranting was just part of the white noise.

When she came out, wrapped in a towel, Dillon was still in his underwear, now watching a basketball game.

Noticing the layers of Band-Aids over the bottom of Dillon's right foot, Angela said, "Did you put peroxide on that like I told you to?"

"You addressing me?" Dillon asked.

"Yeah, I'm talking to you," Angela said. "Why wouldn't I talk to you?"

Dillon went back to watching TV. He muttered along with the play-by-play, "Move yer ass mothfookers," trying to sound like a New Yorker.

"So?" Angela said, putting on a bra. "Did you or didn't you put peroxide on that?"

"Couldn't be bothered," he said.

Angela leaned forward, taking a closer look at the foot.

"You probably need a shot for that, you know, or you'll catch tetanus."

"I'll catch anorexia if I don't get me grub," he said.

Angela finished getting dressed—putting on jeans and a black T-shirt with "My Boyfriend's Out of Town" in red across the front. She sat down on the bed next to Dillon and rested a hand on his lap. For a while there was silence except for the sports commentator babbling, then Dillon said, "I was watching *South Park* before and Kenny is dead again, you see that one?"

"I think so," Angela said.

The food arrived and Angela and Dillon sat on the bed together eating the shrimp lo mein and barbecued spare ribs directly from the cartons. Finally, Angela decided it was a good time to break the bad news.

"Something happened today," she said, "but before I tell you you have to promise not to get mad at me."

"What?"

"You have to promise."

"What is it?"

"You're gonna get angry," Angela said. "I can tell it already."

"Just tell me what the fook it is, you're spoiling me dinner." Christ, she thought, she never saw a man eat so much and still stay skinny as a wet rodent.

Dillon's nostrils flared. He looked the same way he did before he stabbed that cop.

"All right," Angela said. "Remember how I told you I was with my boss last night at that hotel?"

"Yeah," he said.

"Well something happened that we didn't know about. Something that could be bad."

"Stop whining and tell me what it is."

"Well, there was this guy," Angela said, "and he took some pictures of us."

"You mean like a Guard?"

"No, not a cop—definitely not a cop. He was in a wheelchair and—anyway, he came to the office today and he showed the pictures to Max."

"What were the pictures of?" Dillon asked.

"Just of us, you know…in bed together."

"So? What's he going to do with them, beside play with his own self?"

"If the police see them it'll show that me and Max were together, that we could've planned the murder."

"But the police haven't got the pictures, the gimp in the wheelchair does."

"That's where the bad part comes in. He wants money for them. A lot of money."

"You mean he's trying to blackmail you?"

"He's trying to blackmail Max."

"And you're sure this fooker isn't a Guard?"

"I don't know what he is," Angela said, remembering again how Bobby Rosa had looked at her. "But Max thinks it's a big problem. He wanted me to get you to get rid of him."

Dillon sat calmly for a few seconds and Angela thought, Hey, that wasn't too bad. Then he suddenly threw his carton of food against the wall on the other side of the room. Angela covered her ears as Dillon stood up and kicked the top of the TV set with his right foot, then roared as the pain hit his already inflamed sole. He said, "You're going to get the hiding of yer life, you hoor's ghost!"

Dillon began hitting her in the face, slapping her with his open hands. Angela didn't know how she got out of the apartment. She ran down the stairs, nearly tripping several times. She walked toward Second Avenue, not realizing for several minutes that she was barefoot.

She went into the Rodeo Bar, on Second Avenue and Twenty-eighth Street. She sat at the dingy half-empty bar and then realized she had no money. She told the bartender she was "waiting for a friend" and stared at the hockey game on TV.

She became aware of a guy sitting on the stool next to her. He was young, around twenty-three, in a business suit and she saw a couple of other guys—his friends—giggling to each other. The guy said, "Hey, is this Woodstock or something?"

Angela was confused for a second then realized he was making fun of her for being barefoot.

"Just leave me the feck alone, yeh arsehole!"

The guy, looking terrified, went back to his friends.

Angela left the bar and headed toward home. She approached her apartment building, hoping Dillon had calmed down a little. Food and weed usually took his edge off, but she knew it was only a matter of time before he really lost it. Then she thought about Bobby Rosa again. The guy was really into her—that much was obvious. And, yeah, he was in a wheelchair, but there was something about him that made her think he could take care of himself. But could he take care of Dillon?

Angela didn't have the key to her apartment. She kept ringing the buzzer, but Dillon wouldn't answer it. Finally, after nearly an hour, someone leaving the building let her in and she went upstairs. The door to her apartment was open.

Dillon was sitting on the bed, watching videos and reading his damn Zen book. He said, "I wouldn't go in that bathroom if I were you. That fookin Chinese food, it was off."

Angela went to the fridge and poured herself a glass of soda.

Dillon said, "While I was in there on the bowl, shittin' out me organs, I was thinking this guy in the wheelchair is our problem too. I don't trust that bollix, Max. If he cracks, he's taking us down with him. You know that, right?"

Angela didn't answer.

Dillon said, "So my question is how much should I charge?"

"Charge?"

Dillon glared at her like she was stupid.

"For blasting a guy in a wheelchair."

Sixteen

Muggers are plain creepy.
DUANE SWIERCZYNSKI

Max said to Kamal, "Have you ever had herpes?"

They were in Max's kitchen where Kamal was busy cooking Max's macrobiotic meals for the rest of the week. Three pots were going on the stove and Kamal was chopping up beets and potatoes.

"Herpes?" Kamal said pausing with the cutting knife in his right hand. "Why do you ask that?"

"No reason," Max said. "I mean it's not like I think you're gonna infect the food or anything like that. It was just something that was on my mind."

"No," Kamal said, still looking confused. "I do not have any venereal diseases."

"Ah-ha," Max said. "So you haven't been tested for herpes."

"No, I do not believe so. Unless it was part of my regular physical examination."

"Very interesting," Max said. "Very very interesting."

Now Max was almost one hundred percent sure that the little Indian guy had been banging Deirdre, probably had been banging her for some time. The last time Max had had sex with her must have been three or four months ago and he must have caught the virus then.

"You can just admit it," Max said.

"Admit what?" Kamal asked.

"That you and Deirdre were, you know...a couple. Don't worry, I won't fire you or anything like that."

"I have no idea what you are talking about," Kamal said.

"Come on," Max said, "you think I'm blind? I saw how much time you and Deirdre spent together. It's obvious you two were very close."

"I admired your wife a great deal," Kamal said, "but I could never imagine having relations with her."

"Not even one time," Max said, "just for the hell of it?"

"I'm offended that you would even ask me such a thing. I am a Sikh from Punjab—we are very spiritual people. We don't sleep with other men's wives, not even if we wanted to, and I did not want to sleep with your wife. No offense but, western women, they have a peculiar odor—it's from eating meat perhaps. I like the smell of curry and spices, if you can understand."

Max stared at him deadpan, thinking, Is this guy for real?

Then Max demanded, "You swear to God?"

"Why should I—"

"If you didn't do anything you shouldn't have a problem swearing to God about it."

Kamal slid the potatoes and beets into the steamer then said, "I do not believe in God the same way you do."

"Yeah, yeah, whatever," Max said. "Then do you swear to the Buddha about it?"

"The Buddha does not ask anything to swear to it. The Buddha is not a singular being or concept. The Buddha is all things."

Max picked up a plate and held it up. He said, "Fine, so let's say this plate is the Buddha. Do you swear to this plate that you never banged my wife?"

Kamal looked at Max like he was crazy, then said, "I did not do anything with your wife. I'm giving you my word which should be enough, now please, do not say any more disrespectful things about the Buddha. It is very, very hurtful to me."

The little rice eater looked like he was about to cry.

Max stared at him for a few seconds and decided that he was probably telling the truth after all. But if Kamal didn't give the herpes to Deirdre that meant that Max must have gotten it from Angela.

"Eh, just forget about it," Max said. "What difference does it make anyway?"

Max went to the fridge and poured himself a glass of skim milk.

"You know, you should really consider joining me at the ashram sometime," Kamal said, stirring the big pot of brown rice. "I think it would very healing for you."

"I'm Jewish," Max said.

"Our guru welcomes people of all faiths," Kamal said. "And meditating and chanting can be very cleansing. It can help you to become at peace with your inner self."

"I'm not gonna sit on the floor and chant like some hippie," Max said. Then he wondered if he could meet some classy Indian woman at the ashram. Hell, he could do rice and, for a decent lay, he'd chant till the crows came home or till the whatever fucking birds they had in India came home. Besides, what the hell was he doing with Angela anyway? He used to think he was in love with her, but lately he wasn't so sure. She had a nice body and that great accent, but there wasn't much more going on there. What had he been thinking?

"Lemme ask you something," Max said. "Do women come to these ashrams?"

"Yes, of course," Kamal said. "The spiritual journey is not just for men."

Kamal was trying not to smile. Was something funny?

"Yeah, lemme ask you something else," Max said. "Are they well-endowed?"

"Excuse me?"

"Tits. Do they have big tits?"

Kamal waited a few seconds, checking the vegetables, then said, "Some of them do, yes."

"In that case, maybe I'll give the hippie shit a shot," Max said. "I mean after I get through with my mourning of course."

Then he looked away and glanced at the copy of the *Daily News* on the table. Some Jap tourist got his throat cut on Forty-second Street and the police had no suspects. Max chuckled, thought, *I guess Times Square ain't no Disneyland after all.*

Seventeen

I lose it, flapping about in the rain and kicking the hell out of the dog. I don't deserve this. I don't fucking deserve all this fucking bad luck and this stupid fucking life.
RAY BANKS, *The Big Blind*

The next day another Manhattan murder was the lead story on the six o'clock news. The rat-gnawed body of forty-one-year-old Homicide Detective Kenneth Simmons of the 19th Precinct had been discovered by some children in an empty lot in Harlem. The body had two gunshot wounds and a stab wound to the chest. The police had released a police sketch of a suspect in the case—a white male, approximately five-five or five-six, maybe 130 pounds, with gray hair, last seen wearing an old leather jacket and dirty blue jeans and new sneakers. On Monday morning, the suspect had been spotted in a pawnshop on Bayard Street in Chinatown selling jewelry that was stolen during the recent murders of two Upper East Side women. Police believed that he might be a suspect in those murders as well since Detective Simmons had been working on that case when he was killed. People with any information regarding the case were urged to call a special police hotline number or 577-TIPS.

Watching the news report on the TV in his living room, Max had no doubt that the guy in the police sketch was Popeye. His face was too fat and his eyes and nose looked different, but everything else, down to the leather jacket, was definitely him. Max didn't know what that guy was going to fuck up next. Was the stupid prick determined to wipe out the population of Manhattan? He'd read once that the Irish were truly demented. Well, no argument there.

Sitting at a table in the back of Famiglia Pizza on Fiftieth and Broadway, Max saw Popeye limping up the aisle. After Popeye sat down, diagonally across from Max, with a big cupful of ice, Max said, "What happened to your foot?"

"Fook me foot, yah suited prick," Popeye said. Then looking around nervously he said, "Nobody followed yeh here, right?"

Dillon was fingering a gold pin in his leather jacket, like it was a talisman or something. The Irish and their goddamn superstitions.

"Not that I know of," Max said.

"Yeah, well you better be sure," Popeye said. "I shouldn't even be here now. I should be in Florida, writing me poetry."

The idea of this bloodthirsty animal writing poetry was too much for Max. What was that old joke? If you threw a stone in Ireland, you'll probably hit a poet, usually a bad one.

Smiling, Max asked, "How do your poems start? Roses are red?"

Popeye had the cup up to his mouth, sucking out an ice cube. When his eyes peered over the cup, Max said, "Don't look at me."

Sucking on a cube, Popeye said, "What?"

"You heard me, you little cocksucker." Max laughed. "Just sit there and keep looking straight ahead and don't look at me. If you look at me one time I'm getting up and leaving here and you'll never see me again."

"I like that, the little bollix showing some spunk," Popeye said. "But are you on medication? *You're* the one who can't look at *me*."

"Not anymore," Max said. "Now *I'm* calling the shots."

"You'll be calling the fookin mortuary, I haven't time for this shite."

"Then find time, because you'll be here as long as I want you to be here."

"Yeah, and if I get up, walk out, what will you do, use more obscene language?"

"Go ahead. You're the wanted criminal, not me."

"If I'm fooked, you're coming to hell with me."

"You can't prove anything," Max said. "What are you going to do, say I hired you to kill my wife? I really doubt that the police'll take your word over mine. I'm a respected businessman. Who the fuck are you?"

"Did you say fook to me?"

"I told you not to look at me."

"Bollix, I'm legging it."

"I don't think that would be a wise idea."

Popeye paused, half-standing, then sat down again and said, "Why not?"

"Think about it. You need this guy out of the way as much as I do. You don't know what evidence the police have on you. Maybe you left something in my house that night—something you forgot. Or maybe they found some of your blood or hair there or they got something off that piece of shit you left on my rug—thanks very much for that, by the way. What was that, your idea of a fucking housewarming present? It wasn't very bright, with DNA and all that other shit the cops have these days. I don't know what it feels like to die by lethal injection, but I imagine it's not very pleasant."

Popeye stayed still for a few more seconds then settled back down in the seat and stared straight ahead. Finally he said, "So where does the crippled fuck live?"

"First let's talk about the important *shite*," Max said, trying to put on a brogue, wanting to give Popeye a taste of his own. "My money. I want to revise the offer I made to you over the phone this morning."

"You said twenty large."

Max loved the way Popeye's tone was weakening. Jesus Christ, Max felt the power going straight to his head.

"Yeah, well, a lot has changed since then," Max said. "For instance, you've made it on to the NYPD's Most Wanted list, so I've decided you owe me a freebie for this one."

"Like fuck I do."

Max ignored this, said, "You have as much stake now in this as I do. You can't disappear until this Rosa guy is out of the way and you know it."

Popeye's eyes narrowed into slits.

"How will you find his address?"

"I already called Information," Max said. "They told me they didn't have any Bobby Rosas. I said, what about Robert Rosas? They had one in the West Village—the fudgepacking district. The Rosa I met didn't look like a guy who talks into the mike, if you know what I mean. They also had one at one hundred West Eighty-ninth so I said gimme that one."

"But how you know it's the same fellah?"

"I did something you're not used to doing—I used my fucking head. I called the building and said to the doorman, 'Does a Robert Rosa in a wheelchair live at your address?' The guy said 'Yeah,' and I hung up. You have any more stupid questions?"

Popeye started to say something, but Max interrupted and, with his best Oirish accent said, "Good, then you can get the *bejaysus* out of here."

Popeye looked stunned for a couple of seconds, mumbling something about "tinkers." Then he stood up and said, "You shouldn't take the Lord's name in vain, tis bad luck."

✷

About twenty minutes later, when Max got out of the cab in front of his townhouse, a man said, "You Max Fisher?"

Looking at the guy, Max thought, Jesus Christ, what now?

The guy took out his shiny gold badge and said, "Ortiz—Homicide. I think you better come with me."

Eighteen

*I wanted to say they busted apart as do dried-up dreams,
or public trust, but, truly, they flew apart exactly like
yesterday's shit.*
DANIEL WOODRELL, *Give Us a Kiss*

The doorbell rang and Bobby said, "Come in," sitting in his wheelchair about ten feet from the door, his Glock 27 compact pistol resting on his lap. In walked Max Fisher's executive assistant. She was wearing a short red leather skirt, matching pumps and a tight top. Like the other night at the hotel, her hair was big and blown dry, but tonight she had on thick red lipstick, plenty of eye makeup, and silver hoop earrings.

After looking her up and down again and then waiting a couple of seconds, Bobby wanted to say, *Holy fuckin' shit,* but went with "Can I help you with something?"

"Sorry to bother you like this," she said. "I mean I would've called, or tried to call and tell you I was coming over, but I didn't think I'd have time. It's just I heard my boss talking on the phone today and I had to come over to warn you."

Man, that Irish accent was sexy as hell. He was trying to remember whether he'd ever banged an Irish chick. He had—a few of them—but they were Irish-American. They didn't sound like this girl, that's for sure.

"Warn me about what?" he asked, hiding the gun between his leg and the side of his chair.

"I think you're in big trouble," she said. "My boss said he's sending somebody over here to hurt you, or maybe worse. I don't know what's going on, but I heard him mention your name and address."

Bobby stared at her for a few seconds. She was biting her lower lip, in a naughty schoolgirl way, and he wished he could give her something else to bite on. He wondered if she'd dressed up just for him. The other night, at the hotel, she'd been wearing jeans and a tube top.

"So who's this guy that's gonna come after me?" he asked.

"He calls himself Popeye."

"Popeye? I gotta look out for Olive Oyl too?"

Angela smiled, said, "I just heard Max talking about Popeye."

"And how does Max know a guy like this 'Popeye'?"

Angela shrugged.

"Is he the guy with the gray hair and the screwed-up mouth I saw a sketch of on the news?"

"I really don't know anything else," Angela said. "I mean I guess it could be the same guy."

Bobby looked her up and down again, said, "Wanna sit down?" and Angela said, "Sure."

As Angela passed by Bobby caught a whiff of her perfume and said, "You're wearing Joy."

"Yeah," Angela said, smiling. "How'd you know?"

"I bought some of it for an old girlfriend one time. I love that smell."

Bobby watched her sit down on the couch. He liked the noise her leather skirt made when she crossed her right leg over her left. She was exactly the type of girl Bobby would have gone crazy for before he got shot. He would have taken her to one of those classy Italian restaurants downtown in the West Village, then to some club on Seventh Avenue, and then back to his place for an all-night screw fest.

"This is a really big place you got here," Angela said looking around. "You live here all by your own self?"

"Yeah," Bobby said. Then he lifted himself up in his wheelchair to do a pressure-relief and said, "But I'll probably sell it one of these days and move into something smaller." Noticing an empty pizza box on the coffee table and glasses half-filled with soda on the end pieces he said, "Sorry it's such a dump."

"Oh, don't be ridiculous," Angela said. "If you want to know a secret, my apartment's a real mess too."

Bobby was staring at Angela's mouth, loving how when she stopped talking her lips stayed slightly apart. He said, "So you know why Max wants this Popeye guy to kill me, don't you?"

"No," Angela said.

"You don't know anything about the pictures?"

Angela shook her head.

"Well," Bobby said, "I sort of took these pictures the other night of you and your boss...in that hotel room."

Bobby was watching Angela's reaction closely. She seemed genuinely surprised, but he couldn't tell for sure.

"You're saying you were the guy who—"

Bobby nodded.

"And you took pictures of me and Max..."

The funny thing was, it almost seemed the idea was getting her hot. He nodded again.

"I can't believe this," Angela said, but not in an angry way. "What are you, a detective or something? Did somebody pay you to follow us?"

Bobby laughed.

"No, it was just chance. It could have been any two people. It didn't have to be you and your boss."

"I don't get it," Angela said. "Why would Max want somebody to kill you?"

"Well, the meeting we had yesterday...I'm not really sure how to put this. I went to Max with a business proposition. I'm a businessman, like he is—except my business is a little different than your boss's."

"I don't get it."

"Yeah, I didn't think you would. Let me put it this way—I was trying to squeeze some money out of him. It was just a racket I got involved with because I had nothing else going on and it got a lot bigger than I ever thought it would."

"A racket? What kind of racket?"

"Taking pictures of people fucking in hotel rooms and trying to blackmail them."

"That's amazing," Angela said.

"What is?"

"That you could be so honest about something like that. I mean a lot of guys would've made up some bullshit story. You just sat there and told me the truth. I can really respect that about a person."

Bobby liked that. "Thanks."

"I mean, I have to admit I'm a little embarrassed that you have those pictures and that you saw me...you know...but on the other hand I can understand why you did it."

"But you don't have to worry," Bobby said, "once your boss pays me the money I'll throw out all of those pictures and the negatives. They won't wind up on the fuckin' Internet if that's what you're worried about."

"Oh, I'm not worried about stuff like that. I really don't care about Max. As far as I'm concerned he can go rot in hell."

"Really?" Bobby said, loving how she said *hell*. You could almost feel the flames. "I thought...I mean, going by the way you two looked that night..."

"I made a huge mistake," Angela said, looking at her lap. "It's the story of my life—things just seem to get really fucked up. I was on the rebound, you know? Max kept asking me out and asking me out and finally I just said yes. I guess I just thought he was a different person than he turned out to be."

Her accent had become full-blown Irish, and had a trace of little-girl-lost in there too, a sucker punch for most men, and for Bobby, who hadn't felt anything for a woman since Tanya, it was a K.O.

"Did he pay this guy Popeye to kill his wife?"

"I don't know for sure, but after hearing him on the phone today...I'm almost positive he did. He was going crazy for me, getting really obsessed, you know? I kept telling him it was nothing serious and that we should end it. But he wouldn't get the message and then he must've gone ahead and got this guy to kill his wife. Believe me, if I had any idea anybody was gonna get hurt there was no way I would've stayed with him."

Angela uncrossed her legs then crossed them again, her leather skirt making that rubbing sound. Her bottom lip was moist and, he didn't know if it was just him or something about the way she was sitting, but her bust looked bigger than it had when she walked in.

"But you were with him the other night," Bobby said, "after his wife got killed."

Angela looked away for a moment, toward the front door. When she turned back, tears were streaming down her cheeks and her face was all scrunched up and ugly.

"I was afraid," Angela said, her voice cracking. "I wanted to break it off, but I've only had my job for a few months and he told me if I didn't keep going out with him he'd fire me and give me a shitty reference. And I was lonely, I guess. Maybe you can't understand, but women get desperate when they get lonely. They do things they wouldn't ordinarily do. Plus my mother was putting a lot of pressure on me."

"Your mother?"

"My mother died a while ago and she was, you know, real salt-of-the-earth."

Bobby loved how she pronounced it *sall-t*. She could even make a condiment sound sexy.

"She had a hard death," Angela went on, "and before she passed, she held my hand and begged me to find a good man someday, not to end up alone." She took a tissue from her bag, dabbed at her eyes, then said, "Maybe you can't understand it, but my mother always had a lot of control over me."

"Actually, I know exactly what that's like," Bobby said.

"You do?"

"My mother and I were very close."

"I'm sorry," Angela said.

"Oh, she's not dead. She's in a nursing home. I still go visit her all the time, but she's really out of it."

"I think that's the most beautiful thing I've ever heard in my whole life," Angela said, starting to cry again. "A son who visits his mother in a nursing home."

Bobby was feeling something he'd never thought possible—he was feeling *noble*, like a fucking good guy. He had no idea how that had happened, but he kind of liked it. He saw himself like Tom Cruise in that flick, *Born On The Fourth of July*, having fucking dignity in his disability.

"I only go a few times a week," Bobby said.

"A few times a week! I hope when I'm old I have a son like you who'll always love me."

Now the tears were starting to flow freely down Angela's cheeks. Bobby noticed that the tissue she had was drenched so he wheeled into the kitchen and returned with some paper towels. He gave one to Angela and she dabbed her eyes a few times and said, "I have a confession to make. There's something

I lied to you about before and I feel really bad about it."

"Shoot," Bobby said.

"See, the truth is, I *could've* called to tell you all of this instead of coming here. But after I saw you leave the office, I just couldn't stop thinking about you. I thought maybe if I came over here...I don't know...I just thought maybe something could happen between us. Believe me, I usually don't do stuff like this—I mean get so forward with guys—but after all the hell I've been through lately I figured things couldn't get much worse than they already are. I just think you're a very attractive man and...I feel like such an idiot. I should probably just go home now."

Bobby's face was hot. He hoped he wasn't blushing.

"Well, that's definitely very flattering," he said.

"It is?"

"Of course," Bobby said. "I mean you're a good-looking girl and—"

"You mean that?"

"Mean what?"

"That I'm good-looking."

"Of course. Believe me, if I wasn't in this wheelchair..."

"Oh, I don't care about that."

"You don't?"

"If you want to know the truth I think a wheelchair's kind of sexy. I mean it's not like I'm some bleedin' pervert or anything like that. I don't go out trying to meet guys in wheelchairs, but it's not like I have anything against it and you're so, like, courageous about it. You don't whine or moan—you just go on with your life. Max can use both of his legs and he never, and I mean never, stops whining."

"I don't think you understand—"

"You know who you're like? You're just like Tom Cruise in

that movie about the Vietnam vet in the wheelchair. My mother loved that movie. She'd say, God rest her, 'See that? That's a man of character.' "

Bobby couldn't believe she'd said that. It was like they were *fucking communicating mentally*. How great was that?

Angela was gazing at Bobby with her eyes wide open and her lips parted slightly, like she wanted to be kissed. In the old days, Bobby would have sat next to her on the couch, gone in for some tongue action, and the rest would have been history. But now he felt like it was his first time alone with a girl.

"I have an idea," Angela said, maybe sensing his awkwardness. "I'm a really good cook. I could go out and get some stuff and cook you a really great dinner. Are you Greek by any chance?"

"No, but people sometimes think I look Greek. Why?"

"My father's Greek and you sort of remind me of his side."

Shit, why the fuck didn't he just say he was Greek? He could do Greek. Hell, anyone could do Greek. Just don't shave and grunt, what's so hard about that?

"Hey, I have an idea," Angela said, her face brightening. "I know how to make a great pasticcio and I could make a big Greek salad to go with it. How's that sound?"

Bobby said that sounded dynamite. While Angela was out shopping for food Bobby got dressed as quickly as he could. He put on one of his good silk shirts and a pair of chinos. He wished he had time to take a bath and trim his beard, but by the time he finished getting dressed Angela was already back from the supermarket. Bobby had Thin Lizzy going, figuring he'd impress her with some Irish rock.

Angela heard the opening riff of "Whiskey In The Jar," shrieked, "Oh my God, that's like, my favorite song."

Bobby had a feeling she was full of shit. He liked that, though —showed she was into him.

Coming back with some bullshit of his own, he said, "Yeah, I love Lizzy, man. My opinion, they're better than AC/DC. I got everything they ever did on cassette."

Angela told Bobby to wait in the living room while she was cooking because she wanted the meal to be a surprise. It took a long fucking time, but she finally told him dinner was ready and he wheeled up to the table. By the way Angela was looking at him he knew that after dinner she was gonna be up for some dessert. He hoped he could give it to her. Phil Lynott was into "The Boys Are Back in Town" and Bobby figured, hey, it had to be an omen.

The pasticcio was only so-so—okay, it tasted like horseshit—but Bobby told Angela that it was the best Greek dinner he'd ever eaten. They sat at the table afterwards, drinking Merlot and talking. He told her all the highlights of his life, including how he had wound up in the wheelchair.

"I was dating this black girl named Tanya," Bobby explained. "It was nothing too serious, you know? We were just going out a lot, having a good time. Then one night we were at her place, up in the South Bronx, listening to some tunes. I remember the fucking song that was playing—Guns N' Roses, 'Sympathy for the Devil'—when her boyfriend comes into the room."

"She had a boyfriend?" Angela said.

"It was news to me too," Bobby said. "He was a big black guy, like six-four, and he was angry as hell."

"So what happened?"

"He starts saying, 'Why are you fucking my woman?'—shit like that. I didn't know what was going on. I just said to him, 'Look, you two better settle this yourselves,' and I got up to leave. That's when I heard the shot. Next thing I know I'm on the floor and I can't feel my legs."

"Did he go to jail?"

"No, he ran away and I didn't press charges."

"Why not?"

"What was the point? It wouldn't get me my legs back."

Bobby didn't want to tell Angela the rest of the story, how when he got out of the hospital he took a bus up to the project in the Bronx where the guy lived and pumped six bullets into his back. But just thinking about how he'd plugged that fucking bastard and then put a couple in Tanya when she came home made his blood bubble.

"You okay?" Angela asked.

"Yeah," Bobby said. "It's just the memories are, you know... painful."

Angela shook her head in sympathy then said, "You know what I think? I think you're lucky."

"Why's that?"

"Look at you—you're strong, healthy, not too old. If he shot you in the head you would've died and you never would've met me."

"Yeah, I guess that's true," Bobby said, thinking only somebody who wasn't paralyzed would say a thing like that. He remembered what it felt like, lying on Tanya's floor, realizing he was a cripple. In twenty-plus years, pulling heists and shit, he never got a scratch. Then some jealous fuck walks in a room and shoots him in the back. There was nothing lucky about it.

They started to talk about other things. Then Angela said she had to go to the bathroom, but instead she stopped behind Bobby and started kissing the back of his neck, running her hands over his chest. He had no idea what to do next. He felt sweat building under his arms and he couldn't remember if he'd put on deodorant. He was positive that he reeked and that he was going in his pants. Angela rotated the wheelchair around, away from the table, and climbed on top of him. As she undid his chinos he said, "There's something you gotta know."

He told her how he couldn't stay hard for more than a couple of minutes and how he didn't think he'd be able to screw. It was hard for him to say all of it, to find the right words and then get them out, but when he finally did he was surprised how much better he felt. Still, he was ready for her to make up some phony excuse and go home. But instead she put her hands over his cheeks, and moved her face right in front of his, looking into his eyes and said, "Don't worry, everything's gonna be okay. Think of my mother looking down at us." Bobby was going to say, Think of that black fuck looking up at us, but managed to keep it to himself.

After about ten minutes had gone by, Bobby was going to tell her that it was a waste of time, that they should just forget about it. But then Angela looked up at him and by the way she was smiling he knew they were finally getting somewhere. She climbed on top of Bobby in the wheelchair and started thrusting. At first, all Bobby could think about was how he was going to shit and make a big asshole out of himself. But then when he saw Angela starting to come Bobby felt a way he never thought he'd feel again.

"See?" she said. "I told you everything was gonna be okay, didn't I?"

Later, they went into the bedroom.

"Hey, who took all these pictures?"

Bobby was afraid Angela would think he was some kind of loser, but he didn't see any point in denying it.

"I did," Bobby said. "Why? You like them?"

"It looks like something they'd have hanging in a museum," Angela said. "You didn't tell me you were an artist."

"It's just a little hobby of mine," Bobby said.

"I love the way they're all different sizes. It's like you're saying that women are different, but they're the same, like—I don't know what I mean, but I like them."

It crossed his mind that maybe she wasn't playing with a full deck.

Now that they had gotten the first time out of the way, Bobby's old confidence was back. They went at it again and this time Bobby wasn't worried about anything. He couldn't believe how lucky he was to meet a girl like Angela who didn't treat him like he was a freak.

Angela lay next to him in the dark. Cool jazz was playing, the soft music seeming to fit the mood. Angela was running her long fingernails through Bobby's thick, sweaty chest hair.

"You know it could be easier for you the next time we get together," Bobby said. "I can use a vacuum pump or get one of those injection devices. You just shoot some medicine into the side of your dick and you stay hard for hours."

"Maybe you could take Viagra."

"Tried it," Bobby said. "Didn't do shit for me."

"You know what would be great?"

"If you moved in here and I could fuck you stupid every night?"

"That too." Angela caressed his chin and stared into his eyes. "But it would be great if you could get rid of Popeye."

"What do you mean, get rid of him?"

"You have that gun. I mean, I saw it. Maybe you could, like, scare him, or do something to make him leave, go back to Ireland."

"That's where he's from?"

"Or maybe you could…I don't know. I'm just worried about him, that's all. I think if he kills you, Max might send him after me next."

"Kill me? Whoa, I did two tours in Desert Storm. Nobody's

gonna kill me, especially some crazy, grey-haired Irish fuck. No offense."

"So you'll protect me?"

Angela was twirling the hair below his bellybutton now and he couldn't believe it—he was getting more liftoff.

"Don't worry, sweetheart, I'll take care of Popeye," Bobby said, grabbing Angela and pulling her back on top of him. "Now how about you take care of me?"

Nineteen

I pictured his mouth open and the powerful cleaning fluid filling his mouth, his lungs, stomach—pooling in his ears, penetrating into his skin, burning through the tiny pipe of his cock, tearing its way like a knife up his asshole. He would soon be cleaner than any human ever got. His stench would be filtered and dumped with the toxic waste.
VICKI HENDRICKS, *Miami Purity*

Homicide Detective Louis Ortiz pressed the RECORD button on the digital recorder on the desk and said, "As you might've heard we have a suspect in the case. There's also been another victim."

"Why are you taping me?" Max said. "I don't get it—am I being interviewed or interrogated?"

"Maybe you should answer that question for me."

"Look, I don't know what's going on here. I thought you were going to fill me in on what happened to my wife and niece. But if this is some kind of—"

"If you want to call a lawyer you can."

"What do I need a lawyer for? Only guilty people need lawyers."

"Then shut up and answer my damn questions," Ortiz said. "As you may have heard, my partner, Kenneth Simmons' body was discovered this afternoon."

"Yeah, I heard about that on the news."

"What did you hear?"

"That a Detective Simmons was killed."

"And you realized that this was the same man who was working on your wife's murder case?"

"The name rang a bell."

"Did the news come as a surprise to you?"

"Excuse me for getting off topic here," Max said, "but I don't see why you're talking to me. From what I heard on the news the suspect you're looking for is a skinny guy with gray hair. Does my hair look fucking gray to you?"

Max had some extra edge in his tone, letting this prick know he was a respectable businessman, a pillar of the community, the guy who paid the cops' goddamn wages.

Ortiz breathed deeply then said, "Kenneth Simmons was following you when he was killed."

"Following me?" Max said. "What the hell for?"

"That's not important now," Ortiz said. "What's important is we found his car in front of the Hotel Pennsylvania on Thirty-third Street. Can you tell me what the car was doing there?"

"I haven't the foggiest idea," Max said. He had always been a horrible liar, especially under pressure. *Foggiest*. What the fuck was he, British?

"Maybe it'll come back to you," Ortiz said. "I questioned the clerks at the hotel. They said at around eight o'clock on Monday evening, Detective Simmons inquired at the desk about a couple that had checked in under the name Brown in room 1812. You don't have an idea who that couple is, do you?"

Max was shaking his head.

"I don't have to tell you what I think," Ortiz continued. "Unfortunately, the woman who was working at the desk that night said she couldn't remember what the couple looked like, but I have people taking a look at the security video from that night and I think it's going to show you and a woman checking into that hotel. Now if you're as innocent as you say you are you could just save us some time and tell us who that woman is."

"I don't know what you're talking about," Max said as calmly as he could. "I was never in that hotel."

"All right," Ortiz said. He turned off the recorder then got up and went behind Max. Resting his hands on the back of Max's chair, his mouth almost touching Max's left ear, he said, "You wanna do this the hard way, we'll do it the hard way. But I'll tell you right now—if I find out that was you in that hotel I'm gonna make your life a fucking nightmare. You ever get fucked up the ass? Well, I hope you enjoy it because I'm gonna put you in a cell with a psychotic, white-boy-hating motherfucker who's got a big, fat, fourteen-inch dong. Then we'll see how much you like fucking around with Louis Ortiz."

Ortiz stayed there for a few seconds, letting his words sink in, then he returned to his seat and turned the recorder back on.

Max felt wetness on the back of his neck—either sweat or his spray-on hair was dissolving. He wasn't sure what he was accomplishing by not admitting he was in that hotel; when Ortiz saw that surveillance tape that ridiculous wig would be no disguise. But, at this point, he didn't see what he had to lose by continuing to lie.

"Look, I want to do everything I can to help you," Max said, "but I think you're forgetting that my wife and niece are *dead*. You know what it's like to come home and find the brains of your loved ones splattered on your wall? Believe me, it's not very pleasant. But what's even worse is having to put up with some ignorant fucking detective, making up ridiculous stories, trying to implicate you. Don't you people have any sense of decency?"

Max thought that his speech had affected Ortiz and was proud of himself for performing so well, but then Ortiz said, "You want me to spell it out for you, Fisher? I think you hired somebody to kill your wife. I think your niece was just unlucky, got mixed up in it by accident. Detective Simmons thought the same thing—fact, he was more sure about it than I was. That's why he was following you that night. Oh, and by the way I do know what it's like to lose somebody close, like a partner you've been working with for the last seven fucking years."

Max said, "That's it. I'm not doing any more of this bullshit without my lawyer."

"I thought you told me only guilty people need lawyers?"

"Guilty people and people who are being harassed."

"All I'm asking is that you tell me the truth."

"I'm telling you the fucking truth, but you don't want to hear it."

"All right," Ortiz said, "then tell me—where did you go Monday night after work?"

"I took a cab home."

"You have anybody who can vouch for that?"

"Not unless you can find the cab driver who drove me."

"Speaking of cab drivers," Ortiz said, "we *did* find a driver who claims he picked up a man fitting Kenneth Simmons' description in front of the Hotel Pennsylvania at approximately eight-forty Monday evening. Simmons ordered him to follow another cab which ended up going to the corner of Twenty-fifth and First. A woman got out of the first cab—the driver couldn't ID her except that she was white and had 'big blond hair'—and Kenneth Simmons got out of the cab and followed her. The driver of the cab that the woman was in hasn't been found. You don't, by any chance, know anybody who lives around that area, do you?"

Shit, Twenty-fifth was Angela's block. But she hadn't mentioned anything about talking to a cop that night.

"No," Max said after taking a few moments to mull it over. "I don't."

"What about a gold pin, two hands almost touching? You ever see one of those suckers?"

Max had no idea what Ortiz was talking about, said, "I have no idea what you're talking about."

"My partner had a pin. It wasn't on his body when his body was discovered."

Then Max remembered the weird pin that Popeye had been wearing at the pizza place. Like the idiot didn't have enough heat on him already, he had to steal the pin off a cop he'd killed.

"Lemme ask you something," Max said. "Let's say I was in that hotel with a woman that night—which I absolutely wasn't—and let's say we checked in under—what did you say the name was?"

"*Brown.*"

"All right—let's say we checked in under the name Brown. How the hell would that help you find out who killed my wife?"

"We think the gun that was used to kill Kenneth Simmons was the same one used to kill your wife and niece. He was either killed on Twenty-fifth Street or else he was taken to Harlem and killed up there. But the only reason he ended up in either place was because he followed your girlfriend—excuse me, Mrs. *Brown*—out of the Hotel Pennsylvania. If we know what went on in that hotel it may tell us why he followed her when she left."

"I guess that makes sense."

"So, then, Mr. Fisher," Ortiz said, "are you ready to tell me anything?"

Max thought for a moment, then shook his head.

"What about the man in the sketch?" Ortiz took out a copy of the sketch from his drawer and slid it across the desk for Max to look at. "You ever seen him before?"

Max stared at the sketch of Popeye for a good ten seconds, trying to make it look like he was really studying it, then said, "No, never."

Ortiz glared at Max. "Where were you before you got home today?"

"I was at work. You gonna try to book me for that too?"

Ortiz pressed the STOP button on the recorder.

"Maybe we should do this again," he said. "This time without all the bullshit."

"I'd rather not."

"How about taking a polygraph?"

"Not without my lawyer."

"It won't matter anyway," Ortiz said, "after I take a look at that surveillance tape."

Twenty

A rotting old woman in the bedroom in black plastic bags
would be a sure tip-off. He had to find a way to get rid of her.
Feed her to some dogs or something.
JOE R. LANSDALE, *Freezer Burn*

Dillon's book of Zen wisdom wasn't weaving its magic no more. He poured a shot of Jameson, the bottle nearly empty. Everything was running down. The tinker he'd killed crossed his mind and he gave an involuntary tremor. He downed the whiskey, then waited for the hit and muttered, "That shite burns."

To erase the tinker, he dredged up another memory, a dog he'd owned. Mongrel called Heinz, cos of the 57 ingredients it had. That mutt loved him, completely. He'd deliberately starved it for a week, see how it fared. Not so good—lotsa whining in there. He'd got back to the shithole he was living in then, put out his hand to the pooch and the fooker, the fooker bit him. He almost admired the sheer balls of the little runt. But, of course, no one, no thing, ever bit Dillon, at least not twice. He got his hurly, made from the ash, honed by a master craftsman. Dillon had never used it, except to bust heads. He'd stolen it at a match in Croke Park, and if he remembered correctly, Galway had their arse handed to them by fookin Cork.

The dog had backed away and Dillon cooed, "Come on boy, come get yer medicine."

Took him fifteen minutes to beat the little fook to death, gore all over the walls, the tiny animal not going easy.

For devilment, Dillon had told this story to Angela, hoping to get a rise out of the bitch.

She'd been horrified and then he asked, "You ever been hungry, alanna?"

She didn't know what he meant and he said. "There's a little moral here mo croi, and it's don't bite the hand that feeds you."

Then, near to tears, she'd said, "I don't know what you mean."

And he laughed, delighted, said, "And isn't that the bloody beauty of it?"

Bobby popped a wheelie coming out of the D'Agostino supermarket on Columbus. He was in a good mood, still thinking about last night with Angela. He couldn't wait to call her later—maybe she'd want to come over and listen to some Ted Nugent.

Then, looking over his shoulder, he saw the guy walking about ten yards behind him. It was him all right—same thin, gray guy with the lips who was in the police sketch on TV and in all the newspapers. He was wearing faded jeans and his hands were tucked deep into the pockets of a leather jacket.

It was cooler than it had been on recent nights and there were still a lot of people on the street, shopping or coming home from work. Bobby didn't think Popeye would try to shoot him here, with all these witnesses—but he might use a knife.

Instead of crossing Columbus, Bobby turned left on Eighty-ninth and headed toward Central Park. It was a darker, emptier, quieter block, with mainly four-story brownstones. Bobby rode at a slow, steady pace and listened closely to what was happening behind him. He had always had great ears. In Iraq, he used to hear the towelhead snipers even when they were a hundred or so yards away. Now he listened to Popeye's footsteps, hearing them get gradually closer. There was something unusual about the way he was walking. He was taking one solid step, followed by a softer dragging step, like he had a limp. But the footsteps were definitely getting closer. Just before he reached the darkest part of the block, which was shaded by dense, overhanging trees, Bobby braked and wheeled around. The bag of groceries fell off his lap and crashed onto the sidewalk, gushing dark purple liquid. He raised his arm in one fluid motion, taking his Glock from his jacket pocket and aiming it between Popeye's eyes.

Obviously surprised, Popeye stopped about ten feet from Bobby, his left arm by his side and his right hand in the lower pocket of his leather jacket.

"Look what you did, asshole," Bobby said. "You broke my fuckin' grape juice."

Popeye started to move his right hand. Bobby went, "Move one more fuckin' inch I'll put a hole in your head."

"Jaysus, take it easy fellah," Popeye said. "No harm, no damage done. Just take it fookin' easy, me man."

Wondering if the guy knew how stupid he sounded, Bobby said, "Take your hand out of your pocket slowly. It comes out with anything—I don't care if it's your fucking house keys—I'm gonna start shooting."

For a moment, Popeye remained still, then he showed his empty hand.

"Now your jacket. Drop it on the sidewalk, and take five steps backwards."

Cursing in Irish under his breath, Popeye slowly took off his jacket and let it fall.

"Now back up."

Popeye backed away a few steps, then Bobby slowly wheeled himself forward one-handed. Keeping the gun aimed, he leaned down, picked up the coat and removed a switchblade from one pocket and a .38 from the other. He put the gun and the knife in the pocket of his windbreaker.

"Okay, dickhead. We're going for a walk."

Bobby said to his doorman, "I want you to meet my cousin Popeye—he's visiting from out of town."

"It's a pleasure to meet you, Popeye," the doorman, an old guy, said.

Inside his apartment, Bobby ordered Popeye to sit on the couch and Popeye said, "Okay, so who told you about me? Fisher?"

"What do you mean?"

"You knew my name. Jaysus, I knew I should never've trusted that prick. When did he put you on to me?"

"I think, under the circumstances, I should be the one asking the questions," Bobby said, aiming the gun.

"You think I'm gonna sweat you, some fuck in a wheelchair? Lemme tell yeh, fellah, I've had weapons aimed at me by the very best. I've had an Orange bastard, fueled on anti-Papal hysteria, believing the only good Catholic was a dead one, put an AK-47 in me mouth and I survived that, so you think I give a shite's fuck about you and yer feckin' Glock?"

"I said I'll be asking the questions," Bobby said calmly, "and this is the last time I'm gonna tell you that."

Popeye didn't flinch—he barely even reacted. The guy must be a pro, Bobby thought. He was keeping his cool anyway, like he really didn't give a shit if he lived or died.

"Why'd you kill those two women?" Bobby asked.

"I didn't kill nobody."

"It's not exactly a big secret anymore. The police have that picture of you going around."

"You mean that snap in the *Post*? You telling me my nose looks like that?"

"Did Max Fisher hire you?"

"Ary Christ, what do you care, you're not a Guard."

"A what?"

"A cop, yah bollix."

"No, I'm not a cop," Bobby said. "I'm just the guy holding a gun on you. I'd think you'd want to answer my questions, but maybe you don't. Maybe you just want me to shoot you."

Popeye thought about this a second. Maybe he did want to live because he said, "Yeah, okay, he hired me."

"To knock off his wife?"

"Yeah."

"And what about the college kid—the girl?"

"T'was a bit of bad timing, as the tinkers say back home."

"And what about the cop?"

"Him I would've killed for a shot of Jameson."

"What?"

Popeye smiled out of the corner of his scarred mouth, said, "Where I come from, a Guard is a bonus." Then he pulled up his shirt to cover his face and said, "Jaysus, what the hell is that smell?"

Bobby couldn't smell anything unusual, but it was possible he had farted or shit in his pants. He was about to check when Popeye lowered his shirt and started sniffing some more.

"Me lady been here?"

"Who?"

"Colleen with a bust on her to die for. Name of Angela. Was she here?"

Bobby shook his head, smiling, thinking, *I should've fuckin' known*. All that bullshit, saying, *If you want to know the truth I think a wheelchair's kind of sexy*. She'd just been manipulating him, playing a game with the poor cripple, leading him around by the nose—or by the dick, more like it.

Still smiling, Bobby said, "Angela, huh?"

"Yeah, Angela, the hoor's ghost. Funny, smells like her scent mixing with the shite. Would you open a window? It's killing me, mate."

Bobby, not smiling anymore, didn't answer right away. Then he said, "Open a fuckin' window yourself, if you want to. I don't give a shit."

Popeye slid one of the panes open, letting the noise of traffic and blaring horns into the apartment along with the breeze.

"So how did you meet *Angela*?" Bobby asked.

"I met her in Ireland, at a pub."

"And you guys live together?"

"More than that, I gave her a Claddagh ring."

"So it was Angela's idea to knock off Fisher's wife?"

"Would love to take the credit me own self, but the idea was hers."

Bobby, thinking, *That bitch*, said, "And what were you planning to do then?"

"She was going to marry him."

"Then what?"

"The best part. I'd get to blast Fisher."

"And you thought this would work?"

"Was working till you came along, fellah. Now, come on, why don't you put the gun down? If you shoot me what'll you do with me body? You have the doorman right downstairs. So how about you just let me go? When I get Fisher's money, I'll give you a nice cut, how's that?"

Bobby, keeping the gun aimed at Popeye, wheeled to the bookshelf and took down a folder with several pictures.

"Why don't you take a look through these?"

Popeye came over and snatched the envelope from Bobby. He looked through the pictures quickly, then handed the envelope back and said, "So?"

"So?" Bobby said. "That's your Angela, right? What do you think now?"

"I knew you had these. Angela told me all about them."

"Does she look like she's enjoying it?"

"Are you trying to get me riled?"

"You know why you thought you smelled her before, you fuckin' idiot? Because she was here."

"Why was she here?"

"To fuck my brains out, for one, and, I gotta admit she was pretty damn good at it."

"What do I care? She fucked Fisher too—lots of times. I don't do jealousy, mate."

Feeling stupid and sick, Bobby said, "She also came here to try to get me to kill you."

"Eh, that's bollix."

"She told me you were coming after me. She wanted me to get rid of you for her."

"Why would she want me dead?"

"Who the hell knows? Maybe her plan was to marry Fisher and then kiss your ass goodbye, man. Hell, maybe she was even planning to hire a hit man to knock you off."

"Ah, you're talking shite, that dosh was for us. I fooking earned that."

Bobby put the gun down in his lap, said, "That's just what she told you to get you to kill Fisher's wife. All along they were planning to fuck you over. If I hadn't come along they probably would've ratted you out already, but then they thought they still needed you, to get rid of me."

"I'll tell you what I think. I think you would have made a good Brit, cos you like fookin with me head."

"Jesus Christ, why the fuck would I lie to you? I have the pictures, I have the gun, I don't have to help you. I'm just telling you the way it is. They're gonna tell the cops you killed those two women, they'll say they had nothing to do with it. They'll say you were fucking Angela, you got jealous, you broke into

Max's townhouse to kill him, but he wasn't there and the women were, so you did them instead. And who's the judge gonna believe? You know a guy like Max Fisher is gonna hire some hotshot lawyer. The judge won't give a shit about you. And once the press starts calling you a cop killer too, forget about it. Meanwhile, Angela and Max'll be living happily ever after."

There was no sound in the room other than the noise of the traffic in the street outside. "So what're you saying?" Popeye finally asked.

"It's up to you how you wanna handle this," Bobby said, "but I know what *I'd* do."

"What's that?"

"I'd go by Angela's tonight, teach the bitch a fuckin' lesson."

"Keep talkin."

"Then, I'm just gonna throw this out there—maybe after you take care of Angela we can work together."

"Doing what, changing your diapers?"

"What I did before I landed in this fucking chair, asshole. Hit banks, jewelry stores, anywhere where there's money."

"Why would I want to do that?"

"To make some money, Popeye. You like money? First we'll soak Fisher for all he's worth, then we'll move on to bigger and better things. See, this picture shit—it's just a sideline for me. I'm into armed robbery—pulled some of the biggest jobs on the east coast. I got a few jobs I'm lookin' to pull right now and you can be in my new crew."

"What do you need me for?"

"I can handle a gun, but I can't muscle people the way I used to. You ever do any muscle work, Popeye?"

"You're fooking codding me, muscle work is me middle name, leaning on fookers, tis me birthright. I did some protection work for the Ra, the IRA to you."

"The IRA?" Bobby said, impressed. "That's great. So you already have some useful experience. So what do you say?"

Popeye thought about it, said, "What about the Guards? I can't be waiting around New York, you know."

"You ever hear of Willie Sutton?"

"Is he gonna be in our crew too?"

"No, he was a bank robber from the old days, the best who ever lived. Anyway, when the cops were coming after him he used to dress in disguises. One time he was living right next door to a police station and they never found him."

"Fookin A. My kind of fellah."

"So what we'll do," Bobby said, "is put you in some disguises. Or—I got a better idea—I know a guy out in Long Island City —you know, a plastic surgeon. He specializes in cons on the run."

"Any chance he can make me look like Colin Farrell?"

"Those guys can work fucking miracles."

Popeye smiled, stuck his hand out, said. "In that case, tis a deal, mate."

Twenty-One

I put on the suit and hey, I was Dillon Blair; same shit-eating smile.
You wear a suit like that, you get a hint of why the rich are so smug.
Later, in Bedford Hill, a hooker said
"Suit like that, you want to play busted?"
"Play what?"
"I sit on yer face and you guess my weight?"
Like I said, the suit was a winner.
KEN BRUEN, *The Hackman Blues*

Angela woke up when Dillon came home and turned on the light. He was wearing his leather jacket and was holding a big white shopping bag. He looked angry. Angrier than usual. Without saying a word to Angela, he went into the bathroom, still wearing his jacket and carrying the shopping bag.

Squinting, still half-asleep, Angela remembered what was supposed to happen tonight and obviously hadn't happened. Bobby was supposed to take care of Dillon for her, but something had definitely gone wrong. Was Bobby dead? He must be if Dillon was still alive. Angela prayed that she was still sleeping, that this was a nightmare and that she'd wake up any second.

Dillon came out of the bathroom, still wearing his leather jacket.

"So?" Angela asked. "How did it go tonight?"

Dillon stared at Angela for a couple of seconds then said, "How did *what* go?" His tone had a combination of sarcasm and amusement, but he wasn't smiling.

"You know what—with Bobby Rosa, the guy in the wheelchair." She swallowed. "I mean did you kill him like you were supposed to?"

"Why the fook do you care?"

"I'm just asking. Jaysus, I have a right to ask, don't I?"

Again, Dillon stared at Angela for a few seconds. His mutilated lips seemed to be wet, like a pair of ugly snakes. Angela had no idea what was going on. The only thing she could think of was that he had found out about her and Bobby's plan. But this didn't make any sense. Bobby would never've told Dillon about that unless Dillon had tortured him. Imagining Dillon torturing a poor guy in a wheelchair and enjoying it—she *knew* he'd enjoy it, all right—pissed Angela off big time.

"What's wrong with you?" Angela said. "Why are you looking at me like that?"

"I can look at you any way I want to," Dillon said.

"Well, I don't like it when you wet your lips like that, so just stop it."

"You think there's something wrong with me mouth?"

"I don't think anything," Angela said. "I just don't like it when you do that. It gives me the creeps."

Dillon stuck his tongue out and slowly ran it along his upper lip, then his lower. Then he said, "I'm going to miss that shite you talk."

"What do you mean, *miss* it? Where are you going?"

"I'm not going anywhere," he said, still smiling.

"Look," Angela said. "I wish you'd just tell me what's going on here. It's late and I have to get up to go to work tomorrow."

He laughed out loud, said, "Missing work is not really something you'll have to be bothered about."

"Did you kill Bobby Rosa?" Angela asked. "Did you torture him first?"

"Why you care so much about Bobby Rosa?"

"I don't. I just want to know what's going on."

"Maybe I did have some fun with the bastard. What's it to you?"

Dillon's left hand came out of the jacket pocket holding the gun he had used to kill those women and the cop. He aimed it at Angela. There was glint in his eye, part sexual, part adrenalin. He was having the time of his life.

"What's that for?" Angela asked.

"It's for you acting like you're a tinker and you just stole me wallet."

"Stop pointing that thing at me."

"I never told anyone about the tinker, you know."

"I'm gonna scream my feckin' ass off," Angela said.

Dillon grinned, said, "Go on. Pretend you're trying to steal me money."

"I'm serious," Angela said.

"Try, go on, put yer hand in me jacket."

Dillon's right hand came out of the other pocket holding a switchblade. The blade sprang open and he lunged forward, slicing Angela across her right thigh. A deep gash opened and blood spread in a thick stream down Angela's leg. Dillon laughed. Again, Angela was struck by the thought that this had to be a nightmare. She didn't feel any pain yet, and everything was happening too fast, like it wasn't real. But then the pain kicked in, like a stick of dynamite exploding in her leg, and Angela knew that in dreams you weren't supposed to feel pain like this. She grabbed a pillow from the bed and put it over her leg to stop the bleeding. It didn't help. Her leg was wet and hot. She sat down.

Dillon sat next to her on the bed and held the switchblade against her neck. He said, "Snatch me wallet yah tinker."

Angela's mouth was trembling. She couldn't speak. Dillon

was grim-faced now, ordered, "Go for it, go for me cash."

"No," Angela said.

Dillon looked like he might slash Angela again. She started to scream as he pushed her down onto the bed. All she had on was a pair of panties; he got one hand in under the waistband, slid the switchblade roughly under the fabric, and sawed through it with two strokes. He yanked the tatters off her body. Holding her down with one hand, he took down his jeans and underwear with the other. Angela cast around desperately for a weapon. Dillon had the switchblade in the hand that was holding her down—she didn't know what had happened to the gun.

There was a glass on the night table where she'd left it after swallowing a couple of Midols before going to sleep. She grabbed the glass and smashed it against the side of Dillon's head. He let go of her, brought his hand to his head and brought it away bloody. Angela looked at her hand and saw she was still holding about half the shattered glass, a jagged, splintered wedge dripping water and blood. She slashed the edge across Dillon's throat.

Dillon tried to scream, but couldn't make a sound.

Angela freed the blade from Dillon's fist and managed to slide out from under him. He turned to reach for something, maybe the gun, and Angela lunged forward, sinking the blade in his back till it couldn't go any further. She tried to pull it out, but the blade was stuck. Angela stood back in horror as Dillon stood up. He stumbled a few steps, looking into her eyes, then he collapsed in the middle of the floor, where the circular throw rug beneath him promptly soaked through.

She couldn't believe it had been so easy to kill the fucker.

Angela turned on the stereo to some pop station. It was eighties night and Debbie Gibson was singing "Only In My Dreams."

The pain in Angela's thigh, which she'd forgotten in the

moment, was back now in full force and blood covered her entire leg. Angela stepped over Dillon and went into the bathroom and rinsed her leg in the shower. She knew she should probably get to a hospital, but she also knew there was no way she could do that now. She didn't have any gauze, so she put some paper towel over the wound and wrapped it up with painting tape.

When she turned off the water, she thought she heard a noise in the other room. She waited, even held her breath, but there was nothing; the sound must've come from another apartment. She remembered what always happened in those horror movies, how whenever it seemed like the killer was dead, it turned out he was still alive. Angela wished she had taken the gun or something with her into the bathroom. She opened the bathroom door slowly and peeked her head out. She relaxed when she saw Dillon still lying on the floor in the same position she'd left him in, his wide-open eyes looking up at nothing. It annoyed her that the bastard looked so fucking relaxed, even Zen-like.

Angela had no idea what she was going to do now. With Bobby dead, she had no one left in the world to help her, except Max, and she knew Max would never get involved in something like this. He'd probably go to the police and say the whole thing had been her and Dillon's idea, that he'd had nothing to do with it. The police would probably believe him too.

Then Angela noticed the white shopping bag that Dillon had left in the bathroom. She looked inside and saw five containers of Drano. She could only think of one thing that Dillon could've been planning to do with them. Well, as her mother used to say, *waste not, want not.*

Holding him by the feet, she dragged Dillon's body into the bathroom, leaving behind a long streak of blood across the floor. Her arm ached, and it was hard to lift him up to put him into the bathtub. But she forced herself, lifting Dillon's legs up first then standing in the bathtub and pulling the rest of him up and over.

Next, she put the stopper over the drain and poured a container of Drano over Dillon's body, saying, "Who's the tinker now, huh, you prick? Who's the tinker now?" She added the other four containers and then she pulled the shower curtain closed.

Back in the main part of the apartment, it crossed her mind to throw his Zen book in after him. But she decided not to, thinking it wasn't worth having to see his face again. Besides, maybe Max might want the book. God knows the guy could use something to help him relax.

Only then did Angela realize how stupid she'd been. How was she supposed to wash up now with Dillon in the bathtub? She could use towels to clean her leg, but she hated washing her hair in the sink.

She had small cuts on her hands from the glass. She poured peroxide all over her wounds, wincing from the pain, and then wrapped the worst of them with more paper towel and painting tape.

Angela was exhausted. She just wanted to get some rest and worry about everything else in the morning. It wasn't as if she could solve all of her problems tonight anyway. She turned the dial on the stereo to an easy-listening station and lowered the volume. There was still a huge bloodstain on the floor, in the middle of the room. She didn't feel like mopping now, but she felt uncomfortable sleeping next to a pool of blood all night, knowing it had come from Dillon. She pulled the bed out, away from the wall, to cover the blood—that was better. Then she shut off the light and lay back down, listening to the soft rock music. She decided she'd just have to go over to Max's tomorrow night and take a shower at his place.

Then, as she was falling asleep, she thought she heard faint laughter. It reminded her of a tinker she'd seen in the park when she was a little girl, one who had been laughing his mad head off. But one thing she was sure of—it wasn't Dillon. At least she had one less nightmare to worry about.

Twenty-Two

He might have tried to hide it by dressing in a smart, well-cut suit and putting an easy smile on his face as soon as he saw me, but I could tell this straight away: Roy Fowler was one of the world's guilty.
SIMON KERNICK, *The Murder Exchange*

In 1979, when Max needed a lawyer for his business, he had picked Sid Darrow out of the yellow pages, figuring that a guy with the last name Darrow must know something about the law. But it turned out Darrow wasn't nearly as good as his namesake, bungling a couple of simple contract negotiations that wound up costing Max thousands of dollars. Later, Max found out Darrow's name had been shortened from Darrowicz, but Max didn't fire Darrow for this misrepresentation or for his incompetence. Through the years, he had kept Darrow on the payroll, mainly because he was too lazy to look for someone else and because he figured that all lawyers were basically the same anyway.

When Max called Darrow for a reference to a good criminal lawyer Darrow asked Max what the problem was. Max explained how the police had questioned him last night about his wife's murder.

"If you want my opinion," Darrow said, "you shouldn't have answered any of those questions."

"I don't want your opinion," Max said.

Darrow gave Max the name of a criminal lawyer—Andrew McCullough. Max couldn't think of any famous lawyers named McCullough, but he didn't have time to be choosy. Once the police played back that security tape and saw him and Angela arriving at the hotel the situation would be way out of control. Max knew that Angela wasn't bright enough to keep her story straight and it was only a matter of time until she mentioned Popeye and the murders.

McCullough wasn't in. Max said to his secretary, "Well, can you tell him to call me as soon as he comes in?...Yeah, it's fucking urgent—the cops're trying to nail my ass!"

As Max slammed the phone down there was a knock at his door.

"What?" he yelled.

The door opened slowly. Harold Lipman entered.

"What the hell do you want?"

"I could come back later if..."

"No, come in," Max said. "Sit the hell down."

When Harold sat down across from him, Max could tell by the way Harold wouldn't make eye contact with him that he hadn't made any progress.

"Let me guess," Max said, "you lost the sale?"

Lipman nodded slowly, looking at his lap. Sweat glistened on his forehead.

"What happened?" Max asked.

"He went with someone else," Lipman said dejectedly. "I did the best I could, but our prices just weren't competitive enough. The guy's quote was twenty, thirty thousand dollars lower than ours."

Max was seriously pissed.

"I told you what you had to do to close that sale."

"I'm sorry," Lipman said, "but there was nothing I could do."

"I'm sorry too," Max said, "but your best obviously wasn't good enough. The company can't afford to keep you on, paying you the draw that you're making now, when you're not producing. I'm sorry, but I'm going to have to let you go."

"You're firing me?" Lipman said. "Just like that?"

"You have a half an hour to clean out your desk and leave the premises. And don't take any leads with you—all leads are property of NetWorld."

"Come on, Max—give me another chance. Please. I swear I'll do better."

Max was shaking his head.

"I gave you solid sales advice and you refused to take advantage of it. I'm sorry, but the decision is final—you're terminated."

Max had always loved firing people. In fact, when it came right down to it, it was probably his favorite part of running his own business. He loved controlling people's lives. It made him feel like...well, like God.

He knew he still had a lot of deep shit to climb out of, but tried to focus on the positives. Last night Popeye had killed Bobby Rosa. Now Max's only problem was Angela. He couldn't fire her right away. He'd just have to tell her he wanted to let things cool for a while and hope she kept her mouth shut. Then, after enough time passed, he'd terminate her Greek-Irish ass and hope he never saw her again. His only other problem would be that hotel videotape, but it wouldn't be nearly as harmful as Bobby Rosa's pictures could have been. All the videotape would show was him and Angela checking into the hotel that night, but it wouldn't be real evidence of an affair. A hotshot criminal lawyer like McCullough would be able to get around it somehow and then he'd be home free.

He retrieved the bid that Harold hadn't been able to close from a file folder and called the guy up.

"Hello, Mr. Takahashi? Max Fisher calling—I'm the president of NetWorld, how are you today?...Good, I'm glad to hear that...I just had a conversation with Harold Lipman and he said you decided to go with someone else for your networking job, is this true?...Well, we try to keep our costs as low as possible...Yes, I understand....Oh, of course....No problem, Mr. Takahashi, but can I just ask you one semi-personal question and then I'll let you go?...Are you married?...The reason I ask is I'd like an opportunity to re-explain this quote to you....I understand, but there's a place I'd think you'd love—I know I love it. Have you ever been to Legz Diamond's?...That's right, and I sort of get VIP service there. I know this one stripper there—you don't have anything against black people, do you? ...I didn't think so. Anyway, this black girl they got there is dynamite. She's a personal friend of mine too and, I assume you like women with large breasts, Mr. Takahashi...Well, wait till you see this girl. I'm talking 44 triple-Ds...I'm serious. You didn't sign that other quote yet, did you?...Good. I'm gonna show you a time you'll never forget. How's tonight at six sound? ...Six-thirty's terrific. I'll be outside your building in a cab. You won't be disappointed, Mr. Takahashi."

Max hung up, shouted, "Baby!"

The quote was for $220,000 and Max knew that there was no way Takahashi wasn't going to sign it after the night he'd have tonight. And this was only the first job for this client. Their network had over one hundred users and there could be ongoing work there. Harold had been working on this quote for weeks and hadn't gotten anywhere and now Max had practically closed it in less than one minute. No one could sell computer networks the way Max Fisher could—no one.

Max buzzed Angela—he was hungry and wanted her to order him some breakfast—but there was no answer at her desk. He thought this was strange, since it was after nine o'clock and she was usually in by eight-thirty. He buzzed the receptionist to ask if she had called in sick or to say she was going to be late, but the receptionist said that she hadn't called.

A few minutes later, Max was on the phone with a software vendor when there was a knock at his door.

He assumed it was Lipman, coming to beg for his job back, and Max put the vendor on hold and yelled, "Go away!"

But the knock came again, a little louder, then Max said, "Who the hell's there?"

The door opened and Bobby Rosa wheeled into the office. Seeing the bearded cripple again made Max's throat close up. He reached for a mug of day-old coffee on his desk and swallowed the murky crap as fast as he could. Bobby had closed the door and was smiling now, watching Max. Max looked at Bobby's black sweatshirt with the words *Average White Band* inscribed on it and thought, Jesus, what's this guy, in the KKK or something?

"Surprised?" Bobby asked.

"No," Max said, forcing a smile. "Why would I be surprised?"

"I don't know. I just thought it would be natural for a guy to be surprised when someone he sent a hit man to bump off shows up in his office the next morning alive. But hey, that's just me."

"I really don't have the foggiest idea what you're talking about," Max said. There it was again, *foggiest*.

"You want to keep playing games, be my guest," Bobby said. "It won't matter soon anyway."

"How the hell did you get in here?" Max said, his throat tightening again.

"Don't blame the girl at the desk," Bobby said. "I'm good at getting into places I'm not supposed to be. But I think you already know that."

"Look, if you're not out of here in two minutes I'm calling the cops."

Bobby laughed, then said, "You still don't realize what kind of trouble you're in, do you? You sent Dillon after me, but that was your last card—you shot your load."

"Dillon?" Max said. "Who the hell's Dillon?"

"You know him as Popeye, but his real name's Dillon. It doesn't matter now anyway because he's out of the picture."

"What do you mean, out of the picture?"

"Not what you think it means. He's working with me now."

Max couldn't believe this was happening, that this freakazoid in a wheelchair was really here again, trying to ruin his life.

"Oh, and your executive assistant," Bobby went on, "the one I got in that picture with you—Angela, I think her name is. I don't think she'll be coming in to work anymore, so you might just want to clean out her desk."

"Why? Is she working with you too?"

"No, she's really out of the picture, and I think you know exactly what I mean."

Max picked up the phone and said, "That's it. I'm calling the cops."

"I'd think about that a second," Bobby said. "I mean what are you gonna tell them?"

Max paused, realizing Bobby was right, and replaced the receiver.

"Why are you doing this to me?" Max said, feeling like he might start to cry. "What did I ever do to you?"

"You were just in the right place at the wrong time," Bobby said. He took out a mini-cassette recorder from the pocket of his windbreaker and placed it on the desk. He said, "You want to do the honors or should I?"

Max didn't move so Bobby went ahead and pressed the PLAY button.

> *"Did Max Fisher hire you?"*
> *"Ary Christ, what do you care, you're not a Guard."*

Max looked at Bobby, but Bobby was looking down at the tape recorder, smiling. There was more conversation, something about Bobby holding a gun, then Popeye said:

> *"Yeah, okay, he hired me."*
> *"To knock off his wife?"*
> *"Yeah."*
> *"And what about the college kid—the girl?"*
> *"T'was a bit of bad timing, as the tinkers say back home."*
> *"And what about the cop?"*
> *"Him I would've killed for a shot of Jameson."*

Bobby pressed the STOP button and said, "Oh, one other thing. I don't want a quarter of a mil anymore."

"Yeah?" Max said weakly. "What do you want?"

Bobby leaned forward in his wheelchair, then said, "Everything."

Before Angela left for work, she checked to see how Dillon was doing in the bathtub. The Drano had burned through the top layer of skin on his face, turning it yellow and gooey, but at this rate it was going to take weeks until his whole body was dissolved, if it dissolved at all. Meanwhile, the room stank so bad she could hardly breathe. It figured that Dillon would come up with some stupid idea that had like zero chance of working.

Then she saw something glinting in the gooey yellow. For one awful moment, she thought maybe his gold tooth fell out and her stomach heaved. But it wasn't a tooth, she realized, it was the pin, and she muttered out loud, "What's with that feckin' pin?"

She picked it out, real careful not to touch any of Dillon, going under her breath, "Sweet Jesus, oh Sweet Mother of all Heaven."

She put the pin on the sink, figuring she'd stash it in her handbag later. The pin was tarnished from the Drano, but compared to Dillon himself it was in great shape.

Angela had already mopped up most of the blood off the floor and reluctantly she washed her hair in the kitchen sink. Even after she blew it out, it still looked flat. And, to make things worse, although the wound on her thigh had stopped bleeding, it still looked pretty bad and she couldn't wear a skirt to work.

She was running so late she decided to take a cab. It was a nice, cool day and it felt good to get out of that stuffy apartment. As the cab headed up Third Avenue, Angela decided that she would have to slowly get her life back together. First she was going to have to get the apartment clean and wash Dillon down the drain, then she could start worrying about a relationship again.

But now that Dillon and Bobby were both gone, she wondered if she should go back to her original plan and get married to Max. She still thought he was an asshole, but the whole experience with Dillon had taught her that she had no idea what she was doing when it came to judging men. At least Max was rich and, when it came right down to it, what was more important than money?

It was ten-fifteen when Angela arrived at NetWorld. The door to Max's office was closed and she didn't feel like bothering him. So she turned on her computer and started to catch up on some work. When Max came out of his office he stopped and stared at Angela for a second or two, like he was surprised to see her.

"What happened to you?" he asked.

At first, Angela thought Max was talking about her being an hour and a half late, but then she realized it had to do with the bruise on her face. Where Dillon had punched her she had a big black-and-blue mark that her makeup couldn't hide.

"Oh, *that*," Angela said. "My roommate swung another door into me again. She's a real ejit."

"You should get rid of those swinging doors," Max said seriously, "or that stupid roommate."

"Yeah, that's a good idea," Angela said, thinking about Dillon dissolving in the bathtub.

"Why don't you come into my office?" Max said. "I need to dictate a letter."

Angela followed him into his office and sat down on the couch. Max was already sitting at his desk.

"First of all," Max said, "I have to talk to your cousin."

"My cousin? What for?"

"Never mind what for, just give me the goddamn number."

"I don't have it."

"What do you mean, you don't have it? You had it yesterday."

"Why do you need to talk to him?"

"To find out if his friend Popeye—I'm sorry, *Dillon*, is still alive."

"Dillon?" Angela asked.

"That's Popeye's real name," Max said. "At least that's what Ironside told me."

Angela was confused.

"Mr. Average White Man in the wheelchair," Max continued. He was here about a half hour ago. He told me that you 'wouldn't be coming in anymore' and that Dillon was 'out of the picture.' But since you're here I'm starting to think he's full of shit about everything."

"Bobby Rosa was here?"

"Yes," Max said. "Don't you pay attention to a goddamn word I say?"

"But he's dead."

"Then I guess it was a ghost who was just in here, trying to blackmail me again. And my question is, Why? If this Popeye—*Dillon*—is supposed to be on our side, why isn't he killing the people he's supposed to kill? Why is he telling Rosa that I hired him? The only thing that makes sense is they're working together, and that they've been working together all along. Why else would Bobby go into that hotel room that night unless he knew we'd be there? So what I'm gonna do is call that little mick and say 'Tell the cripple to back off or I'm taking you down.' And I'm serious. I have the name of a top-notch lawyer now and I'll pin this whole thing on him. I don't need all this bullshit in my life right now—I have a business to run."

Max's face had turned red during his long speech and he was breathing heavily. He looked like he might croak at any moment. But Angela had something bigger on her mind—Bobby was still alive. She had to talk to him, figure out some way to get him off their backs.

"Sorry, Max," Angela said standing up. "I have to go to the bathroom. Oh, but wait, I have something for you." She rummaged in her bag and took out the book. "It's a present. Sorry I didn't have time to wrap it."

It had crossed her mind to give him the pin too, but she kind of liked it.

Max took the book cautiously and Angela said, "Don't worry, it's not gonna blow up."

Max gave her a look as if he wasn't so sure. Then, squinting at the book, holding it at arm's length because he didn't have his reading glasses on, Max said, "*Wisdom of Zen*? What's this crap?"

"It'll bring you peace," Angela said, thinking about Dillon again, lying there in her bathtub, all yellow and Zen-like.

"I get enough of that Zen peace talk shit from my asshole

chef," Max said. He flipped the book onto his desk then demanded, "What about your cousin's phone number?"

"I think I better call him," Angela said.

"Why can't I call?"

"He has a bad temper—you know how Greeks are. If you call and he thinks things got messed up he might start going crazy."

"I thought your cousin's Irish?"

"Half Greek, half Irish. Like me."

"I don't know what the fuck's going on anymore," Max said, shaking his head in frustration. "Just get me another meeting with Popeye today before five or I'm calling the cops. And close the door on your way out, will ya? I have to do my breathing exercises."

Diane Faustino from Accounting was talking to Sheila in Payroll near Angela's desk and Angela wanted to talk to Bobby in private. So she went to the back of the office, to the supply room. She called, but there was no answer. She went back to her desk, but it was impossible to concentrate. Max came out of his office every couple of minutes and asked if she had made "that call yet." Angela kept saying, "Yeah, but he's not home."

Max was getting to be a real pain in the ass. Angela couldn't believe that less than an hour ago she was seriously considering spending the rest of her life with that loser.

After waiting for about half an hour, Angela went back to the supply room and dialed Bobby's number again. This time he picked up.

Bobby was about to get into the bathtub when the phone rang. He lifted himself back into his wheelchair and went out to the living room. He answered the phone on its sixth ring.

"May I speak with Bobby Rosa please?"

It was an official-sounding older woman. Bobby figured it was another one of those asshole telemarketers. Even though he'd put himself on the national do-not-call list, those fucking cold callers kept hassling him twenty-four-seven. If she was a telemarketer, he was going to do what he always did when those pricks called his apartment—tell her Bobby Rosa had died. That usually got him off whatever list he was on.

"Why do you want to talk to him?" Bobby said.

"Is this Mr. Rosa?"

"Maybe, maybe not."

"It's very important that I speak with Mr. Rosa."

"Yeah? And why's that?"

"My name is Estelle Sternberg from the Jewish Home for the Aged. I'm afraid I have some bad news regarding his mother. Who am I speaking with please?"

"What happened to his mother?"

"I'm afraid she passed away last night," the woman said.

Bobby paused, letting the news sink in, then he said, "Yeah, well, this is Bobby so you can tell me what happened."

Ms. Sternberg explained that Mrs. Rosa had died in her sleep the night before. She asked Bobby if he wanted any assistance in making the funeral arrangements.

"No, I'll take care of it myself," Bobby said, thinking, Well, at least I didn't have to shoot her.

When he hung up, Bobby realized he was starving and he decided to take his bath later. He hadn't had pancakes in a long time so he cooked some up the way he liked them, with a lot of butter. Then, as he was eating, it hit him. He lost it, wheeling around his apartment, screaming and throwing things. It wasn't good enough—he needed to start shooting shit up. He was on his way to the closet to get a piece when he heard the phone ring.

He picked up, going, "What?"

"Bobby?"

Fuck, it sounded like Angela. How was that fucking possible? Was Dillon completely fucking incompetent?

"Yeah," he finally said.

"You know who this is?"

Straining for a Mr. Nice Guy tone, he said, " 'Course I do, sweetheart. How's it going?"

Why, why was that cunt still alive and his mother was dead? What kind of fucked up world was this?

"I can't talk much right now," Angela said. "I'm at work. You won't believe what's been going on. I can't even believe I'm talking to you."

"Yeah," Bobby said. "Me neither."

Angela lowered her voice to a whisper, said "We don't have to worry about Dillon, I mean Popeye, anymore...I got rid of him last night."

"What do you mean *got rid* of him?"

"I can't talk about that right now."

"Is he dead?"

"Yeah," Angela said.

"You killed him?"

"You know, Bobby, I really think we should talk about that somewhere private. Can you meet me somewhere or something?"

Bobby might have left Angela alone—forgotten about her—but it was too dangerous now. She knew about three murders and had committed one herself, meaning the cops would be after her soon, if they weren't already. If she was arrested she'd flip on Max Fisher, and after that the million-dollar photo of Max and Angela would be worth about as much as any of the other pictures he had taped to the walls.

Besides, he was in the mood to go kill somebody, let off some steam.

"Sure," Bobby said. "I can meet you. Let me think a sec."

"How about tonight?" Angela said. "I could stop by your place on my way home from work."

"Nah, I don't think we should wait that long," Bobby said. "I wanted to get out of the house anyway today. I know, let's meet in Riverside Park this afternoon. How's two o'clock work for you?"

Twenty-Three

I would extricate myself, I was sure, though I thought, too, of what I'd told the police, how the killer was still out there, and I felt a sense of danger beneath the veneer of the moment, everything about to break loose.
DOMENIC STANSBERRY, *The Confession*

When Angela told Max she was taking a late lunch, Max said, "What about that phone call?"

"I'll try again from the street," Angela said. "I have to go—I have a two o'clock appointment at my hairdresser."

Angela had just said this as an excuse to get out of the office, but on the way downstairs she decided that getting a haircut would be a good idea. Maybe she could get a blow out and a wash every day until she could start using her shower again.

Angela took the 1 train from Times Square and got off at Ninety-sixth Street. Bobby had said he wanted to meet on the Riverside Park promenade, between the Hudson River and the tennis courts.

Angela's bruises and cuts were still bothering her, especially the one on her thigh, but she knew she'd feel better once she figured out a way to get Bobby out of the way. Maybe she'd sleep with him again if she had to. He had B.O. and he wasn't the best-looking guy in the world but, she had to admit, there was something kind of hot about wheelchair sex.

She entered Riverside Park at Ninety-sixth Street and walked toward the river. She came to the underpass Bobby was talking about and went through to the promenade. It was a clear, sunny day, about seventy degrees. There were a few old men sitting on benches and other people out jogging and walking their dogs. Angela got to the spot Bobby had described and looked around. She didn't see him anywhere. She checked her watch—a few minutes after two.

She was tired and her thigh was hurting worse than before. She wanted to sit down, but all the benches nearby were either taken or covered with bird shit. She went back toward the water, leaned against the railing, and stared out toward New Jersey.

Bobby was waiting on a path on the wooded hill behind the tennis courts. The trees had blossomed a few weeks earlier so there was good cover. From his position, he had a nice, clear view of the promenade. Angela wasn't there yet, but when she showed up he'd be ready for her. In the big front pocket of his windbreaker he had a stainless steel .44 snub nose Mag Hunter. Yeah, fuckin hardware—it made the man.

Angela would be about sixty yards away—a tough shot for most people, but point-blank range for Bobby. He was already getting flashbacks of all the towelheads he'd taken down in Iraq, the sheer rush he'd get when he had those sand rats in his sight.

A few minutes later, Bobby saw Angela walking along the promenade. For some reason she was limping. She looked pale and drawn, not nearly as sexy as she had the other times Bobby had seen her. He remembered what she'd said, about the wheelchair being "kind of sexy." An old song began to play in his head, *Where was the love?*

When she got to the spot where they were supposed to meet Bobby took out the Mag and fitted on a silencer. Man, just holding a loaded gun again got Bobby juiced.

He looked around to make sure there was no one nearby,

watching him, then he raised the gun and aimed at Angela's chest.

Angela limped toward a bench and looked like she was about to sit down, then she turned and went back toward the railing of the promenade. She put her hands on the railing and looked out across the river. Bobby was locked in on a spot right between her shoulder blades, figuring he'd give it to her in the back. But when Bobby fired, the bullet tore through Angela's right thigh instead, his chair bucking from the recoil. Angela fell back against the railing, then her legs buckled and she coiled onto the cement. Bobby fired again, but the angle was shitty and this time he missed completely, the bullet whizzing by above Angela's head. Bobby cursed and fired again. The bullet hit the concrete on the promenade and ricocheted into the Hudson. Angela was on her knees now. He fired two more times—one bullet entered the left side of her stomach, the other, finally, ripped through her chest. Now Angela was on her side, covered in blood. Bobby twisted off the silencer, put it and the Mag back inside his windbreaker, and wheeled out of the park, thinking, Who sang that goddamn song?

Twenty-Four

Everyone knows what he has to do next and sticks to it. It's a simple way of life, and one that allows a man to get the most out of his simple pleasures, without cluttering up his swede with plans stretching too far hence.
CHARLIE WILLIAMS, *Deadfolk*

Sherry, today's temp receptionist, buzzed Max's office and told him there were two police officers here to see him. Was there a tiny smug tone in her voice?

"Shit," Max said. "Tell them I'll be right out."

Max had been calling Andrew McCullough all afternoon and the bastard wasn't returning his calls. And Angela still wasn't back from lunch so Max didn't know what was going on with her cousin and Popeye. As he opened his office door Max promised himself that this time he wouldn't say anything without some kind of lawyer present, even if he had to use fucking Darrow.

Louis Ortiz, the detective who had questioned him the other night, was standing next to the reception desk, next to a tall, older man with a mustache whom Max had never seen before. Ortiz and the older guy were both wearing plain gray suits and they both had serious, angry expressions.

Max thought, *Uh oh*, and wished he'd taken a look at that freaking Zen book. Maybe if he had he'd be relaxed, he wouldn't be shitting fucking bricks right now.

"Hello, gentlemen," Max said, trying to stay as calm as possible. "Can I help you with something?"

"You can get your coat," Ortiz said.

"Am I under arrest?" Max asked, trying to make it into a joke.

"We're taking you in for questioning," Ortiz said.

"What if I don't want to go?"

"You don't have a choice," Ortiz said.

"I don't understand," Max said. "What's going on?"

"Angela Petrakos was shot earlier today," the tall man explained, "in Riverside Park."

The words took a few seconds to register.

"Angela Petrakos?" he said. "You mean the Angela Petrakos who works for me?"

Several people in the office had been eavesdropping. Now people were talking at once, asking the detectives what was going on. Finally, Ortiz, talking above everyone, said, "This is police business. You'll all be briefed as soon as it's appropriate. Right now we need to talk to Mr. Fisher. Mr. Fisher, are you gonna come with us or am I gonna have to cuff you?"

Ortiz had a malicious grin, looking like he wanted to cuff Max more than he wanted his next meal.

Suddenly, the office was quiet. Although he was still looking at Ortiz and at the other detective, Max could sense that everyone else was staring at him. He remembered watching *Law and Order,* the ones with Jerry Orbach, and he was tempted to say, *I think I need to get lawyered up*. But instead he said, "Let me just get my coat," and he went back into his office. When he came out, wearing his sport jacket, a larger crowd had formed.

"This isn't a vacation day," Max said, above all the other voices, using a tone of authority, of steel. "Come on everybody, let's get back to work."

A few people went back to their desks, but a large group remained near the front of the office. No one seemed to feel sorry for Max. Actually, the bastards seemed happy to watch him being taken away. Max couldn't understand this. He'd always been a good boss. He only fired people when they deserved to be fired and hadn't he just announced a ten-percent raise?

On the way to the precinct, Max remembered the appointment he had made with Mr. Takahashi for this evening at six-thirty. Sitting in the back of the car, Max asked the detectives up front how long this questioning was going to take.

"As long as it needs to," Ortiz said.

"Seriously," Max said. "I have an important appointment with a client in less than two hours. Am I gonna have to reschedule it or not?"

The detectives looked at each other as Max reached into his jacket for his Blackberry. The car stopped short. Ortiz got out and opened the back door.

"Give me that fucking thing."

"What's the big deal?" Max said. "I'm just making one call."

Ortiz reached for the Blackberry. Max wouldn't let go and, turning away, he elbowed Ortiz in the face.

"You fucked up big-time now," Ortiz said. "I'm gonna book you for disorderly conduct and assaulting a police officer."

Max thought Ortiz was kidding until he pulled him out of the car and cuffed him.

At the precinct, after he was booked, Max used his one phone call to call McCullough. McCullough was still in the office, thank God, but he was in a meeting and couldn't be disturbed. Max screamed at the secretary, demanding to speak with him. The secretary said, "I don't enjoy being spoken to this way" and was about to hang up. Max begged her to stay on the line and then he left a message that he had been taken into police custody and to please come to the precinct as soon as possible.

Max was put in a holding cell with two other men who looked homeless. One of them was lying on the bench, passed out, handcuffed to the bars. The other guy was squatting in the back of the cell, his hands crossed in front of his knees, mumbling to himself. They were both wearing ripped, dirty clothes. The whole place smelled like piss.

Max had been waiting in the cell for nearly two hours when McCullough finally showed up. Max was disappointed by how he looked. He was expecting an older, seasoned guy, but McCullough looked like he was right out of law school. He had short blond hair and light blue eyes and he didn't look a day over thirty. He pulled a chair up outside the cell and spoke to Max through the bars.

"Sorry I couldn't get here any sooner," McCullough explained, "but I've had a chance to speak with a couple of detectives, so hopefully I can give you an idea what's going on."

"Just get me the hell out of here," Max said.

"I'm working on that, but legally they can hold you overnight, or until a judge can see you downtown."

"If you think I'm spending a night in jail—"

"Let's not worry about that right now. The important thing right now is *why* you're here. I understand you assaulted Detective Ortiz."

"I didn't assault anybody," Max said. "I was just trying to use my Blackberry and I accidentally elbowed the guy in the face."

"Yeah, well, you've got bigger problems anyway," McCullough said. "The detectives seem to think you had something to do with the murders of your wife and your niece and Detective Kenneth Simmons, as well as the attempted murder of Angela Petrakos. Now before I can agree to represent you I need to know the truth—did you have anything to do with any of those crimes?"

Max remembered *The Godfather*, Diane Keaton asking Al Pacino if he was in the Mob. Max stared into McCullough's eyes for a few seconds, trying to get his face to look like Pacino's, then said, "Absolutely not."

"Alrighty," McCullough said, opening a small notepad, "so now we can get down to business. Let's talk about Angela Petrakos first—she's your executive assistant, I understand?"

Max nodded.

"She was shot this afternoon in Riverside Park, a little after two o'clock." Max thought there was a prissy tone in McCullough's voice and he noticed that the man's teeth were capped. The caps were bad news. They were a sign of self-absorption, the last quality in the world you wanted from your lawyer.

"Who shot her?" Max asked

"They don't know yet. They haven't had a chance to speak with her. She's still in critical condition at Columbia Presbyterian."

Fuck, Max had been hoping she was dead. If she lived, it would be a freakin' disaster. The police would grill her and, in her condition, she'd probably spill everything. Wasn't he ever gonna catch a break?

"So, do they think she's gonna make it?" Max asked, praying the answer would be no.

"It's hard to say," McCullough said. "Her injuries are quite severe."

"Shit," Max said, hoping "severe" meant brain damage or something like that.

"Unfortunately, that's not all the bad news," McCullough continued, reading from his pad. "About an hour ago, the police entered Angela's apartment on East Twenty-fifth Street and discovered a body decomposing in her bathtub."

Max blinked. "A body?"

"Apparently the neighbors had complained about the smell. According to the police, she or someone else had poured Drano all over the corpse."

Jesus Fucking Christ. She was a psycho. It was as simple as that. Max couldn't believe he'd fallen for her. If he'd just had a thing for flat-chested women none of this would have happened.

"The police haven't been able to get a positive ID on the body yet," McCullough said, "but going by some other evidence they found in the apartment, they're almost certain the dead guy is Thomas Dillon. Does that name mean anything to you?"

Max tried not to have a reaction. If he'd learnt one lesson in business, it was never show the person sitting across the table from you what you were thinking. He shook his head slowly.

"They've talked to some people who'd seen Dillon around the neighborhood, and they said he used to carry a book around with him, a book about Zen. They think it's the same book they found on your desk in your office."

"Wait a minute!" Max said. "Angela gave me that! This morning, she said it was a fucking gift."

"Unfortunately, she's not in a position to corroborate that right now. In the eyes of the police, it's a connection between you and Dillon."

Max shook his head miserably, thinking, What next?

"The police also found a gun in the apartment," McCullough said. "A Colt Lady .38. They think this was the gun that was used in the three murders."

"So Angela killed my wife?"

"Or Dillon," McCullough said, "or both of them. The police definitely don't think it was just a coincidence that Angela works for you. They think you were having an affair with her and conspired with her, or with her and Dillon, to kill your wife."

"That's ridiculous," Max said.

"Well, we'll have to convince a judge of that," McCullough said. "Which means we need a better explanation for what happened. For instance, maybe Angela had the idea to rob your house, talked Dillon into doing it, and gave him the code to your alarm, but then your wife and niece came home during the robbery and everything went to hell. I don't know how that cop got killed, but I'm sure he'll fit into the picture somehow."

Max hesitated for a second, then said, "There's one problem you need to know about. A big one."

McCullough looked at him, waiting. Max wasn't sure he could trust the guy, but what choice did he have? He had to figure out some way to take care of Rosa and he couldn't do it if he was spending the rest of his life in jail.

Max leaned close to McCullough and whispered through the bars, "The problem is, it's true, I *was* having an affair with Angela. And there's this guy—his name's Bobby Rosa—he has these pictures of Angela and me…"

"What kind of pictures?"

"He got into our hotel room the other night," Max said, "while Angela and I were…well. We were in bed, and he took photos. Then he came to me and asked for a quarter million dollars. I said no, of course. What am I gonna do, start paying off a blackmailer, right? But if those photos get out, it would be bad. I mean, wouldn't it?"

"The detectives told me about that hotel room. They say they have surveillance video from the hotel showing the two of you going into the room. I don't know that having photos of you actually in the room would make things a lot worse."

Max didn't have an answer to that. He wanted to tell McCullough the rest, wanted to tell him about the cassette Rosa had played for him, about Dillon admitting to Rosa on the tape that Max had hired him to kill his wife. But he couldn't.

"I agree the affair makes things a little more complicated," McCullough continued, "but your case isn't impossible. If it turns out Angela's the one who killed Thomas Dillon and poured Drano on him, it'll be easy to show she's unstable. As long as you're telling me the truth, I think we'll be able to build up a solid defense."

As long as you're telling the truth. Always a goddamn catch.

"What about Bobby Rosa?" Max said, trying again.

"So he has some pictures of you having sex. So what? It's not like he has pictures of you killing somebody."

This was hopeless. He'd have to find a way to handle Rosa himself.

Max shot a glance at the homeless guy on the floor and lowered his voice further. "Do me a favor, don't tell anybody about Rosa, all right?" He hated that he was almost pleading with this teenager, this freaking child. "Forget I ever mentioned his name."

"Mr. Fisher, if it's going to come out, it's better if we're the ones who disclose it—"

"Don't. Just don't."

"But—"

"No." Max wanted to grab him and bang his head against the bars, get him to fucking pay attention for Chrissakes.

"What if Rosa had something to do with the shooting? What if he was working with Thomas Dillon—"

"Look," Max said, "we didn't discuss your fee yet, but you came highly recommended and I'm willing to pay top dollar for you to take me on as a client. But if I'm your client that means you work for me. Those pictures Rosa has could be a big embarrassment, especially if turns out Angela is involved with the murders. I don't want the police finding the pictures and the whole story going public. Do you get it?"

Reluctantly, McCullough agreed not to bring up Bobby Rosa's name to the police. He stayed with Max for a while longer, discussing strategy, then an officer came and led them into a small interrogation room with a square table. Ortiz and the tall detective sat on one side of the table, and Max and McCullough sat across from them on the other. In the middle of the table a little recorder was going. Ortiz began grilling Max, asking many of the same questions he'd asked the other night. Before answering each question, Max looked at McCullough, but McCullough had a blank expression, like a kid in the back of the class who didn't do his homework assignment, and didn't interrupt one time. These days it seemed like they handed out law degrees on street corners—you can probably get one online; answer a few questions and, boom, you're a lawyer. Max just hoped this McCullough knew what the hell he was doing. But Max had to take it easy. He knew the cops would love it if he started chewing out his own goddamn lawyer in front of them. His lawyer was his ace, his only good card in a shitty hand. His father, a poker addict, used to say, *Doesn't matter about a bad hand, it's playing it badly that matters*. Max finally understood what the hell the bastard had been talking about.

Then Granger, the tall detective, asked Max if he was "involved" with Angela Petrakos.

"Yes," Max said. "We'd been having an affair for the past few months."

"How come you didn't tell me that the other night?" Ortiz asked.

"I didn't want it coming out," Max said, "out of respect for my dead wife and her relatives." He made sure he hit the right somber note. He didn't go overboard, wiping at his eyes and sniffling, but he let the words hang there.

Max looked at McCullough who blinked once as a sign of approval, or maybe just to show he was actually alive.

"We might as well tell you, then," Ortiz said, "we talked to some people at the Hotel Pennsylvania and they ID'd you and Angela Petrakos. So it's just as well you admitted it. Now, you want to tell us where you went after you left the hotel that night?"

"I went home," Max said. It was nice to tell the truth for a change. Being honest was so foreign to him it gave him a rush. He'd have to try more of it.

"You never saw Detective Simmons that night?"

"Absolutely not."

"Did you ever meet a man named Thomas Dillon?" Granger asked.

"No," Max said, hoping the British accent wasn't coming out again.

"Were you aware that Angela Petrakos had been living with Dillon?"

Now Max felt feverish, realizing what an idiot he'd been for believing all those stories about Angela's roommate. He would've killed for a half bottle of Stoli.

"Angela led me to believe that she lived with a woman."

"So you never went to her apartment?" Ortiz asked skeptically.

Max shook his head.

Ortiz and Granger continued to grill Max for about another half an hour. Max continued to deny knowing anything about Angela and Dillon's relationship or any murder plot to kill his wife. When Ortiz suggested the possibility that there might be "a fourth person," someone Max had hired to try to kill Angela this afternoon, Max could tell McCullough wanted him to bring up Bobby Rosa, but Max told the detectives he had absolutely no idea what had happened in the park today. He was going to add, *What the hell's happening to our city?* but was scared it would come out in that fucking accent.

Finally Max was taken back to the holding cell. About a half an hour later, McCullough came to the cell and said, "I have some good news for you—they're dropping the assault charges."

"That's very nice of them since I didn't assault anybody."

"And they're going to let you go on your own recognizance."

"For good?"

"No, just for now. They want to see what happens with Angela and get her side of the story. If they get a confession out of her you might be off the hook, so let's just hope, for your sake, she pulls through."

Twenty-Five

Little Girl Lost
RICHARD ALEAS

Bobby couldn't stand lying in bed anymore, staring at the fucking cracks in the ceiling, so he went into the living room and lifted himself out of his wheelchair onto the couch and turned on NY1, the local twenty-four-hour-a-day TV news station. He watched the same bit on Angela's shooting three times, wondering each time, How the fuck could she not be dead? What the fuck was with that?

Finally, he fell asleep. When he woke up, at a little after six, the news was running a different segment about the shooting with a different reporter live on the scene. The reporter said that Angela was in critical but stable condition. He also said something about the cops finding a body in her bathtub soaking in Drano, which he figured answered the question of what she'd meant by "got rid of." Bobby still didn't know how the hell she'd survived those shots. He'd thought the one in her chest had gotten her for sure, but the bullet must've just missed her heart. He didn't get this because Bobby Rosa never, *never* missed a fucking target. Was he losing his touch? It was bad enough that he couldn't walk and that it took the stars aligning just to be able to bang a chick, but now was being in a wheelchair affecting his ability to kill people?

Bobby knew there was no way he would be able to fall back asleep now. He put on some clothes and went down to the deli and bought a couple ham and egg sandwiches on rolls, a large black coffee, and a copy of the *Daily News*. Back in his apartment, he wolfed down the sandwiches and read the newspaper articles about the Riverside Park shooting. Like on TV, there was no mention of Max Fisher and no mention of any possible suspects. He didn't know if this was good or bad. Fuck, he didn't know shit about anything anymore.

Later, Bobby was finishing his bladder routine when he noticed something funny and muttered, "The hell is that?"

It looked like a blister down there, then he looked closer and noticed that there were others clustered around. Bobby laughed. If he'd caught herpes a few years ago he might have been upset, but now he couldn't feel any pain down there so what the hell difference did it make?

Bobby started to plan his mother's funeral. He got hold of a funeral home on Amsterdam Avenue and arranged for them to pick up the body from the morgue at the nursing home. Then he called Information in Brooklyn and got the phone numbers of a few of his mother's oldest friends. One of them, Carlita Borazon, had died a couple of years ago, her husband told Bobby, but her two other close friends—Anna Gagliardi and Rose-Marie Santos—were alive and well. They both seemed very upset when Bobby broke the news.

After he got off the phone with Rose-Marie, Bobby turned on the TV. There was an update on the Riverside Park shooting. A spokesman from the hospital said that Angela was out of her coma. She was awake and alert, but still in critical condition.

"Fuck!" Bobby shouted and threw the remote at the TV.

He got the address of Columbia Presbyterian Hospital from the phone book, then went down to the street and took the Broadway bus uptown to 168th Street. The hospital lobby was crammed with reporters and camera crews, but no one paid much attention to him, some guy in a wheelchair. It took a long time, but Bobby finally made his way through the halls to the nursing station and found a clipboard that showed what room Angela was in. He half expected to see a pair of cops stationed outside the door and was prepared to just keep rolling if there were, but the door was open and there was no one outside it, so he just went in.

Angela looked like shit. Her face was white and there were tubes coming in and out of her body. How the hell had she survived? The luck of the Irish, that's how. Ask any Brit—it's friggin' impossible to kill those mothers. No wonder the Irish made such a big deal about funerals. It was so hard to put a mick in a box, they actually celebrated when they got one there.

Bobby wheeled close to the bed. The easiest thing would have been to smother her with a pillow, like what that Indian did to Jack Nicholson in that *Cuckoo's Nest* movie. But that would be crazy with the door open and cops in the building.

Angela was sleeping or resting, but when Bobby touched her wrist her eyes opened. She turned her head slowly in his direction.

"Don't try to talk," Bobby said. "I just came by to see how you were doing."

"I'm doing okay," Angela said weakly.

She squeezed Bobby's hand. Bobby felt uncomfortable, but he left his hand there anyway.

"Did the cops talk to you yet?" Bobby was trying not to sound too anxious.

Angela shook her head.

"That's good," Bobby said. "That's real good. What about what happened in the park? Did you see who shot you?"

Again Angela shook her head, then said, "All I remember is lying on the ground bleeding."

"Some kid with a gun probably took a pot shot at you," Bobby said. "Fucking kids these days—running around, shooting people for kicks. I ever get my hands on them..."

He let the threat hang there, to show how much he cared about her. Man, he was a great actor.

Now Angela was squeezing Bobby's hand tighter. She was trying to say something, but Bobby couldn't hear her.

Then Bobby said, "Don't worry, everything's gonna be all right. I just talked to your doctor and he said you'll be walking out of here in no time, so you don't gotta worry about that. Understand?"

Angela nodded.

"But listen," Bobby whispered, "the police are gonna want to talk to you and it's very important what you say to them. You listening? They found Dillon in your bathtub, but you don't have to worry about it. He came after you and you killed him in self-defense—it's as simple as that. But here's the important thing—when the police ask you about Fisher hiring Dillon to kill his wife you have to say you know nothing about that. Remember—you knew nothing about that. Whatever you do, don't finger Max. I don't wanna see you get in trouble and this is your only way out of this mess. So just tell the police you know nothing about Max—tell them the robbery was all Dillon's idea. Max had nothing to do with it, got it?"

She managed to smile, then said weakly, "Oh, I understand, Bobby. It's really sweet of you to try to protect me. But there's one thing you've got to understand, too." Her voice was fading and she had to pause to take a breath. Bobby had to lean close to hear her say, "I get half the money."

That night Angela was the top story on all the newscasts. She claimed that her live-in boyfriend, Thomas Dillon, had killed Deirdre Fisher and Stacy Goldenberg and that Fisher's husband

Max had nothing to do with it. She also said that Dillon killed that cop, Kenneth something.

Bobby knew he could do it now. He could show up at Fisher's office Monday morning and go for his full bank account, his stocks, his cars, get him to sell that fucking townhouse. It was all there for him to take. Even half the take would be a nice score. But, for some reason, he couldn't get psyched up about it. Part of it was the idea that he'd have to split the money with that lying bitch, but that wasn't all of it. He needed to *do* something, to show that he still had what it took to get the job done. The business in the park had really gotten to him, shaken his confidence. He had to prove to himself that he hadn't lost the touch.

He called Victor. He got his voicemail, said, "I'm gonna leave an envelope at the desk for you. Don't say I never gave you nothin' you dumb fuck." Then he hung up, feeling nice and pumped.

Yeah, he knew exactly what he had to do next.

Twenty-Six

I love storms.
GANDHI

Monday morning, Max wasn't expecting a party in his office, but he thought there would at least be a few smiling faces. Instead, no one even said hello to him. Max didn't understand it. Didn't anyone read the papers or watch the news on TV? Didn't they know that Angela had cleared his name? He'd fire all these bastards, see what they thought then. Christ, couldn't an innocent guy get a break?

Max went to Diane Faustino's desk and asked her to please come into his office. He had steel in his voice, thinking, *You wanna play hardball, baby? All right, then come to Daddy, sweetie. Come to Daddy.*

"What for?"

"I'm your boss—I don't need a reason." He let his eyes turn to stone. He'd seen Eastwood do that.

Diane breathed deeply, then followed Max.

In his office, Max asked her to shut the door then he said, "All right, now what the hell's going on here?"

"Going on with what?" Diane said coldly. She was still standing near the door, looking like she was staring down a man who'd raped and killed her family.

"The silent treatment," Max said. "You'd think I was Charles Manson or something."

"The police came back here Friday afternoon, after they took you away."

"So?" Max said.

"They were talking to everyone, asking a lot of questions."

"That's what police do," Max said, trying to seem patient. "When somebody gets shot they go to their office and ask a lot of questions."

"You don't care, do you?"

The question confused Max. He wasn't sure whether Diane was trying to change the subject or not. "Care about what?"

"You really don't know, do you?" Diane said. "You're pathetic."

"That's out of line," Max said. "If you don't—"

"Everybody thinks you did it."

Max stared at Diane. He couldn't believe she had the balls to talk to her boss this way. What the hell was happening to the world?

"Did what?" he said.

"Hired that guy to kill your wife," Diane said, "hired somebody else to shoot Angela."

"I didn't hire anybody to shoot Angela."

"But you hired somebody to kill your wife?"

"I didn't hire anybody to do anything."

"I don't believe you. Nobody believes you. We knew you were an asshole, I just can't believe I've been working all this time for a murderer. And no, don't bother firing me—I quit."

"Will you just calm down?" Max said. "Jesus, I hate it when you get hysterical." He wondered if she had any valium. Women always had that stuff and God knew he could use some too. He'd been having chest pains again lately and needed something to ward off a heart attack. How much could one decent man take?

Diane stormed out of the office, letting the door slam behind her. To hell with her, Max thought. If an employee wasn't loyal to her boss, what use was she? Besides, accounting people were a dime a dozen and it was a known fact that the Chinese were better than Italians anyway. He'd make a call to a headhunter and tomorrow morning there'd be ten Chinese guys lined up for Diane's job. His heart pounding, he looked at his Rolex, went to the drawer, poured a large glass of vodka, and gulped it down, spilling some on his tie, thinking, *Aw, c'mon, gimme a break.*

There was a knock on Max's door. Diane begging for her job back? That was fast. But instead it was Thomas Henderson, NetWorld's CFO. He told Max that he was resigning, that he just couldn't work here anymore. Max said this was fine with him. A CFO would be harder to replace than an ordinary accountant, but fuck it, Max didn't want anyone working for him who didn't have loyalty to the company.

Eleven more people resigned during the next half hour, including four of his Senior Network Technicians, a few cable installers, and two of his best PC technicians. Goddamn it, his whole company was hemorrhaging. Now Max was starting to get frightened and more than a little drunk. As they filed in and out of his office, he said to one guy, "When the going gets tough, the tough get fucked." He knew that wasn't right, was it? What-the-fuck ever. He said to some woman, "Easy go, easy come for me, baby." Like he didn't give a goddamn, but he did, oh yeah. After another glass of Stoli he screamed at another woman, "Get out of my fucking face!" Max realized he was losing it. It was one thing to lose a couple of people, but all of a sudden his entire company was falling apart in front of him.

Max ordered the temp who was answering phones today to call all the headhunters NetWorld dealt with and to transfer them to his line as soon as she got through. Later, when the headhunters returned his calls, Max told them to set up appointments to interview people for the vacant positions. This made

Max feel a little more at ease, until clients started calling. He realized he was slurring and the damn vodka was empty, *How the hell'd that happen?*

At first, there were just a few smaller clients, calling to cancel their service and consulting agreements. They were five- to ten-thousand-dollar-a-year clients that Max wouldn't miss, but then a few bigger clients, where Max had placed full-time consultants and did steady business, called to say they were planning to look for a new company for network support. All of the clients had the same story—they didn't like the bad publicity that Max and NetWorld were getting so they had decided it was best to take their business elsewhere. Max tried desperately to save the clients, but nothing he could say worked. It was like he was shouting and the world was, what, deaf? He hated how he sounded, like he was fucking *pleading*. Then, craving another drink, he went to the stash of Chivas Regal he kept for special clients. He poured a glass, some going on his tie, thought, *Fuck it*, and started guzzling. Vaguely, he remembered the hangover from hell the last time he mixed vodka and whiskey, but he didn't let that slow him down. He hit the intercom button and ordered his temp to go out to get some pistachios, figuring they'd soak up the booze.

Ten minutes later, clutching the bottle of Chivas, Max wobbled out to the temp's desk and said, "Where the fuck are my nuts?" Then he said, "Wait I know where they are, they're right here," and grabbed his balls.

The girl mumbled something with the word "disgusting" in it and Max interrupted, "Hey, you talking back to me? Don't you know, I own your arse!" He smiled, realizing he'd channeled Thomas Dillon, old Popeye himself.

Now the girl was saying something about quitting and Max said, "You know, you're getting just a tad on my nerves." Then he thought, *Tad?* How fucking British was he gonna get? And where the hell was that Zen book? Hadn't the police returned it? How was he gonna mellow out if he couldn't find the goddamn thing?

The girl got up to leave. No big loss—she was thin, had no shape.

"And Zen there were none!" Max yelled at her as she ran out of the office.

He opened the Chivas for another dose and then shouted, "Fuck!" as the cap cut into his index finger, blood leaking out. In the bathroom, full-blown panic set in as he rinsed his finger, watching what he was convinced were pints of blood go down the drain. He was gonna bleed to death from a Chivas bottle cap—how pathetic was that?

The bleeding finally stopped, but he was convinced he'd lost vital amounts of blood and back at his desk, he drank from the bottle, trying to replace the fluid, thinking, *Yeah, like that was gonna work.* Then, thinking out loud, he said, "Did I just think out loud?" Fook on a bike, as that Irish cow always said. Why wouldn't the bitch do the decent thing and fuckin' die? Was it so much to ask?

Max stood straight up, muttered about getting focused, even though he was seeing double. He was determined to save his business. Then, the whiskey pumping him up, he thought, The office? Why stop there? He could save the world, maybe give Angela's buddy Bono a run for his money.

Then Jack Haywood from Segal, Russell & Ross called to tell Max that his company wanted to sever ties with NetWorld. Max nearly cried, *No, not fucking Jack.*

"Come on, Jackie baby," Max pleaded, "after all we've been through, all the lap dances and hookers? Come on, buddy, you know what kind of guy I am? You know I'd never get involved with any of those sleazeballs you're hearing about in the news, I thought we were tight, man?"

There was silence on the other end of the line. Max thought Jack might have hung up, then he was saying, "I want to believe you, Max, but I saw you with that stripper the other night and I've seen you with strippers before and I know how you were always putting down your wife, talking about how you sleep around—"

"Jack," Max shouted, "that was just bullshit I say when I'm selling. You don't really think I...whatever you do, Jack, please, don't tell the police that!"

"It's not my decision anyway," Jack said. "If it was up to me, I'd keep you on, but the partners don't like it. But hey, listen, I'll keep your number in my rolodex. If I ever move to another company, I'll give you a call. Maybe we can do something." There was a long pause then Jack asked, "Are you drinking?" Then, "I mean, it's none of my business, pal, but you need to stay sober if you want to regain any credibility."

Max squinted hard, said, "Regain?"

Wasn't that the shit to save your hair? Hell, maybe it could save his firm.

By the end of the day, half his client list was gone, kaput, *finito*. And the other half would've been gone too if, at some point, he hadn't stopped answering the phone.

Twenty-Seven

You have a saying "to kill two birds with one stone."
But our way is to kill just one bird with one stone.
SUZUKI ROSHI

With a gym bag resting on his lap, Bobby wheeled into the liquor store on the corner of Amsterdam and Ninety-first. The same old Pakistani guy Bobby always saw there, morning or night, was working the counter. What was with that? Did they sleep, like, standing up?

There were two customers in the store—a Chinese woman and a black man. Bobby wheeled to the back of the store and started browsing in the Merlot section. Meanwhile, in one of the overhead mirrors, he was watching the activity at the checkout counter up front. The Chinese woman paid for her purchase in small bills, even counting out coins to give exact change, for Chrissakes. But eventually she finished, took her bag, and left. Now it was only Bobby and the black guy in the store. Bobby felt like he could get out of his chair and walk.

The black guy moved to the checkout counter. Bobby thought he saw the Pakistani guy looking in the mirror, watching him, maybe suspiciously, but Bobby wasn't worried. He was in the groove—nothing could get to him now.

"Thanks," the black guy said.

When the door closed and the little bell above it rang, Bobby moved—not fast, casually, toward the front of the store. The Pakistani guy was looking down, writing something in a pad.

Bobby opened his gym bag and took out an Uzi. The rush he felt when he had the weapon in his hand—yeah, this was the old Bobby.

"This is a stick-up," he announced. "Don't try to be a hero. Just fill up this bag up with money and you won't get shot."

He had just the right amount of hard-ass and viciousness in his tone, just like the good ol' days, just like Isabella had taught him.

Everything the Pakistani guy did was magnified. Bobby could hear his breath, see the sweat spreading out of his pores. Was he imagining it, or did the guy smell like the back seat of a cab?

Then he saw the guy's right arm start to move. Bobby imagined that a lot of guys might have missed this, guys who weren't as sharp and quick as he was. This was what he had learned from twenty-plus years in the life—to notice the little things. Maybe the guy was going for an alarm or maybe he was going for a gun, but Bobby wasn't going to wait and find out. He started firing, unloading half a round in an instant. He had a flashback to Desert Storm, the time a sniper was running across the sand and Bobby shot him in the neck so many times his head fell off, but his body kept running a few feet before it dropped. Then he saw flashes of himself on jobs—running out of jewelry stores and banks. This was where he belonged—in the action, on the front line. Bobby was smiling now, watching the little towelhead store owner flying back against the back wall in slow motion. The bullets shredded the little fucker to bits.

Then Bobby heard footsteps behind him. When he turned around he didn't see another towelhead, but an old woman, probably the owner's wife. She had a gun, a little revolver, in her right hand and she was screaming in a language Bobby didn't understand. Bobby didn't want to fire, but when he saw her trigger finger starting to move he had no choice. What, he survived Desert Storm to let some old broad get the drop on him?

Getoutta here. He sent the screaming old woman into a wine rack, shattering glass and spilling red liquid everywhere. Red with meat, right?

The store was quiet again. Moving quickly, Bobby hoisted himself up onto the counter so he was sitting next to the register and reached into the open cash tray. Then he wheeled himself to the back room and found some more money in the old woman's pocketbook. The whole score only came to a thousand bucks and change. It wasn't as much as if he'd gotten them to open the safe, but what could you do? He'd just have to make it up on the next job and the job after that. He put the money and the Uzi into his gym bag, closed the zipper all the way, and, with the smell of cordite rocking his brain, wheeled out into the twilight.

Heading across the street, Bobby saw the cops get out of the squad car before the cops saw him. He went for the Uzi again when he saw another cop across the street aiming a gun at him, yelling "Stop, police!" Shit, why'd he put the Uzi away? He had his hand in the gym bag when the first bullet went into his leg. He laughed, didn't even feel it, but the bullet sent his wheelchair out of control. The laundry truck, shit, it was coming right at him.

Twenty-Eight

*He was one of those "There but for the Grace of God" guys;
one of those guys that thought if you went out of your way to ignore
someone else's bad shit then the same bad shit was liable
to boomerang and smack you in the head.*
JOHN RIDLEY, *Everybody Smokes in Hell*

Max was on line at the checkout counter at Grace's Marketplace on Third Avenue, buying some vegetables to steam for dinner, when he heard these two young guys talking.

The bigger guy said, "Did you hear what happened on the West Side?"

Max's hangover had kicked in big time and, although the guy was talking in a normal tone, it sounded like he was screaming directly into Max's ear with a bullhorn.

"No," the other guy said, sounding just as loud. Max had taken two Advils, but they were doing shit.

"This afternoon," the big guy said, "couple hours ago. This guy in a wheelchair robs this liquor store on Amsterdam Avenue and loses it. He goes in with an Uzi and starts shooting up the place—kills the owner and his wife."

Now Max was straining, listening closely, as the guy went on, explaining how the guy was run over and crushed to death by a laundry truck.

"That's it," the other guy said, shaking his head. "I'm moving to fuckin' Jersey."

As the guy went on, talking about something else, Max said, "Excuse me," then more softly because of his aching brain, "excuse me, I just overheard what you were saying—about this guy in a wheelchair."

"Yeah," the guy said. "Pretty fucked up, huh?"

"You didn't, by any chance, hear what his name was, did you?"

"Yeah, it was, I don't know—something Spanish. Ramirez, Rojas..."

"Could it have been Rosa?"

"Maybe," the guy said. "I wasn't really paying attention too much to that part."

He was staring at Max like Max was some wino or something. Max didn't get it. Before he left the office, didn't he have all those Altoids? There was a goddamn guarantee on the packet, wasn't there?

Max left the vegetables in the shopping cart, and jogged back to his townhouse, nearly out of breath when he got there. His heart, fuck, it felt like it was about to explode.

He turned on the TV, expecting to find out that it was all a big mistake, that there were two crazy cripples with Spanish names in this city. But, sure enough, the reporter, live at the scene, said, "...police are releasing no other information about the gunman right now, but we have learned that Robert Rosa was an ex-convict who had been arrested several times for gun possession, armed robbery, and related charges. He was not married and it is not known whether he has any relatives."

At first, Max was elated, but then he realized that his troubles were far from over. The police were probably searching Bobby's apartment at this very moment. It was only a matter of time until they found that cassette.

Max turned off the TV and sat on his living room sofa in silence, the only noise coming from the refrigerator buzzing in the kitchen. At any moment, the police would come to the door, demanding to be let in.

He had to see Angela. He'd been thinking about her all last

night, and most of the day today, wondering what was going on in her head. He knew she still loved him or why would she have lied to the police to protect him? Sure, she was covering her own ass as well, but she could have done that just as easily by letting him burn. Unless she figured he'd turn on her if she turned on him. Which he would have.

He needed another drink. He chugged a quarter bottle of Stoli then, thinking *That was the problem, never should've switched to whiskey*, left the townhouse and headed toward Third Avenue to hail a cab. Was he staggering a little? Nah, just nerves, that's all. It was all perspective, how you looked at the picture. He muttered, "*So you had a wee dram.*" Then, horrified, he thought, What was that? Scottish? Jesus. "Coulda been a contender." Fuck, get a grip.

"Columbia Presbyterian Hospital!" he shouted at the driver.

The twenty-minute cab ride sobered Max up a little, but at the hospital he was still half-drunk and it took him a while to find Angela's room.

A cop on duty recognized Max immediately.

"Hold it right there, Mr. Fisher."

The cop was short, heavyset, with curly hair. He stood up with his hands on his hips, sticking out his chest.

"I wanna see Angela Petrakos," Max said.

"Yeah, I bet you do, but I can't let you in there."

"Why not? I'm not charged with anything."

"I still can't let you in there."

"Did someone tell you I couldn't see her?"

The officer thought this over for a second then said, "No. But I still think it's best."

Max was in that weird zone of half hung over and feeling like he was seeing everything through glass, very dirty glass. For a mad moment, he was ready to take a swing at the guy.

He said, "Unless you want to embarrass yourself when I start making phone calls to your boss, I would suggest you let me inside there. The woman works for me, for Christ's sake."

Max was trying to summon up the old powerbroker Max, before his life went in the toilet, and maybe it was working. He thought the cop looked a little worried. Nothing like sticking it to the boys in blue to restore the old Max Fisher confidence.

The cop said, "All right, you can talk to her, but just for a couple of minutes, and I'm comin' in there with you."

Max was expecting Angela to look like hell, but it was just the opposite. She was sitting up in bed, watching TV, and she looked almost normal. She wasn't wearing as much makeup as usual, but she was wearing bright red lipstick and her hair was nice. Her breasts looked great too. Who said hospital gowns weren't sexy? He looked over at the cop and had a feeling the guy was thinking the same thing.

Looking back at Angela's face, Max couldn't tell if she was happy to see him or not. He had to be very careful now.

"Surprise," Max said.

Angela continued to stare at Max with a blank expression, then she smiled slowly. But Max still couldn't tell what she was thinking.

"What are you doing here?" she said.

"I just thought I'd stop by and pay a little visit," Max said, "see how you were doing."

The cop was standing in the corner of the room, watching them.

"I'm doing okay," Angela said.

"Yeah, I can tell that," Max said. "I mean it. You look dynamite." He nodded toward the TV. "I see you're watching the news. So I guess you saw about the robbery. That guy in the wheelchair. Crazy, huh?"

Angela nodded slowly.

"So...you should be feeling a little better, I'd think. Not out of the woods yet, but things are looking better."

"The doctors said I was really lucky," Angela said. "If the bullet in my chest had been an inch over to the right I'd probably be dead. They still think it's a miracle I made it with all the blood I lost."

Max's vision was still blurry and it was hard to concentrate. He knew there were things he wanted to say to Angela, important things, but he couldn't think of what the hell they were.

"So is that why you came here, just to see how I was?"

"No," Max said, "I also came here to tell you that I miss you —at the office I mean. I miss having you around, and I miss...I miss a lot of things about you."

"The doctors told me if I keep improving I might be out of here by next week."

"That's terrific," Max said. Out of the corner of his eye he saw the cop raise his arm and point at the watch on his wrist. "Look, I just want you to know that I appreciate your sticking up for me. It showed me that deep down you really do care. It meant a lot. Everyone else at the company walked out on me, pretty much. First sign of trouble and it was adios, amigo, sayonara, nice knowing you. But you were loyal, and..." He felt something swelling up inside him, the same feeling that had hit him that night years ago in the bar of the Mansfield Hotel. And look how well that had worked out for him. But, hey, sometimes, you just feel what you feel, and you've got to go with it, or whatever.

"I know none of this was your fault," he said, some of the words slurring, "and I just want you to know that I don't blame you for anything. The thing is I can't stand living in that big house all by myself. What I'm trying to say is, when you get out of here, I think we should get married."

Angela looked shocked. Her mouth sagged open. "Are you serious?"

"Oh, I know it'll be hard for a while," Max said. "I mean, getting over everything and everything. But eventually we'll get used to it."

"But the police are still—"

Max waved his hand dismissively, knocking into some big tube. "I have a good lawyer, and I'll have him handle your case. And then when it's all behind us, we can do everything we talked about doing—travel, go places, see things. What do you say?"

"I can't believe you'd propose to me after...after everything," Angela said, and he thought she looked like she was about to start crying.

"Say yes," Max said. "I hope I didn't have to schlep all the way up to Harlem for nothing."

She still wasn't answering. He was about to get on his knees, do the proposal in style, when she closed her eyes, maybe to squeeze back tears, and said, "Of course I'll marry you. Why wouldn't I?"

That night Max made a decision. If he somehow got through all of this, he was going to change his life—make up for everything he'd done. Innocent people had died and, while he knew it wasn't all his fault, he also knew he was at least partly responsible. He was a stand-up guy, could take some blame. He was going to quit booze and start going to a synagogue. Better yet, he'd read that damn Zen book, if he could ever find it. Yeah, that's right, to hell with Judaism, he was going to finally see what this Buddhism shit was all about. Maybe there was something to meditating—maybe sitting Indian-style, thinking about nothing, was the answer to all his problems. He didn't care what he had to do, he was going to make big changes in his life and things were going to be different.

Max woke up feeling refreshed. His memories of the previous day were a little foggy, but he remembered proposing to Angela. Eh, what the hell? Maybe it wasn't something he would have done sober, but that didn't make it a mistake. After all, what were the odds of him having two fucked up marriages in a row? Maybe marrying Angela would be the best thing that had ever happened to him.

After he showered and shaved, he took a walk over to the newsstand around the corner and bought a copy of the Sunday *Post*. He felt great, whistling the song from *The Bridge on the River Kwai*, then he looked at the paper and the screaming headline PERVERT! Under the headline was a big picture of Bobby Rosa. He read the article standing in front of the newsstand. There were two full pages, all about Rosa. The police had discovered hundreds of pictures in his apartment of women —women in bikinis, women in their underwear, peeping tom shots taken through windows, upskirt shots, downblouse shots. Many of the pictures were hung up on the walls in his bedroom and bathroom, but the police had found boxes of additional pictures in his closet, including the ones of Max and Angela having sex. But the most shocking news was that the police had found a gun in Bobby's apartment that had been used in the Riverside Park shooting. Max couldn't understand this at all. He knew Bobby had some screws loose, but the maniac had gone biblical. Max definitely didn't feel like whistling anymore.

The whole thing was so confusing now, Max had a throbbing headache. He bought copies of the *Times* and the *Daily News*, but their stories basically repeated the same information as the articles in the *Post*. The only good news, as far as Max was concerned, was that there was no mention in any of the papers of the police finding the incriminating cassette tape in Rosa's apartment. But how long would it be before they did?

He had a feeling that his life was about to go down the shitter again.

At a deli on Lexington Avenue, he bought a bouquet of red and pink roses, then he took a cab up to the hospital. A different cop was on duty in front of Angela's room. This one let him into the room without a hassle. Angela was sleeping. Max tiptoed up to the bed and woke her up with a soft kiss on the lips. Not his special, the hot one that never failed, but one with concern, damn it, plenty of real compassion in there. Angela's eyes opened suddenly, like she didn't know where she was, but then she saw Max's face. There was a moment of horror at first and then her expression softened into a smile though her eyes still looked strained and unhappy. He figured he must've woken her out of a bad dream or something.

At work the next morning, Max had his receptionist get Andrew McCullough on the phone.

"I have another job for you," Max said. "I want you to represent Angela Petrakos."

"Angela Petrakos?" McCullough said. "You're kidding, right?"

He hated the prick's tone, like he thought he was so high and mighty because he was the lawyer and not the guy who constantly needed one. "Why would I kid about that?"

"Since when do you care what happens to Angela Petrakos?" the dick asked.

"Since I asked her to marry me," Max said.

Max spent most of the day on the phone with his remaining clients, trying to shore up relationships. He also called some of the clients who had canceled their service agreements last week and asked for second chances. Most said they were sorry, that they were still going to take their business elsewhere, but he was able to sweet talk some into saying yes.

For the first time since before Deirdre was murdered, Max felt like his life was getting back on track. He was the kind of guy who worked best under pressure; it showed what he was made of.

He went to the gym in the morning, worked hard all day, then went to visit Angela at night. He was feeling healthier than he had in years. He felt a little bad about some of the things he'd done, but he also knew that somewhere inside him there was another Max Fisher, a better Max Fisher, and somehow he was going to let that Max Fisher out. He couldn't wait to let the world see the new model. Hell, he might even start leaving tips.

Nah, no need to get stupid.

In the mirror that morning, he said to himself. "You're a good person. Sure, you've had some tough luck, but suffering makes the man."

He was pretty sure the Zen book would have this type of crap in it.

A minor hitch developed in McCullough's case when the doorman at Bobby Rosa's building came forward, claiming that Angela and Dillon had visited Bobby's apartment on successive days. McCullough claimed that his client had been blackmailed by Bobby, and that she was at the building that night to ask for the sex pictures back. McCullough also speculated that Dillon was "the jealous type" and that he may have gone to confront Bobby, suspecting that Bobby and Angela were having an affair. As for the body in the bathtub, McCullough claimed that Angela was trapped in an abusive relationship and had killed Dillon in self-defense. The Drano was evidence of how desperate and illogical she had become. Angela's cuts and bruises backed up the self-defense claim and several people at the office came forward and vouched that they'd seen Angela arrive at work with a nasty black eye prior to the murder. Regarding the other sticking point, the code to the alarm, McCullough suggested that Dillon had forced Deirdre Fisher to give him the code to the alarm the evening of the murders, which was why he was able to reset the alarm before he left.

Max didn't think there was any way in hell the police would buy McCullough's bullshit. They were going to indict Angela and then, under pressure, she'd break down and implicate him. But then McCullough called him at work with the incredible news. The police had held a press conference announcing that the investigation was officially closed—Thomas Dillon and Thomas Dillon alone had committed the murders of Deirdre Fisher, Stacy Goldenberg, and Kenneth Simmons. Apparently, although it was clear that Max and Angela were having an affair, the DA's office didn't think they had enough evidence against Max to pursue a case against him. They also felt that Angela, as a battered woman, would be viewed as sympathetic by a jury, especially after it was announced that Dillon was also linked to the vicious slaying of a Japanese tourist. According to an Op Ed piece in the *Post*, the Mayor may have urged a quick resolution to the case as well, the start of the summer tourist season being a bad time for stories about a tourist having his throat cut to be in the news.

Two days after the case was closed, Angela was discharged from the hospital. She was transported out of the premises in a wheelchair and then she stood up and limped into Max's arms. Thanks to his Viagra he had a powerful hard-on, wanted to bang the living crap out of her right there. That night, he took her out to a romantic candlelight dinner at Demi on Madison Avenue and surprised her with a two-carat diamond engagement ring from Tiffany's. It was worth every penny it had cost to see the way her eyes lit up when she held it. Who said money couldn't buy happiness? Some dumb bastard who bought discount, probably.

❖

Max started to go to the ashram a few times a week with Kamal. He listened closely as the swami talked about "the universal unconscious" and "the inner self." He started to read books on Buddhism and Eastern philosophy and he did relaxation exercises and meditated two or three times a day. Hell, he was born for this shit. Even the itching had eased and the blisters were fading. That Buddha, he delivered, no question about it.

One weekend, Max took Angela to a yoga retreat in the Berkshires. They had a great time meditating, chanting, going to yoga and exercise classes, eating macrobiotic food, and taking long walks in the woods. When they came back to the city, Max felt completely cleansed. He felt as if he had been asleep his whole life and had finally awakened. The new Max Fisher was a kinder, more relaxed person who treated his newly hired employees with respect. He realized that for most of his life he'd been on the wrong path. His ego and desires had been controlling his actions while his true self was trapped underneath. Though he knew this didn't justify or make up for anything he had done, he also knew the things he'd done weren't his fault either. His ego had decided to kill Deirdre, and now that his ego was gone, the killer was gone too. He also felt a new sense of humility about himself and sensed that people understood he was a man who'd risen above great suffering to become even more compassionate. He knew it wasn't just his imagination, people were looking at him differently. There was no use for false modesty now—he might as well display it for the goddamn world to see. He couldn't wait to talk about his entire journey someday on *Oprah*.

Then, one afternoon, his new executive assistant—a petite Indian girl whom Max had hired because she was a Buddhist; her breasts weren't even B-cups—came into his office and said there was a man waiting to see him.

"Who?" Max asked.

"He wouldn't say, but he said it was important."

"All right," Max said. "Send him in."

Max shut off the CD of Tibetan chants he was listening to on his PC and then a short, very thin man, completely bald, with a big crooked nose entered his office. He was wearing jeans, sneakers, and a hooded sweatshirt, so he definitely wasn't a salesman.

"Can I help you with something?" Max asked, smiling.

"Yeah, I think you can," the man said. His voice sounded very hoarse, like a chain-smoker's, or maybe even one of those people you saw sometimes who'd had throat cancer and talked through a machine.

"Why don't you take a seat?" Max said. "Make yourself at home."

"That's all right," the man said weakly. "I don't mind standing. I've been standing all my life, you know what I mean?"

Max thought, *Yeah, standing, waiting for a bus*, because he wasn't the type who'd ever have a car. Max had a message for him, *The bus wasn't coming, pal,* but with his new spirituality, he decided to treat the poor loser like one of the Buddha's own. Yeah, he was a loser, shit on the bottom of his heel, but Max wouldn't be the one to tell him.

Max assumed the man was looking for work, maybe as an installer, doing punchdown for machine rooms, something like that. Max decided that because the man looked like he was in need he would hire him no matter what his skills were. The Buddha would be pleased as hell about that, right?

Max noticed that the man was looking above him, at the framed picture of the Dalai Lama he had hung above his desk.

"You meditate?" Max asked.

"No," the man said in that scratchy voice.

"You really should try it. If you want, you can come down to my ashram some time. I'll introduce you to some people."

"Nah, that's okay," the man said. "I don't believe in that religious shit."

Feeling sorry for the man for being unenlightened, Max said, "Well, you just call me if you change your mind. So do you have a resume?"

"What?"

"Do you have a resume with you?"

"Why would I give you a resume?"

"To get a job. That's why you're here, isn't it?"

The man smiled. It wasn't a pleasant smile.

"I didn't come here for a job. I just came to talk to you, Mr. Brown."

Max glared at the man, suddenly dizzy. He had quit drinking, but he suddenly craved vodka. Fucking Buddhism, where was it when your nuts were in the blender?

"Sorry," Max said. "What did you just call me?"

"Mr. Brown."

"I think you're in the wrong office," Max said. "My name's Fisher—Max Fisher." He wanted to rip the Dalai Lama to bits.

"I know your name," the man said.

"I get it," Max said. "This is some kind of joke, right? Angela put you up to this."

"Nobody put me up to anything," the man said.

Max hoped that this wasn't happening, that there was some explanation he couldn't imagine.

"Then why are you here?" Max's voice was almost as weak as the man's.

"I want one million dollars in cash by tomorrow at five P.M.," the man said. "I'll come back here to pick it up."

"Whoa, whoa," Max said, standing up. "Who the hell do you

think you are, barging into my office like this? You know what I think I'm gonna do? I think I'm gonna call the cops."

Max reached for the phone.

"I don't think that would be a smart idea."

"Really? Why not?"

The man took a mini-cassette player out of his sweatshirt pocket and held it up for Max to see. Max stared at the little machine, as if in a trance. He barely heard Dillon with that death-knell accent say, *"Yeah, he hired me,"* before his left arm went numb.

Later, sitting in the bar of the Mansfield, Max was getting shit-faced on Gimlet, whatever the hell that was. He wasn't even sure how he'd gotten to the bar. He remembered realizing, finally, that he wasn't dying of a heart attack—no, the fucking Buddha wouldn't put him out of his misery that easily; that Buddha, his ass was so fired—and running out of the office. At first, Max was planning to head to the ashram to center himself, but then he thought, Fuck it, and went to a bar. He started on Stoli, and worked his way up to liqueurs and other shit. He'd hit one or two or maybe three other bars on his way to the Mansfield—*hey, who was counting, right?*—and was still wearing his business suit, although it was wrinkled and stained and where the hell was his tie?

He finished his third Gimlet, screamed for another, then fumbled for his Blackberry. Muttering, "Where the hell…goddamnit…shit," he checked his two jacket pockets at least five times each before finding the thing in one of them. He thought he'd called Angela something like four hours ago to tell her how fucked they were, how they were gonna have to give the man everything, and to come meet him at the Mansfield. He called her again and was leaving another goddamn message when the next Gimlet arrived and he screamed, "Just get your ass over here, woman!" and he clicked off, knocking over the Gimlet in the same motion. The liquid stained his pants, making it look like he'd wet himself.

After Angela passed through Homeland Security—the guy had given her a nice little squeeze—she headed for the bar. The bartender smiled and asked her what she was having.

"A large Jameson, please."

"Are you Irish?"

"I am."

"Going on vacation?"

"I'm going home." Her engagement ring sparkled in the light for a moment and she added, "Home is where the heart is."

"Yeah, like that book I read in high school," the guy said smiling, "*The Heart is a Lonely Hunter*."

Angela didn't get it, said, "I don't get it."

Then she noticed the guy staring at her chest.

"I like that pin," he said, although she knew it wasn't the pin that interested him.

She took a breath, expanding her bust for a couple of moments —why not make the poor guy's day?—then she let the breath out slowly and said, "Thanks, it belonged to me mother, the only legacy she left. It represents our hands reaching out to each other. It's my new good luck charm, I think."

"Wow, that's so cool," the guy said. He must've polished that same glass, what, five times?

Angela finished the Jameson in one long gulp, said, "Ta," and walked away, swinging her hips, her chest fully expanded.

Hey, you got it, you gotta strut it, right?

SLIDE

For Chynna and Grace

and

*For Paul, Eileen, Colleen, and Nicole, the whole gang
at Dead End Books on Long Island (www.deadendbooks.com)*

and

*For independent booksellers everywhere,
without whom…*

One

Some people never go crazy.
What truly horrible lives they must live.
CHARLES BUKOWSKI

Max Fisher opened his eyes, looked at the blurry mess around him, thought, *Where the fuck am I?* He managed to turn his head, stare at a wall. It was a white wall. The walls in his apartment were white—okay, he was probably home. What day was it? He thought it was Monday because yesterday was Sunday, right? Didn't he see a football game on TV, at the bar he was drinking at? Or was that two days ago? Wait, it wasn't football, it was baseball. It was July for Christ's sake. The Fourth was just, what, last week? He remembered loud noises, explosions, fireworks. Yeah, it definitely wasn't football season.

He rolled over toward the night table, misjudged it, fell onto the floor. Right on his hip. Must've been a bad fall because the pain killed even though he was still smashed.

"Aw, Christ," he said, wincing, tasting vomit.

He stayed like that for a long time, might've passed out, then managed to struggle to his knees. The pain in his hip was excruciating, but he figured if he'd broken something he wouldn't be able to move.

Using all his energy, he squinted, trying to focus on the digital clock. There was a 7 there and a 1 and was that a 5? No, it was an 8. 7:18. There was light outside behind the curtains so it was morning—okay, things were coming together. Then he made out the letters above the numbers: W E D S. Fuck, it was

Wednesday morning—a workday. He had meetings to go to, people to see, deals to close.

Holding onto the bed, using all his might, he was able to stand. It was hard to stay upright, though. What was with the floor? He needed to shower, put on a suit, get to the fucking office. He took a couple of steps, almost fell, then a voice reminded him, *You don't work anymore.*

Then it all came back to him, how his whole life had been ruined by his former executive assistant—and, briefly, ex-fiancée—that Greek-Irish whore, Angela.

Angela. Max wished he could strike that name from his brain, like they did in that Schwarzenegger movie, *Total*...what the fuck was the name of it? Max couldn't even watch TV anymore. *Angela's Ashes*, Angela Lansbury, Angela Bassett. Suddenly Angelas were fucking everywhere. Even on the street there were reminders—the hair, the tits, the sickening Irish accent. One day Max heard a tourist near Rockefeller Center go to his friend, *I'd fancy a pint me own self,* and Max wanted to strangle the Guinness-loving fuck.

The first time Max had laid eyes on Angela and her incredible bust, he should've known how things would turn out. Big tits meant big trouble; every guy knew that. Max always listened to his instincts, but the one time he let his guard down—kaboom.

Things had been great before she came along all right; yeah, his life had been hopping. He was the fucking man, the head honcho, the big enchilada, you ask anyone. He was a player and he had freaking mega plans, he was riding that gravy train all the way to the goddamn zenith. He owned a successful computer networking company, lived in a spectacular town house on the Upper East Side. Then Angela came along. Fucking Angela. She was like a living curse, a goddamn virus.

And not only had the cunt wreaked havoc all over his perfect life, she'd given him herpes! When you see those blisters in the morning while you're having a long lazy piss, you see agony, you see fucking terror.

After Angela ran off to Ireland—charging the flight on his AmEx—he'd gotten revenge. One night he was drinking at some bar in the Bowery and he met a witch, Glinda. Her name wasn't really Glinda—he didn't know what the hell her name was—but that was what he'd called her in his mind. Anyway, Max went to her, "You mean you can cast spells?"

"Of course I cast spells," she said, as if offended. "I said I'm a witch, didn't I?"

Max glared at her, then said, "Yeah, well, I want you to put the evilest spell you can come up with on my ex-fiancée. Make her life and everybody's life around her a total living hell."

The witch cast the spell, said it was the harshest she'd ever done. Did Max sleep with her afterward? He vaguely remembered some wild, crazy woman, babbling about Wicca while he was banging her, but that could've been a dream.

The witch's spell might've ruined Angela's life, but it didn't make Max's any better. So Max had been trying to drink Angela out of his mind. It had been working, too. Or at least he'd thought it had been working until he wound up here. Wherever here was. And the sad truth was this wasn't the first time something like this had happened. Blackouts, those holy rollers in twelve-step programs called them. But this was worse than usual. Before now he'd never gotten fucking *lost*.

After stumbling and wobbling into the bathroom, Max looked at a mirror, almost not recognizing the bum with swollen, bloodshot eyes and pasty white skin and strings of greasy gray hair hanging over his face. And why were his teeth all yellow, and was one *missing*?

"Aw, Jeethus," he lisped. Or Jaythus, as that Irish cunt would say. "Not a toof gone. Gimme me a fucking break."

Max's big problem was, despite all he'd been through over the past few months, his ego was all there. He might've looked like a cesspool on the outside, but inside, he was still the same happening, suave, debonair, hip Max Fisher he'd always been.

He splashed some cold water onto his face and toweled off and something clicked. The towels—they weren't his. And the vanity and tiles—this wasn't his bathroom. Where the fuck was he?

He stutter-stepped back into his bedroom. Wait, it wasn't his bedroom, it was a fucking hotel room. He parted the curtains and brightness stung his eyes like he was Dracula getting out of his coffin. His eyes finally adjusted and he saw a parking lot. He was in a motel, on the ground floor.

"Jeethus H," he said.

It took him a while to find his pants on the floor. They had stains all over them. He put them on, inside out first, then the right way.

"Shirt, shirt, hell's my shirt?" he said, fumbling and stumbling around the room.

Finally he found a wife-beater T slung over a chair and put it on.

When he opened the door, the sunshine stung his eyes again. He went to the front of the motel, to the office. A young unshaven blond guy was on the phone.

Max stood there, rolling his eyes, while the guy took forever to get off the phone with his girlfriend or whoever. Max felt like raising hell for this kind of treatment—write letters, make phone calls, get this jackass fired. Firing people, this was Max's gig, how he'd risen to the top. And, by Christ, he'd rise again.

Finally the guy hung up, said, "Can I help you?" and Max went, "Where the fuck am I?"

The kid gave Max a look like he'd never heard the word fuck before, then said, "The Golden Star Motel."

"Where the fuck's that, Jersey?"

Another long look. Max wondered if the guy was retarded, had one of those learning disabilities. Or maybe he was dyslexic, was hearing everything backwards, like he thought Max was speaking Hebrew.

Finally the kid went, "You're not serious, are you?"

"Do I look like I'm not fucking serious? I don't see buildings anywhere so I know I'm not in goddamn Manhattan."

No pause this time, just, "Sir, you're in Robertsdale, Alabama."

Max looked at him like he was full of shit, said, "You're full of shit."

The kid showed him a business card, a brochure. Shit, Alabama. And the kid's accent wasn't Jersey; it had southern hick written all over it. That also explained why he was so slow, like everything Max said seemed to have to bounce off a satellite before reaching his brain. Didn't they fuck sheep or their sisters or both down here?

"How the hell did I get here?"

Long delay then, "Well, according to what it says here on the computer, you checked in yesterday afternoon."

"But how?" Max said. "I live in fucking Manhattan."

The kid didn't have an answer to this, just stared at Max with a stumped expression.

Max said, "So where is..." He squinted at the brochure, holding it arm's length away because he didn't have his reading glasses. "...Robertsdale."

"About forty miles from Mobile, sir."

Jesus, sounded like the name of a freaking Glen Campbell song. And gee, like that really helped. Like the whole world knew fucking *Mobile*.

Baffled, Max returned to his room. He sat on the foot of the bed, racking his brain, trying to piece together the last few days of his life. He didn't make much progress. He remembered seeing that baseball game on TV at a bar in New York. It was definitely in New York, he was sure of that. Wasn't it that place in Hell's Kitchen he'd been drinking at? Yeah, he remembered the bartender, the black guy, trying to cut him off, telling him he had a drinking problem. Max, who'd been schmearing the guy for weeks, must've given him five hundred bucks in tips, said, "Are you fuckin' kiddin' me?" He realized he wasn't when the bouncer carried him out of the place, dropping him on a pile of garbage.

Max had no idea why the bartender wanted to get rid of him, but the idea that he had a drinking problem was the biggest joke ever. Max Fisher couldn't handle his liquor—yeah, right, that was a good one. Max knew he'd been drinking a lot lately —well, pretty much all the time—but he knew his limit; he knew when to stop. He was just in an alcohol phase that's all. He was de-stressing, doing what he had to do to get by till it was time to get back in the game. Look at all the big players in every sport, didn't they all have a time out for abusing *something*? Fuck, it was almost mandatory. It was freaking un-American not to have some *issues*. Dr. Phil built a career on it, for chrissakes. Besides, Max knew he was in total control and could kick the habit whenever he wanted to. That was the key.

All this thinking about drinking was making Max crave one. The few empty bottles of vodka and scotch strewn on the floor whetted his appetite even more. He went around the room, going, "Booze, booze, where the fuck are you? Come out, come out, wherever you are." He needed the wag of the dog, or whatever the hell it was called. Finally, under the bed, a bottle of Stoli, one quarter full. To hell with the glass, it tasted best straight from the bottle. Mmm, yeah, like that. Yep, it was hitting home big time. Max Fisher was back, all right.

Reenergized, Max formulated a POA—get to Mobile, fly back to the city, figure out some way to straighten out his life once and for all. But, whoa, big problem: his wallet was on the dresser, but there was no cash, no credit cards. For all he knew, somebody had stolen his identity, was going around New York, pretending to be him.

Max tossed the wallet away, grabbed the bottle of Stoli, muttered, "Welcome to fucking Robertsdale," and went bottoms up. The booze started weaving its dark magic almost instantly—reason you drank the shit, right?—and Max thought, *Okay, you need a plan, Maxie, that's all. One simple plan and get back in that goddamn saddle, let the suckers know Maxie is back. Think, Maxie, think.*

At that moment there was a knock on the door—talk about kismet—and a Mexican woman outside went, "Housekeeping."

Then it came to him out of, like, nowhere. He sat up, energized, muttered, "But have I got the *cojones*?"

The last gulp of Stoli assured him he had.

Two

A hole is nothing at all, but you can break your neck in it.
AUSTIN O'MALLEY

He was one dark, dangerous, lethal motherfucker. No one knew the truth of this better than his own self. They called him Slide because he didn't let anything slide, ever. He'd killed thirteen and counting. Counting like the ritual psycho he was. Counting on there being more—lots more. He was, as they say, only getting warmed up.

The name, trademark, signature if you like—that's right, he had a *signature*—came from what he'd whisper to his victim before administering his *coup de grace*.

"Know what, partner?...I'm gonna let it slide."

Ah, that sheen of hope, that desperate last dangling moment of reprieve. It got him hot every time.

He had looks to kill, like a wannabe rock star. Long dark hair, falling into his eyes, always the black leather jacket and the shades, knock-off Ray-Bans. He wore a thin band on his left wrist, woven by the tinkers. He didn't come from the classic horrendous background. He was that new comfortable Irish middle class—lots of attitude, smarts and a mouth on him. Raised in Galway, he'd been to the best schools, never wanted for anything. His passion was all things American.

He'd adopted a quasi-New York tone, learnt from movies and TV. His dream was to live in the Big Apple. Yeah, he actually called it that. His vocabulary was a blend of John Wayne, *The Sopranos* and De Niro. He was twelve when he discovered his talent for murder.

He had one sister, always in his face, taunting him about his long hair, his huge blue eyes that girls would swoon over. They'd been swimming, his sister and him, and literally, in a second, the voice said, "Drown the bitch."

He did. Whispered to her, "Was gonna let it slide."

The rush was near delirious, better than any jerk off to *Guns & Ammo*. And fuck, even better, he made it look like he'd tried to save her. Got all the kudos that brought.

His father was into hunting, a successful attorney. Gentry and shooting pheasants, made his dad feel like a player. Slide shot him in the back. Terrible hunting accident, shame these things happen.

Slide was suitably traumatized. Yeah, right. Laughing his arse off as they comforted him. Duped everyone except for his mother. She knew, maybe had always known. The morning of Dad's funeral, she confronted him, said, "You are the devil."

He didn't let that one slide.

Maybe the world didn't know it yet, but Slide was gonna be one of the greats. Dahmer, Bundy, Ridgway, Berkowitz, Gacy, and Slide. The only problem with this killing gig was it didn't bring in any dough. He couldn't sell his memoirs and film rights till he was dead, or at least on death row, right? He also knew if he really wanted to make his mark, he would have to move to America. In the world of killing, the land of opportunity was the big leagues. It was easier to get guns and ammo and there were lots of people who needed killing. Compared to Ireland, America would be a goddamn playground. But he needed cash to finance his dream. Piles of it.

And that was how Slide got into the kidnapping biz.

It hit him one day that he was great at abducting people. He'd done it plenty, leading up to a murder. But wasting a victim right away was a major, well, waste. He thought, Why not hold onto a few, ask the relatives for some cash, and *then* waste them? Call it his Oprah moment.

To master the art of kidnapping he studied American films like *Ransom, Frantic, Hostage,* and *Don't Say a Word*. He knew the mechanics of abduction, but had trouble on the follow-through. He knew how to do ransom notes and torture his hostages, but having a man or woman bound in his basement was way too tempting, and sometimes instead of collecting ransom, he'd kill them, chop up the bodies in his bathtub then bury them. His backyard was like downtown Baghdad—start digging, you were likely to hit bone somewhere. No one amused him like his own self and once, when his shovel clanked against an old victim, he muttered, *Boner*.

Late one evening he was out in Dublin, searching for a victim, when he saw a woman walking alone along Dawson Street, near the Mystery Inc bookstore. Now come on, was that an omen right there or what? She had acid blond hair, a full figure, kind of reminded him of a few hookers he'd offed. But she was classier than a hooker; you could see that from across the street. A woman like her, some guy would pay a fortune to get back.

The pick-up was usually the tricky part. If you're going to stuff a girl in a car, you had to move fast before she screamed her arse off. Or if you were going to lure her, you had to be clever, pour on the charm. But this woman turned the tables—she came up to him. Rushed up, more like it. Slide was baffled. This had never happened before. All his victims in the past had sensed the danger, the looming moment of truth. But this woman was fearless. Even ol' Ted Bundy would have been confused.

She sized him up, smiled, went, "Hey, I'm Angela, wanna buy me a drink?"

The rest, as they say, was history.

Three

At four in the morning, nobody's right.
THE ODD COUPLE

Angela Petrakos had arrived in Ireland with big dreams, an engagement ring, and ten grand in cash. She also had a gold pin of two hands almost touching. The pin was her lucky charm, or at least it was supposed to be. She wore it everywhere she went, figuring the luck part would have to kick in eventually.

Her first day in Dublin she sold the engagement ring to a pawnshop and blew the proceeds in about a month. Then it was time to piss away the rest of her money. The ten thousand dollars had been Max's "emergency fund," a wad he'd kept hidden, with a roll of duct tape, in a shoebox in his bedroom closet since 9/11. Angela used to go to him, "What's some money gonna do if they, like, drop the bomb?" and Max would come back with, "Who knows? I might have to bribe somebody to drive me out of the city or something." Like he thought he'd simply *drive* through a nuclear wasteland. Had anything that bollix said ever made any sense? Had she really agreed to marry him? What the hell had she been thinking?

At first she stayed in the Clarence Hotel on the Quays in Dublin, and jeez, did that Liffey stink or what? The hotel was owned by U2, but had she seen Bono, or the Edge, or even a fucking roadie? Had she fuck.

When she'd arrived her money had seemed like plenty to get started with but hey, no one told her about this strong Euro. When she'd changed her Franklins, she couldn't believe how it translated, almost cut her nest egg in half. And cash wasn't her only problem. She'd been born in Ireland but raised in the States. In America, her accent was always recognized as Irish and a definite plus. Here they heard her as a Yank and kept busting her chops about Iraq. Like she sent the troops in. She didn't even know where the shithole was.

One day she returned to her room and discovered her key card was no longer working. Beautiful, right? Bono was canceling world debt but not, it seemed, hotel bills. Leaving the hotel, down in the zero, she fingered the pin in her lapel. It was like a prayer she almost believed.

She needed more Euro and she wasn't about to go looking for a job. After a string of bad jobs in America she'd had it with working. Besides, the demand for office assistants who typed twenty words a minute wasn't exactly staggering. A man had always been her first step to money, to getting on track. *Get a guy, get centered* was her motto. The fact that men had fucked her over each and every time had slipped her mind.

She walked along Ormond Quay, passed the very fashionable Morrison Hotel. Unfortunately she didn't have enough to buy a goddamn coffee in there. She continued, her hopes sinking as she watched the area take an Irish dive. Then she hit the fleabags, where the "non-nationals" were housed, and found the River Inn. It reminded her of some of the shitholes she'd seen on the Bowery and the Lower East Side.

The guy behind the desk snarled, "Money up front, no visitors in the rooms and..." The motherfooker gave her the look, sneered, added, "No clients in the rooms unless you want to pay extra."

She was mortified, like the scumbag was calling her a hooker.

She roared, "You'll get yours, you bastard."

He would, but not in any way Angela could possibly have foreseen.

Angela's room was shite, simple as that. When she turned on the light, the roaches scattered, as if they didn't want to be there either. Cum stains on the bedspread—God only knew what the sheets looked like—crusted snot on the pillow cases, dirty towels thrown on the floor, and a turd floating in the toilet. Jaysus, good thing she wasn't planning to spend very long—maybe, if her prayers were answered, not even a single night. Dressed to kill, in fuck-me heels, the micro skirt and the sheer black hose, she set out to score.

She went to Davy Byrnes on Duke Street. Her *Lonely Planet* guide—and fuck they got that right, she was as lonely as a banshee without a wail—said it was the watering hole for the yuppies, the moneyed young whizzers. Mott the Hoople's "All the Young Dudes" had unspooled in her head when she read that.

Well, the place had men all right—older men. Okay, she could do old, long as they had the moolah.

Guy in his fifties hit on her right away, said he was an accountant. His name was Michael. He was bald. He was barely five feet tall. But, most importantly, he owned lots of stock and property—including a place in the South of France—and, the clincher, he drove a Merc. Want to find a good man, find out what kind of car they drive. Michael gave her some shite about James Joyce drinking at Davy Byrnes. She thought, *God, is that his line?* She thought she'd heard them all, but a guy trying to win her over with Joyce was a brand new experience. Over the next year, she'd be hard pressed to enter a pub that Joyce hadn't rested his elbow on. She'd sometimes wonder, when did he get the time to write all them impossible-to-read books? If he was drinking that much, no wonder the writing was so incomprehensible. And another thing, everyone in Ireland bored the ass offa her about him but no one had seemed to have actually read him. They'd seen the Angelica Huston movie and that was the whole of their Joyce expertise. Go figure.

She moved in with Michael pronto at his flat in Foxrock. No zip codes in Ireland, probably because the wild bastards couldn't count. They uttered some neighborhoods in hushed tones, with the appendage Dublin 4, and that was enough.

Foxrock was most definitely Dublin 4 and Michael was lovely, as the Irish say, for a while. He took her out for nice posh meals, bought her silk lingerie from Ann Summers, Dublin's version of Victoria's Secret. Course, being a man, he bought stuff he liked that no woman would ever wear. She brought it all back, got the cash, building towards a nest egg. Good thing. Like so many times before, with so many other guys, he turned. Once they'd screwed you, once you were, as Irish men so delicately put it, well shagged, they lost interest. Michael's personality turned too. Where was the accountant who'd seemed like an Irish version of Jason Alexander? All the weak bollix had ever hit was the books and now, now he was walloping her! The silver-tongued devil.

One night, after watching *What's Love Got To Do With It?* and listening to Nancy Sinatra, Angela felt empowered and took off. Went right to an ATM and withdrew as much of Michael's cash as she could. Angela's rule: before you let a guy ride you, you get his account details. In his case, it was easy. The code for his ATM was JOYCE. She couldn't make this shit up.

It was back to the River Inn and the sneer of the gobshite at the desk. So began a year of hell, the search for Mr. Right. There were ups and downs—mostly downs. Men supported her for a while, seemed to truly like her, but there was always a flip side. Married men told her they were single just to get laid, underage guys told her they were eighteen. One night, she was date-raped by a lawyer. Angela managed to get to the bathroom, grab a can of Lysol, and spray it into the cunt's eyes, but she was starting to see a disturbing pattern here. She was a magnet for trouble. She was seriously thinking about packing it in, going to play for the other team. She wasn't attracted to women, but she wasn't attracted to a lot of the guys she was sleeping with either. Besides, it seemed like every guy she got involved with wound up hurting her. And it wasn't just emotional pain. No, these men were leaving visible scars.

Self-help books were no help. *Richard and Judy*—fuck 'em. Even a talk with a shrink didn't do crap. She didn't go into formal therapy, but one night she started talking to a woman who was staying in the room next door to her. The woman mentioned she was a counselor and Angela invited her to a pub for a drink. When Angela started to describe some of her experiences with men, the woman started checking her watch, suddenly announced she had "an appointment." Angela never saw the woman again.

Soon afterward, she hit rock bottom. It was her thirtieth birthday. Her clock was ticking. She didn't have many eggs and she knew she'd be a great mother, she knew she had so much to give. It was back in the fishnet hose, back to pumps, back to the same old same old.

After a night of fending off the usual losers, she headed back to the hotel. She was wondering if it was all worth it and was considering a life of celibacy. Was it too late to become a nun?

Then she saw him, watching her from across the street. It was Bono. Well, close enough anyway. He had the rock star gig going on full force, with the hair, the sunglasses. Not Bono-style glasses—they looked like knockoff Ray-Bans—but, hey.

She was tired of waiting for guys to come up to her, being so fucking passive. Didn't the psychology books say she had to assert herself? So when she saw him staring at her, she thought,

Who the fook cares anymore, and went up to him, and said, "Hi, I'm Angela, want to buy me a drink?"

The line worked like magic. Better yet, she could tell he had a good soul, that she'd found the real thing. Had it always been this easy?

He offered to skip the drink part and go right back to his place. Angela wasn't opposed. With a ticking clock, you had to move fast. Hell, if he asked her to marry her in the morning she'd say yes. As long as he was decent in bed, was willing to support her and her children, what did she have to lose?

There were a few things early on that caught her attention. He drove a Toyota. No Merc but, hey, it wasn't a mini either. She noticed a strange odor in the car, like he'd washed it with ammonia. On the dashboard was a St. Bridget's Cross, and when she asked him where the name Slide came from, he said, "From the Old Irish." She wasn't sure what this meant, but she figured, he was a religious guy—good sign. Then again, the micks, they'd kill you for a five spot and confess in the morning.

They went to a small house—more like a cabin—on the outskirts of the city, some place named Swords.

When they entered, Angela went, "Ted Kaczynski live here?" but for some reason the joke fell flat. Okay, so maybe he didn't have a sense of humor and he wasn't much of a talker either, but he was still cute as hell. She was dying to be kissed or—who was she kidding?—humped. If this didn't lead to a relationship, at least she'd get a good lay. She hadn't gotten any in over a month and when Angela Petrakos wasn't getting any, look out world.

His place was, if not dirty, in need of a woman's touch, that was for sure. There were beer cans on the couch, garbage on the coffee table. Then she saw rope and chains, which got her hopes up—maybe he was into kinky sex? But when she asked him about it, he muttered, "Haulage business," and changed the subject, going, "Sorry me flat is such a wreck."

She didn't want to tell him that she was *way* into the whole chain thing. At this early stage, she didn't want to make him think she was *that* kind of girl or anything. Much later, she'd learn all about restraints, the kidnapping, but not yet.

There was more painful silence as she watched him go around, cleaning the place.

Then she asked, "Do you read Joyce?" figuring she'd get that nonsense out of the way fast.

He gave her the look, the same one he gave her when they met on the street. His eyes had, what? A shine? A light? No, more like a fevered intensity. She liked them...a lot.

He said, "I've done Joyce, but I prefer non-fiction, *mi amor*. You familiar with *The Road Less Traveled*?"

What was with the Italian and was he trying to talk with a New York accent? He must've been trying to impress her, because she'd lived in New York. He was so cute, the pet.

Liking him more and more—which usually meant there was trouble ahead and lots of it—she asked, "You haven't ever been an accountant, have you?"

After a rich, warm-the-cockles-of-yer-heart laugh, he said, "Baby, the one accounting I do is off the books."

She laughed her own self. Christ on a bike, how long since she'd done that? A year? Not since New York, and even then there wasn't exactly a lot to laugh about.

He got a turf fire going, gave the room a nice glow, and then they began to fool around a bit. Nothing heavy, the guy wasn't all over her. He was tender almost. Then he made some hot toddies, even added cloves, saying, "Cloves, cos, I'm like the devil, baby."

Things heated up. They got naked and he said, "Turn around

for me." Like an order, but she was into it. Then he took her fiercely and abruptly and she came with a scream.

Lying alongside her afterward, not even breathing heavy, he asked, "You know I was planning to kidnap you, right?"

Angela, playing along, still nearly breathless, gasped, "Kidnap me anytime you want, baby."

Four

*I grabbed her thin wrist, jerking her onto the bed. I was
more than brutal, savage really; I didn't even go through
the preliminary of kissing the dumbfounded girl.*
CHARLES WILLEFORD, *The Woman Chaser*

Max's big plan: mug the chambermaid, use her five bucks to ride the Greyhound outa this shithole.

The maid knocked again, went, "*Hola,*" and Max was ready to rock 'n' roll. He stuck his hand under his wife-beater like a concealed gun, opened the door, and went, "*Hola* right back atcha, sweetheart." Then he took a closer look, saw a young smiling pregnant girl holding a stack of towels, and he couldn't go through with it. What was he gonna do, roll some knocked-up Spanish broad for her last *pesetas*? What kind of guy was he? Okay, okay, he was desperate, but come on.

He took the hand out of his shirt, said, "Sorry, *señorita*, it was just a joke, *Avril* fools," and slammed the door in her face.

What the fuck was he gonna do now? He still needed a way out of this mess. If he had to spend any more time in Alabama his brain would start to erode, he'd become as stupid as that kid at the desk. Next thing, he'd be eyeing sheep.

Okay, he thought, *Who can I call? Who can bail me out?*

He couldn't think of a single name and, at some point, passed out.

When he woke up, his head was splitting, felt like it was falling off. Then, he realized that was because it *was* falling off. Well, off the bed anyway. Not really, but he was lying on his back, with his head at the foot of the bed, his mouth sagging, like he was doing a backwards, upside-down blow job scene in a porn movie.

He called his bank in New York. He was surprised to find out he only had $632 to his name. How the hell'd that happen? He thought he'd had two grand last time he checked. He arranged to have money wired but since it was Saturday and because he was no longer a preferred client—what the fuck?—he would have to wait until Monday morning before the money arrived.

This was crazy—how would he survive two more days in Robertsdale? He needed food and more booze, not necessarily in that order.

He left the room, headed back to the motel's office. The sun was as bright as car headlights shining directly in his face. Did the sun, like, ever set in the south?

The blond kid at the desk was on the phone again. Max had to wait till he was off, but this time he had to be polite about it—after all, the kid could be his meal ticket.

When the kid ended the call, Max offered his widest, most congenial smile, and said, "I have a bit of a… um…er… um… problem."

Max let the smile linger and then realized the kid was looking at him in a weird way. Max was clueless for a few seconds, wondering if staring was another side effect of the kid's mental disorder, and then realized it was because of the missing tooth.

"Oh, yeah," Max said. "Cap fell out last night. Fucking dentist. When I get back to the city, his ass is so fired."

Max continued smiling.

The kid went, "So how can I help you, sir?"

Southerners, they were so goddamn polite. You can stick a knife in a guy's back and he'd go, *Thank you, sir. Have a good day now, hear?*

"Yeah, well, I seem to've, um, er, lost my wallet. Not my wallet itself—I still have that five-dollar piece of shit. I'm talking about what was inside it—the cash, credit cards. You know, my money."

"Sorry to hear that, sir."

Sure he was.

"So I was just curious," Max said, "did I happen to leave a credit card with y'all at the desk?"

That was the way, slip in "y'alls" and Southern-speak whenever possible. Max wanted to show the kid that deep down, despite all their differences—like level of intellect, etcetera—they were one and the same.

"No, actually, sir, you're all paid up."

What the fuck? Max never, ever paid for anything in advance. He almost shit himself—literally. He cut a nasty booze-fart then asked, "What?"

"The Chinese guy paid for your room, up front in cash, sir."

The kid was smiling, like he knew. But knew what?

"Chinese guy?" Max said. "What Chinese guy?"

"He seemed like a friend of yours. He had his arm around you."

The kid gave another knowing, smirking look.

Max remembered, when he'd woken up, feeling some pain in his rectum. He'd thought, *hemorrhoids?* But was it possible that....

Oh, God, Max didn't even want to go there. If this wasn't a wake-up call he didn't know what was. From now on, no more mixing Scotch and vodka. He had to draw a line somewhere, right? And didn't Chinese, like, wear off fast? Five minutes later, you wanted more? Holy shit.

"Whatever, whatever," Max said. "So the room's paid through the weekend, right?"

"No, actually, sir, you were supposed to check out today. The Chinese guy—that's right, said his name was Bruce. Yeah, he took off early this morning."

Max was thinking, *Bruce!* Fuck, if that wasn't a gay name, what was? Wait, Bruce Lee wasn't gay. He'd had a kid anyway. And Bruce and Demi had had a whole litter, hadn't they? There was still hope.

"Look, here's the bottom line," Max said. "I don't have any money, and I won't have any money till Monday morning. So what I need you to do is front me."

"Sir, we can't—"

"Look at me, kid. Understand who you're dealing with. I'm Maximilian Fisher. I'm a man of wealth and fame."

The kid looked confused. Shit, the missing tooth, the dirty wife-beater, and the farting wasn't helping Max's cause.

Max went, "You're not superficial, are you...sorry, what's your name?"

"Kyle," the kid said. "My mom and dad, they were big *Twin Peaks* fans."

Not in the mood to hear the kid's life story, Max said, "Okay, okay Kyle...Look, what I need y'all to do right now is look beyond what you see in front of you. Ignore appearances, ignore perceptions." Max realized he was using big words; he had to dumb it down, keep it to one or two syllables, or the kid would get confused. Max went, "Just because I don't look rich, don't mean I ain't." Shit, that was too dumb. He didn't want to offend the moron. Bringing the level of conversation back up, Max said, "Look, Kyle, I've dabbled in Buddhism, okay? I'm not a monk or anything like that, but I meditate, get into myself, you know? And what I've learned from my studies, I mean the bottom line of all of it, is that the real world is bullshit, it doesn't even exist. What really exists is what doesn't exist at all—the inner self. So let's talk to each other, one inner self to the other here and—"

"Sorry, Mr. Fisher, I can't front you on the room."

Fuck Buddhism. Max wanted to strangle the dumb hick.

"You have Web access at this shithole?" Max asked.

"Yep, we sure do," Kyle said, "but—"

"Lemme show you a thing or two," Max said.

Max got behind the desk and went online. Although his company, NetWorld, had gone belly-up, the website was still live. When Kyle saw the picture of Max sitting on the red Porsche with the two D-cup blond bimbos alongside him, below the company slogan NETWORLD OR BUST, his eyes nearly left their sockets.

"You like those knockers, huh?" Max said.

"Yes, sir, I sure do but—"

"Would you like to meet these girls?"

Long pause, then Kyle asked, "Are they here?"

"No, but I'll tell you what I'll do," Max said. "Next time I'm in Alabama, I'll bring Cindy and Bambi with me, and you can take them up to a room with you, and spend the whole weekend banging their brains out. How'd y'all like that, Kyle?"

"That would be pretty nice," Kyle said. "But when y'all planning to be in Robertsdale again?"

Thinking, When fucking hell freezes, Max said, "Next weekend. I'm here on business and I'll bring the girls with me. What do you say?"

Kyle stared at the monitor for a while longer—did Max see drool? The kid had probably never met a girl outside of church.

Finally Kyle got a hold of himself, said, "Okay, sir. Sounds cool."

Max shook Kyle's hand firmly, sealing the deal. Then Max felt his stomach rumble—the mini-mart on the other side of the office, with the Cheez Whiz and the Pringles and the cans of Bud—especially the cans of Bud—was looking mighty good.

"I'll tell you what, Kyle," Max said. "How about we add a little rider to our deal? Cindy has a twin sister, Lolita, looks exactly like her except her garbanzos are a cup size larger. Lolita loves Southern guys. How about I toss Lolita into the mix and you let me raid the mini-mart this weekend?"

The prospect of three girls at once was too much for Kyle. He looked like he was going to have a stroke, or an orgasm, or *something* massive and, yep, that was drool all right.

He went, "G-g-go on. You can take all the food you want, Mr. Maximilian, sir."

Max went up to his room with a few six-packs of Bud and munchies to last the weekend. He had never been a beer man —the low alcohol content didn't work for him—but as he began to guzzle the brews he found after nine or ten he had a pretty good buzz going. Then he kept up a "maintenance level" of one or two an hour, like he was on alcohol cruise control.

In New York, he'd been eating healthy—well, trying anyway. He had a bad heart; even with Lipitor, his cholesterol was a mess and when was the last time he'd taken Lipitor? The Pop-Tarts alone were probably clogging the shit out of his arteries, but, Eh, the beer was cleaning 'em out. Checks and balances, right? You take some shit, then you wash it down with good vibes. Max was so blasted he had no idea what the fuck any of this meant but, hell, he'd drink to that.

Sometime Friday night, Max passed out. When he woke up on Saturday—unless he'd missed a day, not exactly beyond the realm of possibility—he started drinking again. The routine was getting old fast, but unless he went sober, he had to keep the brews flowing.

On Sunday night, Max ran out of munchies. He went down to the office, saw the kid at the desk with some black guy. He looked like a gangbanger, with the dreadlocks or whatever, wearing a Denver Nuggets jersey with SPREWELL 8 on the back, and a black stocking on his head. What was up with that anyway? Next thing, they'd be walking around with garters around their necks.

Kyle and the black guy were having a hushed conversation but stopped talking when Max came in. The black guy glared at Max, looking like he wanted to pull out his piece and blow him away. Kyle looked like he was shitting bricks.

"I'll check you later," Kyle said to the black guy, and the guy said, "Yeah, whatever," and walked by Max, bumping into him hard with his shoulder, going, "'Scuse me," but not like he meant it.

When the black guy was gone, Kyle said to Max, "If you want more Budweiser you can go 'head and take it."

Max, toasted but still plenty with it, went, "What're you doing, making drug deals down here?" He asked it as a joke, but going by the kid's reaction he realized he'd hit the nail on the head. Fuck, Kyle the slow-talking church boy was a dealer. Who would've thought?

"N-n-no, sir," he said, shitting some more bricks. "He's just an, um, old friend'a mine from, uh, high school."

"Don't worry," Max said, "I'm not a fucking narc. C'mon, gimme a break, kid—wise up. If I was a fuckin' cop would I really be hanging out here, OD'ing on Bud and Cheez Whiz? I mean, going undercover is one thing, but would I torture myself to make a bust? So what kind of shit you dealing? Weed, sense, bud, blow?"

Yeah, that was the way—use all the hip lingo to show the kid he was streetwise, *a player*.

Kyle smiled, said, "Naw, it's not like that, Mr. Maximilian. That there was just my friend, Darnell, and me and Darnell, we was just—"

"Look, you don't gotta bullshit me, all right?" Max said. "Truth is, I've got some dealing experience myself. In seventh grade, I dealt weed, shrooms, and speed. How do you think I got to be such a respected businessman? The drug business is just like any other business. You have a product, you have a customer, and you have margins. I was growing the shit in my closet. Had a tree up to the ceiling, and got some serious bud off it. So you don't have to beat around the bush with me, kid—no pun intended."

Max laughed. Man, he was on fire tonight. Fuckin' smoking. That old Bud, maybe it cleaned out the debris, let his razor-sharp mind get cooking.

Kyle stared at Max for a while, then said, "Can I pat you down?"

"Ah, Jesus Christ," Max said. Then, realizing the kid wasn't joking, went, "Go 'head, go 'head."

Kyle frisked Max, doing it so slow Max started to wonder, Is this kid from Brokeback Mountain or what?

Finally, satisfied Max wasn't a narc, Kyle said, "It was crack, sir."

Max went, "Crack? You're shitting me. Didn't that go out in the nineties?"

"You'd be surprised," the kid said. "There's still a good market for it. A niche market, but still."

Listen to this kid, *niche market*. Like he was on goddamn CNBC.

"You using or selling?" Max asked.

Kyle hesitated, as if wondering, maybe it wasn't such a good idea to divulge he was involved in crack deals to a total stranger, even if that total stranger wasn't a narc. Then, looking like he was thinking *Well, told him this much—mise well tell him the rest*, Kyle said, "Selling."

Kyle a crack dealer! Max was beside himself, almost started laughing. He remembered Angela had had a whole other spin on *crack*—freaking mick-speak. Over there, they spelled it *craic*, which meant "party on" or some shit. But why was he thinking about that bitch now?

The kid was asking, "You want to check some out?"

Max had done coke *mucho* times before. Fuck, he'd spent half the eighties at Studio 54 and the Palladium, snorting mountains of blow. But he had enough trouble in his life. He didn't need a goddamn crack habit.

"What do I look like, some low-rent nigger?"

God, had he said that out loud? Hello, filter, where are you? Thank God Darnell wasn't around to hear that one.

"I mean negro," Max said. "I mean person of colored. What-the-fuck-ever."

"Actually," Kyle said, "that attitude is a misperception."

"What is?" Max asked, surprised Kyle knew such a big word. Four syllables—Jesus.

"That African-Americans make up the majority of crack users," Kyle said. "My clientele is all races. Heck, I'm white and I smoke it."

Kyle on crack. This Max had to see.

Max said, "This I have to see."

"You're already seein' it," Kyle said. "I was basin' with Darnell about ten minutes ago."

Max knew Kyle wasn't fucking with him, but he didn't get it. Weren't crackheads supposed to talk fast? This kid sounded like Gomer Fucking Pyle. If this was the way he spoke on crack, Max couldn't imagine how slow his brain worked normally.

Maybe this crack wasn't as powerful as they said it was. Maybe it wasn't all it was cracked up to be.

"Cook me up some of your shit," Max said.

Keeping his tone casual, like he was one cool dude. Like whatever you had, bring it on.

Kyle hung the BE BACK IN FIVE MINUTES sign on the door and took Max to the back room. As Kyle prepared "the rock," he was telling Max all about his dealing business, how he was taking in a grand a weekend and he only worked at the motel so his parents—"I was raised by good ol' God-fearin' Christians"— would think he was holding down a decent job. Max was feeling something he thought he'd forgotten, that elusive goddess— hope. If Kyle could pull down a grand a week as a crack dealer, imagine what a savvy city slicker like Max Fisher could rake in. Was the sky the limit or what?

The pipe was ready. Max took it, then hesitated, wondering if this was such a great idea. After all, he had an addictive personality. Then he thought, C'mon, how was he gonna endorse the product if he couldn't road test it? You gotta try it before you recommend it. That was the first law of the American corporate bible, right?

Max inhaled. A few seconds later he was fucking flying, like he was fucking God. Even better—like he could kick God's ass.

"This shit is good," Max said.

Man, it was great to finally crawl out of the hole, to have that old Max Fisher energy back. Yeah, get all that Bud outa there and put the rock in its place. Talk about wake-up calls. This was the mother of all wake-up calls. Fuck the ashrams and Om sessions—the secret to true enlightenment was a crack pipe. Man, Max's brain was working as fast as it could. Yeah, he could probably go on the wagon for three weeks and he would've still failed a sobriety, but he was thinking one thing—he could make a fortune with this shit.

Max said frantically, "Can Darnell mule this shit up to me in the city? Well, can he or can't he? Answer the goddamn question."

Kyle started to answer, but Max couldn't wait all day for the slow fuck.

Max went, "Say hello to your new business partner," then brought the pipe back up to his lips and took another hit of enlightenment.

Five

He decided to let it slide,
let the shades do the talking, like rock stars did.
KEN BRUEN AND JASON STARR, *Bust*

Slide was getting his shit together. He had his kidnap victim, Angela, tied up in bed, and now he needed some—what did the brothers call it? Oh, yeah, *mo…ti…vation*. Get that Harlem laid-back emphasis going on.

Angela had told him about the guy in the River Inn, calling her a hooker, *dissing her*. Thing was, Slide hadn't offed anyone for, like, eons. What had it been, a week? And he especially hadn't done somebody for, you know, fun. He'd done the last schmucks for cash, but when had he done one for the sheer heat, the rush, that fucking adrenaline gig? That was what he was talking about, brother.

He got his carpet cutter out, honed the edge. The Guards stopped you, you went, "Hey man, I'm a carpet layer, tools of the trade." That he'd never laid anything but broads was beside the point.

He left a note for Angie, after handcuffing her to the bed. Went:

> *Babe*
> *T.C.B.*
> *El.*

In the car, the thought struck him, Would she know that El was the King and that T.C.B. was, like, his mantra?

Sure, for fook's sake. She was a Yank, had to know all that shit.

He got to the River Inn and sure enough, a punk at the counter, sneer in place.

Slide asked, "Got a room, mate?" Using his English accent.

Slide knew if you wanted to make them record books, you better have a shiteload of talents, mimicry for one. The Brit was simple, just act like you had a lump of coal in yer mouth and act like a complete prick. Piece of cake, or rather, piece of crumpet. Jolly fooking hockey sticks.

That Slide was shite at accents never occurred to him.

The counter guy stared at him, as if thinking, *What's with this wanker?* Asked with a smirk, "You got twenty Euro?"

Slide was delighted. The guy was even better than he hoped—he was giving mouth.

Deciding to fuck with him, Slide adopted a timid voice, went, "Why?"

The guy, not hiding his disdain at all now, said, "You got twenty Euro, I might have a room."

Slide took a quick look around. Coast was clear and, best, no CCTV. What'd you expect, the place was a kip.

He plopped a wad of crumpled notes onto the counter, mumbled, "Is that enough for ya?"

The guy sighed—he could have sighed for Ireland—and leaned down to sort the notes.

Slide grabbed the mother by his lanky hair, going, "Jeez, you ever hear of shampoo?" and then slit his throat from left to right. He stepped back, there was always a geyser. Sure enough, here it came—fucking fountain of the red stuff, *whoosh*, there she blew. Slide never ceased to be struck with admiration by the pure power of the splurt.

The guy was gargling, emitting strangled moans, and Slide

said, "Was gonna let it slide, know what I mean? Running yer mouth there, mate. Well, let's fix that. You think?"

He took off the guy's lips. It took a while—harder than you'd think to slice evenly. Sometimes you got gum—not chewing gum, the other kind. Though sometimes you got chewing gum too.

Slide took the fuck's wallet. It had, like, fifteen Euro and a photo of a dark-haired woman. Slide kept that. Figured he'd show it to some chick sometime, say the girl in the photo was his childhood sweetheart who broke his heart. Always good for a pity fuck, right?

He was outa there, the lips in his jacket. For a moment, he imagined the lips talking, giving it large. He had such a hard-on, couldn't wait to ride Angela with the handcuffs. Then, mid-orgasm, *hers*, he'd kiss her with the guy's lips, go, "No lip from you now."

She'd get a kick outa that.

Six

*It started as kind of a joke, and then it wasn't
funny anymore because money became involved.
Deep down, nothing about money is funny.*
CHARLES WILLEFORD, *The Shark-Infested Custard*

Angela tried to open her eyes, couldn't see, and thought, *Jaysus, have I gone blind?* Or, wait, it was the mascara glued solid. She knew she always overdid the goo, an echo back to her brief stint as a goth chick. But no, this was, like, what, her eyes were covered?

And what the hell was up with her right hand, like it was suspended, and when she pulled, she felt metal grate on her wrist. She managed to sit up and, with her left hand, tore off the covering on her eyes. A blindfold? What the fuck? Then it came flooding back.

Slide, the demented bastard, telling her blindfolds were a huge kick and pouring vast amounts of Jameson down her throat, not like she was fighting it. A year of near poverty in Dublin, was she going to turn down some decent hooch? Yeah, right.

But, Jesus, she needed to pee and now.

Then she saw that the handcuff on her right wrist was attached to the bar above the bed. She yanked at it and it chaffed her wrist, probably tore off some skin. She didn't remember agreeing to that kink.

Or had she?

She did remember, after the first time, when he took her fast, doggy-style—that was nice—they did shots of Jameson. Then he suggested another go and, Jaysus, it was even better the second time—hot, heavy, fevered and wild. It had been a while since she'd lost control like that—not since her old boyfriend, Dillon. Dillon had turned out to be a raging psycho but, boy, he knew how to screw.

Slide, it seemed, had a little Dillon in him. She vaguely recalled him shouting, "Ride me yah bitch, go on yah wild thing!"

The Irish male—they might not be subtle but, Christ, they sure were vocal. When he came, she felt a delicious frisson, and then he roared, as if he was dying, "Ah sweet mother ah fook me!....Yah hoor's ghost!....Aw bollix, I love yah!....Yah filthy cunt!" Celtic terms of endearment, right?

And the other thing, every one of them, when they had an orgasm, screamed not blue murder but green mothers. Angela shuddered, realizing that the Irish matriarch wasn't exactly what she wanted to think about in the throes of a ferocious hangover.

She roared, "Slide, I want to be released now! Joke's over and goddamn it, I need to pee. You hear me?"

She listened but, nope, no sign of the Irish fucker.

Then she had an epiphany—she no longer thought of her own self as Irish. How did that happen? She'd been raised in New York, in a Greek-Irish home where the Irish influence was the dominant theme. She knew more about the Boyos than the Yankees, and had bodhrans, spoons, accordions, all around the house. Oh, there'd been plenty of melancholy. Everything, we're talking every single thing, was a tragedy. Her dad had always said, Give a mick lots of grief, pain, sorrow and he was as happy as a pig in shite. Maybe all that rain had something to do with it. They had to occupy themselves somehow so they spent their time pissing and moaning. And Jesus, could they moan.

"Slide, you fookin cunt bastard, I'll have your eyes out, ye demented fool!"

Yep, her year in Dublin had literally robbed her of her Irishness all right. And she wasn't the only one losing it—the whole fookin country wasn't Irish anymore. Everybody spoke in bad American accents, wore Harvard or Knicks sweatshirts and watched *The OC, The Sopranos, Deadwood,* and *The Simpsons.* And, get this, on Sundays, Sky TV showed baseball! Irish guys who wouldn't know their Mantle from their Aaron were talking about *stepping up to the base, second innings, pitchers, catchers* and the *World Series.* How fucked is that?

At a pub one night, Angela asked a baseball fan, "What happened to hurling and shillelaghs?" and the guy went, "Shut yer mouth, woman. Jeter's batting."

And, sin of sins, the guy was drinking Coors Light, for God's sake, with a glass of water as a chaser, as if the shite wasn't watered down enough already.

Truth was, Angela missed America. She wanted a real goddamn sandwich. In Ireland, they gave you slices of thin white bread. No rye, no whole wheat, no fookin pumpernickel. Then they added a shaving of something called *ham* and some sort of dead leaf they claimed was lettuce. Lettuce pray for fucking patience! She wanted to go home, get some meatballs and mashed potatoes, where you didn't have to pay for a second shot of coffee, where a hero was a real sandwich and where people spoke real English.

"Slide, you cunt bastard!"

She'd had enough of the game, if that was what this was. She had to pee like hell, and Christ, she needed a hit of nicotine. Yeah, yeah, she'd started smoking again. How could she help it? Despite the ban in Ireland, it seemed the whole country huddled outside pubs, smoking their fool heads off. Then, one night, she'd learned the reason why. Some girl told her it was the new way to hook up—flirting with a smoke. Slirting or some shite they called it. Well, she'd been slirting her ass off and what good did it do her? She was half-drunk, chained naked to a bed in some cabin on the outskirts of Dublin, waiting for a man who was possibly deranged to come free her.

The cigs were on the table, tantalizingly out of reach. If Slide had done that deliberately, she'd cut his balls off. See if she wouldn't.

She roared, "C'mon yah bollix, enough with the screwing around, like hello, game over?" And she figured she must still be a bit drunk as she added in a screech, "What's a gal gotta do to get a drink around here?"

Then she heard a car pulling into the drive. A few moments later, there he was, and she launched, "Yah prick, yah storming major asshole, yah…"

From the tent in his pants, her tirade was turning him on and, guess what, she was a little heated her own self.

Then he was on her and they were at it like mad things—sweaty, perverted, debauched, and delighted.

Jesus, she was on fire, hollered, "Kiss me yah bollix!" and Slide slipped his hand into his pocket and then seemed to rub something onto his lips. She thought, *Chapstick now?*

Then he was kissing her. Felt weird, kinda cold—was it some new kind of oral condom or something? And, fuck, she still had to mention the little item of her having, um, you know, herpes.

Before she could say anything, he whispered, "Lips to die for," and he was between her legs again, giving it, as the Brits say, *large*.

God, she roared like a hyena. And, Jesus, those lips—it was like Angelina Jolie was going down on her.

When he'd finally surfaced, he tossed something into the litter bin, said, "Loose lips sink ships."

The fuck was he on about? He got out of bed and she admired his bod. Then he was uncuffing her and she finally got to have that pee. When she returned, he had two cigs lighted and there was a glint in his eye. If she didn't know better, she'd have suspected he wanted to burn her. Yeah, like she was going to let that happen. In New York, she'd dated a married Puerto Rican guy for a while. Not one of her better choices in men but, hey, he looked kind of like Ricky Martin. Okay, in the right light, from the right angle, with beer goggles, but she'd been in a slump with the guys. One night he whispered to her in a sexy Latino tone, "You wanna golden shower, baby." Not as a question, but as if saying, You're getting a golden shower and now. Christ, she was so innocent then. She thought they'd cover themselves in gold leaf or something, hop in the shower and, like, well, maybe lick it off each other. You know, something romantic. So imagine her shock when he'd started pissing on her. She went along with it—what the hell?—but when he broke the news about his family in San Juan she kicked him right in the nuts, shouted, "You won't be pissing, golden or otherwise, for a Spanish month, yeh bastard!"

If Slide tried to burn her, God help him.

But, no, he let her take one of the cigs. As she took a long drag of it, he said, "Let's go out, have a jar, I want to run something by you."

She thought, *The romantic fool, is it marriage?* She knew she'd been good in bed, but was she *that* good? She'd only known him what, a few hours, but, hell, she wasn't about to let an opportunity like this slip away. She didn't want to be one of those single women in their forties who look back at their lives, regretting the one that got away. Though she had some, well, concerns about Slide, she had a gut feeling that he was a good man, and would make a wonderful father. Her gut feelings had rarely been right, but she figured, bad luck didn't last forever, right?

The place was called the Touchdown Bar and Grill. As they got out of the car, Angela went, "Jeez, how Irish is that?"

A huge sign inside proclaimed, KARAOKE TONIGHT, and she wondered, Were they, like, trying to scare business away?

The place was hopping—three deep at the bar and all shouting for Bud Light, Corona, and Miller.

On the stage, a middle-aged woman, looking like a very poor man's Desperate Housewife, was massacring "I Will Survive."

Angela shouted at the stage, "Not if you don't stop that singing, you won't!"

When the woman got to the part about how she was going to walk out the door, Angela said, "You and me both, lady," and then she said to Slide, "I need some air. There's a pub down the road, how about we go there instead?"

Slide wasn't keen but she rubbed his crotch, purred, "If staying here is what you want, then, okay."

She was wondering, Does he have a ring? If he did, it better be a fookin' diamond—a big one. And if he was the typical Irishman and tried to propose to her with a Claddagh ring, Lord help him.

Slide led her through the crowd, going, "Lady coming through."

They found a space at the bar, ordered large Bushmills with Guinness chasers.

She whined, "Don't I get to choose my own drink?".

He shoved her glasses at her, said, "You have what I have."

Mr. Taking Command, but she liked it.

A huge painting of—what else?—a baseball player hung on the wall and Slide sneered, "I see your point about this baseball shite, babe. What do we know about American sport?"

Without thinking, Angela corrected, "*Sports*. We say American *sports*."

Slide gave her a look that shouted, *Never correct my American again, ever*.

Then he toasted, "Here's looking at you, kiddo."

She was going to correct him, go, It's *kid*, but had a feeling she'd better keep her mouth shut.

They did a few more of The Bush and that sucker slid on down so easy, packed its own potent wallop. Next thing, Slide was on stage, doing "My Way," the anthem of macho losers the world over. He wasn't awful but, then again, anything was a relief after having to listen to that dame sing disco.

Angela felt eyes on hers and saw a well-dressed guy smiling at her. She noticed the gold Rolex and the deep tan. Yeah, he was a player. And he had great teeth. In Ireland, that translated as, Cash and lots of it.

In the back of her mind, she was already thinking, *Slide? Slide who?*

Then Slide was back, asking, "Did you like my singing?"

She gushed, "God, it was beautiful, you could make a career of it."

Dumb fuck believed her too. Was there one man on the goddamn planet who if you told him he was the greatest, didn't buy it?

He gave a *Gee shucks* almost shy grin, said, "Remind me to do 'Stairway to Heaven' for you, I improvise all the instruments too."

She suppressed a shudder, went, "I can hardly wait."

Slide got a six-pack to go and they were in the parking lot, his hands all over her.

Then they heard, "Hey, wait up," and saw the Rolex guy swaggering over.

"Hey, where you dudes headed?"

Dudes, with a thick Irish accent.

Slide thumbed a bottle from the six, asked, "Like a brew, dude?" Then he smashed the bottle on the car, put the jagged shards into the guy's face.

Grinding the bottle in, he went, "There you go, dude, it's Miller time."

Then he took the guy's wallet and Rolex and shouted to Angela, "Get in the car, we're so outa here. You drive, baby."

Looking at the wailing guy trying to pull the bottle out of his face, she said, "But, Slide, why did you have to—"

"I said get in the fookin' car and drive, woman."

Angela got in. It took her a moment to figure out the gears, as she was accustomed to automatic. But by luck more than skill she got the thing in gear and got out of there, fast.

Slide was going through the guy's wallet, shouting, "Jesus wept, there is a god, there's a shitpile of cash in here, this bastard was seriously carrying, you know what this means, babe?"

She knew what it meant—her new boyfriend was seriously deranged. The casual violence, the way he'd chopped down the poor guy. There was something romantic about it, but still.

She said, "Did you have to, you know, go so far?"

Slide gave her a mega smile, crooned, "I did it my way."

Slide was modeling the Rolex, turning it on his wrist, letting the light bounce off of it. Angela was thinking, *So, how come you get the watch? You wanna tell me that?*

But Slide was high all right—wired on the blood and the violence, pacing the room, his eyes neon lit with frenzy. Once again, he was seriously reminding Angela of Dillon, that psycho poet nut job, but it was possible that Slide was even more out there, really way perched on the precipice.

Now he was speaking, the words spilling over themselves, tumbling out like floods of rap dementia, going, "Babe, we're a team, we're on a hot streak and we should keep the level up and I have just the plan to get us some serious wedge, how do you feel about kidnapping?"

And she thought, Kidnapping, another term for marriage without the rings.

She said, "Wait, you mean how do I feel about you kidnapping me?"

"No," he snapped as if she'd asked a stupid question. "How do you feel about joining up with me in the kidnapping biz?"

So, what, now she was going to be the Irish version of Patty Hearst? Least she'd remember to wash her hair. What was that girl thinking, letting CCTV pick her up on a bad hair day. Christ, you rob a bank, at least make the effort, put a little blusher on, a hint of eyeliner.

She went, "Kidnapping biz?"

He slowed a tad, said, "You'll have noticed the chains and shite around the house, right?"

Like you could miss them?

Before she could say, You mean it wasn't a kink? he went, "I'm in the kidnapping biz, a pro, been doing it for a while."

And fuck, he looked so proud, like he was really doing something important, his bit for the new prosperity. Meanwhile, she was thinking, *And how successful have you been? You live in a shithole, can barely buy the drinks, drive a freaking banger, and have to roll some poor schmuck in a car park.*

Here he was again, now looking like he was about to bestow some great honor, going, "I've decided to let you be my partner."

She loved *decided*. Like he'd been deliberating over it and wasn't she lucky she'd been *picked*.

Then she thought, A kidnapper, an Irish well-groomed version of Patty Hearst. She had to admit, there was something glamorous about it. And if you did it right, shite, there could be a real payoff. Christ, wouldn't she just kill to be rich?

She asked, "But nobody gets hurt, right?"

He gave her a bashful smile, said, "See, that's my motto right there, no pain, lotsa gain."

This from a guy who put broken bottles in strangers' faces.

She went, "You're a caring man."

He literally hung his head, whispered, "I put the C in care. Sometimes, I think I care too much."

She nodded, thinking the C applied if you meant cunt, then asked, "Have you someone in mind?"

He sang, *"You can always get what you want."*

Real pleased he was using *can*, not *can't*.

Then, scaring the shite out of her, he did a hip swivel that was supposedly Jagger, but came off like Jim Carrey in *The Mask*.

"Go on," she said. "Who?"

"Who?" he said. "Jagger or Richards, one of those fookers. The Stones are in town, and someone'd pay plenty to get those lads back alive."

"The Rolling Stones," she said.

He looked at her, nodded.

She said, "You want to kidnap the Rolling Stones? That's your plan?"

"The fook's wrong with it?" he said.

The idea started to grow on her. The Stones weren't so young anymore, probably couldn't run like they'd've been able to back when.

But would there be room here for the lads? And of course she'd need a whole new wardrobe. Mick liked his women in the newest gear. God, she was already seeing Mick's lips on her neck. So, okay, he had a few wrinkles but fuck, he still had those buns and, come on, if you haven't sucked a Stone, have you really lived? Have you?

She could see herself on *Oprah*, Oprah's fattish face, full of curiosity, asking, *And when did Mick give you the diamond ring?* Then Angela would modestly flash the huge stone on her engagement finger. She'd make a joke about it, go, "I've got my Stone all right." She pictured her and Mick spending winters in the south of France, and lots of little Stones with Angela's eyes.

"So what do you say?" Slide said. "You in or out?"

Imagining herself and Mick getting married on an exclusive island off the coast of Who The Fook Cares, Angela sang in a voice much worse than Slide's: *"Wild horses...won't keep me away..."*

Seven

"OK," I said. "Forget the whole thing."
"Really?"
"Order are orders," I said. "The alternative is
anarchy and chaos."
LEE CHILD, *The Enemy*

Max Fisher was the shit all right. He was living it up—the kingpin of New York, another goddamn Scarface. His crib—he called it FisherLand—was a penthouse sublet on East Sixty-sixth Street and Second Avenue. He'd always liked the building because it was made of dark black glass, like the windows of a limo, and to Max, it oozed class, was a place The Donald would've loved before he started naming buildings after himself.

Yeah, everything was going Max's way, all right. He was making five grand a week in profit as what he liked to call himself, "a high-end crack dealer." He had the freshest clothes, a live-in sushi chef named Katsu, and best of all he was getting some of the finest poontang in the city from his steady ho, Felicia, a former stripper he'd known from Legz Diamond.

Yeah, it was hard to believe how far Max's life had come since that weekend from hell in Alabama.

How many other slick brothers like himself could've got out of that hole? No cash, a chink in your ass, literally, and not only had he kissed that shithole goodbye, but he'd set up a mini-empire in Manhattan. And we're not talking years here, buddy. He'd put this shit together in—what was it that Irish cunt used to say?—oh, yeah, *jig time*.

Where was that Irish bitch now? he wondered. If the curse

he'd paid to have put on her worked, she was probably in an Irish prison, sucking some prison guard's meat in the hope of a free lunch. Yeah, Angela had fucked Max over but good, but who was laughing now, bitch? Who was the player in the toughest game in town and who was on her knees, taking it large in some skank Irish prison? Huh? Huh?

Man, if Max had known the crack business would be such a gold mine, he wouldn't have wasted years of his life selling goddamn computer networks.

The thing was, unlike a lot of businesses, it was so easy to get the ball rolling as a crack dealer. The start-up costs were miniscule, and the obstacles to entry were virtually non-existent. All he needed was product and steady customers. And the great thing about the business was you didn't have to worry about shit like "competing technology." Once you hooked a customer, he was yours for life.

The way Max got the action started: a week after he'd hightailed it out of Alabama, Kyle had sent a mule, some high school kid, up to the city with Max's first supply of rock. He had the merchandise; all he needed was the customers. In his days as head honcho, Max had had to do with whatever was necessary to close sales, including, for many important clients, scoring coke. Max figured that all had to do was "transition" the fucks from coke to crack and he'd make a mint. Easy, right? And of course Kyle had been all for the idea, even though the putz was only getting twenty percent, and it was twenty percent of the *profits*, and Max had no intention of paying it to him anyway. Poor fuckin' Kyle. The kid was so in love with the idea of having a foursome with the blond bimbos that if Max had told him to go up to Harlem and stand in front of the Magic Johnson movie theater wearing a FUCK YOU, NIGGERS T-shirt, the stupid moron would've done it.

But, yeah, Max's drug dealing business was a huge hit. He started small, with addicts he knew. Like one of his oldest steadies, Jack Haywood. Jack was the VP of Information Technology at a major midtown investment banking firm. He was a closet cokehead and Max had been taking advantage of this for years, plying the asshole with coke and table dances in exchange for inking six- and seven-figure IT deals.

So when Max had received his first shipment of rock, he'd called Jack at work and gone, "Don't hang up on me. I've got something good for you—"

"I can't do business with you any more," Jack said nervously.

"It's not about business," Max said. "It's—"

"I'm sorry," Jack said. "It's not you. I think you're a decent guy, but my bosses—they don't want me, well, associating with you anymore."

Max had expected this attitude from Jack. When NetWorld had gone under, Max had gotten into a little trouble with the police. Something about a bunch of murders he didn't commit. None if it had been any fault of his—blame it on booze and that ditzy bitch, Angela. Call it "the dark period" in his life. But that was all in the past. He was a new Max Fisher now, a Max Fisher who had discovered the wonderful world of crack cocaine.

"It's not what you think," Max said. "I just want to get together, for old time's sake."

"I'm sorry, I can't—"

"I have some new candy for you," Max said.

Candy was the old code word that Max and Jack used to have for coke.

There was silence on the line, then Jack said, "I don't like candy anymore," but Max could tell the idea was very appealing to him.

"This is really sweet, really delicious candy," Max said. "I tried some myself the other day."

A longer silence, then Jack asked, "How sweet and how delicious?"

Max punched the air, thinking, *Gotcha, sucker*. What was that line from *House of Games*, and two to take 'em? No, that wasn't it. What-the-fuck-ever.

Max took Jack out, got him hooked. Before long, Jack was spending a thou a week on Max's shit, and that was only one customer. Soon Max had twelve other Jack Haywoods and his profits started to explode. Hell, Jack had even hooked his wife on crack. That was the beauty of the business—you could gain new customers so effortlessly. It was all word of mouth. You didn't need to advertise, you didn't need to invest a lot of money in having a pretty office. There was no one to impress. All you had to do was get people addicted and you were golden. They would get others hooked, and so on and so on. This was better than TiVo and the George Foreman Grill.

Max had been smoking crack himself—but he was taking it easy, kept it to two pipes a day. Well, maybe more than that sometimes, but he didn't go crazy or anything. He found that crack actually kept him balanced. If he was having too much booze, he would smoke a crack pipe to pull himself back up, and vice versa. It kept him levelheaded, in control. And, just like he was avoiding mixing alcohol, he stuck to crack and crack only. The stupid fuckers who got addicted to the rock—like Jack Haywood and his wife—were the ones who cut it with brown. Yeah, that was right, Max called heroin *brown*. He was up on all the current, hip drug lingo all right. He listened to Naz, Ja Rule, Busta Rhymes, and 50 Cent. He even knew how many times 50 had been shot—nine. See how hip he was?

To keep the hip vibes flowing, he had gangsta movies playing on his massive Sony 64-inch LCD TV, twenty-four-seven. Classics like *Boyz n the Hood*, *Menace II Society*, *Gang Related*, and, of course, the granddaddy of 'em all, *Scarface*. One of Max's favorite ways to pass the time was to smoke some good rock while watching *Scarface* and trying to keep track of how many *putas* Pacino blows away. When he got into the twenties he always lost count.

Max learned lots of hip lingo, but *chill*—ah, chill was by far his favorite new word. Man, he loved saying chill. And it was such a useful word; it had so many meanings. Chill could mean to relax, as in, "Chill out, my man" or "I'm just sitting in here in FisherLand, chillin' with my bee-atch." But it also meant to be cool, like, "I'm chill, baby, I'm chill." And it meant, "Hang out," like when you say to somebody, "Wanna chill?" But the best way to use chill was in place of fuck. Like sometimes Max would go to Felicia, "Yo wassup, my bee-atch? You wanna get in bed and chill, baby?" Or sometimes, while she was going down on him, Max, high on crack, would go, "Yeah, chill on my rod for a while, baby. Yeah, like that, my bee-atch."

Was hiring Felicia as his round-the-clock ho the best move he'd ever made or what?

When the money started rolling in, one of the first things Max had done was go to Legz Diamond in midtown, where he used to entertain his networking clients back in the day. He bought a lap dance from Felicia, and as she was squatting over him, those great fake tits—had to be quadruple Ds—inches away from his face, he whispered to her, "Can I ask you a personal question?"

"They ain't real," she said.

"I know that," Max said. "I was curious about something else. How much're you making?"

She thought about it, went, "You mean dancin'?"

"No, I mean the whole enchilada. Dancing plus whatever else you do on weekends. How much you make in a week?"

After a long pause, she went, "On a good week? Two thousand."

Max went, "Say hello to your new boss—I'm paying you four."

And that was it, done deal. Talk about closing a sale.

Felicia moved into the penthouse with him and Max only had one rule: she had to walk around topless at all times. He didn't care what she wore on the bottom, but he needed to see those tits constantly. Her knockers were like his goddamn *inspiration*. He could be feeling down about something, self-doubt creeping in, and he'd go, "Yo, Felicia, come here bee-atch and chill on my lap," and life would have meaning again.

The most chill thing about Felicia was how she knew her place in the world, and how she accepted it. She knew she was a ho, a bee-atch, and she didn't give Max "no talkin' back to." Most of the other women in his life had been a lot more sensitive. Angela, forget about it. If he called her a bee-atch, she'd would've bashed his face in. And his ex-wife Deirdre, God rest her soul, hadn't exactly rolled with the punches either. If Max had let one slip, called her a cunt or something, she would've had a big fit, going on about how he was "verbally abusive" and "a misogynist" and a "womanizer." Yadda, yadda, yadda. Thank God he was through with all of that shit, right?

But, yeah, Max was in heaven with Felicia. If there was such a thing as an ideal woman she was it. At home, it was like she was his beck-and-call girl, his Pretty Black Woman, but nothing had ever made him feel more like a player than the times he took her out on the town. He'd be in one of his new mustard-colored suits, and she'd be wearing something really skimpy, showing as much of her boobs as was legally allowed, and just to see the looks on people's faces was priceless. Everybody was so fucking jealous, especially the guys. They'd look at him, their mouths sagging open, and he could read their minds. All the jealous fucks were wishing that they could be Max Fisher, just for one day, just to see what it was like.

Sometimes Max took Felicia out clubbing to all the hip spots. Max felt like he was back in the good ol' days at Studio 54. So what if he was the oldest guy on the dance floor and the kids called him "Gran'pa"? Max Fisher still knew how to get jiggy wid it and he and Felicia had a fucking blast.

But Max's favorite place to take her to, to be seen, was the QT hotel on Forty-fifth Street. There was a hip swimming pool bar on ground level in the lobby and it was where all the current happening players hung out with their beautiful young ho's.

Businessmen on their lunch breaks would stop by, not to swim, but just to leer in through the glass at the spectacular women in bikinis, wishing that some day their wildest dreams would come true and that they could score some of that fine poontang for themselves.

Max knew what it was like because he used to be one of those losers himself. But now he'd turned the tables. Now he was the one in the water with his beautiful smoking hot bee-atch, and the guys in suits were looking in at him. Man, it felt good to be a winner, on the other side of the glass.

The only little issue Max had had with Felicia was one day when he went into his safe in his office to put away some cashish, and noticed the wedge of green was looking a little low. He did a count and sure enough a thousand bucks was missing.

He said, "That fuckin' *puta*'s stealing from me?"

Sounding like Pacino without even trying.

He went under his bed, took out his rod. You wanna be a drug lord, you better talk the talk. Max knew shit about guns, had never even fired one, but man, just holding a piece in his hand made him feel like his dick was six inches longer. Which would make it, what, a solid nine-and-a-half inches?

He started toward the bathroom where Felicia was showering,

then he decided he needed to get pumped for this. He hadn't smoked any crack in about an hour—Jesus, it was like he was going cold turkey. He didn't have time to cook up some shit, so he took out the little silver wrapper, did some fast lines. This was nothing like the rock, barely a notch above a double espresso, but, man, it hit him like a train, fast and hard. He did a little dance, rapping a little of the gangsta stuff he'd been listening to, doing a little 50 Cent. He sounded great and thought he could release a rap album and it would go fuckin' platinum. But he'd need a cool name, have to use numbers or initials or something. What about M.A.X.? Yeah, that had a ring to it and man, he could rap. He'd go on stage in a suit—didn't P. Daddy, or whatever the hell his name was today, do that?

But Max knew if he wanted to go gangsta he'd have to take it all the way. He'd get all the right threads. Shit, when he was The Man, the designers would be giving him clothes for free—they'd want their clothes to *be seen* on The M.A.X. He liked that, put *The* in front of his name, to highlight that he was the one and only M.A.X., the *official* M.A.X., that there was no other. Yeah, and he'd have buy a Jeep, get some customized *The M.A.X.* plates for it. Man, would that look bitchin' or what? He laughed, *bitchin'*. He was getting' down with the homies all right. The coke loosening him, he was flying, ideas hitting him, like a zillion a second. When he was a big-time rap star he knew all the brothers, all the bee-atches, would look up to him, like he was a mother who'd been around the block a few times and they best be showin him some respect. Yeah, he'd seen that respect, no, *fear*, from his bee-atch, Felicia. Her eyes fucking dazzled at his genius. They'd be in the hood, hanging with his homies, and he'd be her Mr. Wall Street. Like how many guys could pull off corporate America and be down with the gangstas? Yeah, it was time to pull some attitude on that sista.

Max went into the bathroom, slid open the shower door, and pointed the gun right at her face, holding it sideways, the way the brothers did.

He went, "You wanna get up in my face, bee-atch? Or maybe you wanna suck on some of dis?"

Not this—*dis*.

Felicia knew she was in some deep shit. She started begging, *pleading* for him to put the gun down, going "Don't do nothin' crazy" and "Don't shoot me, please don't shoot me." It was great watching her squirm, being at his mercy. Now he knew what Pacino was talking about. Guns, drugs, tits and rap—what else did a man need?

Max went, "Where's my fuckin' money, bee-atch!"

He was so juiced he nearly squeezed off a round. Saw himself as Pacino, going, *Fuck you, how's at?* And blowing the *puta* away.

She was still begging: "I swear to you, baby. I didn't take nothing. Why I need yo' money? You be givin' me so much already. Think about it. You know that shit's stupid, right?"

She went on, whining, and Max felt like he was losing his edge. Why did he do that bullshit coke? He couldn't wait to get his lips around that fucking crack pipe.

He interrupted whatever she was babbling about and screamed at her, "I got ears, ya' know! I hear things!"

Shit, Pacino again.

"I don't know what the hell you talkin' 'bout," she said. "Just get that gun out my damn face! Get it out my face!"

"What happened to my fuckin' money?"

"How I know what happen to it? I ain't seen it. How'd I even get in yo' damn safe? I don't know the combination. I don't know what you even accusin' me for, pointin' a gun in my fuckin' face like a crack-up, dumb ass, street ho motherfucker."

Desperate for some rock, feeling dizzy, Max went, "I know I'm a thousand bucks short."

Felicia fired back, "So why you think I took it? Maybe yo' damn sushi chef stole it."

Max thought about this. Katsu steal from him? It didn't add up but, hell, nothing added up right now.

"What the fuck ever," Max said. "But if I ever find any money missing you better watch your ho ass because next time you won't be so lucky. Next time I'm gonna slap you silly."

Later on, when he finally got some good crack into his system, Max wished he could've taken that last line back. *Slap you silly*. That didn't sound hip and cool at all. What the hell had he been thinking? He worried if this was a side effect of crack. It was supposed to speed you up, but it seemed to be slowing him down. Maybe that explained Kyle.

It had to be the crack because Max used to be the type of guy who could always think of the "big line" at the right time. Like when he was working in sales, going for the bulldog close, his brain never failed him. But now, lately—well, in the last couple minutes anyway—he was losing his edge.

He had to get the crack out of his system, get some food into the mix.

"Katsu, get your nip ass out here!"

Max's sushi chef came into the living room, bowed. Max liked that—showing his boss respect.

"Make me three spider rolls," Max said. "Pronto. And skimp on the caviar again, I'll shoot you. Got that, slant eyes?"

Jeez, did he really say slant eyes? He took a deep breath, thinking, *Easy, big guy. Chill*.

"Yes, Mr. Fisher," Katsu said. "I make spider roll for you right now, Mr. Fisher."

"It's The M.A.X.," Max said. "My name's initials now with 'The' in front of it. Got that?"

Katsu bowed and went into the kitchen to make the sushi.

The missing thousand bucks was still eating away at Max. A

business was like a ship. When there was a hole you had to plug it up fast or the whole fucking thing would go down.

Max went into the kitchen, said to Katsu, "You didn't happen to pocket a thousand G's of my moolah, did you?"

Katsu looked confused. What now? He's accused of stealing, suddenly the skinny little nip can't speak English?

Max took out his piece, jammed the muzzle into Katsu's ear and said, "You best not be lying or I'll slap you silly. I mean, I'll slap you really hard. I mean, I'll...Ah, fuck..."

Marching out of the kitchen, he couldn't believe he'd blown the big line again. He had to cut down on the crack. There was no doubt about it, it was fucking up his brain big time.

He needed an antidote—a little weed, or throw some Valium into the mix. You can never be too mellow. Mellow yellow Max —that would be his new thing. Fuck, rap, it was horseshit anyway. He'd go acoustic, sing peace songs. C'mon, how hard was it to sound better than Cat Stevens anyway?

Yeah, the Val was kicking in and Max was chilling big time now. Easing on down the road, he cracked open a bottle of Merlot. Wine had become his drink of choice. Had to lay off the hard stuff and after Alabama he didn't want to see another bottle of Bud for as long as he lived. But you want the class and culture of wine you gotta fucking show it. So he had bought a shitpile of Merlot, had racks of it on display. He knew Merlot was where it was at after he saw that movie, *Sideways*. What was wrong with that idiot anyway? The divorced blond chick was horny as hell, wanted to fuck him stupid, and he kept blowing her off? And Max was supposed to take wine advice from that loser?

Max poured a large glass, took a lethal wallop. He swirled a little of the stuff in his mouth and didn't they spit it out then and say, tad fruity?

He spit some out and said, "Tad fruity?"

Then he made *mmmph* sounds and swirled some more, went "1987, late fall," then said, "Ah, fuck it," and drained the glass in one gulp.

He felt the munchies coming on fast and, thank God, Katsu brought out the spider rolls just in time.

"Sorry about before," Max said, going for a super smooth, jazz musician-type voice, like he was a DJ on fucking Lite FM. "Katsu, I think you're a really cool cat, man. I didn't mean to frighten you or anything with that gun. That was just the crack talking, that wasn't me. But I'm chill now, I'm real chill. So what do you think, man? We chill?"

"Yes, we are chill," Katsu said, and he bowed and returned to the kitchen.

Max wolfed down the sushi—man, that was good shit, but he was starting to get sick of it. He'd been having sushi three meals a day for, what, two months? It was classy food, but still.

Scarface was playing on the TV. For a little change of pace, Max put in *Carlito's Way*. What could he say, he couldn't get enough of Pacino. And come to think of it, didn't he and Al look more than a little alike? Yeah, they both had that smoldering gig going on, the half-lidded eyes.

Max whispered, *"You wanna piece of me?"*

Maybe Pacino would play Max in the movie of his life. And, make no mistake, Max's life was ripe for the big screen. They loved riches-to-rags-to-riches stories, didn't they? And, whoa, hold the phones, what about HBO? His life could be a series—God knew there were enough plot twists—and he had a title already, *Maxwood*. Speaking of which, he was starting to pop a little wood.

"Beeeee-atch!"

Max called for Felicia again and a couple of minutes later

she was busy on her knees, chilling. It was great to have things back to normal with his bee-atch and he could tell she was digging the whole mellowed-out Max Fisher deal. Had to be better than having a gun in her face anyway.

Later on, he and Felicia were chilling with Merlot, watching Pacino, when the phone rang.

"Maximilian?"

It was fucking Kyle.

Shit, had the pot and the Val brought him that far down? It even seemed like Kyle was talking fast.

"My name's not Max, it's The M.A.X."

"Oh, sorry 'bout that, sir, I guess I have the wrong number."

"It's me, you stupid fucking moron," Max said, thinking was this a put-on or what? Could a human being be this retarded? "Hey, and I was about to call you. Where is the mule with my candy? We were supposed to do that deal today? Ten grand, remember?"

"That's why I'm calling," Kyle said. "I have some bad news for you about that."

Felicia was eating a spider roll, not paying attention.

"I'm warning you," Max said. "I'm an emotional guy lately. You don't want to say anything that might rub me the wrong way."

"I can't send you any more candy, sir."

"Maybe it's the Southern accent or the insane amount of coke I've done today, but I don't think I understood you. I thought you just said you can't send me any more candy."

"I'm sorry," Kyle said. "It's out of my hands."

"Whoa, whoa, what the fuck're you talking about, 'any more'? You trying to say you're cutting me off? No one cuts off The M.A.X.!"

Looked like mellow Max Fisher was a thing of the past. That didn't last long.

"Please don't be mad at me, sir," Kyle said. "It's not my fault, sir."

"Who is it then? Is it that nigger, Darnell?"

Felicia gave Max a nasty look. Max mouthed, *Sorry*. Should've added, My bee-atch.

"No it's not Darnell either, sir. It's our friends in Colombia. They don't…maybe we shouldn't be talking about this on the phone."

"Paranoia's no way to live your life, Kyle. What the fuck is the Colombians' problem?"

"Well, they don't trust you, sir. They said until they get a chance to meet you we can't send it up to you in New York."

"Did you tell them who they're dealing with?"

Long pause, then Kyle said, "I told them your name."

"Not my name, you idiot. Did you tell them who I *am*. Did you tell them I'm a mogul, I'm a kingpin, that I'm a respected businessman, that nobody ever, ever calls the shots with The M.A.X.?"

"I'm sorry, sir," Kyle said. "I'm just reportin' the facts as the facts were reported to me."

"Stop the slow talk and just fucking listen to me," Max said. "I have twenty grand sitting here and I have no candy. Do you understand my predicament? I have customers who have very sweet tooths, or teeth, or whatever the fuck, and I need to get them their goddamn candy."

"Maybe if we can arrange a meeting—"

"You mean an audition? I don't audition for nobody."

Did Pacino ever say that? If not, he should've.

"I'm sorry, Max…I mean, The M.A.X. If they can't meet you, they won't do the deal."

Max let out an angry breath, shook his head, said, "If those cocksuckers think I'm going down to Alabama they're out of their minds."

Yeah, that was the way—put the peons in their place. *Peons* —he liked that, but he wasn't sure what it meant. Did it mean people you pee on? Yeah, probably.

Kyle was saying, "They said they want me to bring them up to New York. Somethin' about how they want to see you on your own turf or somethin', see what you're all about."

"I hope you realize how insulting this is," Max said. "But if you think I'm letting them walk into my apartment you're out of your mind. I'm not letting any scummy Colombians into FisherLand. Dis be my crib, homey. You all wan' in, you waits like for the in-vite."

Felicia was still on the couch next to Max. He didn't want her listening in on his important business and said to Kyle, "Wait a second," then went to Felicia, "Baby, do me a favor, and chill in the bedroom, okay?"

She got up slowly and Max watched her walk away. There was no question she had all-star knockers, but her ass was on the big side; you might even call it fat. He'd have to have a little talk with her about that at some point. Maybe she'd have to cut down on the desserts, start using Splenda.

When Felicia was gone Max said to Kyle, "Okay, here's the way we're gonna work it. They can come to my town. That's right, New York is my town, I fuckin' own it. But we do it on my terms. I pick the time and the spot and I'll let them know what the time and the spot is when I want to tell them what the time and the spot is. You got that?"

Yeah, this was the old wheeler and dealer talking. Nobody could pull a power play on The M.A.X.

"I'll let them know all that," Kyle said. "But there's just one other thing."

"Yeah, what is it? Come on, talk, I don't have all day."

"You think, maybe, when I come up to New York you might have the girls there ready for me?"

Max didn't know what Kyle was talking about, said, "What the hell're you talking about?"

"You know," Kyle said, "the girls from the Internet— the ones on the Porsche and the sister too. Bambi? Cause you said you were gonna bring 'em down here, but you never did and—"

"Have you ever heard the word chill, Kyle?"

"Yes, sir, but—"

"I have the girls all primed up, ready to meet you. Bambi was just saying to me the other day, 'Why can't I meet Kyle already? I really want to meet him.' And I went to her, 'Easy, baby. Chill.' And now I'm telling you the same thing."

Long dead silence then Kyle went, "I don't get it. So the girls'll be waitin' for me up in New York City?"

"Only if you stay chill," Max said, and clicked off.

Max got up. Whoa, nelly. He felt a little unsteady but, hey, you're doing major, like, biz with Colombians, you're gonna be a tad unsteady. Shit, there was that *tad* again, his inner Brit coming out.

Then it suddenly hit him and he screeched, "Fucking Colombians!"

Was he in the big time now or what? Colombians, fucking drug lords, were coming up to the city to meet with him. This was his moment, his time. Like Pacino, he'd eat the savages for fucking breakfast. Didn't Pacino take all these dudes *mano a mano*? Wait, that was Cubans, not Colombians. Eh, same shit.

Yeah, everything was going The M.A.X.'s way now. Keep Kyle happy, get him some sleazy hookers, let them fuck him stupid. Well, could he be more stupid? Now he was sounding like Chandler from *Friends*. How talented could one man be? Voices, business acumen, well hung, and he was a good man too, promoting diversity in his work force. Christ, he wanted to hug himself.

He shouted, "Yo, bee-atch! Git yo' sweet ass in here, de man need his pipes blown!"

Maybe he'd let the ho sit on his face, she liked that, and she sure had enough on there to cover his neck as well.

He took off his boxers and settled back on the couch. Shut off Pacino, put on Snoop Dog for some *mood*.

His stomach rumbled, all that goddamn sushi. Fuck the diet food, an *hombre* like him needed some goddamn calories. He could see a porterhouse steak, mashed potatoes, mountain of gravy and some heavy wedge of cheesecake to top it off. Needed some meat on his bones to deal with the *Cubanos*.

Felicia came into the living room. Looked great topless but, man, that ass.

She went, "You ready for me, baby?"

Time for a little *Scarface*. Max, in his best Tony Montana, went, "Okay, fuck me, how's 'at?"

Eight

*Chico took a bloody baggie out of his
shirt pocket and handed it to Bock.
"What's this?"
Chico laughed. "A bonus. Remember the tall one,
I cut that out of his asshole."*
CHARLES WILLEFORD, *The Way We Die Now*

Slide was waiting at the bottom of Grafton Street. He looked around, making sure no one was in sight, then ducked into the alley that runs alongside the rear entrance to Lily's Bordello. *Lily's!* The hottest venue in Dublin, where Bono held court and any celebrity just had to show up. You did a gig in Dublin, it was *de rigeur* to hit Lily's after. Slide had heard that the Stones were in town and he knew those geriatric bastards would have to show up at Lily's after their gig.

Slide muttered, "You better fooking believe it."

His plan, half baked as usual, was to nab Keif—Keith Richards. Figured Mick had too big a posse but Keith—yeah, he was getable. This alleyway, with the new smoking ban in force everywhere, was where the celebs nipped down for a hit of the nicotine or weed or what-the-fook-ever they were inhaling. Keith, he'd be first down, grab his own self some major drag of some substance, and Slide would be waiting. He'd grab him fast, get the fook outa Dodge.

Jaysus, how much would the Stones pay to get the Keifer back? Slide's mind boggled at the prospect of, like, millions! Then fecking Mick Jagger would bankroll his record-breaking killing spree. Satisfaction that.

The side door opened and in the half-light he saw a thin figure, leather jacket, shades, white hair, skinny as a rodent, lined face. Shit, it looked like someone took a cookie cutter and drew deep wedges on his cheeks.

Slide was momentarily taken from left field, thinking, *Has to be Keifer*.

They say the camera adds twenty pounds, so it figured in person he'd look damn near anorexic. Or *damn near dead* was more like it. Sure enough, Slide heard a click of a Zippo, that was the clincher. Keith would definitely be a Zippo kind of dude.

Slide pulled the black sack from his jacket, moved like a shark, had the bag over the guy's head and shoulders and chest in jig time. But was he breathing in too much pot smoke or something, or did the guy go, "The fook you doing?"

Keith with an Irish accent? What the fook? That couldn't be right. But, yeah, probably being in Dublin, the Keifer figured to go native.

The guy was going, "The fecking cigarette has burned me lip."

Slide nearly said, *You're half in the bag*. Instead, let the crowbar do the talking—walloped the fuck on the head and that's all she wrote. He bundled the guy over his shoulder—the guy weighed, what, seven stone?—and started away, when the side door opened again.

"Ar, bollix," Slide muttered as he ducked with Keifer behind some leaking bags of garbage and almost passed out from the stench. Not of the rubbish—of Keifer. How much cologne was the dude wearing? Did all rock stars drench themselves in that shite? Even through the sack the guy reeked to bloody high heaven. No wonder Mick got all the babes.

The door opened and closed—the coast was clear. He didn't see anyone else till, at the top of the alley, a bouncer looked over.

Slide said, "Garbage run." To hear the music papers tell it, the Stones had been rubbish for the last decade, right?

Slide thought he was fooked, but the bouncer was distracted by the arrival of a white limo. Slide slipped past him, moving towards his car, parked on Nassau Street.

He threw the guy in the front seat, buckled him in, and burned rubber outa there.

Outside the city limits, he pulled into a lay by. He wanted to see the famous guitarist up close. But then, pulling the sack off the man's head, he echoed his favorite words of James Joyce, going "Aw shite...shite and onions."

Whoever this guy was, he wasn't Keith Richards. He was in his fifties, thick lips, with a scar to the right of his mouth, a button nose and blue eyes. The guy had to be fooking Irish.

The guy came to, seemed completely lost for a while. Then he focused, looked at Slide, and asked, "What the hell is going on?"

Slide nearly whined, "You're not Keith Richards?"

The guy gave a laugh, no humor in it, a sound that seemed to reflect a life where shite happened often and always.

The guy went, "Don't you know me?"

Slide didn't, said, "I don't."

The guy sighed, as in *Give me patience Lord*, then said, "I'm a crime writer."

"A what?"

"A crime writer. I've won the Macavity for—"

Slide shut him off, roared, "Ary Christ, shut the fook up or I'll remove all your fookin' cavities and your tonsils too! Are you somebody? Anyone give a damn about you?"

The guy looked crestfallen, stammered, "I-I got starred reviews in *Publishers Weekly* and *Booklist*...well, maybe I caught them on an off day b-but—"

Slide gave him a slap in the mouth, said, "I don't want to

hear about your bloody career. I want to hear somebody will pay cash, lots of cash to have you back."

The guy rubbed his face—poor fuck looked like he'd been beaten and hard, many times—and went, "Maybe my agent...." The bastard paused, reached in his jacket and took out a pack of Major and the Zippo. He lit up and asked, "Got any Jameson?"

Slide was suddenly thrown into that total rage that sometimes just snuck up on him. He said, "Shut the fuck up. I need to think and I need you to shut the hell up, can you do that?"

The writer couldn't. Began to list the titles of his books and how he'd once been nominated for an Oscar, or Edgar, or some other odd name, and how the U.K. had a hard-on for him.

Slide said, "I'm gonna let it slide, hear?"

But a moment later he had the crowbar in his hand and was beating the bejaysus outa him.

The thin fook was going, "I wrote a book with another guy. Maybe he can—"

But he never got to finish as Slide lashed the crowbar into his teeth, then took out the bastard's left eye with an almighty swing. "Keep yer eye on the main chance," he muttered.

Then Slide looked up to see a family in a nearby car, looking on in horror.

Slide panicked. He opened the door, kicked the body out, and went, "That should sell some books." Then he drove off like your proverbial bat out of hell.

Looking in the rearview, with the pedal to the floor, Slide knew one thing—the kidnapping biz in Ireland had gone bust. He and Angela were going to have to get the fook out of the country, and fast.

Nine

*One day he told me he wasn't going to eat meat anymore
because of mad cow disease. I said, "Ron, you're mad already,
that's why you're locked up in Broadmoor."*
KATE KRAY, WIFE OF RONNIE KRAY

Felicia didn't know how much more Max Fisher she could take. Letting him touch her—shit, that was the easy part—it was everything else about the man that was driving her crazy.

At first she thought it was gonna be easy. She was sick of dancing anyway, was looking into doing something else. Thought maybe she'd be an escort. She'd do it high end cause, damn, she knew girls didn't have half her ass making a thousand a night. Or maybe she'd get back into pornos. She used to do that shit, back in the nineties. But she was thirty-six now and knew if she tried to get back into films them fat white-ass producer motherfuckers with the cigars hanging in their mouths like big-ass dicks would tell her she was too old, too fat, too this, too that. She'd want to say to them, Look who's talking about fat, bunch of hairy, sweatin', beer-gut assholes can't even bend down to tie their own damn shoelaces. Then they'd be going on, telling her her tits were hangin' too low and she needed more surgery. Yeah, like 44 double-E's wasn't enough. Shit. So then, after she went on, got all her surgery, lost the damn weight, she'd have to give 'em blow jobs, maybe fuck 'em too. Then maybe they'd say, "Sorry, baby, you ain't what we lookin' for." Or, if she got *lucky*, they'd give her a role. Yeah, but not in the good movies, like the ones Jenna Jameson gets in. No, she'd have to bust her ass, doing the "mature" movies—you know, the ones with words like "old lady" and "granny" in the titles. She'd be lucky if she got five hundred a film and how was she supposed to pay her rent and all her damn bills with that bullshit?

So this was where her mind was at when Max Fisher walked into the club and asked for a dance. She remembered Fisher—this practically bald-headed white-ass businessman in a suit, acted like he was all that and shit. Did something with computers, always talking about it like it was some hot shit she gave a damn about. Dropping big-ass computer words, like he thought he was Billionaire Gates or something. She used to play along, suck up to him, tell him how smart and cute he was, when really she thought he was as dumb and asshole-ugly as all the rest of 'em. Stuck-up motherfucker always talkin' the way he did about his Porsche and his town house and how much money he had, all that trying-to-impress-her bullshit when the truth was all she cared about was the next twenty-dollar bill he was gonna stick in her panties.

Another thing about Fisher—he was a titty man. When she was doing a dance he didn't look at nothing else but her titties. It was like that was all she was—two titties, and it was like her nipples were made of metal and there were little round magnets in his eyeballs. Too bad he wasn't making the porno movies because her tits were fine enough for him.

Then, one day, she saw something about him in the paper, how he was mixed up in some shootings or whatever. The cops even came to talk to her, wanted to know where he was the night his wife or girlfriend or somebody got shot. She was surprised, never thought a man like that would ever get involved in something like shooting people. Thought he was all bullshit, no action. Finally the man'd done something impressed her.

But after that, she didn't hear nothing about him for a long time. He didn't come into the club no more and she forgot all about him. Then, there he was, back in his seat, asking for a dance. While she was going at it, he asked her if she wanted to be his live-in ho, paying her double what she was making dancing. She thought maybe it wouldn't be such a bad idea. She get to rest her feet and it was better than regular hoin', goin' man to man. And shit, it was lot better than having to suck off some scumbag movie producer for a role in *Horny Grandmas 11*. She'd get to live in a penthouse on the Upper Rich Side, eat as much sushi as she wanted. Ain't nothin' wrong with that shit, right?

What she didn't know, she was getting in with a crazy damn crack dealer.

Man was on the rock all the time. He said it was just balancing him out or some shit, cause of all the drinks he be having, but Felicia knew that was bullshit talking—the man was just a big stupid-ass crackhead who didn't know how to keep his damn mouth shut. Talking like Al Pacino, thinking he knows shit about hip-hop, and calling her bee-atch all the time. Or how about he's calling people nigger around her, dissing her race and shit? Motherfucka was lucky he was paying her or he woulda wound up with six in his back real quick.

And how many times was the man gonna say chill? Sometimes, listening to him, Felicia would think, does he know how stupid he sounds? And how about the way he treated her, giving her orders, making her walk around topless all the time so he can always be looking at her titties? And, shit, she had to give him lap dances and blow jobs whenever he wanted them. Yeah, he was paying her, but treating her like she was a damn sex slave was bullshit. Crack-smoking dumb-ass motherfucker had no respect for women and shit.

Sometimes he took her out—yeah, like she was a dog that

needed walking. Meanwhile, she knew it was only cause he wanted to show her booty off to the whole damn world. Sometime he'd take her to restaurants and clubbing—damn, somebody had to give that man some dancin' lessons—but his favorite place to go was that swimming pool near Times Square. In the middle of the day, he'd make her get in the damn water with him, so he could be sipping on his drinks with the little umbrellas inside them, showing off her booty for all the white-ass businesspeople looking in.

Shit, being around that asshole twenty-four-seven sure as shit wasn't worth the four grand a week he was paying her. Actually, she was making more than that, because she was screwing Katsu, the man's sushi chef, on the side. Yeah, like sometimes when Max was asleep, she'd go into Katsu's room, be on his body, and then she'd go back to Max. One time he went, "How come you smell like fish?" and she thought she'd got busted. She told him she was hungry and went to have a tuna sandwich in the kitchen and the stupid-ass believed her.

She was also making some money going in Max's safe. One time Max was so shit-ass wasted he gave her the combination, so she was going in, taking fifty, a hundred bucks, figuring the man was so high he wasn't gonna keep count.

The money was good but, no, it wasn't worth being around Max, twenty-four-seven.

She was all set to quit—go back to dancing or whatever—when one day Max sent her out to buy some Cuban cigars and a white guy in an ugly-ass plaid suit—shit went out of style in 1974—came up to her and went, "Hey, Felicia."

Just like that, like they was old friends and shit. She never seen him before in her whole damn life but, shit, all you had to do was look at that motherfucker and know he was a cop.

Pretending she didn't know what was going down, she went, "What the fuck you want?"

And then he laid the shit on her straight up. His name was Detective Joe Miscali, NYPD, and he was gonna bust her ass hard for prostitution, possession, whole mess of charges, if she didn't give him some shit on Max Fisher.

She was like, "Shit about what? I don't know shit about nothing."

Playing hardball with the cop, waiting to see if he was for real or not.

Turned out the motherfucker wasn't playing. Said he was on to Max, was ready to take his ass down hard, and he gave her two choices—cooperate or go away. Shit, she didn't want to do no jail, so she said, Yeah, she'd help. What the fuck? She didn't like helping cops, but she'd love to see Max go down, give the old bald-headed bitch some payback for the way he been treating her.

She started trying hard as she could to get Miscali some shit on Max. She was listening in on conversations, trying to always be by him all the time, whatever. Then, one night, he came into the shower, pointing the gun in her face. She thought, *Fuck, he musta found out I'm gonna snitch on his ass*. Then it turned out it wasn't about that at all; it was about the stupid money from the safe. Played it right, denying all the shit he was saying to her, and he finally left her alone.

Later, she heard him talking to his boy Kyle on the phone about some drug deal was gonna go down with some Colombians. He told her to get out of the room, but she was listening in on the call on the other line in the bedroom. Okay, so now she had the info for Joe Miscali and she could stop being Max Fisher's ho—praise the Lord.

But then she got to thinking—a drug deal, and didn't they say it was twenty thousand dollars? There was gonna be product there too and she was thinking, *Why I gotta tell that shit to Miscali?* Felicia been thinking about getting away, leaving New York. She was tired of ho'in, being worried about money all the time. She had her friend Ramona in St. Louis, was always calling her, saying they should open a beauty salon together. But she need money to do that and no bank was gonna start giving no stripper no loan. But maybe if she could figure out a way to get that twenty grand she could go half with Ramona on the salon, get a whole new life started.

Shit, she barely slept the whole night because she was thinking about one thing—how to get that old stinkin' crackhead's money. Then it came to her—her cousin Sha-Sha from Brooklyn. Damn, why didn't she think of that shit straight up?

Sha-Sha was her second cousin on her mom's side. Felicia was six years older than him and funny shit was he was the first trick she ever turned. Happened when she was nineteen and he was thirteen. He was just hitting puberty and he was a horny little thang—nasty too. He was always walking around, touching his dick, asking her to do shit with him. Finally, sick of hearing him talk, she went, "You wanna fuck, I'll fuck, but it's gonna cost you five bucks." He must've gone and stole five bucks from his momma, Felicia's aunt. Was the fastest five dollars she made her whole life.

Felicia told Max she needed to go get a haircut. Meanwhile, she was really going to meet Sha-Sha in Brooklyn, in Canarsie. She took the L train out there and maybe she should've worn some different clothes. In this short leather skirt Max had bought her every guy on the train was wanting to bone her.

Sha-Sha was living in Breukelen Houses, off the L train. It had been a long time since Felicia had been back to the projects and she wasn't missing none of it. When Sha-Sha answered the door she didn't even recognize the nigga. She went, "Sha-Sha here?" and he went, "The fuck you talkin' 'bout?" Yeah, that sounded like Sha-Sha, but what happened to his body? He used to be fine looking—well not too fine, he wasn't no Denzel—but he was big and strong and his face wasn't too bad either. But now the man was fat. She was talking Rerun fat, like the man be eating ten meals a day.

She looked around at all the pizza boxes, Chinese containers and shit and said, "Damn, how much you be eatin'?"

Sha-Sha went, "That how you say hello? How'd you get so rude, bitch?"

"Fuck you," Felicia snapped. After listening to Max call her bee-atch all the time she wasn't gonna take that shit from her damn cousin.

"Sorry, baby," Sha-Sha said smiling. "Come to me."

He held open his arms for a hug but, damn, Felicia felt like she was only getting her arms around one-quarter his body. She was glad she wasn't hookin' no more, havin' Sha-Sha-size men on her body. Nigga that big fall on a girl's body he kill her and shit.

Then Felicia felt one of Sha-Sha's hands grabbing her ass and she shooed it away.

"Don't be grabbin' my ass," she said.

"Shit, you lookin' good," Sha-Sha said. "Smellin' good too. I bet you nice and tasty."

Listen to the nigga, talkin' to her like she was food. She better watch out—the fat motherfucka might eat her.

When he started kissing her neck—sucking on it more like it—she pushed him away. Tried to push him away. Nigga didn't budge.

"The fuck you doin'?" Felicia said. "Ain't you forgettin' we cousins?"

"Shit never stopped you before," Sha-Sha said.

Sha-Sha grabbed her ass again. She slapped his hand hard and went, "I ain't playin'," and he finally let go.

He moved some pizza boxes off the couch and they sat down, got caught up and shit. He asked her if she was still dancing and she said "Yeah," leaving out that she was Max Fisher's ho. Then she asked him if he was still dealing and he said, "Yeah," and she was thinking, *I wonder what shit he's leaving out.*

Felicia didn't want to spend her whole damn day bullshitting in the projects. Yeah, Max was a bitch-ass motherfucker, but living in a penthouse—shit, she could get used to that. So getting right down to it, she went, "Yo, there's this white motherfucker I know. You know, I dance for him and shit. Motherfucker's dealing rock."

"Who's he with?" Sha-Sha asked.

"Ain't with nobody," Felicia said. "See how stupid his ass is? He don't even know he keep it up the gangs're gonna be coming down on his ass. His clients—yeah, motherfucker calls 'em *clients,* are all rich-ass white people like he is. Nigga's getting' all the white people in Manhattan smokin' rock and shit."

"Damn," Sha-Sha said smiling.

"So I be thinking," Felicia said. "Why wait till the gangs come down on him, know what I'm sayin'? How 'bout I find some way to get down on his ass first?"

"Shit makes sense," Sha-Sha said.

"Shit makes lotta sense," Felicia said. "So nigga's on the phone last night, talkin' about this deal's gonna go down with these Colombians, for twenty thousand dollars and shit. Then I think about you and your boys and I'm like, 'Yeah, we can get in on that shit.' Know what I'm saying?"

Sha-Sha was into a pack of Chips Ahoy, eating the shit two at time. Piling that shit down his throat like his damn life depended on it.

"Shit, you eatin' or listenin'?" Felicia asked.

Sha-Sha gave her a long look, swallowing cookies, then said, "Keep talkin' to me."

"What I been saying," Felicia said. "All I gotta do is find out where the drug deal's at, right? Then you and your boys, whatever, bust in on that shit, know what I'm sayin'? I get the money, you get the rock. Shit, Max—that's the nigga's name—payin' twenty for it, shit's gotta be worth forty, right? You know how much pizza and cookies and Pringles and whatever the fuck else you been eatin' make you so damn fat you can buy for forty thousand dollars?...A lot, that's how much."

Sha-Sha thought it over for a few seconds, stuffing more cookies down his mouth—looked like he was swallowing them whole—then went, "Max huh? And you say the nigga don't got no back-up?"

"Ain't you listenin' to me?" Felicia said. "It's just him, he's alone. Oh, yeah, and some white boy from Alabama. Name Kyle or some shit. Max and Kyle. That sounds like two scary-ass motherfuckers, right?"

Felicia laughed.

Sha-Sha wasn't laughing, went, "What about them Colombians?"

"What about 'em?"

"You say this is twenty thousand dollar, right? Shit, ain't no high-level deal for no twenty thousand dollars, know what I'm sayin'? Sound like some street-level bullshit to me."

"Yeah, yeah, I know. So? That makes the whole thing even more easy. How hard's it gonna be for you and whoever else you got backin' you up, do whatever you gotta do. Shit gonna be stupid easy, you ask me."

"Yeah, I guess maybe I can get my boy Troit in on it with me," Sha-Sha said. "We split up the rock together and shit."

"That's right," Felicia said, "and I get the money. That's all I want—the twenty grand. I don't care if they got a hundred grand worth of rock there. All I want is the cash."

She liked the deal, but she didn't like the sound of Troit. If he was in with Sha-Sha, he was probably some sick-ass, that was for damn sure.

Sha-Sha was quiet a few seconds, like he was thinking real hard, then said, "You know I might gotta cap this Max motherfucker, right?"

"Shit, you wanna cap him, go 'head," Felicia said. "You be doin' me a favor, wanna know the truth. Cap his ass in the head, serve him right for the way he been treatin' me. Walking around with my titties showin' all the time, makin' me do him whenever he get a hard-on, which is like what, five, six, seven times a day? Man's little dick be hard all the time with all the Viagra he be takin'."

"A'ight, I'm in, yo," Sha-Sha said. "Let's bust this Max nigga hard." Then he pushed the Chips Ahoys aside, said, "Man, I'm getting' sick off these cookies. Man need some real dessert, know what I'm sayin'?"

Felicia smiled, like she didn't know what Sha-Sha was saying, and said, "Yo, I should be gettin' back. I don't want Max getting suspicious or nothin'. I told him I was gonna get a haircut but it ain't gonna be no shorter when I get back. Not like his cracked-up ass would notice."

As Felicia headed toward the door Sha-Sha said, "You think I'm playin' with you?"

Felicia stopped, looked back at him. He had his legs spread and he was undoing the buckle on his belt.

"Come on, Sha-Sha, don't be doing that shit. We cousins."

"You want me to do shit for you, you better do some shit for me. Know what I'm saying?"

Felicia knew she had no choice. Shit would end fast anyway. Besides, had to be better than Max, right?

When she had her panties down and was climbing on she went, "You better be quick. And you tell our mommas about this shit, I'll kill you."

When Felicia was done screwin' Sha-Sha she took the train back to Manhattan. Man, it was a relief being back in Manhattan, being back in *the city*. She was through with all that being in Brooklyn, back in the projects bullshit. She had class now and she wasn't gonna be poor ever again. All she needed was the time and place of the meeting with the Colombians and Sha-Sha would take care of all the rest. She'd have her money, be able to open her salon in St. Louis, her life would be all set up.

That night, when she was in bed with Max, she figured there was no use not getting right to it and she said, "When's the drug meeting with the Colombians at?"

She figured Max would just come out and tell her. Why'd he have to keep it a secret?

But either he thought something was up or he was just being an asshole, cause he said, "Why the fuck do you care?"

Shit, why'd she have to be so straight up with him? She shoulda tried to work it out of him, or waited till they were in the swimming pool at the QT and he was in a good mood and shit.

"No reason," Felicia said, twirling her finger in his sweaty gray chest hair, acting all lovey dovey with the damn asshole. "I just wanna know where my man's gonna be at, that's all."

"Hey, let's not forget your role in this relationship," Max said. "I'm not your man, I'm your boss. You got that?"

Damn, she wanted to bitch slap his ass.

"Yeah, I got it," she said. "But ain't I gonna come with you to meet the Colombians?"

Max laughed then said, "Honey, this is business, complicated stuff. Your role is to be waiting for me when I get back. I'm gonna be very worked up after that meeting and I'm gonna to need my bee-atch to relax me. Now make yourself useful and roll me a joint, will ya?"

She knew it was because he'd caught—well, almost caught—

her going into the safe. Now he wasn't gonna trust her with nothing.

In the morning she was ready to give up, say fuck you to the whole busting in on the drug deal idea. She was gonna call Detective Miscali and give him whatever he wanted and then she was gonna get her ass outa, what'd he call it? Oh, yeah, *FisherLand*.

But then the next morning Max's boy Kyle arrived up from Alabama. One look at that white boy and Felicia knew she was back in action. When she first saw him she even said out loud, "Damn, that boy be white."

Serious, if there ever was a white boy, it was Kyle. Damn, nigga put the white in white boy. She didn't know how he was from the South because his skin looked like he was one of them albinos, like he hadn't been out in the sun his whole hillbilly life. Probably because he spent all his time in church, that's why. The boy be carrying around his bible all the time, talking to Max about crack—how fucked up is that? Max had told her something about how he was gonna set Kyle up with some ho's when he came to the city, wanted to know if Felicia had any "references," but Felicia knew the only ho on that boy's body was gonna be her.

And she could tell the boy was hard up, looked like a dog that wasn't getting none. Whenever he looked at her his mouth hung open, like he couldn't believe what he was seeing. She kept him in heat, brushing her titties up against his arm, touching his ass with her index finger, and all the time she kept thinking, "She-itt, this boy be white."

And the way he talked, like some southern gent and calling her "Ma'am." Ain't nobody ever called Felicia ma'am and she had to be real careful not to laugh in his damn fool face.

But, shit, she kind of liked the way he was worshipping her, treating her with respect. Aretha said it right—ain't no girl on the planet gonna turn down some r-e-s-p-e-c-t. And, hell, being called ma'am was better than being called bee-atch, right?

One time, in the kitchen, she moved up close to him, her titties right up against his chest, and tried getting the drug deal info from him but he clammed way up, stuttering, "I-I-I don't think the The M.A.X. w-w-would like me talking 'bout that, m-m-m-a'am."

Stuttering and shit, he was so nervous. She wanted to slap him upside his head, get some sense in his dumb Southern boy ass, but then she needed that information. There was only one way she knew she could get it out of him—fuckin'. There wasn't a man alive didn't talk like a jackrabbit when he got some pussy with the promise of more to come. Besides, she was screwing her own damn cousin, what was one more little white boy?

Later that day, Max went out to sell some of his crack to somebody and Katsu was out buying fish in Chinatown. Felicia put on some of the lingerie Max had got her and went out into the living room. Kyle was sitting on the couch and when he looked up at her he almost dropped his damn bible. She didn't say nothing, just looked him up and down and then went to the stereo and put on some Mary J. Blige. Then she got a bottle of bourbon, two glasses, piled some ice in there and then splashed lots of booze in each. Holding the glasses in one hand, like she'd seen in a movie, she strolled across the room to where Kyle was now sitting straight up, like he was an army man, and went, "Girl sure does hate to drink alone, suga."

He took the glass, his hand shaking, and she eased down next to him. He gulped the bourbon straight down, swallowed the ice too, like he needed it to cool off.

Squeezing up nice and close to him, she went, "What you readin'?"

Kyle could barely speak, he wanted it so bad. He went, "E-E-Ezekiel eigh-eighteen twenty-seven."

"Ooh, that sounds nice," Felicia said, puckering up her lips. "What it say?"

"N-nothing much, ma'am," Kyle said. "Just that, um, uh, 'When the wicked man turneth away from his wickedness that he hath committed, and doeth that which is lawful and right, he shall save his soul alive.' "

"Oh, yeah, that sounds real pretty," Felicia rubbed his leg—damn, he had a tent in his sweatpants already—then went, "You know, I go to church all the time too?"

"Really?"

She wanted to laugh in his face, but she had to keep this shit going.

"Yeah, I always sit up close, in the first row, so I can hear what the reverend say loud and clear. You know, I'm related to Dr. Martin Luther King?"

Damn, she wished she could take that shit back. Boy was from the south, might be some kind of racist or something.

But, nope, turned out it was the perfect way to go because he went, "Wow, Dr. King, that's real impressive, ma'am. I'm a big, big fan. How're you and the Reverend related?"

Shit—questions. She wasn't expecting that.

"He was my mom's cousin twice removed on my sister's side. But he and my mom was real close—like brothers. I mean brother and sister." Figuring she had to get off this subject real quick, she went, "You know what I like about you?" She was tickling his leg a little, happy to see that big tent coming up already in his pants—yeah, boy was ready to go campin' all right. "You real polite, that's what. Callin' me ma'am all the time. I like that shit. Wanna know something else? You real pretty too."

She almost said *purty*, but figured they were past that.

She grabbed the bible from him, tossed it onto the floor, and climbed on his body.

"Don't worry none about your bible, honey chile. We can have our own private bible class. I be Eve, you be Adam, and our asses are stuck in the Garden of Eden."

"O-okay, ma'am," he said. He could barely talk. Shit, he could barely breathe.

She grinded up against him, putting his face right between her titties, then said, "Ain't there a snake in the garden of Eden?" and undid the snap on his Levi's.

"H-hold up a second, ma'am," Kyle said. "Ain't you Max's...I mean The M.A.X.'s girl?"

"Honey, I ain't nobody's girl," Felicia said.

She got his pants down, then pulled his shirt up over his head. Then she took his Y-fronts down and she couldn't believe what she was seeing.

She went, "Damn, boy, you are *hung*."

And she wasn't lying neither, like when she told all them pencil dicks that they got the biggest cocks she ever seen just to boost their egos and shit. Sometimes she even told Max he had a big one. Meanwhile, sometimes she couldn't even feel the shit. He'd roll off her and go, "I'm done," and she didn't even know they was started yet.

But, Kyle, man, he was the real deal. She'd been with half the Knicks and most of the brothers in Canarsie and, shit, none of them had nothing on this white boy.

"Thank you, ma'am," he said.

"Naw, thank *you*," she said, and they got at it. She didn't want him to shoot too soon, because those southern boys—even the gents like Kyle—turned real mean when that happened.

Felicia was letting loose, coming like the goddamn D-train, shrieking like a crack ho who'd had her shit taken away.

Meanwhile, Kyle was going, "Am I hurting you, ma'am?"

She just screamed at him, "You da man, you da man, you da man!"

When she finished up she turned over and let Kyle do his thing. When he blew he didn't make a sound. Boy was too polite to make noise.

Sitting up on the couch after, Felicia went, "I ain't been fucked like that in a long, long time, suga."

Then she saw he was crying, big-ass tears going down his cheeks.

"What's the matter, baby?"

He could hardly talk, he was crying so bad.

Then he went, "I've betrayed The M.A.X. What am I gonna do now?"

Boy was so messed up he didn't even remember to call her ma'am.

She caressed his cheek, went, "Ain't no power on earth can stop love, honey."

"You really mean that? You...l-l-love me?"

"Why you think I'm here with you right now, baby? I ain't usually the type of girl who gets with a man real quick, know what I'm sayin'?"

Lucky she wasn't Pinocchio or her nose'd be blowing a hole through the door, past the elevators, out the damn building and shit.

Kyle said, "But The M.A.X. said that you're a...a... a ho."

"That's bullshit," Felicia said. "Don't listen to anything Max be saying to you cause that man got his head inside his ass, know what I'm sayin'? I ain't no ho. I'm just a woman, a lonely woman lookin' for love, and now I found it."

She saw his eyes well up and let him kiss her, trying not to laugh, then said, "You love me, too, don't you? I can see you do. I can see it. And listen, baby, if you love somebody, you tell them everything. There ain't no secrets. So why don't you tell me where that drug deal's gonna be at?"

"Can I ask why you want to know?"

She wanted to go, "No, you can't," but went with, "Cause I just like to know where my man be at, that's all.... You are my man, ain't you?"

She saw the way he was looking at her and that was it, piece of cake. He told her everything she wanted to know about the drug deal—the time, the place, who was gonna be there, everything.

Then he said, all scared and shit, "You sure you won't tell The M.A.X., ma'am? I mean, I know it's no big deal and all, but I don't think The M.A.X. would appreciate it if he knew I told you something I wasn't supposed to."

Yeah, Kyle had a big dick but Felicia had never seen a pussy like him her whole damn life. Never saw a sucker like him neither.

"Don't worry," she said. "Be our own little secret." Then she climbed back on him and she said, "You like Britney?" Kyle said yeah and she said, "Then what you waitin' for? Hit me one more time, baby."

Ten

Sideswipe
CHARLES WILLEFORD

Joe Miscali was a good guy. You ask anyone and they'd go, "Joe? Yeah, he's a good guy." It seemed like everybody loved Joe and you had to wonder—where's the flaw? what's wrong with this picture?—since Joe was a cop and, yeah, a damn good one.

He'd worked out of the 19th Precinct so long that they called him Joe Nineteen. Even the bad guys kinda had a soft spot for Joey Nineteen. He was divorced—sure, came with the doughnuts and the buzz haircut—but even his ex old lady had nothing but nice things to say about him. She'd go, *Joe? Oh, yeah, Joe, he's a good guy.*

Joe didn't work at being Mr. Nice. He was just one of those rarities, a good man in a bad situation.

He was built like a brick shithouse—pug face, broken-veined complexion, hands thick as shovels. A typical Joe Miscali outfit: polyester pants with a nylon shirt and a plaid sports coat. Note to Norman Mailer: *Good guys wear plaid.* He was born in Queens, loved the Mets, Jets and Nets. He watched re-runs of *The Odd Couple*, like, a lot. He loved to quote from the show, insert lines into casual conversation even if no one understood what the hell he was talking about. Silly, yeah, but Joe got a kick out of it.

His lineage was that old volatile mix of Italian and mick. So how'd he wind up with such a sunny disposition? Go figure.

Joe had a pretty good record of closing cases. Not that he

was a great cop but he was smart, knew snitches were the way to go. He'd been lucky, often getting to the right snitch at the right time. Thing is, like luck, snitches had a very short shelf life, so you got as much as you could from them before their mouths or dope took them off the board.

If there was a sadness in Joe's life, it was for Kenneth Simmons, an old buddy from way back. They'd gone to the Academy together and the son of a bitch had been a hell of a cop—relentless, never let go. Joe admired that, but it would turn out to be Kenny's downfall. Last year, he was after Max Fisher, a smarmy, smug businessman who was on the hook for killing his wife and another woman. Over brews one night, Kenny'd told Joe, "The schmuck is guilty and I'm gonna nail him."

But someone'd nailed Ken before the case got up and running, and no one had ever really gone down for it. Joe kept an eye on the Fisher punk, knowing that somehow, in some goddamned way, he'd been the cause of Kenneth's death.

Kenneth had had a partner, a cocky mother named Ortiz. Joe could never figure the deal out—Kenneth, a sweetheart and Ortiz, a badged prick. But, hey, like marriage, you never knew what glued people together.

After Kenneth bought the farm, Ortiz had let the case go. Time to time, Joe would ask him if anything was breaking on the deal, but it seemed like Ortiz had given up. Then, one night, Ortiz was killed instantly in a smash-up on the Jersey Turnpike on his way to A.C. to—rumor had it—screw some bimbo he had down there. And this with a wife, eight months pregnant, home in his apartment in the Bronx. Nice guy, huh? What was left of Ortiz they shoveled back to some small town in Santa Domingo.

Joe kept an eye on Max, hoping to get some closure for Ken. Yeah, it had become personal to Joe. There was sure some weird karma around that Fisher fuck, like everyone round him got wiped and he just kept on keeping on.

Then Fisher went off the radar. Joe heard he'd fallen on hard times, gone broke somehow, was drinking his ass off, got into a couple of bar fights. Did Joe shed any tears? Like fuck he did. He was secretly hoping that Max would piss the wrong guy off at some bar, get his ass nailed to the wall.

A couple months went by and Joe didn't hear much of anything. Then imagine how surprised he was when he heard that Fisher was back and, word was, he was dealing. You fucking believe it?

Joe put a tag on Max. Yeah, he could've nailed him for a couple of small-time crack deals, could have at least slapped him with Possession with Intent. But the DA wanted the whole deal and didn't want Joe to move in too quick. So Joe got a hold of a new snitch—a stripper-slash-prostitute named Felicia Howard. No surprise there—Fisher was as smarmy as they came and he had a thing for busty broads. Fisher's old flame, Angela Petrakos, had also been built.

Felicia was promising—Joe had scared her and good. He had her on prostitution charges for taking money from the clients she danced for and was hanging three-to-five, no parole, over her head. He could tell she was probably sick of Fisher herself. There was no way in hell she'd go down for that jackass.

The early stages with a snitch were always tricky. He had to build up trust, or if not trust, at least a relationship. He never had any problem with paying his informants. Some cops, they used intimidation, bullied the poor fucks into giving up information but Joe knew, that way you only got half the story. First thing Joe did, always, was slip them a few bucks and it worked every time. Nothing like cash money to loosen up somebody's lips. And paying hookers for info usually worked out really well.

If they'd give away their bodies for some green, why wouldn't they give up info?

But Joe had been working with Felicia for over a week now and he was getting impatient. He felt like she was stalling.

He arranged to meet her at the Green Kitchen diner on Seventy-seventh and First. They did some mean meatloaf there, not a bad rice pudding either. When Joe was seated at a booth toward the back he spotted a dog-eared paperback with a torn cover that somebody had left on the cushion. He could barely read the title—was it *Cockfighter?*

Whatever, he thought, and shoved it aside.

Felicia arrived. It was hard not to notice her in the short skirt and with all the cleavage. Practically every male head in the diner turned to watch her pass. A few women too. When she sat across from Joe, he smiled. He gave great smile. Ask anybody.

He gave Felicia that look, then went, "You need anything?" and took out his wallet, showing her the corner of a twenty sticking out. Figuring he'd whet her appetite right off the bat.

"Why you so good to me, Detective Miscali?" Felicia said. "I ain't used to kindness."

He knew she was full of shit, went, "You're full of shit." And yeah, here was his handkerchief, all sympathy and bull, and he said, "Felicia, I'm your friend, I'm gonna get those minor charges wiped but you gotta give me something on Fisher, you know, keep my bosses happy. And call me Joe, okay?"

She nodded, wiping daintily at her eyes, and said, hesitantly, "Maybe I do got something for you...Joe."

He was all focus now, cop antennae on full alert. Asked, "What is it?"

"Hold up," she said. "What am I gonna get?"

"You get not to go to jail."

"I mean what am I gonna get's green and white, has presidents on 'em."

"Look, Felicia," Joe said. "Just because I haven't played hardball with you yet, doesn't mean I'm not capable. Yeah, I'm a good guy, but I have a hardass side to me, too, and, trust me, you don't want to meet it."

Joe was trying to intimidate. He knew it wasn't working—hell, she knew he knew it wasn't working—but he kept the glare going anyway.

She nodded, said, "I'm just playin' with you. You know how bad I wanna help you, right? But I just hope there's more twenties like that in yo' wallet, know what I'm sayin'?"

"How many twenties we talking about?" Joe said, smiling.

"Fifty," Felicia said.

The smile went. Joe said. "Look, if you think I'm giving you a thousand bucks you're out of your fucking mind."

"Five hundred," Felicia said.

"Two hundred," Joe said.

"Deal," Felicia said.

Joe, feeling like he'd been taken, went, "Do you have anything for me or not?"

"Yeah, I got somethin' good for you," Felicia said. "You gonna be thankin' me for this shit. He's in with some Colombians."

Joe waited a second then said, "You mean Colombian Colombians. *From* Colombia."

"Ain't talkin' about no District of Columbians," Felicia said. "He's movin' up—way up. Motherfuckers are from some drug cartel or some shit. They having a big meeting in Staten Island tomorrow night. You show up there, you can get 'em all."

Felicia gave Joe all the info about the meeting and Joe didn't think she was bullshitting. When you worked with snitches you had to have a good bullshit detector, and Joe had one of the best in the business. He wrote everything in his pad, meticulous to get every detail down. After a few minutes or so of this, he looked up at Felicia and said, "Can I ask where you got this?"

"How you know Max didn't tell me?"

Joe gave her a look, like, Was I born yesterday?

Felicia recognized the look, went, "From Kyle, some white boy from Alabama. The boy's hung, know what I'm saying?"

Joe smiled at his snitch, proud of how well everything had worked out.

"Nice work," he said. Then he grabbed a menu and went, "Now how about we get some food on the table, you hungry girl you."

Eleven

Burn
SEAN DOOLITTLE

Angela was fuming, not from the cigs she was chain smoking but from waiting for Slide again. W*here the fook was he?* He'd said he was going to kidnap the Rolling Stones. It seemed like a great idea at the time, but only because she'd been three sheets to the Jameson wind. Yeah, bring back the Stones, way to go, Slide, good on yah. Bloody Jameson, it was worse than any drug. Not only did it tell you you could do anything, it downright persuaded you that the maddest, most insane scenario would work. How else can you explain Riverdance?

But he seemed gung ho on the idea and she knew men well enough to let them do all kinds of crazy shite and then she'd reap the reward. She heard the car pull up and then Slide was running towards the house—alone. What, no Jagger? No Richards? Not even Charlie Fookin' Watts?

Slide came bursting in, going, "Gotta have me big drink."

She wondered what happened to, *And how was your day, sweetheart?* Fucking men—me, me, me. But she got a glass, poured a large Jameson, then asked in a cold tone, "Ice with that, sweetheart?" Leaning on the endearment, like they even had a fucking refrigerator.

Then she noticed Slide was dripping with sweat. And was that blood?

He gulped the drink, belched, said, "Sweet Jaysus." Then he said, "We gotta get out of here, now, and I mean not just outa here but, but outa the country."

She had to know, asked, "What happened?"

The booze seemed to calm him a bit. He took a deep breath, said, "I took the wrong guy, all right? A fookin writer, and turns out he's related to one of the Boyos, you know, the IRA?"

Was he kidding? She knew who they were. More important, she knew you don't, like, ever fuck with them. There wasn't much that scared Angela. Growing up in New Jersey, her friends used to worry about the Mob. Like if Angela picked up some Soprano at a bar her friends would tell her she was crazy, she didn't know what she was getting into. But Angela would just laugh, knowing a Soprano was a kitten compared to a Boyo.

She nearly shrieked, "Are you sure?"

If Slide had really kidnapped one of their relatives, oh Sweet Jesus, that was like fookin' suicide.

Slide gave her the look, said, "No, I'm making it up." Then went, "Of course I'm sure. He even had a Belfast accent and he said they'd cut me balls off."

That convinced her. She knew, alas, that was exactly what they'd do.

She asked, "Did you give him back?"

He seemed stunned, said, "Are you stone mad? It's not like a pair of jeans that didn't fit, I couldn't *return* him. I didn't, like, keep the receipt. Oh, and here's the worst part."

Christ, what could be worse, unless he killed him? The blood, she realized with a sinking heart.

She said, "You didn't—"

Slide interrupted, went, "I was seen, all right? Well, at least the car was and they got me number, they'll be able to track us in jig time."

She wanted to scream, *Us? You stupid prick, it's you.*

He read her mind, asked in a chilling voice, "You wouldn't run out on me, would you?"

Angela shuddered as the past danced before her eyes. She

mostly suppressed her past, kept it locked nice and tight. Like they said on *Seinfeld*, It was in the vault. But sometimes it came out to play.

Her mother had had connections to the Boyos. Time to time, some shadowy figure would arrive, literally off the boat, with that thick Belfast accent and thicker manners. Her mother would feed him and he'd get Angela's room.

One freezing February night, before Angela left home for good, one of these guys arrived. Had that Marine Corps look about him, ramrod straight, shaved head, menace oozing from him.

Angela's mother was at work—she worked with a cleaning crew that serviced the Flatiron Building, supplemented her income by stealing books from a publisher who had offices there and returning them to various bookstores around the city for credit. Angela arrived home to find this guy in the kitchen, dressed in just a string vest and combat trousers and reading *An Poblacht*, some paper Sinn Fein sold in the Irish pubs. Her mother had warned her, severely, *Don't ever, ever talk to these men*.

Like hello. You tell a woman like Angela to stay away from a certain man and, gee, guess what?

Angela was in man-eater attire, the mini, the sheer hose, heels. The *wanna fuck?* jobs. They were killing her, naturally—did men actually believe women enjoyed wearing these things?—and was heading out when he spoke, startling her.

"What's yer hurry, *cailin*?"

He put the paper aside and she saw the gun. He'd taken it apart and was cleaning it. It looked sleek and ugly. He was wearing Doc Martens and used his boot to push a chair aside.

He ordered, "Take a pew."

Mainly, she wanted to take her goddamn heels off but his whole languid lethal attitude was strangely exciting.

He said, "You'll be knowing why I'm here."

She didn't, said, "I don't."

He snapped the barrel of the weapon in one fluid motion and the gun was assembled. He laid it on the table and said, "I've a bit of business in Arizona. A bollix stole from us and I'm going to recover it."

He was smiling, but no warmth or humor came from it. She felt sorry for the poor bastard in Arizona.

"They tell me tis fierce hot out that way," he said, and she said, "Dry heat."

He laughed, more like the sound of an animal's grunt, and said, "Only in America. Back home, you could say we have wet rain...lashings of it."

She was tempted to say, "How utterly fascinating."

Now he rolled a cigarette, expertly, like Bogart in the old movies, with one hand. He licked the paper and produced a Zippo with a logo on the side, *Fifth of*...something. She couldn't see the rest.

One flick and he was lit. He drew deep, then exhaled right into her face and said,

"Afore I go, I have a wee job to do for yer Mammie."

She knew better than to ask.

He seemed to know she wouldn't and said, "Yer Uncle Billy, he used yer Mammie's name to get a loan and the fooker, he's welshed on the repayment, left her in a right old mess, and old Billy, he supports the English Team."

The latter seemed to be the greater crime, if his expression was any indication. He offered her the cig, the butt wet from his lips, and she was too rattled not to accept.

As she took a full pull he grinned and said, "You like it unfiltered, don't you, gra?" Then he took it back, mashed it on the floor, and went, "I'm going to tell you what's coming down the pike for our Billy, so you know…never…fooking never…piss on the Movement or yer own kind. We never forget and we never fooking forgive, you got that?"

Hard not to.

She nodded slowly, hoping the wetness between her legs didn't show in her face, though she felt a burn on her cheeks.

"First I kneecap him," he explained, "and then, as he called yer mammie a toerag—see, the hoor's ghost is using Brit words—I'll cut off two of his toes and shove them down his gullet. Make him eat his words, and every time he hobbles around, he'll remember…" Then he sat straight up, asked, "Don't you have work to do?"

She tried to stand but her knees were shaking.

He went, "Any chance you could make a fellah a decent cup of tea?"

She never saw him again, though she did see Uncle Billy, with a cane and about twenty added years in his face. She couldn't help wondering if he'd been able to pass the toes, though she imagined that looking in the toilet bowl must have been a fascinating adventure for him from then on.

Now, looking at Slide in horror, she couldn't believe he'd screwed with the lads. Oh sweet Jesus, they'd make him eat both legs—and as for her, she was, in their eyes, one of their own.

She wanted to scream. "You crazy bastard, you've really put your foot in it. Where are we supposed to go?"

"America," Slide said.

And so they sat down, hatched out a plan to get some serious money and fast. In spite of all the fear, all the anger she felt toward Slide, Angela was excited about the thought of returning to New York. Oh God, she realized how much she missed it.

She gave Slide her full look, drilled her eyes into his, and she couldn't help marveling at the piercing blue. His expression, as usual; was impossible to read, though. You never knew if he was planning murder, mayhem and general madness, thinking about sex, or some of each.

"Okay," she said. "Here's what we're going to do and this is how we're going to do it."

The plan: They'd hit the bars, the posh ones where the suits and the money hung. She'd lure some schmuck outside and then Slide would do his gig. She was estimating if they hit maybe ten pubs, they'd score, say, in six, and have the run-like-fook-away money.

Slide was game, said, "Game on."

As long as violence was in the mix, he was up for it.

She cautioned, "And try not to kill anyone, can you fucking do that?"

He smiled, said, "I love it when you talk dirty to me."

Twelve

*If a man should challenge me now, I would go to that man
and take him kindly and forgivingly by the hand,
lead him to a quiet retired spot and kill him.*
MARK TWAIN

Max was gearing up for the big meeting with the Colombians, trying to learn as much *Español* as he could. He'd sent his bee-atch out to get him the tapes and he was listening to them whenever he had time, which wasn't often because he was *mucho* busy. *Mucho*, see how he intuitively knew this shit?

The idea to learn Spanish came to Max one morning on the bowl when he was thinking because, like, thinking was his forte.

See, when you were a clued-in dude like The M.A.X., you not only got to use words like *forte*, you had a reasonable idea of what they meant. He'd been telling himself like a mantra, *know your market*, and *know the guys you're dealing with*. He hadn't built up this hell of a business without being savvy, and he liked to think of himself as straddling both sides. Yeah, the boardroom, piece of cake, he could do the biz gig in his sleep. Sometimes he believed he was born with the Dow Jones in his mouth. Your regular working stiff, he read the sports section of the *Daily News*, moved his lips as he read, but The M.A.X., he didn't just read the business section, he fucking devoured it. *Wall Street Journal*, man, he subscribed, and knew his name was in every editor's address book over there. Come on, if you were a journalist in the business world and didn't have an in with Max Fisher, then who the hell were you anyway?

Who knew, maybe one of these days the *Journal* would ask Max to do a regular column for them and if Max was in a philanthropic mood, had some free time on his hands, felt the need to *give back*, maybe he'd accept. He'd call the column, what else, *The M.A.X.* Have guys in all the happening bars going, "I was reading in *The M.A.X.*..." or "*The M.A.X.* says..." Yeah, he could see it. The double hit of coke he'd had with his croissant and skim milk latte helped the visualization. And, hey, it could happen. But the bottom line was Max was too busy. The guy who came up with *multitasking*, shit, that guy had The M.A.X. in mind.

So, anyway, Max was thinking that the Colombians were coming to town, and those dudes spoke, like, Spanish, right? So, you were going to be in bed with them, you better, like, speak their lingo. Seemed to make sense. And it was this kind of preparation that had made Max the *hombre* he was today.

Hombre. Man, he was getting this shit down fast.

He listened to the Spanish tapes whenever he got some downtime and when you were as freaking busy as Max, running a goddamn crack empire, there wasn't a whole load of free time floating around. He listened when he was eating, on the shitter; he even wore the fucking headphones in bed, letting that crap seep into his subconscious, so even his sleep gig was, like, working. Did The Donald know that little trick?

And sure, okay, it was a little uncomfortable—damn earpiece fell out and poked you in the eye and the wire got wrapped round your throat—but who said knowledge was easy. Fuck, you ever hear old Stephen Hawking complaining? And that dude was wired if anyone was.

Max laughed out loud, loving his wit.

A few times there, yeah, when he'd gotten a little carried away with the crack, the booze, he'd put on the tapes, let it crank, played that shit loud till Felicia had screamed, "The fuck is wrong with you, put on some Lil' Kim!"

The reason why she'd always be a follower, didn't grasp the big picture. The bee-atch just didn't get it.

One odd sidebar—the voice on the Spanish tapes had this, like, posh accent, like some Spanish royalty or shit, and Max could only speak the lingo in the same aristocratic tone. There was this Lopez dude doing the lessons and Max was incapable of speaking in a halfway decent Spanish accent if he didn't add "Señor Lopez" to everything he said, in that upper-class tone. Like if he wanted to say *"Puede ayudarme?"* in a normal tone he sounded like shit. But if he said, *"Puede ayudarme, Señor Lopez?"* he sounded like a native.

Man, he sure as shit hoped one of these Colombians was named Lopez.

Another problem, his vocabulary wasn't exactly massive. He wasn't going to be entering any Spanish Scrabble tournaments any time soon. And a lot of the phrases he knew weren't exactly useful. Like how many opportunities would he have to say, *"Usted tiene gusto de dos limones y de dos naranjas, Señor Lopez?"* Would you like two lemons and two oranges, Mr. Lopez? Or *"A que hora abre la oficina de correos, Señor Lopez?"* What time does the post office open, Mr. Lopez? Or, *"A donde esta un buon restaurant in este ciudad, Señor Lopez?"* Do you know where there is a good restaurant in this city, Mr. Lopez?

The Colombians might find it a tad odd that he was asking them what time the post office opened and where the good restaurants were since he was the one who lived in fucking New York. Or, make that *Nueva York*.

Eh, The M.A.X. would pull it off somehow. He always did.

He pushed the CD player away, went, *"Usted tiene gusto de más blow, Señor Lopez?"* and cut a fresh line.

Sha-Sha shifted on his water bed, couldn't get comfortable. When you weigh in at four hundred pounds and change, comfort, man, that shit's hard to come by.

He was twenty-six years old and where was his life at? Nowhere, that's where. He was doing the same old, same old all the time, every day, and he was getting tired of all that bullshit. He was still out there on the corners, busting his ass and for what? He wasn't The Man—shit, he wasn't even on his way to being The Man. Niggas sixteen and seventeen were above him, bossing his ass around and shit, goin', "Do this, Sha-Sha, do that, Sha-Sha, smoke that dude, Sha-Sha, how come you fucked up, Sha-Sha? Where's my money at, Sha-Sha?" Man, he was thinking about going out there one day, blowing all their asses away. He get a piece and a hundred bullets and solve all his damn problems.

But Sha-Sha knew why he was where he was at—cause he was a sick-ass, that's why. How many times he go to nigga above him and say, "I wanna move up," and the nigga go back to him, "Fuck you"? Sha-Sha knew it was his own damn fault, cause he had no damn self control. He didn't know how to stop hurting people and even the gangs, man, they didn't need no crazy-asses hangin' around. Like sometimes Sha-Sha would be walkin' down the street, and he didn't like the way some nigga was lookin' at him, or he didn't like his sneakers, or the way he smelled, or sometimes there was no reason at all, and he'd take out his nine, pop the motherfucker in the head.

Sha-Sha didn't know why he was so fucked-up—it was just the way he was. It was probably the reason why he got so fat. Whenever he got down about his life and shit, he'd go for the menus, order in a whole mess of food. Then he'd get on the scale, see he'd gained another ten, fifteen pounds, and he'd feel so bad about it, he'd go out and shoot somebody. Then he'd feel bad about how fucked up all that shit was and he'd start with burgers and pizzas again. It was like his life was going round and round in circles and there was no way out.

When he saw he'd passed four hundred pounds he was all ready to say, Fuck it, and go out and start killing people, and kill himself while he was at it. Didn't make no damn difference anyway and, besides, how long before the cops got off their asses and busted him? They'd already had him in for questioning three times for killing three different motherfuckers. Yeah, he'd been away, but never on a murder rap, and his fat ass wasn't gonna be doing no thirty-to-life upstate. Them niggas loved big boys and he wasn't gonna be gettin' jammed like a pin cushion for no thirty years.

Then Felicia, his ho cousin, showed up at his crib. She was looking fine too, with that big ghetto ass, but what she'd do to her titties? Every time he saw her they got bigger and bigger; now it looked like they was ready to explode.

He went to hug her, was ready to push her head down so she could start sucking on his dick like when they was kids, but she pushed him away, started dissing him about his weight and shit. Man, he was ready to smoke that ho, then she hit him with some big idea. Shit didn't seem so bad neither—get some cash and product off some white people and dealers from down south and shit. Twenty grand was bullshit, but maybe they could get forty for the product. That made sixty grand and that wasn't too bad. It got Sha-Sha thinking, anyway—maybe he didn't have to go out, start killing people after all. Sixty grand, shit, he could use that—start up his own crew with his boy Troit. They could be the ones ordering all 'em niggas around and shit. Yeah, Sha-Sha saw his whole life changing. He'd go on the Slim Fast and Lean Cuisine, drop a couple hundred pounds, be able to get up out of his water bed without feeling all that shame and shit.

So when Felicia talking, Sha-Sha kept saying Yeah, yeah, let's do it, let's take the white man's money. Stupid ho thought she was gonna get twenty grand, meanwhile she wasn't gonna get a damn cent. Then he fucked her good and sent her ass back to Manhattan.

A few days later, she called him, told him she knew where the drug deal was at. But she was acting all smart and shit—said she wasn't gonna tell him nothing over the phone, that she had to be in the car with him and Troit and then she'd tell them where it was at. Yeah, she was smart all right. Soon she was gonna be dead too.

Felicia came back to Brooklyn the day before. In the elevator going down, Sha-Sha pulled stop and made Felicia blow him before they went to pick up Troit. Sha-Sha had hooked up with Troit up at Sing-Sing. Troit looked the opposite of Sha-Sha, bone thin, no meat on his whole body, but he was just as fucked up in the head. They called him Troit, cause he was from Dee-troit. Rumor had it he'd killed so many brothers over there he had to come to Brooklyn to cool down. Most times when niggas started going on about all the people they popped, Sha-Sha knew that was bullshit talking. But he'd seen Troit in action and the boy was stupid-crazy. Sometimes after Sha-Sha killed somebody he felt bad and started eating and shit. But Troit, man, he didn't give a shit.

So they was all three in a jacked BMW—Sha-Sha driving with Troit up front next to him, and Felicia in the back seat. She was all excited and shit, talking about the twenty grand she was never gonna get. She even had a damn suitcase, said she was gonna leave New York tonight, get on a bus to St. Louis and open a beauty salon or some stupid shit like that. She still wouldn't tell Sha-Sha where the deal was at—just kept on with the "Make a left here, make a right there" bullshit, like she was Miss Shadow Traffic. Man, Sha-Sha was sick of taking orders, specially from his ho-ass cousin.

They took the Belt Parkway, round to the BQE. Looked to Sha-Sha like they was heading to Queens someplace. Sha-Sha and Troit just wanted to listen to jazz, have some peace and quiet in the car, before they had to go start killing everybody. But Felicia kept going on and on, givin' more mouth. She was talking about Sha-Sha's body again, saying how he was too damn fat, and should go for one of them operations where he could get his stomach sewn up or cut off or some shit. Then she started getting into it with Troit, telling the man he was too thin, that he looked like a skeleton. Sha-Sha couldn't believe it. Didn't the ho know who she was talking to?

Troit couldn't take any more and turned round and said, "Bitch, you better learn how to shut up."

Felicia still couldn't keep her mouth shut, said, "You better stop callin' me bitch. I gotta listen to that shit all day long from Max, and I sure as hell ain't takin' that shit from y'all niggas."

Sha-Sha saw Troit's hand go for his piece, knew what was gonna happen next. And he couldn't let that shit happen—not till they knew where the drug deal was at anyway. Sha-Sha turned to Troit, gave him a look that said, *Later, man,* and Troit put the piece down.

Felicia didn't shut up the rest of the ride.

One point Troit said to Sha-Sha, "Later, yo, she mine."

Felicia, all bitchy, went, "What he say?"

Sha-Sha, smiling, went, "Nothin'."

Thirteen

*I would have killed more but I was out of ammunition
and I was afraid to buy more.*
FRANCIS BLOETH, WHO SHOT
THREE PEOPLE ON LONG ISLAND

To get cash for New York, Angela and Slide ran a series of fast guerrilla hits. Went like this: Angela would go into a bar, lure some sucker, checking out his wallet first, and then bring him outside where Slide got up close and personal. They did seven of these stunts in two days, knowing the Guards would be on them fast. Three paid real fine dividends and the others, well fook it, they were a bust, what can you do?

Still, they had their stake and Angela booked Continental direct to New York.

They ditched the shack they lived in and the car, well, you couldn't give the frigging thing away, so Slide stripped the plates, left it at the airport.

He was like a kid, excited at his dream coming true. Annoying the goddamn shite out of her with the endless questions: Can we go to a Yankees game? Can we live in Tribeca? Can we buy a Chevrolet? Can we go to Niagara Falls? Can we, can we, can we, till she roared, "Can we give it a fucking rest?"

He bought a new suit. It was June and she told him it was going to be hot, hotter than a motherfucker, so he bought a linen job, and was pissed when it creased on the plane. And, yeah, he bought a fedora, in white, looking like a poor relation of Truman Capote, and new shades—the real deal, Ray-Ban aviators. When the flight attendant came by with the beverage cart he ordered a Tom Collins and when that wasn't available, he went Bogey, snapped, "Gimme bourbon, rocks, Bud chaser."

To hear this in an Irish accent is to have lived a little beyond yer sell-by date.

Angela had a large vodka, hold the mixer. She wanted that raw burn of alcohol in her gut and she got it all right.

The in-flight movie had Tom Cruise in it and Slide went, "I love the Cruiser. Maybe we should become Scientologists, there's serious wedge with those dudes."

Angela had some Xanax stashed in her purse and over dinner, with those mini bottles of wine, she knocked those babies back and it knocked her right out. The last thing she heard was Slide asking the stewardess, "You got a carton of, like, Luckies?"

She thought she might seriously hate him.

Entering Kennedy Airport, Slide's first response was, "Holy fook!"

Angela's response was slightly different. She felt relief, hearing the accents, seeing the American flag, like, everywhere, and knowing she was, if not home, at least on familiar terrain. New York was her town; she knew how it worked.

Slide's Irish accent had got him through Immigration and he got the 90-day visa. Angela had her American passport and she got, "Welcome home."

Outside Kennedy, they had to join a line for a cab and Slide was marveling at everything, going, "Fook, the taxis are *yellow*."

He wanted to skip the line, said, "Let's jump the queue."

She explained two things, slowly and patiently because her head was, like, fookin opening from a migraine: "One, you want to get killed in New York, try skipping the line. And two, that's what we call it here, a *line*."

Nothing could dampen Slide's enthusiasm and he said, "Could do me a line of coke right about now."

Online, she'd found a hotel in the Village, got two weeks at a decent rate, the Euro finally working in her favor.

The driver, a surly black guy, said, "The flat rate is forty-five bucks, plus tolls."

Slide, into it, went, "Jaysus, I'm being mugged already."

Either the black guy didn't understand the accent or he could give a fuck.

When Slide saw the size of the hotel room, he said to the bellboy, "Okay, we've seen the closet, now where's the room?"

Angela shushed him said, "Give him five bucks," and then tried to explain to Slide about tipping.

He listened with astonishment, then said, "Scam city, what a con."

Angela said she needed a shower, a big drink, and a lot of sleep.

Slide said, "You grab some z's, babe. Me, I'm gonna paint the town red." Angela was going to have to talk to him about his awful idea of what constituted current American speak, but she was exhausted from the flight and decided the slang lesson could, like, wait.

Slide hit the street, figuring he'd off his first American after a cold one or two. He fully intended chasing the serial killer record and he was in the right city to start. As he entered a bar he hummed a few bars of *New York, New York*.

The place was quiet. A guy at the counter was alternating between sipping a Coors Light and a pint of water. He had on those grey-tinted shades that shouted, Serious intelligent dude. He was reading the sports page.

What the hell, Slide was in the mood to talk, so he grabbed the stool next to the guy and asked, "How you doing?"

The guy shut the paper with a sigh, turned round, gave Slide a serious intensive look, then asked, "Irish?"

Slide was a little put off, thought he'd got the New Yorker thing down, but said, "You got me, pal."

The guy flicked his hair and said, "I know an Irish guy and, well, what can I say? He sure can talk."

Slide wasn't sure if this guy was fooking with him so he shouted to the bar guy.

"Hey, before Tues, right?"

That's some New York speak for ya.

The guy took his sweet time getting his arse in gear but finally came over and said, "What do you need?"

Slide didn't like the guy's tone, thought maybe he'd off both of the fucks, get a jump start on his record. Then he said, "Gimme a Wild Turkey, beer back."

The guy next to Slide exchanged a look with the bartender and Slide thought, *You guys dissing me?* Then he asked the guy, "You want to join me in a brew?"

The guy said he'd have another water. The fook was wrong with him?

The drinks came and the bar guy asked, "You running a tab?"

Slide stared at him, wondering what the fook was he on about.

The guy beside him said, "He means would you like to pay now or pay when you're done? How it works, you put some bills on the counter, and he takes the money as you go along."

Without thinking, Slide went, "Touch my cash, he'll be touching his right hand, wondering where his fingers went."

The guy laughed, as if he thought Slide was joking.

Slide knocked back the Turkey, drained the beer, belched, and put his finger in the air, doing a little dance with it, signaling for more booze. He'd seen that in a movie and always wanted to do it. You tried it in Ireland, you'd be waiting a wet week for service but the Americans, they liked all that signal shite, ever see them play baseball, nothing but fookin signals, anything but actually hit the damn ball.

The second Turkey mellowed Slide a notch and he felt that familiar heat in his gut. He'd had enough of these guys and asked the bartender for directions to the nearest betting parlor. As a child, his old man used to take him to The Curragh, the racetrack in Kildare, and Slide could pick winners simply by looking at the horses in the parade ring. It was a weird and wonderful gift, but erratic, not always dependable. If Slide could have depended on that gift, he wouldn't have ever got into the kidnap biz.

Slide cabbed it to the Off-Track Betting tele-theater on Second Avenue and Fifty-third Street. It was five bucks to get in and he was going to argue but said, *ah fook*. Then, as he paid, the woman went to him, "You need a shirt with a collar."

Said it as an order, like this was the Plaza Hotel and he was, what, some low-life shitehead? He heard the voice, prodding him to lean over and strangle the old wench, but he thought, *Whoa, buddy. Easy now, partner*. There was probably CCTV everywhere around here and after the whole Keith Richards fuckup he wanted to be a little more choosy about his next victim. The last thing he needed was the NYPD breathing down his arse.

He cocked his finger and thumb in the gun gesture, said, "I'll be seeing you in, like, jig time."

Around the corner on Third Avenue and down a couple blocks, he found a sporting goods shop. Bought a golf shirt with a collar and dashed back to the OTB. He was already twenty-five in the hole and his stake was only a hundred to start. He needed to pick winners, and fast.

Unfortunately the horse-picking talent he'd had as a child in Ireland eluded him in Manhattan. In the race going off at Belmont, Slide loved the look of the seven. He bet half his stake on the horse, only to watch the jockey pull the rat up on the backstretch.

Quickly Slide's stake eroded. He was down to his last ten bucks. He was waiting by the TV for a glimpse of the next post parade, when he noticed a guy celebrating, high-fiving with other gamblers. The guy had long straight hair, a strong jaw—kind of looked like a poor man's Fabio.

Slide had heard the guy cheering home the winner of the last race, the race where the pig Slide had bet on finished dead last.

Slide went up to the guy and said, "Had the winner, huh?"

"You kidding?" the guy said. "I hit the Pick Six for the first time in my life. Can you believe it?"

Slide, real happy for him—yeah, right—went, "So how much that get yeh?"

"A lot," the guy said, smiling widely. Was Slide imagining it or was the smug bastard trying to rub it in?

"What's a lot?" Slide asked.

"Eh, about five thousand bucks," the guy said, still with that self-satisfied tone, like one lucky ticket had transformed him from lifelong loser to king handicapper. "For me that's not a big deal. I've been hitting winners left and right for weeks. Who'd you play?"

"The seven."

"The seven!" The guy said it so loud, people were looking over. "You played that piece of shit? That was the first horse I crossed out in my *Form*. I can't believe you played the seven."

Slide, gritting his teeth, went, "So you some kind of expert on American racing or something?"

The sarcasm couldn't have been more obvious, but the guy missed it.

"Yeah, you could say that," the guy said. "I mean, they say only five percent of all gamblers come out on top, and I guess since I'm in that five percent that makes me an expert."

A few minutes later, Slide watched the guy collect his winnings. He was such a high roller now that, of course, he tipped the teller twenty dollars, went to her, "Thanks, hon," like he was De Niro in *Goodfellas*. Then he bought a round of drinks for his gambler friends. Offered to buy Slide one too, but Slide declined, going, "I don't drink." He was on a sarcastic roll all right.

Slide stopped betting. What was the point? He had a more surefire way to make his stake.

The smug guy hung around for the evening harness racing programs. He won a few more races, bragging to the teller, "I'm so hot, you're gonna have to hose me down."

When the guy finally left, Slide tailed him around the corner. It was getting late—there weren't many people around. Near a construction site, Slide grabbed the fook by the shirt, pulled him beside a Dumpster.

And get this, the guy goes, "Hey, come on, easy on the shirt, man, you know how much that cost me at Banana Republic?"

Slide needed to get the guy to focus so he broke his nose for openers. The guy, hurting and seriously pissed off, whined, "Whoa, come on, I have to do a big photo shoot tomorrow for *Crime Spree*!"

"Crime spree this," Slide said, then he shut the fook up with a few rapid punches, blackened both his eyes. Slide went, "Nothing personal," and then he kneed him in the balls and took his wallet. His heart sung at the sheer weight of the cash. Meanwhile, the guy was groaning, "Help me, help me," but it sounded like, *Halle, Halle*.

Slide bent low, face in the guy's face, and, almost lovingly, moved the guy's long hair from his ruined features.

It seemed to finally dawn on the ejit that he was in, like, deep shite and he croaked, "Are you going to kill me?"

Slide went, "Naw, I'm going to let it slide."

He paused for a second. Then he reached out and crushed the fucker's windpipe.

The guy had a very flash watch, looked like one of those high tech jobs. Slide helped himself to that, then gave him a kick in the head for luck. He laughed, said, "Lights out." Then he sauntered off, going, "No hard feelings, all right, buddy?"

Fourteen

*All I have in this world is my balls and my word,
and I don't break 'em for no one.*
AL PACINO AS TONY MONTANA, *Scarface*

This was going to be the day of The M.A.X., the big enchilada, the coming out party, the date that Max showed Señor Lopez who was *el jefe*.

The meeting with the Colombians wasn't till nine PM, but Max had been awake since five in the morning, running the details in his mind, a nagging worry about *Los Colombanos* refused to go away. The stress was really starting to get to him so he decided, Fuck it, and had a little pick-me-up, nothing too heavy, just a few tokes on the crack pipe to go with his caffeine fix. And he was thinking, *I should eat, get something in my stomach*, but he couldn't, so, what the hell, he had another tiny hit.

But the dilemma kept weighing on him—what the hell was he gonna wear? What were folk wearing to dope deals these days anyway? Did you go all biz, the suit, the power tie, handmade shoes? Or dress lethal, like you were casual but, hey, watch your mouth, buddy, cause I might look like Bloomies but I'm carrying, like, major heat so tread real fucking careful, you stupid Lopez fuck.

Yeah, that could work, he liked that touch of swagger, he was preening in front of his full-length mirror. Had his eyes developed that Clint Eastwood hardass glint? He tried narrowing his eyes but he couldn't see for shit when he did that.

Whoa-kay, chill baby, chill way on down and he would but his goddamn heart was like pumping a mile a second. He needed to look chill, so he put on a Yankees shirt, it was black, had the logo only on the collar, showed he was a sports guy but not, you know, showy with it. Then he put on Tommy Hilfiger black slacks, looking good, all in black, looking...what was that fucking word the French had...*nora*?...no, *noir*. Yeah, he looked noir as fuck.

Then the piece de resistance—the Glock he'd found in Kyle's suitcase. Sure he'd gone through the kid's stuff—you had to know who you were employing—and underneath the copies of *Hustler*, *Playboy*, and *Bust* he'd found it, loaded, with a spare clip. The kid had an automatic in there too, so he'd left that. The kid was too much in awe of him to ask if he'd taken it—one of the perks of being the boss, the help didn't get to quiz you.

He pointed the Glock at the mirror and couldn't get over how fucking *cool* he was. He let out his breath—shit, he could have made it in the movies—said, "Name it, mister," and heard, "Who are you talking to?"

For a horrendous moment he thought his reflection had spoken to him—Jesus, he'd have to ease up on the marching powder—then realized Kyle was behind him. How long had he been standing there and what was with that look, the kid's eyes stuck on the gun?

Max went for aggression—you're in a bind, go ballistic—and said, "The fuck you doing, sneaking up on a person, get your fool self killed that way, son?" He liked the almost black intonation he'd achieved there and the *son*, well, that was pure raw talent. Then he noticed Felicia was gone—he hadn't seen her in at least a couple of hours—and said, "Where the fuck is my bee-atch?"

"She said somethin' about havin' to do some shoppin' or somethin'," Kyle said.

Max noticed he had his bible with him and said, "You're not gonna be reading that around the Colombians, are you?"

"What's wrong with the Bible?"

"Do whatever you want," Max said, "but I think it's a big mistake. Religion—shows you're weak, you're living in fear of *Dios*. We want to show these *hombres* we're fearless, then they'll be afraid of us, get it?"

"I need Jesus by my side," Kyle said.

The dope was definitely cruising in Max's system and he had a ferocious impulse to cap Kyle, just for the hell of it. Max had been at the center of a whole blitzkrieg of murders but, like, get this, he'd never—what was the term? Oh, yeah, *smoked a motherfuckah*. Nope, but he sure as hell had thought about it a lot. It was Peckinpah type stuff—a lingering slow-motion shot of Max, cool as the breeze, drawing on a thin cheroot, and then spittin' some baccy from the side of his mouth. He'd been so loaded one night, he even went and bought some chewing tobacco—that shit was harder to get in New York than heroin. Then back at his apartment, the whole scenario opening up, he'd popped the shit in his mouth and, oh sweet Jesus, the fuck was with that taste? It congealed in his teeth, nearly removing one of his very expensive crowns, and then it nearly choked him. He'd cap some dude *sans* the chewing tobacco, maybe get some Juicy Fruit, leave a lingering freshness too.

He barked at Kyle, "The only good book you need is right here," and then he tapped his heart, thinking, *Fuck, how deep am I?* Maybe he'd go for a doctorate in metaphysics when this gig was wrapped—hell, he already had Buddhism down.

Kyle, the dumb cracker, as usual looked lost, said, "I'm lost."

Max sighed, decent help was, like, freaking impossible to find, he tried to put some fatherly patience in his tone, and like Pa Walton on crystal meth, said, "Son, what you read in your heart is the only line you ever need to remember." Max had lost his train of thought halfway through the sentence and in frustration, said, "We're gonna be dealing with some heavy dudes here, son. They see that book, they're gonna think you got a concealed gun in there."

Kyle said, "The Lord is my weapon."

Max, sick of the whole conversation, went, "The Lord better be packing, then."

Kyle stuck his hand out and Max, puzzled, asked, "You want to shake my hand?"

Sly little redneck grin from ol' Kyle who said, "I'd like my Glock. That piece cost me a whole bunch of bucks."

Max, flying off into another one of his accents, said, "Don't you be giving me none of yer lip, boy, hear? You ain't too tall to take a whupping."

The *whupping* set off a drug hard-on and if Felicia had been there, he'd have given her a real whupping right now. "Now git yer ass in gear, boy, we is set to rock 'n' roll, you hear what I'm saying? You down, bro, you ready to chill with The M.A.X., you ready to ice these spics?"

He liked this rap so much he was sorely tempted to write it down, use it in his HBO series.

Kyle, an edge in his voice said, "Don't call them spics."

Max said, "Long as they don't call my play, *hombre*." He started hunting around for the shit he needed to make a martini. There was enough time, as long as while he was making it Kyle went and got the car. Like, right now.

Kyle stared at Max as he found a pitcher but fuck, no olives. Who the fuck was supposed to be doing, like, the housekeeping?

Oliveless, he turned to Kyle, and in his most sarcastic tone went, "Hello, the car, the ve-hi-cle...like, duh?"

Kyle had the vacant-eyed look back and Max reckoned, no two ways about it, down there they were definitely giving one to family members or sheep. Hell, maybe down there the sheep *were* family members.

He said, "Our means of transportation, son. Or are you thinking we should call a cab, say, Take us to our drug deal, Mohammed?"

He had to get these lines down on paper. Maybe write 'em up as a book one of these days, like those Hard Case books with those women on the covers. Max had never picked one up but, man, those guys knew how to use a pair of tits to sell a book.

Kyle said, "Oh, right," and he was gone, with his bible.

Max downed the martini. Wasn't bad, maybe he could do a second, wash his mouth out, take the acrid dope taste out of his gums. Naw, better not. Say what you like about The M.A.X., he knew his limits—oh yeah, he knew when enough was enough.

He put the Glock down the waistband of his trousers, in the small of his back, and went, "Ouch." Jesus, it was cold. Did he have time to warm it up? Could you microwave a gun? And it pressed against his bum sacroiliac, shit. He took the piece out, got his black suede jacket. It had that expensive cut, you saw it, you whistled, it said taste *and* platinum card. Yeah, after today, it was platinum or bust baby.

The jacket had a large inside pocket and he put the gun in there. Was the bulge too big? Ah, fuck it, he was good to go.

He had a last sip of the martini, said, "Bring it on, *muchachos*."

Max and Kyle headed out to Queens in a Ford SUV. Max wanted to go in a Porsche, show the *hombres* what a hip, happening guy he was, but he figured they'd be in a limo and he wanted to be above them, looking down. Yeah, you need that height advantage in any business transaction. How do you think The Donald did it? And how many millionaire midgets were there in the world?

He had Kyle do the driving. What, you think The M.A.X. had time for trivial shit? Get real, buddy.

Crossing the Fifty-ninth Street Bridge, Max did a line on the dashboard, just to stay nice and juiced.

Kyle said, "Um, you think you should be doing that?"

Max inhaled, felt the rush, went, "Doing what?"

"That coke in the car, out there in the open an' all...you know what I mean?"

Man, that slow, muttering cornpoke drawl could start to get on a person's fucking nerves. Max caressed the Glock, thinking maybe he'd shoot Kyle in the foot, see how he liked that. For fucking Christ's sake, the kid was, what, becoming moral now? Thought he had a bible so that made him what, God? Max wanted to remind Kyle that he was the one who'd turned him on to this shit—the kid looked innocent but he was a goddamn enabler. But he didn't want to get into it now, when he was so focused, so *in the zone*.

About ten minutes later, they approached the meeting spot— the lot behind the abandoned warehouse, right along the East River.

Max didn't see any other cars in the lot. He wondered what the fuck was going on, said, "What the fuck's going on? Weren't the *hombres* supposed to be here before us?"

"There they are," Kyle said.

"Where?" Max said impatiently. He didn't see shit and was that line wearing off already? Goddamn bullshit coke. What happened to the Real Thing?

"Right over there," Kyle said.

Now Max saw two kids, teenagers, approaching the car, squinting at the headlights. One of the kids was wearing a Madonna concert T.

"Who the fuck are they?" Max said.

"The big one's Xavier and the shorter one's Carlos," Kyle said. "They're the Colombians."

Max would've thought Kyle was joking if the kid wasn't dumber than Forrest Gump. These were the cartel, the Noriegas of the zeitgeist? And, yeah, as soon as he found out exactly what zeitgeist meant, he'd use it more often. Meanwhile, he was seriously agitated.

"What kind of bullshit is this?" Max said.

There was no limo in sight; how'd they get here, on their fucking bicycles? They had goddamn piercings. And how old were they, sixteen?

"Hey, bro," Xavier said, still squinting badly. "How 'bout cutting the lights? You blindin' my ass."

The fuck sounded like he was from the goddamn Bronx—how much American TV did they get down in South America? He didn't even have a Spanish accent. Max had been wasting his time with all that Señor Lopez shit for this?

Kyle turned off the headlights and Xavier and Carlos came up to the SUV's driver-side window. The three of them started talking, laughing it up, like they were in a fucking high school parking lot. Fuck, maybe they could all go out for pizza.

Max, needing a pick-me-up big time, was getting set to do another line, about to snort it through a rolled-up hundred, when another car pulled into the lot, headlights blazing.

"The fuck is this?" Max asked.

"Darned if I know," Kyle said.

There was something about Kyle's tone. He sounded very un-Kyle—a little too quick, too prepared. It crossed Max's mind, *Was this some kind of set-up?*

Max felt a drip of white cold sweat roll down his back and he knew that was gonna fuck up the line of the shirt. He was thinking, Uh-oh, good this is not.

Two black guys got out of the car. One was skinny, one was huge, looked like Fat Albert. They were both in oversized basketball jerseys and were wearing backwards baseball caps.

Max went, "What the fuck is this? A goddamn nightclub?"

Then Max spotted the automatic weapons the guys were holding. He was too shocked to react. He just sat there, looking as dumb as Kyle, as the two black fuckers started running toward the SUV, firing. Glass was shattering, Xavier's head exploded. The top of it just like took off, went through the air like some weird Frisbee and Max was thinking, *Oh, holy fuck*.

Covered in blood, Max shouted, "Drive, you asshole! Drive!"

A bullet went into Carlos's neck, made almost a whistling sound—whoosh, and kept right on going, to Colombia maybe. Then Carlos crumpled like a sex doll Max had once had and crushed in his excitement. More glass shattered, and finally Kyle turned on the ignition and the SUV started.

Ducking, Max shouted, "Go!" and Kyle sped away.

Max didn't know if he'd been hit. He didn't feel any pain but maybe his terror had blocked it out.

Bullets continued to spray against the car and then Max remembered he had the Glock. This was it, his *Scarface* moment, a chance to put everything he'd learned to work. He could be Tony Montana, he could kill a couple of *putas*. Seeing himself in one of the drive-by scenes in *Boyz n the Hood*, Max sat up and started unloading the Glock, firing wildly at first, but then he hit one of the guys—the skinny one—right in the chest.

Bullseye, got the bastard dead on. Man, Max could shoot—he'd brought down his first *hombre* and it felt fucking wild, it felt *right*. He should have done this years ago, what a goddamned rush. He couldn't resist screaming, "Hee haw! *Caramba!*" as the SUV sped through the lot.

Then Max looked at the parked car back there near the gate,

caught a glimpse of the back seat. He couldn't believe what he was seeing. Was that fucking Felicia?

He wanted to blow the backstabbing little bee-atch away, but he was too stunned to shoot. Right there, the cunt who'd sold him out, in his line of fire, and he got trigger shy. Fuck, fuck, fuck.

Fifteen

Fuckin' Ruthie, fuckin' Ruthie, fuckin' Ruthie, fuckin' Ruthie, fuckin' Ruthie.
DAVID MAMET, *American Buffalo*

When they drove into the lot, Felicia saw the SUV and the two Spanish dudes talking to Kyle at the window and she said to Sha-Sha and Troit, "Do me a favor, yo—don't kill the white boy, Kyle. He ain't done nothin' wrong and he was the one hooked us up to begin with, know what I'm sayin'? Maybe shoot him in the leg if you gotta, or some shit like that, but don't kill the boy, a'ight?"

She was hoping to hell they wouldn't turn, give her that dead-eye, I-fuckin-hate-you-bitch look they been practicing. Hell, with Troit, there was no practice necessary. Few dudes chilled her ass but, man, this motherfucker was born crazy.

Up front, they were chilling with jazz, goddamn Wynton Marsalis, and Felicia didn't think they was hearing a damn word she was saying. Felicia didn't like all this getting in with Troit bullshit. She didn't know why Sha-Sha had to bring that sick-ass along in the first place, why he couldn't keep it in the family and shit.

Sha-Sha braked the car and cut the tunes and said to Troit, "Hold up," and Troit went, "Fuck that shit." Troit had his piece out and Sha-Sha had to take his out too. Damn, was they AK 47s?

Felicia said to Troit, "See? I knew you was gonna fuck all this shit up."

But Troit was already out the car and Sha-Sha was with him. Before Felicia knew it, they was both shootin' like they was in

Iraq and shit, blowing people's heads off, blood going everywhere. Felicia heard Max screaming and she hoped he was gonna get it next. Yeah, she hoped that muthafucka suffered real bad 'fore he went straight to hell. Shit, she couldn't wait for that ol' crackhead to be dead, and it looked like Kyle was gonna be dead too. Shame, dick like that gotta go to waste, but what you gonna do?

The two Colombians went down—that was good—but then the SUV started moving and, shit, was that Max stickin' his head out the window, screaming his ass off, shooting a piece? That flabby white no good motherfucker was *shooting*? He missed Sha-Sha, but he got skinny-ass Troit down. She couldn't believe it—badass Troit taken down by the most useless piece of white trash she ever had in her mouth.

The SUV went right by Felicia and Max was looking at her, aiming the piece right at her. Funny the shit people'll think about when they think they time's up. She hadn't thought about her momma in years, didn't even send Christmas cards to the old ho bitch no more, but now she thinking, *Momma you save me now, I'm gonna come visit y'all, send some bucks too. Y'all see, I be a good daughter now.*

Max's eyes got all wide and shit, like he was gonna start coming in his pants, but he didn't shoot her. Then the SUV sped away, out of the lot, and Felicia said out loud, "Fuck you, Momma! You never did no bullshit for me anyway! I don't care if I see yo' big, fat, ugly ho ass ever again!"

The money was gone but at least they got the rock. Once they split the profits up, she was gonna be on her way to St. Louis. She was nearly laughing now, so happy to be alive, and she yelled, "I'm goin' to St. Louis. Hell, yeah, baby! Hell yeah!"

Felicia watched Sha-Sha get the rock out of one of the Colombians' pockets. He stared at the guy for a minute, then put two more rounds in the guy's face, turned then as if something occurred to him, and kicked the guy in the head, twice, keep the numbers level, then came back toward her. The fat man didn't look too happy. She didn't know, but Troit, the psycho motherfucker, was Sha-Sha's boy, his back-up bro and shit. And, yeah, Sha-Sha's face showed it. He couldn't believe his boy was down.

Looking down at Troit's shot-up body, Sha-Sha was thinking, *Damn, man, why you gotta be so stupid and start shooting the motherfuckas so fast?* If they got up close first, they could've ambushed the niggas, got the white dudes and the Colombians at the same time, and when everybody was good and dead they could've got the rock and the money both. But cause Troit was so wild and shit, they only got the Colombians, and got his own ass killed too.

His head still buzzing from all the guns and shit, Sha-Sha couldn't believe it. The nigga was *gone,* wasn't gonna come back ever. Man, why was the world like that? Why'd bad shit always happen to good people?

Sha-Sha looked up at the sky and wailed to God, "Fuck you! Fuck you, you sick-ass motherfuckin' piece of shit asshole prick-face motherfucker!"

He went back to the BMW, thinking, *This shit, this shit ain't right, some messed up shit goin' on with this deal.* But he had to get them the fuck outa there fast, cause he could already hear the cop cars coming.

Sha-Sha drove away and Felicia wouldn't shut her ho ass up. She kept going on, bitching about Troit and asking when she was gonna get her part of the money. Sha-Sha told her to shut her ass up, but she kept going on, giving Sha-Sha a damn headache. He was still seeing his boy, running towards the SUV, like the fool thought he be bulletproof. He could almost hear the sick-ass brother's voice, yelling as he ran.

On the Belt Parkway, going past the Verrazano, Felicia was still going on, "I want the money tonight. Let's go see whoever you gotta see right now. And don't give me no bullshit about it neither. You ain't playin' me for no sucker. And if you think I'm gettin' down on my knees again, suckin' yo dick one more time, you crazy."

Sha-Sha couldn't hear Troit no more cause the damn ho was screaming, drowning out his boy's voice. He felt all that acidy shit coming up, spat on his own lap, turned around, and shot a big-ass hole in the middle of the bitch's head.

"That'll shut yo ass up good," he said.

He felt better already. Yeah, he could do with a cold one, a little tote of some crystal, count his profit.

He got off the Belt, drove into some dunes and shit. Left the ho's body there for the seagulls to come eat. He reached down, took her bag, cheap damn Gucci reject shit, like her whole cheap damn reject life. Yeah, he'd heard her back there, hollering for her momma. He'd fucked her momma when he was fourteen and now he'd fucked the whole damn family.

He looked up at the sky, waved his big arms, shouted to the birds, "Dinner time, y'all! Got y'all guys some real fine dark meat!" Then he laughed hard, muttered, "Hope you fuckers like silicone."

Sixteen

There are no saints in this world,
only liars, lunatics and journalists.
IAN BRADY, *Moors Murderer*

Joe Miscali was hot to trot, literally. He'd had to go to the can like four times already, had stopped off at Duane Reade, loaded up on Imodium Plus, and had downed like a half a box of the suckers. Now his guts felt like they were knotted together with superglue. This was it, his day of glory, bringing down Fisher, and for pure bonus, a Colombian cartel.

It had been an uphill battle convincing his superiors that this was the real deal, but his sheer insistence and the opportunity to grab major drug dealers had proved irresistible to the brass. With all the scandals recently involving crooked cops, they needed some solid press. Joe had even called the *Daily News*, got a crime beat reporter named Ward to accompany the team. The SWAT guys were pissed, their commander going, "Fucking civilians, they screw up everything, and press, are you outa your fucking mind?"

The commander was a serious hardass, suited up like Armageddon was imminent, with enough hardware to take down a small army. His team was all much the same—macho fucks who gave him the hard-eye. They chewed gum, racked their weapons and muttered among themselves. Joe had a flask of coffee, not a great idea with the trots, but what the hell. Without caffeine, he'd be like a hooker without the fuck-me heels.

He'd offered the flask around and they gave him looks of

sheer disdain, the commander going, "We don't need stimulants to do our duty."

The parking lot in Staten Island was open, exposed, and they'd arrived at the meet two hours early, quietly getting civilians out of the way. Cops were positioned on all perimeters—no way the dopers were going to break out of this ring of solid steel.

Joe, seeing the expressions of the SWAT guys, had said, "I want Fisher alive."

The commander, rolling the gum along his inside jaw, said, "They give it up, no prob...otherwise..." He let the threat trail off.

Joe was going to have to watch this asshole real close, or else the guy would waste everybody, and with the *Daily News* there, Joe was getting a real bad feeling. He was trying not to look at his watch, but he couldn't resist and the commander caught him and said, "They're late."

Ward, the journalist, had been talking quietly with his camera guy and now turned to Joe and said, "Be a major public relations fuck-fest if your guys don't show."

Joe felt his bowels burn and wondered if he should risk more Imodium. How many had he taken already?

The humidity was building and Joe felt a dribble of sweat roll down his forehead, sting his eyes. Then realized the press guy was staring at him, a smirk in place, and Joe snapped, "What?"

The guy shifted his position so he was right in Joe's face, said, "How's it work for you?"

The fuck was his problem? Joe asked, "The fuck's your problem?"

This seemed to really ignite the guy and he said, "You being Mr. Nice Cop, isn't that your rep? The one who gets results with, what, with *decency* and *understanding*."

Joe said, "Yeah, well, we don't all have to be hard-asses. You do what works best."

The guy was highly amused. He gestured at the very empty parking lot, the non-happening parking lot, and said, "Gee, and I can see it's working out really well for you."

Joe tried not to rise to the bait, especially with the growing panic he was feeling.

He said, "I'm sorry you might not get your story."

The guy was smiling, delighted. "Oh, I'll get my story. A no-show is a great story. All this NYPD/SWAT action, all the taxpayers' money, in an election year, flushed right down the toilet. Hell, buddy, I couldn't ask for a better story."

Before Joe could respond, the earpiece the commander wore began squawking. The commander looked at Joe, then pulled the earpiece out and shouted to his team, "Stand down, abort! Stand down, abort!"

Joe, his guts in shreds, asked, "What?"

Like he didn't know.

The commander was standing, tearing open the Velcro strips on his vest. His eyes like ice, he said, "A drug deal went down tonight, major gunfire, and Fisher may have been involved. But, guess what *Detective*, it's not on Staten Island—it's out in Queens."

Joe, bewildered, said, "Maybe it's another deal...I mean...."

The commander pushed past him, hissed, "Yeah, right. Face it, you just took it in the ass, pal, bent right over for it."

The photographer was snapping off pics of Joe, the SWAT team, and the empty lot. Joe shouted, "Put that fucking thing down!"

Ward said, "No more Mr. Nice Guy, huh? Might lead with that. Whatcha think? Think it works?"

Five minutes tops and they were all out of there, except Joe.

He was left standing in the middle of the lot, his hands shaking, his bowels in full revolt, his mind going, *She couldn't...could she?...Jesus, and I gave her, like, a hundred bucks...with another twenty to come...and paid for the meal, she could've, like, had anything on the menu...I didn't say go for the cheap special...I was nice to her, wasn't I?*

A homeless guy approached him, went, "Yo buddy, got anything for a man down on his luck?"

"Fuck you," Joe said, and then, part of his old good self fighting to re-emerge, he said, "Sorry, buddy," and gave him the rest of the Imodium.

Seventeen

Death makes a person hungry.
CHARLES WILLEFORD, New Hope for the Dead

Max was ravenous. He wanted junk food, Italian, Chinese, mountains of carbs, fizzy drinks, cold brews, a heap of coke. He wanted to go on shooting motherfuckers for hours, capping them good. He wanted, he wanted to kill the goddamn world, but first he was gonna have fucking Kyle's ass.

In the car, leaving the bloodbath, Max tried to figure out if Kyle had sold him out. He even put the Glock to the kid's head, threatened to play Russian Roulette, but the stupid hick still wouldn't spill. He just kept quoting from his bible—Ezekiel, Job, Jonah, fucking Ecclesiastes. Yeah, like any of that shit was gonna help him now.

They pulled over and Max tossed the Glock out the window, into the East River. Even under pressure, with the cops on his tail, riding the high of his first-ever murder, Max knew how to cover the bases. They dumped the bullet-riddled SUV on Queens Boulevard and hailed a livery cab into the city. He knew the cops would find the car, trace it back to him, but he had a story all planned.

In the cab, Max told Kyle exactly what to say when the police questioned them, but he wasn't sure if Kyle was listening to a damn word he was saying. Kyle was still praying, frantically turning pages of his bible, like he thought the faster he read it the deeper the shit would sink in. It occurred to Max, does Kyle even know how to read? Down where he was from didn't they all live in trailers and start working on their momma and poppa's farms when they were, like, thirteen?

When they got up to the apartment, Kyle locked himself in the bathroom, where he sat chanting more of that bible shit. Max, fueled on crack, was banging on the door, trying to get him to open up. Then he had an idea. Bible boy wouldn't like to be the cause of another man's suffering, now, would he? Max stormed into Katsu's room and—oh Jesus, the skinny little sushi chef was jerking off to a Jap porn movie.

Max went, "Fuck, you've been making my salmon maki with those hands!"

Then Max thought about all the sticky rice he'd been eating lately and wanted to yack.

Katsu stood up quickly, his boxers at his knees, covering himself and bowing, going, "Sorry, sir. Sorry, sir."

Max grabbed him by his hair and pulled him down the hallway to the kitchen. He grabbed the butcher knife, put it up to the terrified chef's neck, then dragged him to the bathroom and screamed to Kyle, "Okay, bible boy, get your grits-and-collard-greens ass outa that toilet right now, boy, or sushi man's made his last hand roll."

Katsu screamed, "Max crazy! Kyle, you listen to Max and open door right now! He not fucking round!"

Kyle opened the door a crack, saw what was going on, and said to Max, "All right, all right! I'll come out, just let him be. Let him be."

Sounding like some John Lennon freak, like he was gonna go hold a fucking séance at Strawberry Fields.

"I want the truth out of you," Max said, "and if you tell me I can't handle the truth, trust me, you'll make my day, asshole."

He slit his eyes like Eastwood while going for the Nicholson hardass tone. He almost hoped Kyle wouldn't give in. It would be fun to cut Katsu, to see what it felt like to kill with a knife. He'd already shot somebody today; if he strangled Kyle afterward it would be like hitting the murder trifecta. Yeah, Max felt fucking omnipotent, all right. He used to think that word had to do with, you know, getting it hard, getting a woody, but now he knew what it meant, he fucking knew.

"Okay, okay. I told her," Kyle said, tears streaming down his cheeks. "We were in love, Mr. Fisher. I was gonna take her back down to Alabama and turn her into an honest woman."

"You sold me out? After all I've done for you?"

Max felt seriously betrayed. He was Tony Soprano, getting ready to whack Pussy. He was Pacino asking his brother if he'd ratted him out.

Kyle said, "I tried to stay strong, I tried to do Jesus proud, but I couldn't. I just couldn't resist her. That woman, she did something to me. I think...I think she might be Jezebel."

"Yeah, she did something to you all right," Max said. "She tried to get your ass killed, and my ass too. Who were the guys Felicia was with?"

"I...I don't know."

"Bullshit, she must've told you something."

Kyle waited then said, "She said it was her cousin, I think."

"Did she tell you a name?" Max asked.

Again Kyle wouldn't answer right away, slow annoying fuck, then he said, "Yeah...It was Sha-Sha."

Sha-Sha? What the fuck kind of a name was that? It sounded like a guy in one those new videos Madonna was putting out—her tight and old in purple leotards with black guys hopping around her.

Max smiled, said, "But you don't know anything, huh?"

"That's all I know, honest to God." He clasped his hands together, beseeching. "Oh, please, sweet Jesus, don't invoke your wrath, and may the lord god Abraham, the sons of the tabernacle grant you the true wisdom—"

With his free hand, Max gave him a slap in the mouth, said, "May you shut the fuck up?"

Then Max gave Kyle another wallop, and because it felt good to beat on somebody he whacked his chef on the head too, the fucking jerk-off.

Leaving the two assholes, he went into the lounge, flipped on the TV and fixed himself a tall, dry martini, never letting go of the knife. It was like an extension of him. Maybe he'd be called Max the Knife in the movie. Jeez, then there'd be a musical. Max couldn't wait to see it. Maybe they'd get Hugh Jackman to play him.

He cycled through the channels till he got to NY1. And sure enough, the main story was the shootings in Queens. Fuck, talk about popping wood. They were talking about a lone gunman who took down some of the baddest mothers in these here United States. Well, not exactly but that's how it sounded.

Then someone handed something to the news lady, a sheet of blue paper. Breaking news, she said. An ex-stripper named Felicia Howard had been found, dead, off the Belt Parkway. *Bye-bye, bee-atch*, Max thought, then he heard a pair of loud sobs from behind him. He turned around to see Kyle and the freaking sushi chef, weeping in unison.

The fuck was Katsu crying for? Uh oh—Oprah light bulb moment—the little turd was giving the sticky rice to her as well? Christ, was there anyone in the apartment she hadn't been screwing? If they'd had a dog, would she have fucked him, too?

Max turned back to the news report. A cop named Miscali or something was taking the heat for some monumental screw up. At first Max couldn't follow it, but then he started to get the gist, in bits and pieces. Kyle and Felicia must've sold him out, but she'd given the cops the wrong location. But then who the fuck had shot Felicia? The only one left standing after the bloodbath had been Fat Albert—what was his name? Sha-Sha. But why would her own cousin shoot her?

Max's head was throbbing from trying to follow all the ins and outs of this, not helped by no food, but he was fucked if he'd ever eat another morsel that jack-off chef produced. Also, the sounds of Kyle's sobbing and wailing were seriously getting on his already frayed nerves. He shut the fucking TV off and stormed off to his bedroom, carrying the pitcher of martinis with him.

Max came to around ten the next morning. He was in his good smoking jacket, the one with M in gold on the pocket, and his stomach felt like a very large rodent was trying to gnaw its way out.

He wobbled toward the bathroom, then stopped, a thought hitting his very tender head, *The knife, where the hell was it?*

Nope, not on the floor. Then he thought, *Kyle*, and went to the living room, but the boy wasn't there. He did a quick tour of the rest of the apartment—no Kyle.

Well, screw him, he had to get to the bathroom, like, now. As he sat on the bowl, feeling as if his intestines were pouring out, he decided Kyle had run on home to Alabama. Maybe Sushi Man went with him, the good ol' boys down there, they'd sure appreciate cornholing some yellow meat, good for the skin. As another upheaval hit his tender stomach, he was sort of relieved he didn't have the knife—he might not have been able to resist the urge to slit his own throat, put himself out of his misery.

Then the doorbell rang. What the fuck? The doorman was supposed to screen visitors or God knew what vermin could just come up and ring his bell.

He staggered to his feet, gave his tender ass a wipe, and was about to answer the door when he thought, maybe it's Kyle. Eh, fuck him. Let the backstabbing bible boy sleep in the hallway.

Max started to walk away when a voice shouted, "Police, open up!"

Could Max have imagined it? Some side effect of the dope, the vodka…?

But the banging continued and a voice, said, "Police, open the fuckin' door!"

Max opened it slowly, then they pushed it open all the way. That cop from TV—man, this was some bad trip all right—forced Max onto the floor and cuffed him from behind.

"Party's over, big shot," the cop said. "Time to get your scummy ass downtown."

Eighteen

I want the legs.
MEGAN ABBOTT, "POLICY," IN *Damn Near Dead*
(2006, ED. DUANE SWIERCZYNSKI)

Angela was not a happy bunny. They'd moved from the hotel to a basement apartment on Sixth Street, right under a restaurant called Taste of India. When she'd dreamed of coming back to New York, this was not where she'd imagined being. Yeah, yeah, all New York apartments were small, but come on, you couldn't swing a frigging cat in this place, least not a live one. The ceiling was brown, either from nicotine, mildew, shite, or curry. She prayed it was curry. There was a constant pong of Eastern spice in the fetid air so the curry theory made some sense.

They had, count 'em, three rooms. You think, how bad is three? Well, one was a bathroom, then there was the so-called living room/kitchen—i.e., a hotplate and a kettle and barely enough room to walk—and the bedroom was the size of some closets, with one of those fold-up beds. Can you say cramped? And with Slide on top of her in every sense, she was on the verge of a scream every damn second. And worse, like they said at McDonald's, *he was lovin' it*.

They'd found the apartment, a sublet, on Craigslist. The rent was medieval, and that was before utilities. It didn't help the situation that Angela was beginning to have serious doubts about Slide.

The books he brought home—what was the deal with those creepo volumes anyway?

The Stranger Beside Me
Dahmer: An Intimate Portrait
Gacy, in his Own Words
The Green River Killer
Inside the Mind of Serial Killers

Not exactly light reading. And he didn't just read them, he fecking *studied* them. Told her he was going to write a screenplay someday. Yeah, like she believed that shite. Her last New York boyfriend, Dillon, had told her he was a poet and he'd turned out to be a ruthless killer, not to mention a right bastard. And Slide, the shifty fook, could hardly write his name. Besides, what was she supposed to do, support some writer and his hopeless art? She'd had enough of writers and their constant whining. She wanted a guy who'd hit paydirt.

Speaking of which, when she was doing laundry one day she'd found a wad of cash in Slide's jeans, hundreds of dollars. When she'd confronted him about it he'd said he'd gotten real lucky at the OTB. And that fancy watch—he couldn't even figure out how to use it, but would he part with it? Would he fuck. He said a guy gave it to him when he'd given him some action on his forecast for the playoffs. Yeah, like he knew baseball from hurling.

And the guns: He was collecting them, already he had a Glock, a Colt, and, most worrying, what looked like a small bazooka. He said he'd got them at a stall in the East Village and they were only replicas—yeah, right. Angela knew all about fakes, just check out her tits.

But why would he want such firepower? Then, as she had her first margarita of the day—and sure, it was only a little after two in the afternoon, but a girl needed all the support she could get—she suddenly stood still, the frozen margarita frozen in her hand.

Al-Qaeda.

Jesus wept—he had the dark looks, had begun growing his beard, and was always wearing those shades. Then she gulped the drink, another horrific thought hitting her:

Airplanes.

How many times had he made her watch *Airplane!* on their little TV? God, one time, riding her, he'd even hollered, "We have clearance, Clarence."

And as she began to mix a fresh batch of the margs, she remembered the time he'd taken her from behind, and roared, "Incoming, ground control to Major Tom."

Sweet mother of God, and don't forget his attempts to blend in, to sound American. Didn't they, those sleeper agents, try to, like, assemble? No, that wasn't it, fook…assimilate. Didn't they try to do that? And above them, the Indian restaurant, that fucking stink that permeated everything—Slide never complained; he seemed to love it. Them terrorist types, weren't they like *hot* on spices and shite?

Angela looked at the pitcher of margaritas. Whoa, hey, who'd been sipping from it? It was, like, way down. She'd had, tops, three, if even that, and it wasn't like she'd used that much tequila. In fact, if anything, she'd given herself a priest's ration—that is, mean and measured.

She sighed, thinking, What the fuck? It wasn't every day you discovered you were harboring a terrorist. Homeland Security would probably pay serious bucks to grab this sleeper agent.

As she tried to come up with a way to turn Slide in for cash, maybe become a national hero along the way, she saw, out of the corner of her eye, a large roach emerge from under the table. It was sauntering, like, with *attitude*. Frigging cocksucker, strolling across the puke-colored floor like he lived there. Well, yeah, he did, but not for much fucking longer.

She grabbed the mini bazooka, got it to her shoulder and said, "So, let's see if this baby is just a replica."

It wasn't. She blew a small hole in the wall and she missed the roach. The fookin thing scuttled away under the bed.

Her ears were ringing from the blast and she gasped, "It was fucking loaded." Then added, "I'm fucking loaded," and began to laugh—a high-pitched, hysterical giggling. The smell of cordite was overwhelming and she could hear pounding on the ceiling. What were the Indians going to do, spill some goddamn curry over this? They'd probably put curry on the roach too and call it lamb roachala.

She turned on the radio—Dixie Chicks coming in loud and sassy. Then there was lots of banging on the door. Angela opened it and a small Indian woman, concern writ large on her expressive face, asked, "What happened?"

Angela said, "The hot plate, it, like, blew."

The woman was trying to peer inside, but Angela had blocked better and bigger folk than this. Then the woman pointed and said, "Your eyes."

Angela reached up and realized her eyebrows were gone. She covered, going, "But don't worry, the roach is okay," and closed the door.

She was high on tequila, adrenaline and sheer firepower. She thought, No wonder guys went ape over this stuff. Christ, it was better than coke.

She laid the bazooka down on the counter, went in search of the other weapons, and said, "Lock 'n' fucking load." But to her shattered hearing it sounded like, "Rock 'n' roll."

Axl Rose would have understood.

Later, after she'd passed out and caught a few z's, Angela went to look for cigs. She'd been smoking Kools Menthol, what the Irish called the pillow-biter's cig of choice. There were crushed empties all over the floor, but she figured, let Slide clean up. Right. Fucking A.

She went to the tiny cupboard, and pulled out the drawer that Slide kept his undies in. She rooted around and hello, the fuck was this? Wads of notes, Franklins. Jesus, he'd been holding out on her, the dirty bastard. And, whoa, what was this? Some kind of list?

In his very distinctive script—walloped into him by the Christian Brothers, or so he claimed—it read:

> *THINGS TO DO*
> *Beat the serial record*
> *Load up on weapons*
> *Dump the bitch after*

She paused, wondering, Did he mean her? And after what? A terrorist attack? Fuck on a bike.

Further:

> *Learn American*
> *Hit the gym*
> *Get vitamins*
> *Get hooked up*
> *Don't let it slide*

That was it. She had no idea what the last two things meant, and vitamins? What was up with that?

She closed the drawer with his white Y-fronts—and white they were, the screwball soaked them in bleach like some Magdalen Martyr. Then she counted the bills, thinking, Holy shit, where did he get all this anyway, his pal Osama? Wasn't that guy, like, loaded?

The idea of turning Slide over to the Feds had vanished. She skimmed a few bills, figuring, what was he gonna do, call the cops? Her hair needed a cut and color and she had to get her nails done. Then maybe she'd hit the Village, buy some decent clothes. And if she could, she'd have something done about her legs. Oh yeah, and she'd get some frigging eyebrows since hers were, like, *blown*.

She pulled a chair in front of the hole in the wall. It didn't do much to cover it up and she shuddered, imagining what might crawl out of there next.

Nineteen

Ah, well, I suppose it had to come to this. Such is life…
NED KELLY, BEFORE THEY HUNG HIM

Max knew this drill—the windowless, hot-as-hell room, no water to drink, uncomfortable chair. Fuck, they even tried the good cop, bad cop routine. Did these losers think that textbook shit could crack The M.A.X.?

Detective Miscali came into the room again for, like, the fourth time. Max was still wondering what a guy who looked like an Irish cop from Central Casting was doing with an Italian last name.

Miscali sat across from Max, and they said at the same time, "Did you kill Xavier Rivera and Carlos Fuentes?" Then Max said alone, "How many times are you gonna ask me the same stupid questions?"

"Did you or didn't you?" Miscali asked.

"I told you who killed them," Max said.

"Tell me again."

"The thugs who ambushed my SUV when I pulled over to take a leak."

"Were you conducting a sale of crack cocaine with Rivera and Fuentes when the attack occurred?"

"Absolutely not."

"Were you alone?"

"No, I was with a friend of mine."

"What's the friend's name?"

"You seriously asking me this shit again?"

"Tell me his fucking name."

Max breathed deep, then said, "Kyle."

"Kyle what?"

"I don't know."

Max said this definitively because, unlike practically everything else he'd told Miscali, this was the truth.

"You don't know your friend's last name?" Miscali asked skeptically.

"That is correct," Max said.

"Now why is that?"

"Because I never asked him it."

"Yet he's a friend of yours?"

"Yes."

Miscali leaned back, rolled his eyes, said, "And tell me again, why were you going to Costco?"

"Because I like to shop in bulk," Max said. "Saves money. I might look like The Donald, but that doesn't mean I throw money away. I've got deep pockets but short arms, if you know what I'm saying."

Miscali gave Max a look that screamed, *Gimme a fuckin' break*. Max, looking as bored as possible, gave a theatrical sigh. He remembered that time before, when they'd hauled him in over his wife's murder and he'd been assigned some snot-nosed kid lawyer who didn't know shit from shinola. He wouldn't need some idiot lawyer this time.

"Come on," Miscali said. "You expect me to believe a savvy, successful, sophisticated businessman like you has to go bulk shopping?"

"You cops probably don't have to worry about the grocery bills but a businessman like me, I have to keep an eye on the small stuff, can't pay top whack every time I need a loaf of rye."

He thought, Let them digest that, see who they were dealing

with. The corruption slur, which he hadn't outright said, hung there and the Miscali guy—oh, he got the dig, all right—looked like he might come over the table at Max. Then the other cop, the heavyset black guy named Phillips, came into the room, sat. Before, Phillips had been the bad guy and Miscali had been the good guy. Max wondered if they were going to try the old switcheroo. Seemed that way because Phillips gave Miscali a look, like, *Lemme handle this*, then went to Max in a puppy-dog tone, "Mr. Fisher, you expect us to believe you were traveling in a vehicle with…" He checked his notebook, as if he'd forgotten already, "…this *Kyle*, and you don't even know the fella's last name? And yet you want us to believe he's a friend of yours?"

Max knew the routine, he'd watched his *Law and Order*, had the good cop, bad cop gig down cold. Because he knew it would piss their asses off to no end and he was sick of being so—what was the word?—appeasing, he said, "Detective, when you've been in business in this city as long as I have, you acquire a lot of friends; remembering their last names is a task, alas, that even I, sometimes, am not up to."

That was the way—they wanna use words, right back atcha, asshole. He let the black bastard know who he was, subtly, and let the hint of the juice he might have leak over the words.

Before Miscali could jump all over it, Max added, "I do remember the mayor's last name, by the way. You want me to give *him* a call?"

Max sat back thinking, *Suck on that, detectives*. He watched Miscali's face and the sheer rage there catapulted him into a realization. Man, this guy had such a hard-on, such a ferocity about him, it couldn't just be because of a busted drug deal. There had to be more there.

"Tell me about Felicia Howard," Miscali said.

"You know her last name," Max said. "Good work, detective."

Miscali looked look like he was going to lose it. "Who was she working with?"

Max exchanged menacing glares with Miscali for a few seconds, then the dots connected. Felicia had been snitching to this fuck and now she was meat; the guy was shredded but he had to bite down and not blurt it out. Knowledge was power and Max wasn't yet sure but knowing this, he thought he could get one over on the guy. He went with, "Don't I get a phone call? And a soda would be good now. You guys have any Fresca?"

Phillips—now it was Good Cop's turn—grinned and went, "Aw, c'mon now, Mr. Fisher. You're gonna lawyer up? We're trying to help you here."

Max had the upper hand now, felt the delicious thrill of it, drawled, "Like I said, a soda would be an enormous ol' help right about now, and a phone call, that would be, like my friend Kyle was fond of saying, a gift from the Lord."

Miscali lost it, stormed over the desk, grabbed Max, tearing his good shirt, a Van Heusen, for Chrissakes.

Max went, "Whoa, you know how much these suckers go for in Bloomies?" Thinking, *Two shirts down the shitter in twenty-four hours? For fuck's sake.*

Miscali snarled in Max's face: "You fucking prick. You know the mayor, like fuck you do. You keep this up, you're gonna know a bunch of guys at Rikers intimately, if you get my drift. These guys, they're itching to run a freight through some asshole. You that asshole, Fisher? Huh, wanna make some new friends?"

Max was going tell Miscali that he'd already had a Chinaman in Alabama visit his asshole—been there, done that—but he didn't see the need to dignify the cop's remarks.

"Face it," Max said. "You took your best shots at me and I blew 'em all to bits. Got anything else to throw at me or can I go home now?"

Miscali glared at Max for a few more seconds, then he and Phillips left the room. Max couldn't help feeling seriously proud of himself. Talk about courage under fire.

Then, about ten minutes later, Miscali returned, smiling widely, a big toothy grin.

"Jesus Christ," Max said, "what're you gonna do, be Mr. Good Cop now? How long is this fucking circus act gonna continue, because I have to, like, be places, you know what I mean?"

"I'd cancel my dinner reservations for tonight if I were you," Miscali said. "Maybe you should cancel them for the rest of your life. Well, that's not true, but you'll have no choice of where you eat. And that prison grub will probably be a little disappointing to a classy guy like you. You know what I mean?"

Max didn't know what he meant, went, "What do you mean?"

Still smiling, Miscali said, "We just got some good news. Well, good for us, not for you. We just picked up your friend Kyle at the Port Authority, trying to board a bus to Mobile. It's Kyle Jordan, by the way. Your friend's last name. Jordan. I guess we'll see how the Costco story and the other bullshit you handed us holds up, or doesn't hold up. Meanwhile, I'd suggest you make yourself nice and comfy, Mr. Fisher."

Max knew he was fucked but good. He'd finally hit the end of the line, his winning streak was over. Well, it made sense—after all, how long could all the good cards keep coming his way? He'd been on such a great run for so long, but even the biggest winners in the world eventually had their luck turn to shit.

He just couldn't imagine that Kyle, Retarded Kyle, would be able to keep his story straight. He'd probably get so freaked out about spending eternity in an eight-by-ten cell with a guy named Lucifer on the next bunk that he'd put Max at the scene, put him with the gun, even describe how Max had shot that gangbanger. Yeah, Max was fucked, all right.

The way he saw it, he had two choices: cry like a baby, or go down with class. The old Max would've picked door number one, no doubt about it. But the new and improved Max was beyond all that whiny bullshit.

Max sat in the corner of his cell, got into a lotus position. Okay, okay, so he was about as flexible as a dead tree, but he was almost able to sit Indian-style. He started with the breathing and relaxation, then he threw his mantra into the mix. He wanted to go inward, remove himself from the physical world, but he kept thinking about coke. He'd been okay during the interrogation, but now he was feeling it in a major way. Whenever he'd meditated lately he'd done a line or two, just to loosen up, and without it he felt lost, unstable. Then Max shuddered, thought, *Am I an addict?*

The idea seemed absurd. The M.A.X. a cokehead? He was too strong, too focused to actually become dependent on something. He was using the coke, the coke wasn't using him.

Or was it the other way around?

Now Max was losing his focus big-time—all he could think about was that bag of coke on the coffee table at home. Then he had a thought that terrified him: What if the cops got a warrant and searched his apartment? He'd left a lot of shit around —the coke, some crack here and there and, oh yeah, some pot— and there wouldn't be a shortage of drug paraphernalia. If the cops wanted to bust him they didn't need a confession or evidence he'd been involved in those shootings; all the evidence they needed was in a penthouse on Sixty-sixth and Second.

Max caught a vision of the immediate future—the booking, the circus with the media.

Then the jail time. He noticed the big buck in the next holding cell, one real big mean-looking dude who'd been eyeing The M.A.X. Oh yeah, wouldn't he like to give Ol' Max the railroad treatment. Fucking Miscali—if they'd wanted Max to fess up, all they'd have had to do was *suggest*, just *hint* they were gonna buddy Max up with that Afro-American boy, and he'd have confessed to the freaking Lindbergh kidnapping and thrown in the little beauty queen as well. What the hell was her name? Bon…Bon fuckin' something. Jesus, the powerhouse intellect was winding down, even The M.A.X. got tired. What was it he read somewhere? Homer nods? Like in *The Simpsons*? No shit, he was zoning, going in and out of thoughts, didn't realize he was muttering aloud till the homeboy next door growled, "Shudthefuckup."

Christ, Max tried but the words just came spilling out. This is what happened when you were hyper-aware, mega-bright, the flow couldn't be stopped. You could cage it but, man, you could not contain it.

Max began to weep. What had he done? Really now, come on, hadn't he just tried to get a slice of the American Dream? And tell the truth, was anyone hurt? Okay, yeah, the black guy he'd capped but, man, that was one fucking rush. He wished he had that Glock now—would blast the fucker in the next cell first, cap him right in the balls, then blast his damn way right out of this freaking hellhole.

Was the little girl's name Bon Jovi?

About an hour later a guard approached the cell. Max looked at the guard, anticipating the barked command of, "Get your ass in gear, dickhead."

What he didn't expect the guard to say was, "You're free to go, Mr. Fisher."

Twenty

I like to beat up a guy every now and then. It keeps me hand in.
MONK EASTMAN, NEW YORK CRIME BOSS

When Slide got back to the apartment, some Indian woman grabbed him and started screeching about an explosion in the basement and how she wouldn't tolerate this type of behavior. Slide was tired, wanted to get inside, get a cold one, many cold ones, and here was this mad Indian cow yelling in his face. He was sorely tempted to off her right there, but he sighed, said, "Yeah yeah, I'll take care of it."

She was still hollering, pointing her finger in his face, saying, "I will not stand for this" and "This cannot happen under my restaurant" and a lot of other shite talk. Finally he got away from her, went down to see what the bejaysus was happening in the apartment.

First thing he smelled was cordite. He was confused—had Angela been in a shootout? Then he saw the empty pitchers of margaritas and, worse, his list, his whole game plan, was out on the table. The bitch had been going through his stuff.

She was in the bathroom, the door locked. Slide busted open the door—wait till the Indian cow saw that—and grabbed Angela, pulled her out into the kitchen area. He whacked her good and was about to lay on a whole lot more when she shouted, "Get your fucking hands off me," and whipped out one of his handguns.

Stupid bitch couldn't tell the safety was still on? He grabbed the gun by the barrel, wrenched it this way and that while she fought to pull the trigger. Eventually he tore it from her hand.

Angela shrank back against the wall, went, "Oh, Jaysus, please don't kill me!"

Kill her? Slide wanted to ram her head into the wall a few hundred times, watch her bleed out. But he'd had a long, hard day—he'd killed a rollerblader in Riverside Park earlier—and he wasn't in the mood to kill again, not right now, anyway.

"You didn't call the police, did you?" he said, tossing the gun on the table.

"No," Angela said. "I swear on me mother's grave, no. Nor Homeland Security."

"Homeland Security?" he said.

Angela, trembling, went, "You're in...Al-Qaeda, aren't you?"

"Al-Qaeda?" Slide said. "Are you fookin' mad?"

"'Cause what I've been through, with IRA guys...I can't take another terrorist boyfriend."

"Is that why you blew the place up? Cause you think I'm in with fookin' Osama? Jesus wept, are you stone mad?"

"Well, you're growing the beard...and you're always talking about airplanes and—"

Slide went to the fridge, opened a bottle of Bud, sucked it down in one sloppy gulp.

Then Angela, who'd regained some of her composure and her earlier anger with it, went, "In that case, Mister Not-Al-Qaeda, what's this list, then? You planning to dump me?"

Actually, especially after this, Slide was planning to do more than just dump her. But, because he loved to fuck with people's heads—it's what he lived for—he said, "Never, baby. We're a team for life."

Angela said, "Then why did you write those things?"

"It's for me screenplay," he said. "I have to have some way to get money for us, right?"

"A screenplay, my arse. Try again."

"All right," Slide said, smiling because a brainstorm had come to him just in time. "What can I say. You got me. I been havin' an affair—but I'd already decided to break it off." He picked up the list from the table, neatly tore it in two, put the pieces in his pocket. "It's her I'd decided to dump. Not you."

"You asshole," Angela said, but there was a hopeful glimmer in her eye.

"I love you, baby," Slide said. "You and me."

"You mean it?"

"Cross me heart."

"Who was she, Slide? Was she someone I know?"

"Who?" For a moment, he seemed completely baffled.

"The other woman, Slide. The one you're dumping."

Oh. "Nah," he said. "No one you know."

"Was she…younger than me?"

"Ah, fook, see why I didn't want to tell you? Enough with the questions already. T'would only hurt you to know."

She went over to him, wrapped her arms around him tightly, and said, "I just want things to work out for us so badly, and I don't want any more trouble. I was thinking—maybe we should leave New York."

"What do you mean? We just got here."

"Yeah, but I'm tired of living this way, in this fookin' coffin, with curry dripping from the ceiling. And I'm tired of the whole city grind. I want to move to the suburbs. I want to be a soccer mom. I want to have a big kitchen that I can cook in. I want to live in a big house in New Jersey, like the one the Sopranos have."

He had to admit, the idea appealed to him. Operate in the suburbs, be Mr. Low Key Guy, hold down a job during the day, kill at night—yep, that worked. And the Sopranos' house with that swimming pool! Angela, she could be like Mrs. Soprano.

He could go around killing his arse off and she'd be there at the door at night to kiss him and say, *How was your day, hon?*

"I'd like that too, babe," he said. "But we need a stake to make that happen. I've been trying to get it, but it's just not coming together."

"Well, then," Angela said. "Take a look at this."

She showed him a photo in the newspaper, some business fuck looking smug.

"And that is of interest fookin how?"

Which was when she told him the whole long story, how she got mixed up with Max Fisher before she went to Ireland, had even been engaged to him for a while, and now he'd been connected to some drug dealers.

"You sure it's him?" Slide asked.

"I was engaged to the fooker," Angela said. "You think I can't recognize a snap of him in the paper?"

Slide said, "So he was arrested. What's that gonna do for us?"

"If you actually read the article you'd see that he was released, along with his partner, this guy, Kyle Jordan. God only knows how he got mixed up with that crowd. Max dealing crack—Jaysus, I can't even imagine that."

Slide went, "So what do you want to do? Kidnap him?"

"Not him—somebody close to him, and then make Max pay," Angela said. "See, I know how Max is. He talks the talk but deep down, when it counts, he's what we in America call a wuss. You should've seen him when he found out he had herpes. He was crying like a baby."

"Herpes?" Slide asked.

"Oh, no, he didn't catch it from me," Angela said quickly, obviously busted, trying to cover. "He got it from, um, a previous relationship. And he didn't give it to me either. Honest."

Slide suddenly felt the urge to scratch. He also had the urge to wallop her again, but the lure of money was stronger. He said, "So he's a wuss. What does that do for us?"

"He's in a very vulnerable position, cops breathing down his neck, and if he's dealing drugs these days, he must be seriously loaded. It's the perfect time to kidnap somebody close to him and the panicked bastard will pay."

"I like it," Slide said, "but who do we grab? He got a wife?"

Angela got a strange look on her face, said, "I sincerely doubt that any woman in her right mind would be with that man. But there's this partner—Kyle from Alabama."

"You know him?"

"Never heard of him before, and honestly I can't imagine what Max is doing with somebody from Alabama. I mean, the article says he met the guy down there. When I was with Max he bitched about going to the West Side."

Slide was playing with the idea, tossing it around in his mind. He wanted to get the kidnapping gig down and he knew it would pay serious wedge if only he could stop killing the victims so fast.

"The only problem," Angela said, "is how we do the abduction. After all, Manhattan isn't Backwoods, Ireland. You can't just nab somebody off the street."

"True enough," Slide said, grinning. "But *you* can."

Twenty-One

Denial is the outstanding characteristic of the addict.
ADDICTS ANONYMOUS

Max took twenty minutes to fill out the Cocaine Anonymous addiction test, twenty-three questions asking him things like whether his cocaine use was interfering with his work (*Nope. Moolah rolling in*), whether he'd experienced sinus problems or nosebleeds (*Occasionally*), and whether he felt obsessed with getting coke when he didn't have any (*Si, señor*). He tallied up the yeses—only eight out of twenty-three, nine if you counted the nosebleeds one. Hell, he wasn't an addict, not even close. What the fuck had he been stressing about? And, to think, he'd been seriously considering the idea of cleaning up, going into rehab. Whew, dodged a bullet there.

Max ripped up the addiction test and did three quick lines. Whoops, what was that blood coming out of his nostrils? Nine yeses. Eh, what the fuck ever.

The only downside of not being an addict was he couldn't do one of those rehab gigs. *People* magazine had done a piece saying you were, like, *nobody* unless you'd done at least one stint. That bony Brit chick, Kate Moss—yeah, she'd fucked up big time by being photographed shoving mountains of coke up her dainty little nose. It looked like she was gonna lose all those lucrative contracts—so what'd she do? Yup, that's right, headed right to rehab in Arizona, and *voila*—not only did the dumb-ass public admire her for her courage but shit, get this, she scored more gazillion-dollar contracts. Now that was class. Them Brits, they had some sneaky moves—no wonder they'd once owned India.

So, Max thought, when he had his movie career up and humming, he might do a stretch in one of those places anyway, just for the PR bump. Not long—come on, how long could The M.A.X. be out of the game?—but yeah, some time to deal with "personal issues" would do him good. He could see the cover of *Entertainment Weekly*, The M.A.X. looking contrite and yes, suffering, in real, physical pain, but was he denying it? Fuck no, here he was fessing up, admitting—and this would make a killer headline—*I'm human, too*. A tear would be rolling down his cheek, of course, though they'd probably have to Photoshop that in. God, it would be beautiful and word was, in those clinics, you made the best dope connections so he could, you know, combine business and healing in the one package. And, chances were, he'd meet one of those babes like Paris Hilton, have her hanging on his recuperating arm. Nah, not Paris; he liked the way she'd talked into the mike in that sex video, but she was way too flat-chested and way too bitchy, a bad perfecta if there ever was one. He'd rather have that other one with the implants, Tara Reid? Yeah, that Tara babe would be all over him, oozing love for The M.A.X., and when the press asked he'd simply say coolly, "We're just good friends."

Yeah, he'd be all set if only the blood would just, like, freaking STOP. That stuff, it totally ruined your shirts. He was wearing a white Van Heusen number—it was fucking Goodwill for that baby. How many fucking shirts had he bled on and had to donate? A hundred bucks each for those shirts and they went right down the shitter. Maybe he'd have to start buying black ones, go the Johnny Cash route.

Max was totally gone on this whole vision when his thirst kicked in, an overwhelming, all-consuming passion for gallons of water. Ah, screw that, make it a brew, lots of vitamins in those hops and lots of yeast too, right? Yeah, just a cold one—hell, maybe a few cold ones—and didn't that prove he wasn't a cokehead? You never see a junkie gasping for a Bud, right?

"Kyle, The M.A.X. needs a brewski!"

Kyle was back at the apartment, but the sushi chef was gone. Maybe he ran back to Japan, or at least back to Nobu. Max had given Kyle Katsu's room but, man, Max hoped the kid had changed those sheets.

Max shouted for him again, then pounded down the hall to his room. The kid was watching Meg Ryan movies, a stack of 'em back to back—said he was having himself "a Megathon"—and he actually asked Max, "You think she'd be hard to find in Seattle?"

The schmuck really believed she lived there and, fucking with him, Max went, "I'll ask Hanks if you can have her address."

The kid's eyes got huge and he stuttered, "You know T-T-Tom Hanks?"

Times like this Max wondered—was he fucking with Kyle or was it the other way around? Could someone be alive and functioning and yet be so brain dead?

But Max said, "Me and the Hankster go way back. Yeah, he was unsure about doing this movie with a fucking mermaid, and I told him, go for it Tommy, it'll make a *splash*."

The kid was stunned and Max had to jar him out of it, going, "The brewski. You know before, like, Tuesday?"

Rooming with Kyle, having to dumb it down on a daily basis, was stretching Max's patience mighty thin, but it wasn't like he had a choice. The cops had released Kyle along with Max, with instructions that they couldn't leave town. Max didn't want Kyle living alone someplace where he could fuck up and do something stupid. Max figured he knew the cops' big game plan. They'd searched the apartment while Max and Kyle were being questioned but, guess what, they hadn't taken anything. They could've nailed The M.A.X., but for what? It was his first offense and they could get possession but could they have gotten intent to sell? Maybe, but maybe not. Maybe Max would've gotten six months or, if he had a good lawyer, community service. No, Miscali and those assholes didn't want to send Max up on bullshit charges. They wanted the Big Kahunas, the Colombian suppliers, the behind-the-scenes players. So they figured they'd leave Max and Kyle on the loose for a while—see where that led them. Little did they know that The M.A.X. was one step ahead of the game.

When Max had been released from the precinct, he'd spotted the tail on him right away. *Spotted the tail*—man, he had this shit down cold. He'd also seen cops around outside when he went out for chores—i.e., to buy cigars and load up on booze. The cops weren't uniforms and they weren't holding up NYPD signs, but they might as well have been. Max, especially when he was coked up, knew everything that was going on around him and he had amazing instincts. Put one cop in Yankee Stadium with fifty thousand screaming fans and Max would pick the cop out, no problem. It was like Max was born with sonar for this shit.

One afternoon, when Max left his apartment, he did his usual cop search, immediately spotting the son of a bitch—the black guy sitting at the table in the sidewalk café across the street and up the block. Then, as Max headed up the block, he spotted something else. Blonde hair, big knockers—could that possibly be...?

Max's hand was up, hailing a cab, and a cab pulled up, nearly running over his goddamn foot. When Max looked over again she was gone.

"Come on, buddy, get in my cab," the driver said. "I don't have all day."

Max got in, trying to look back to confirm, *Was it her?*

It couldn't've been, Max decided later. What the hell would she be doing in America, after all this time? Nah, it wasn't her—it had to have been a hallucination. Or maybe it was just paranoia. Okay, okay, so now he was up to 10 out of 23 on that coke addiction test. Maybe he shouldn't've ripped the thing up so quickly.

The hallucination, or whatever it had been, reminded Max of how lonely he was. Yeah, he had Kyle around, but Max was physically lonely. Since Felicia had been killed there had been a big gap in Max's life—well, two gaps, about the size of a pair of 44-double-E's. The thing was, Max was a relationship guy. Without a loving, caring, big-titted woman at his side he felt incomplete. Yeah he was a metropolitan dude, but at heart he was a romantic, a one-woman man. Sure he played around, but no biggie, that was just for show, to impress the troops. But deep down he was a Paul Newman type really—one woman, one love. Damn straight and, hey, maybe he'd invent a salad dressing too. Fuck, the possibilities were, like, endless.

Funny thing was, Max had been thinking about Angela for a couple of weeks now, wondering where she was, who she was with, if she was happy. Maybe that's why he'd thought he'd seen her, because she was prominent in his thoughts. So much had happened since the last time they'd spoken that it was hard for him even to remember what had gone wrong between them. He couldn't remember any fights they'd had or any real conflict. Okay, she'd given him herpes, but aside from that Max could only remember the good times—the blowjobs, the quickies on his desk at his old office. You know, the Hallmark moments.

The next morning Max couldn't get out of bed, depression kicking in big time. Even the thought of getting up for a little nose candy and some *Scarface* didn't have any appeal. Kyle, God bless the kid, noticed Max's state and tried to help, but The

M.A.X. just couldn't be reached. Max was even thinking about retiring the The in The M.A.X. He just didn't feel worthy.

Man, this being depressed shit sucked big time.

Then, the next morning, Max noticed Kyle was gone. He thought maybe the kid had gone out shopping or to Blockbuster to get another Meg Ryan movie, but then it got to be afternoon and there was no sign of him. It was very unlike Kyle to disappear for even a couple of hours without leaving a note, or saying where he was going and when he'd be back. Sometimes Max felt like he was the stupid kid's father. And there was another virtue right there, his fathering side, his nurturing streak. No wonder people flocked to him—he had enough love to go around.

Max wondered if the cops had picked Kyle up and Kyle was busy confessing, implicating Max in the shootings, but the sad thing was that Max didn't really care. Having to spend the rest of his life as some queer's fuck hole seemed like a better option to Max than lying around in bed all day, feeling so, so...so worthless.

Sometime in the afternoon, the doorman called up, said there was a package for Max at the front desk marked URGENT AND PERSONAL. Max didn't have the energy to go down to get it so he had one of the porters bring it up. Max was so not himself that he gave the porter a five-buck tip. The porter, shocked, went, "You feeling okay today, Mr. Fisher?"

Max couldn't even muster the energy to fire back with one of his usual zingers. He just smiled meekly and muttered, "Have a good day."

The package was about shoebox size—actually, it seemed to be a shoebox. But there weren't shoes in it—it was way too light for that. An envelope was attached to the box and there was a note inside the envelope. Max took out the note. It read:

NOW WHO'S A DICK?

Even more confused, Max opened the package. It was wrapped up with lots of tape, and then inside there was crumpled-up newspaper. Max was starting to think it was some prank, maybe that cop Miscali playing head games with him, and then he got to the plastic bag, looked like one of those Ziplock things. There was something inside the bag, something long and pink.

Max held up the bag, studying the contents, and then it hit him. If he hadn't been so depressed he would've screamed—fuck, he probably would've run for his life—but in his current state his only reaction was to drop the bag on the floor and back away very slowly.

Twenty-Two

*There are few more lethal creatures than
an Irishwoman with a grudge.*
IRISH SAYING

Angela had been casing Max's apartment and, Jesus, she'd nearly blown it. The other day he'd come out the front entrance, right on to Second Avenue, and nearly seen her. His face had taken on a stricken look, but then a cab had pulled up and distracted him, giving Angela a chance to duck out of sight.

She hated to admit it, but the bastard looked pretty good. He'd lost weight and was wearing a classy suit—shame about the beige, but it looked like Hugo Boss. He still made her stomach turn, and yet he had a certain air about him now, like he'd finally gotten it together. She liked that he was clean-shaven as Slide's bearded Arab look was starting to bring her down big time, not to mention scare the living crap out of her. She was impressed with how Max had hailed the cab—no frantic arm waving, just a hand barely raised and then the cabbie had screeched to a halt, knowing a player when he saw one.

The next morning Angela was back in front of Max's building when she saw Kyle, the young kid from the newspaper article, coming out the front door. He walked to the corner, waited for the light to change.

He had a forlorn country boy look about him, as if he'd hiked over here from the Ozarks or some place like that. He had a kind of cute face—in a lost, helpless sort of way. Best of all, as she walked up to him, swinging her hips slowly back and forth, she saw he was blushing. Every woman knows that when a guy starts blushing you're going to be adding notches to the bedpost.

Angela said, "Hey, handsome, anybody ever tell you you look like Brad Pitt?"

Angela had used lots of pick-up lines over the years but her "Pitt-Depp technique" had been her most effective by far. It went like this—if the guy had blond hair she told him he looked like Brad Pitt; if he had brown hair she told him he looked like Johnny Depp. Guys soaked that shit up every time.

Although Kyle looked nothing like Brad Pitt, she could tell the line worked big time as he blushed some more, then said, "Wow, thanks, ma'am. And you know who you look just like?"

"Lindsay Lohan," Angela said posing. She'd been to the hairdressers earlier and had asked for the Lindsay Lohan look.

"No, ma'am," Kyle said. "You look like Meg Ryan."

This was one Angela had never heard but, hey, maybe it was an Irish thing—seen one mick, seen 'em all.

She silently blessed that hairdresser, screw Lindsay Lohan, and she put her fingers to her lips and whispered, "Actually I'm Meg's half sister."

She'd meant it as a joke but he stammered, "N-no way."

"Way," Angela said, going along with it, thinking either this kid was putting her on or he was a total moron.

"Man, this is so awesome," the kid said. "I've seen all your sister's movies, like, a hundred times. Wait till The M.A.X. hears about this."

The M.A.X.? What the F?

"Have you seen *my* films?" Angela asked.

"You mean...you mean you're an actress too?"

"One of the best." Had this been Angela's easiest pick-up or what? She moved right in close, his blush getting a notch redder, then she said in what she knew was her huskiest tone, "How would you like a signed picture?"

She could see his boner hit instantly and, she had to admit, that excited the hell out of her.

She added, "I have a small apartment in the city, for when I'm planning a shoot. How would you like to accompany me there? You could help keep the press away."

He looked like he might pass out. Before he had a chance to even consider the sheer implausibility of any of this, she hailed a cab. Yes, she had to wave, a lot, but finally she got one to stop. She squished up close to Kyle, letting her breasts casually rub against his arm.

When the cab pulled up to the apartment on Sixth Street, the kid had zoned out, was in some kind of trance, and kept muttering stuff about Meg Ryan and Jesus. If they hadn't needed Kyle as ransom bait she would've dumped him somewhere because she was getting seriously weirded out.

She slipped her hand in her bag, took out a pair of shades and said, "So I won't be recognized."

She led him down to the apartment. Slide was stretched on the sofa and Angela went, "My agent."

Slide was impressed, asked, "How the fook did you pull it off?"

Angela turned to Kyle, whispered. "Why don't you wait for me in the bedroom and I'll sign the picture for you?" Then added, when he still hadn't moved, "And if you're a good boy, maybe I'll call Meg and let you chat with her on the phone."

Kyle hurried into the bedroom.

"The fook is Meg?" Slide asked.

"Meg Ryan." Angela posed. "You think we look alike?"

Slide gave her a once-over and said, "You're fookin' weird." Then he said, "Okay, better get to it." He went to the counter, picked out a knife with a six-inch blade.

"To what?" Angela feared she might have misjudged a boyfriend yet again. She lowered her voice to a whisper. "We agreed we'd hold him for ransom. You're not going to...hurt him, are you?"

"No, I'll be sure to give him lots of anesthesia," Slide muttered, smiling.

"Seriously, Slide." Angela was panicked. "Remember all the trouble you got into with that Boyo in Ireland. Don't hurt him."

"I'm not going to hurt him," Slide said. "I'm just going to frighten him, that's all, so Fisher can hear some begging and screaming when we make the ransom call. You want the money for the Sopranos house, don't you?"

This seemed logical, but somehow Angela didn't trust him completely.

She said, "Swear to me on the graves of your parents and your sister that you won't hurt him at all."

Slide had told Angela the sad story of how his family had been killed in a car accident when he was twelve years old.

"You know, I think you better leg it," Slide said. "You're ruining me concentration."

"Swear—"

"All right!" Slide exploded. Then more quietly, "I swear. Now would you go take a walk while I get him ready for the phone call?"

Angela turned and walked out, still wearing the dark shades. She headed up Sixth Street. She didn't know how she'd reached yet another new low in her life. For a while things had seemed so hopeful—she'd just wanted to have a happy life in the suburbs, a couple of kids, the swimming pool—and now that poor kid was in that apartment with her latest monster boyfriend, and it was because of her.

Fuck him, she decided. She'd do kidnapping with him, but

she wasn't gonna do murder. That poor kid—he'd really thought she was Meg Ryan's sister, and maybe that he was gonna get laid. The poor, poor fool.

As she reached the corner of Second Avenue, she told herself enough was enough. She was sick of getting pushed around. As she headed back to the apartment, she decided it was time to do a little pushing back her own self.

Twenty-Three

*The fact that I'd mistaken him for anything other than a
typical shithead policeman could mean I was disgustingly
superficial, capable of allowing my entire perspective on
life and law enforcement to be swayed by...what?
A smile? A few kind words?*
ALISON GAYLIN, *Hide Your Eyes*

Joe Miscali was having a very bad day. After the complete fuck-up with the drug bust, the freaking SWAT team on Staten Island, the wrong location, and, oh Jesus, the *Daily News*, his fellow cops had been breaking his balls all day, going, "Hey, Joe, you got any hot tips, don't tell us, okay?"

Like that.

And Felicia winding up dead didn't help. Like he was ever gonna get another source when he let his people get wasted, half-eaten by freaking seagulls?

Joe was biting his nails, one of the reasons his wife had legged it. At the marriage counselor's she'd screamed at him, "I'm sick of you and your fucking anxiety!" Christ, if she could see him now.

His phone shrilled and he was seriously thinking of not answering it, one more shitheel taking a shot at him. He picked up anyway, fearing the worst.

It was Rodriguez, one of his undercovers, who'd been tailing Max and Kyle. Rodriguez had been stationed outside Fisher's building for hours. Now he said there was movement. Kyle, the 'Bama boy who palled around with Fisher, had come out of the building and gotten into a cab with some chesty blonde, maybe an UnSub. Miscali started shouting, telling Rodriguez to get his ass in gear and follow them. Rodriguez sounded real hurt, shot back that if Joe thought he wasn't up to the job, yada yada. So now Joe had to, like, placate the guy for, what, five minutes, telling him what a terrific cop he was, with the rest of the Department lapping it up, until Rodriguez calmed down.

Rodriguez called Miscali back later, said he'd tailed Kyle and the broad to Sixth Street, Little India. He said they went into a building together, then the woman came out alone, and then went back in again a minute later.

Rodriguez went to Miscali, "What am I supposed to do?"

"Do?" Miscali shot back. "Stay the fuck where you are is what you do."

He put the phone down, tried to figure out what the hell was going on, who the hell the broad was.

Slide went, "Fook," as he hefted the kid's weight on his shoulder, tried to get the balance right. He thought, Jaysus, this kidnapping lark is fooking hard work is what it is, how come they never show that in the fookin' movies?

And here was the bold Angela, back in the apartment going, "Put him down, now."

Like she was Miss Super Hero, come to save the day.

Raging, Slide dropped the kid onto a chair, going, "I thought I told you to leg it." The kid had a piece of cloth tied in his mouth as a gag and bruises on the side of his face. He was unconscious.

It was hard to read Angela's expression behind the dark shades. She said, "You promised you wouldn't hurt him."

"Gimme a fookin' break," Slide said, "and get me a cold one, the kid is heavier than he looks." Slide tied the kid's arms behind the chair with a length of chain, then wrapped the remainder of the chain around Kyle's chest and legs. Then he got a basin of water and lashed it into the kid's face, going, "Wakey wakey."

"Thank God," Angela said as Kyle's eyes opened. "Slide, listen to me. I want you to let him go."

Slide laughed.

"I'm not joking," Angela said, and she grabbed the butcher knife from where Slide had left it when getting the basin. Pointing the knife at Slide's throat she went, "Let him go."

"The fook're you going to do with that?" he asked.

"I'm not going to get mixed up in another fookin' murder because of you."

"So what're you going to do, kill me? That's a good way not to get involved in another murder—kill somebody."

"I will if I have to."

"Oh, Christ, just put the knife down and give me a hand here. We're wasting valuable time."

"I'll put the knife down when he's safe."

Slide laughed, said, "That's a great plan. You think he'll go home and decide not to tell anyone he was kidnapped? I guess we'll just hope he sees the fun in it, eh?"

"He might not tell," Angela said.

"Oh, stop with that shite talk and give me the knife."

Slide reached out, but Angela didn't give it to him.

She said, "I'm not going to let you hurt him."

"Don't you get it?" Slide said. "This is the way it has to be. If we hurt him a little he'll be afraid, then when we release him he'll keep his mouth shut. Trust me—I've studied kidnapping and I know how the gig works. We have to hurt him, but I won't kill him, I promise you that. Now just give me the fookin' knife."

Slide inched closer to Angela then he lunged toward her suddenly and wrested the knife away. They stood looking at each other for a moment, he with the knife, watching his own reflection in the lenses of her glasses. For a moment, they both wondered whether he was going to plunge the knife into her.

But he didn't. He swung his other arm around in a roundhouse instead, clocked her solidly on the temple, and she went down like the proverbial steer.

He dragged her out of the way, then got busy, spreading plastic on the floor, especially under the chair where the kid was sitting.

Slide knew he had to cut something off. A finger, an ear, whatever. That's the way it was done. It's how you showed you were serious.

In his chair, the kid was struggling weakly.

"What shall I cut, boy?" Slide grabbed him by the hair, tugged the boy's right ear away from the side of his head. Just like slicing off a chicken wing. *Ear's lookin' at you, kid.* But ears, ears had been done, like, so often, they were fookin' old. He needed something new, something original. Then, bingo, it came to him. Oh, man.

He unbuckled the kid's belt and worked the kid's jeans and Y-fronts down over his hips. The kid was near catatonic with fear.

Slide stepped back to marvel—this kid had a whopper all right.

"Fook, not even the black fellahs could equal that," he said.

He grabbed the dick, and began to cut.

When she came to, Angela heard Kyle whimpering. Slide was nowhere in sight. She went over to Kyle, saw his pants around his knees, saw the crude pressure bandage Slide had put in place, saw the blood all over, and she ran into the bathroom, barely reaching the sink before violently throwing up.

Twenty-Four

He was as attractive as a barracuda.
DESCRIPTION OF ROBERT STROUD,
THE BIRDMAN OF ALCATRAZ

Max knew what he was looking at and it didn't take him long to figure out who it had belonged to. He had once walked in on Kyle taking a leak and had noticed the kid's huge dong. At first he was surprised and—let's face it—jealous, but then he realized it made total sense. Little brain, big dick, right?

Speaking of brains, Max racked his, trying to figure out who could've done this and why. He'd found another note in the box—in addition to the NOW WHO'S A DICK? one—warning that if Max didn't deliver $50,000 in cash to the "phone box" on the corner of Second Avenue and Fourteenth Street by 1:00 PM, more pieces of Kyle would arrive. Yeah, like Max would ever pay a penny to get Kyle back. Shit, Kyle out of the picture helped Max—if the kid was dead Max wouldn't have to worry about him flipping on him for the drug shooting.

But Max still wanted to know who was behind this, if only for his own safety. The one explanation that made any sense to him was that it had to have been the fat guy from the drug deal, what the hell did Felicia say his name was? Shoe-Shoe? Yeah, Shoe-Shoe must've nabbed Kyle in revenge and cut off his dick, the sick fuck.

Then Max had a thought that horrified him a lot more than the sight of the Ziplocked dick lying on the floor. What if Shoe-Shoe came after Max next? The thought of getting his dick chopped off terrified Max to the point where he was ready to call the cops and get his ass arrested pronto. Spending the rest of his life in jail, or even the death penalty, had to be better than walking around dickless.

But then Max managed to calm himself, his old Zen side taking over. He thought, *Okay, be wise, Maxie, be in the now.* Yeah, Shoe-Shoe was bonkers, but maybe this was it—maybe one dick was enough for him. After all, the note had been, *Now who's a dick?* Not, *Whose dick is coming off next?* This gave Max some reassurance.

Max stared at the dick, nudged the bag with the tip of his shoe. He was mesmerized by its size. For years Max had been using pumps and taking pills trying to enlarge his dick, but to no avail. Max wondered—couldn't those things be transplanted nowadays? If they could do hearts and livers they had to be able to do dicks, right? And didn't that guy down south, Bobbitt, get his reattached after his old lady dumped it on the road? Kyle was from the south—maybe there was something about southern dicks. Maybe Max could go for dick replacement surgery or whatever the hell it was called. Maybe he should, like, save the dick just in case. Hell, what if Shoe-Shoe showed up at the apartment later and chopped off Max's dick? Wouldn't it be good to have a spare?

He entertained the idea for a moment, but the moment passed. He picked up the Ziplock with two fingers, went out to the hallway, and dropped it down the garbage chute.

Slide was seriously antsy. He'd been hanging out at the phone box on Fourteenth and Second since dropping off the package. He was waiting for Fisher, but there was no sign of the bastard. What the fook was with that? You get a dick hand-delivered to your building and you don't even show?

He said aloud, "Bollocks."

He was drinking Coors Light, yeah, *Light*, not by choice, mind, he'd hit a deli and that's what they'd had.

He asked himself, What's with Fisher? Why is he ignoring us? Is he scared to leave his apartment?

And right away, he knew what to do.

He caught a cab, went directly to Fisher's building, and told the doorman he was a police officer, quickly flipped his wallet open and shut. Nothing in there but a MetroCard, but Slide must have made a convincing-looking cop, or could've been the Irish accent, because the guy let him right up.

He took the elevator to the penthouse, rang the buzzer. The door opened slowly and there he was, the man himself, looking a little the worse for wear, like he'd been on a speed jag or some such shite.

Max went, "Yes?"

Slide figured this guy would be a pushover, said, "It's about your young friend."

Fisher looked sick, as if he was going to throw up and then said in a weak voice, "Shoe-shoe sent you."

Slide thought, The fook was Shoe-Shoe? but, going along with it went, "That's right."

Max looked disgusted, as if something had stirred some vile memory, and said, "Jesus Christ, you're not fucking Irish, are you?"

Jaysus, and Slide had thought his American had been coming along so well.

"Actually, I'm of British descent," he said, trying to sound miffed.

"Eh, Irish, British, same bullshit," Fisher said and waved him in.

Slide followed, noticing the package on the counter and wondered where the item was. Must be fairly ripe by now.

Slide decided to play it as it laid, went, "My partner, see, he's a psycho, I tried to stop him from cutting the…you know, but he's impossible to control. He wanted to kill the kid. If he knew I was here, he'd kill me."

Fisher's eyes got a sly sheen and Slide knew the guy was figuring the odds. Fisher said, "You're not exactly tight with your partner, huh?"

Slide nearly laughed but kept it reined, and said, "I won't lie to you, Mr. Fisher, I want the cash but some things, they're just not right and anyway my, um, partner, he'd as soon kill me as share the money."

Fook, he was losing track of who he was supposed to be, but Fisher helped with, "So, you'd be open to a new deal, one that, let's say, terminated your agreement with Shoe-Shoe?"

Slide had forgotten the name and was delighted to hear it again. He tried to put on a serious look and said, "What is it you're proposing, Mr. Fisher?"

Fisher looked wired now, as if he'd won a new lease on life. He headed for the bar, asked, "Get you something?"

Slide, in a real mood for playing, went, "Got any Coors Light?"

Twenty-Five

*Showing a woman your pistol is
just like showing her your cock.*
CHARLES WILLEFORD, *New Hope for the Dead*

Angela, still wearing her shades, took a deep gulp of vodka. She'd discovered a bottle of Stoli in Slide's stuff—rifling through his gear was habitual now—and, hello, she'd also found a Browning automatic. She didn't actually know it was a Browning but she sure as shit knew what it felt like—reassurance in her hand. When you had a piece in your hand you knew no one would be fucking with you, least not twice.

Notwithstanding her horrendous year in Dublin, Angela was still prone to all the superstitions that the Irish half of her heritage had bestowed. She checked in her purse and sure enough, there was the gold pin of two hands nearly touching—her lucky charm. The evidence of her life would contradict the notion that the pin had brought her much in the way of luck lately, but hey, the way she was feeling she'd have stuck pins in a friggin doll if it might help. She attached the pin above her bust and the light caught the tiny hint of gold. It gave her a moment if not of peace, then of resolve.

She took a breath and walked out to where Kyle sat. His moans had been ferocious for the hour he'd been conscious.

The gun was in her hand, hanging casually alongside her hip. The kid's face was contorted. Angela peered over the top of her shades at him. Jesus, what a poor bastard. She felt her heart melt.

His eyes opened and he looked at her.

Jesus, she thought. Sweet bloody Jesus. The things we do.

She touched the gun to his forehead, between his eyes. He closed his eyes. She'd been hoping for a nod, but fuck it, you take the signs you get. She intoned, *Jesus, Mary and Joseph, forgive me for I do know what I'm about to do, have to do.*

She pulled the trigger. The recoil from the gun knocked her back. A spray of blood spattered against the plastic.

Then she threw up again. She went back for the Stoli and lots of it, the gun still in her hand. She wasn't letting go of that baby—it was all she had.

She went into the tiny bedroom, threw some things in a suitcase, then came back to the chair. Was it madness or did the dumb-arse kid look…peaceful? She leant over and took the pin from her bust, put it on the kid's bloodstained shirt. The gold seemed to have dulled, and the hands were further away from touching than ever. Then, without a backward glance, she opened the door, and didn't bang it, just let it close softly. Joyce would have been proud of her. What he would have made of the Browning in her case is anybody's guess.

Sha-Sha was in Canarsie, corner of 102nd and L, having his ass a little snack—couple dozen White Castle cheeseburgers. He was eating 'em two at a time, washing them with soda—Diet Coke cause he was trying to lose some weight—when he saw the white man coming toward him. Nigga wasn't no customer—must be a damn cop. But that disguise, man, it wasn't working. Motherfucker tryin' too hard to look undercover, with them shades and the hair and the beard and shit.

Sha-Sha been through this police bullshit a million times before. He made like he was just minding his own, chompin' on the White Castles, acting like he didn't give a shit.

The man went up to him and said, "You'll be Sha-Sha?"

He had this fucked-up accent, like the nigga was trying to sound like damn U2.

"The fuck wants to know?" Sha-Sha asked. He gulped down some soda, tossed the can on the street, like he was sayin', *You can bust my ass for litterin' you want, but that's all you gonna get, nigga.*

But then the Bono dude went, "Answer my fookin' question. Is your name Sha-Sha?"

Sick of playing this bullshit, Sha-Sha went, "Yeah, I'm Sha-Sha, now how 'bout you get the fuck out my face, punk?"

Sha-Sha looked away and spat. When he looked back the dude was holding some big-ass knife, looked like you could carve up a turkey with it. Sha-Sha was thinking, *The fuck kind of cop is this?*

Slide had partied hard with Max at the penthouse, doing coke, pot, vodka, even shared a few hits on his crack pipe. It was some good shite and Max—sorry, *The M.A.X.*—was a great guy, first person in eons Slide didn't want to off. Slide felt like he and Max seriously connected. They both loved American film, especially anything with De Niro or Pacino. And, besides, how could he kill a guy who did a pretty good Brit accent his own self?

Max, high as a kite, had told him about some woman, Felicia, who'd screwed him over by selling him out to her 500-pound cousin Shoe-Shoe who lived in Canarsie. Slide was relieved because he'd had no idea how he'd find this fookin Shoe-Shoe guy, but when Max gave him the bit of info he figured, How many Shoe-Shoes could there be in Canarsie? Wherever fookin Canarsie was.

Max told Slide he would pay him one hundred thousand dollars in cash if Slide took care of Shoe-Shoe for him. Slide couldn't believe this deal—he was actually going to get paid to kill someone? That was like telling a guy who sat around jerking off all day, watching pornos, that he would now receive hard cash every time he ejaculated. Slide wanted to pinch himself.

An hour later, he left Max's, found this Canarsie place on a subway map, and headed out to Brooklyn, to Shoe-Shoe's— what was the term the brothers used?— oh yeah, *hood*.

Off the L train, he asked the first drug dealer he spotted if he knew where he could find a dealer named Shoe-Shoe who weighed about five hundred pounds. No luck there or with the next couple lowlife-looking types. But then he found a skinny, nervous guy outside a schoolyard who seemed to have the info. The fellah wasn't exactly forthcoming, but Slide persuaded him to open up by placing his knife to the fook's throat.

The guy spilled. "His name ain't Shoe-Shoe, man, it's Sha-Sha. He's up on his corner, Hundred and Second an' L. Please don't kill me, man. Please don't—"

Slide stabbed him in the chest. Straight to the heart—in, out, wipe. Would've had some more fun with him but Slide was in a hurry and had, like, important business to take care of.

Then Slide found Sha-Sha. How could he miss him? The bollix was the size of a small car. His mouth was stuffed with food—big surprise there—and Slide went to him, "You'll be Sha-Sha?"

The guy gave him some mouth about who wants to know, and some other shite talk, and then Slide revealed the blade. He didn't have the reaction Slide expected. Yeah, there was terror in his eyes, but he didn't start begging and screaming the way most victims did. He'd probably had machetes, hooks, broken bottles, you name it, put up to him and he did the very worst thing he could've done—he waved Slide away, like he was some minor irritation.

This pissed Slide off to no end. Didn't the fat fook know who he was dealing with? For a moment, Slide nearly leaned over and gutted him there and then, but he chilled, as his new buddy, The M.A.X., was fond of saying. Instead, he grabbed one of the burgers, took a healthy bite, chewed down, said, "Needs a little more ketchup, don't you think?"

Now he had the guy's attention. Yeah, the guy's mouth was hanging open, like he couldn't believe this skinny fellah had taken his food. It was like Sha-Sha had seen all kinds of stuff in his career but the one line you did not cross, ever, was to fuck with his food.

His mouth still full, he'd gurgled something like, "De fu...c... de...ddddoin?"

Slide wondered if the guy was rapping. He knew these dudes rapped on just about everything.

To get him focused, Slide took a nice swipe out of his cheek, just one fast stroke of the blade and there, a nice tribal scar for him. Weren't these guys into all kinds of colors and markings, or was that Indians? What the fook ever.

Slide gave him his best smile—now the guy was all attention—and said, "I like black dudes, really I do. Phil Lynott, now there was one cool cat, you dig? And for a moment there, I was going to let this slide, just mosey on my way, let you finish this little feast you were at, but you know, you gave me cheek." Slide laughed. "Cheek, sorry, I'm a mick, punning is our gig." Then he put the knife in Sha-Sha's throat with maximum force. The knife was so deeply imbedded that it took Slide a few moments to extract it, and he muttered, "Dunno me own strength."

Sha-Sha's knees buckled and he fell onto the sidewalk. He squirmed for a few seconds, belched a few times, then he wasn't moving no more.

Slide reached down, popped a bite of burger in his mouth,

thinking, you could develop a taste for those suckers. He stared at the enormous body on the ground for a moment, thinking, *Trophy?*

He bent down, pulled off one of Sha-Sha's sneakers, stared at it, went, "Got your Shoe-Shoe, Sha-Sha."

He loved that, repeated it to himself all the way back to the city.

About an hour later, back in Manhattan, Slide gave The M.A.X. the sneaker and along with it, the rundown on Sha-Sha's last meal.

"Son of a bitch," Max said, "you really did it." Then he said to the sneaker, in his hip-hop voice, "You be de shoo-in, baby," and tossed it away over his shoulder.

He and Slide cracked up over this—were these guys on the same page or what?

They had a few brews, just two buddies, sinking a few. From time to time they looked over at the sneaker in the corner and toasted to it.

Finally, Slide, much fun as this was, said, "I gotta, like, get moving, so if you can give me the cash, I'll be on me way."

Max suddenly looked pained and Slide hoped he wasn't going to start fucking around. He would really not want to have to gut the likable bastard.

Max raised his hands, let them fall. "I'm broke. I have, tops, eight or nine grand. I might be able to raise more later but right now, that's it."

Whacked out, Max found this amusing, started giggling.

Slide surprised himself, said, "Let's see it."

Max led Slide to the bedroom closet. He opened the safe and took out the wads of bills and Slide, an edge in his tone now, said, "Count it."

Max did. There was nine grand and change.

Slide snatched the cash from Max's hand, stuffed it in his pocket. Max whined, "C'mon, can't you leave me a few bucks for, you know, necessities?"

Slide gave him back two singles, said, "Knock yourself out."

Max didn't argue.

When Slide reached the door, Max said, "I guess this is *adios, muchacho*?"

Slide lunged, as if he was going to stab Max in the gut, and Max jerked back. But, alas, Slide wasn't holding the knife.

"Nope, not *adios* for you yet," Slide said, smiling. "Not if you can round up the rest of my money in, say, two days. Nah, let's make it one."

"But I can't—"

"Sh," Slide said. "Don't say can't. Don't say won't. Say yes I will." He patted Max on the side of the face. "I'll be back."

Slide cabbed it back to the apartment on Sixth Street. He was tired, in need of a bit of grub, maybe a quick violent shag from Angela, and then he was going to have him some serious z's.

But the minute he entered the apartment, he knew something was up.

There was no sign of Angela, no screaming and moaning from the kid. Then he saw Kyle's body, the bullet hole in his forehead. So she'd taken the kid out—fook, Slide was impressed.

This Angela and Max, they were some pair all right. Slide had never come across the likes of them, and he wasn't sure he wanted to again. They had their good qualities, but they were a little too out there, even for him. They were always doing weird shite. It was kind of spooky actually, gave Slide the creeps. He needed to be among ordinary folk, the type you could kill and they didn't screw around, didn't make any big fuss, just took their licks and didn't do anything.

He went to the dresser, packed a few shirts, noticed Angela had taken his Browning. He said, "Mad fooker."

Outside, he was leaving the apartment when a guy approached him and Slide thought, *Cop*.

Sure enough, the guy introduced himself, went, "Rodriguez, NYPD."

The guy was polite enough, wanted to know if Slide had seen a young kid, blond hair, maybe with a woman—blond, sunglasses, a nice shape.

Slide gave him his best smile and his best New York accent, said, "No, sir, and let me say, I sure admire you for the work you do, can't be easy."

Slide started to walk away when the guy said, "Excuse me, sir," and Slide knew this was trouble.

"Yep," Slide said calmly.

"I had a talk before with the woman who manages the restaurant above your apartment," Rodriguez said, "and she said she thought she heard some strange noises coming from there earlier, sounded like someone screaming."

"How do you know it's my flat?"

"Because I watched you go in a little while ago."

Yep, this was trouble, but Slide was looking forward to it. Doing guards always gave him a rush.

"I'm just fookin' with you," Slide said. "It's my flat but there's no kid and no woman in there. Want to take a look inside?"

"If you don't mind," Rodriguez said.

Slide led Rodriguez into the building. In the vestibule, Slide fumbled in his coat pocket, going, "My fookin' key, where is it?" Meanwhile, he was opening the five-inch switchblade he kept in the inside pocket.

Slide turned, ready to slash the cop's throat, when the fook fired his gun and Slide felt pain rip through his side. He was coming again with the blade but the Rodriguez bastard fired again and Slide slid down against the door, till he was seated on the floor, his ass soaking in his own blood. Shite, this was no way for a serial killer to go down. He hadn't even come close to any of the records.

He was looking up at Rodriguez, then everything turned foggy. The cop's face turned into Angela's—the mad cow looking down at Slide, and was she fookin laughing?

Slide was trying to mumble something so Rodriguez leant down, trying to catch it.

Slide gasped, "Was…gonna…let…it…slide."

The cop said, "You lied? You lied about what?"

Slide tried again.

"Yeah, fucking scumbags like you always lie," the cop said.

A gurgle in Slide's throat, and he was history.

Twenty-Six

I am the wickedest man in New York.
THEODORE "THE ALIEN" ALLEN, GANGSTER

When Joe Miscali broke down the door to Max's apartment and entered with a whole goddamn SWAT team Max knew this wouldn't be the usual bust.

Couple of cops pushed Max face-down onto the carpet and cuffed him and Max whined, "Ow, you're hurting me."

Max wondered what the hell had happened to his machismo? It abandoned him at a time like this, when he needed it most? Jesus H.

"You cocksucker," Miscali said. "You thought you could fuck me over, you son of a bitch. You little piece of shit."

"What are you gonna arrest me for?" Max said. "You can't prove anything."

"You think you're so fuckin' smart, you're a fuckin' brain surgeon now, huh?" Miscali said. "For possession of whatever shit we find in the apartment...and, oh, yeah, and for murder."

"I didn't shoot that fuckin' gang kid," Max said.

"I'm not talking about that murder," Miscali said, "though don't think you're not gonna go down for that too. I'm talking about the murder of Kyle Jordan."

"Hey, I had nothing to do with that shit," Max said. "Honest."

"If you didn't kill Jordan," Miscali said. "How come we just recovered his penis in your garbage room? You wanna tell me that?"

"His penis?" Max said. "I never saw that penis before in my life."

"And how about the blonde with the big tits?" Miscali said. "You're gonna tell me you haven't been in contact with Angela Petrakos?"

Max started to smile, thought, *So it* was *her. Son of a bitch.*

"Answer my goddamn questions," Miscali said.

"As far as I know, Angela isn't even in this country," Max said.

"My guy saw her pick up Kyle Jordan in front of your apartment."

"How do you know it was her?"

Miscali showed Max a gold pin. Shit, it was the one Angela used to wear, of two hands almost touching.

"My buddy Kenneth Simmons had this pin because his son had Down Syndrome," Miscali said. "Then after Simmons was killed you somehow got hold of the pin and gave it to Angela Petrakos. That was the theory anyway. Now the same pin winds up on the body of Kyle Jordan. You wanna explain that to me?"

Max, with tears in his eyes—hey, he was a sentimental guy—said, "Wow, the pin. I never thought I'd see that pin again. Can I just, like, touch it?"

Miscali, looking like he was about to lose it big time, roared, "Get this cocksucker out of my sight!"

The cops led Max away in handcuffs. He was still confused about a lot of things, especially why in God's name Angela had chopped off Kyle's dick and then killed him, but he focused on the important thing—she was alive; she was out there somewhere.

Leaving the building, Max didn't know what was going on, said, "Whoa, what's going on?"

Where were the crowds? Where was the media? Didn't the whole city want to, like, come out to see The M.A.X. take his fall?

Eh, the President was probably in town, or maybe it was

Super Sunday or Christmas Day. Yeah, it had to be something big like that.

As they stuffed Max into the back of the police car, Max smiled in a cocky way, like John Gotti did whenever he got sent away. It was like Max was telling the cops, *Maybe you got me this time, but I'll live to fight another day.*

Yeah, The M.A.X. knew that, no matter what, he was looking at some time here, but he was getting into the idea. He was a big-time criminal now, a pro, and pros always had to do a stretch or two during the course of their careers. It was part of the biz; it came with the territory. And, hell, it was better than rehab. Yeah, he knew he'd have a blast behind bars. Celebs like him always got protection from the thugs and women went nuts for notorious prisoners. He'd begin a proper study of Zen, become a master, maybe even bop over to India when he got out, to finesse his calling. And did anyone understand the law better than The M.A.X.? He'd be like Jimmy Woods in *The Onion Field*—the elder statesman, still with a fucking dangerous mind but, you know, not showy with it. Oh, and inside you know he was going to be flooded with love letters and marriage proposals from an assortment of babes. Naturally, Angela would write to him. She'd say how lonely she was and how she was counting the days till his release. Maybe she'd even show up to visit, bring him cakes, and then when his parole came through she'd be waiting for him in a red Porsche. Ah, then he'd have the HBO series, the *Wall Street Journal* column, and everything else he'd ever wanted.

The cop car pulled away and The M.A.X., in the back seat, was grinning his fucking ass off.

The driver looked up at Max in the rearview, smiled, and the other cop next to him, chewing on gum, said something and they both laughed together.

The M.A.X. didn't hear what they were saying but he knew, like all knowledge that had been given to him, that they were trying to decide which of them would ask him for his autograph. He fingered his hair—hell, he was feeling expansive, he might even give them a lock of it, let them sell it on eBay, bring some bucks into their mundane fucking lives.

He thought, *Whoops, I cursed, gonna have to give that up.*

He wondered if he should ask them to put on the sirens, let the little people know a player was en route. But then he decided to ride with the humility gig, no need to be flashy. As the mad Brit had told him while they were freebasing—sometimes you just gotta let it slide.

THE MAX

For Jerry Rodriguez, Megan Abbott and Alison Gaylin
Madison Rules

One

I had no worries about someone fucking me. I was no white bread white boy. If someone said something wrong, my challenge would be quick and if the apology was less than swift, I would attack forthwith.
EDWARD BUNKER, *Education of a Felon: A Memoir*

"Gonna have yer sweet white ass later."

The greeting Max Fisher got from his towering black cellmate, Rufus.

Max thought, Whoa, hold the phones, there's gotta be some mistake. Was he in the right place? Where was the V.I.P. treatment? Where was Martha Fucking Stewart? Where were those bastards from Enron? How come there wasn't a goddamn tennis court in sight? Yeah, Max knew Attica wasn't Club Fed, but he didn't expect *this*. He thought a big-time player like himself would get the, you know, special treatment but, Jesus, not this kind of special treatment. He thought he'd work on his backhand, get some stock tips, learn how to crochet, maybe start working out, lose some of the extra forty pounds he'd been lugging around. Maybe the guard took him to the wrong part of the prison. Didn't prisons have neighborhoods just like cities? Max was supposed to be on the Upper East Side, but by accident they'd brought him to the goddamn South Bronx.

Max clutched the bars, said to the guard, a young black guy, "Hey, come back here, yo." Yeah, Max spoke hip-hop, one of his many talents. The guard didn't stop and Max shouted, "Hey, asshole, I think there's been a little fucking screw-up around here!" Yeah, let the fuck know who was boss, like the time he was dining at Le Cirque and the maitre d' sat him at a table with a dirty tablecloth. Max let that motherfucker have it all right.

The guard, walking away, laughed, said, "Naw, I think there's gonna be a *big* screw up, Fisher. Inside yo' ass."

His laughter echoed in the corridor until a gate slammed. That's when it finally hit Max—he was fucked. Up till that point he'd been living the high life, in every sense of the word, blitzed from morning till night. He'd once been a highly successful businessman, then he'd had his nagging wife murdered by a psycho mick and things had gone south faster than you could shout *bust*. But rising if not from the ashes exactly, he'd reinvented himself as a dope dealer, and not only that, a goddamn *Scarface*. It didn't last very long, though. He enlisted Kyle, a young hick from way down south, and to say the kid got, um, screwed is to put it very politely.

Throughout his more than colorful career, Max had been haunted, okay *plagued*, by an Irish-Greek woman named Angela, AKA heat on heels. She twice fucked up his life and twice walked clean away. He blamed her for his current situation as he blamed her for all his fucking misfortunes. And yet, fuckit, he still got a hard-on when he thought about her. But, Jeez, a hard-on was one thing he did not wanna see right now, in this cage with Rufus.

Scared shitless, Max looked up to God, or at least toward the fucking ceiling, and asked, "Why me?" Yeah, he'd been found guilty of dealing and the judge had thrown the book at him, calling him a, what the fuck was the term? Oh, yeah, "a scourge of our society." But Max didn't think the judge had really, like, *meant* it. During the trial, etcetera, Max had been so out of it on dope, he'd thought he was some kind of rock star, waving to the crowds, and he expected to be found innocent. Yeah, they were some seriously good drugs. Finally out of the haze of the drugs, the booze gone from his system, Max realized he was actually *going to the freaking slammer*. He screamed at his lawyer, "Get me out of this, I don't care what it costs!"

His lawyer had actually smiled, the bollix smiled! Yeah, *bollix*—Max's speech was littered with Irish-isms from all the mad deranged micks he'd encountered the past couple of years.

The lawyer had said, "Maxie, you're broke. You've got like zilch, nada."

Max got the picture, but...*Maxie?* The fuck was with that? *Dios Mio*. See, he still had his flair for languages, even spoke spic after his time dealing dope to a crew of *Colombanos*.

His lawyer had said to him, "Keep your head down."

He'd be keeping his head down all right, on Rufus, it seemed. He'd heard they ran a train through new fish and this was not a train you wanted to board, as it involved lots of guys and your ass.

The reality of the situation had sunk in when the verdict came down but, as he so often did, he'd managed to look at the bright side. Hey, what could you say, he was a positive thinker, an optimistic dude. Maybe this was a reflection of his spiritual training. Yeah, he was a Buddhist, knew how to get into himself, and knew how to not let the negativity of the physical world affect him. He'd asked himself, as he often did during times when his life went to shit, What would Gandhi do in a situation like this? He wouldn't be panicking, that was for damn sure. He'd be getting off on it, acting like, Yeah, a harsh jail sentence, it was a bump in the road, they can beat me up but they can't keep me down.

Like that.

So he'd kept on smoking rock—yeah, he was hooked, so the fuck what?—right up until the day he was due to report to prison, thinking how bad could it be at Attica anyway? Hell, Pacino'd wanted to go there, right? The M.A.X.—that was his dealing name—was a big-time criminal and every famous crime guy had to take a few falls. Look at Dillinger, look at Sutton, look at Capone. It was just part of what you signed up for when you wanted to be the Kingpin, the Big Boss.

As a successful businessman, Max knew that you always had to stay one step ahead of the competition, so to bone up for jail, Max had stocked up on books and DVDs. He'd been given a surveillance bracelet and couldn't leave his apartment, so what the fuck else was he gonna do? He hadn't read anything other than the *Wall Street Journal* since he was in goddamn high school and, let's face it, he didn't read the *Journal*, he just liked to hold it up and stare at it intensely for show, to make people think he was one serious dude who knew his shit. But now he'd started reading for real. The first book: *Animal Factory*. Edward Bunker, now there was one tough mo' fo'. Then he checked out Genet's prison journals till he shouted, "Hold the goddamn phones, this guy is, like, a *pillow biter?*" The fuck with that. But *Stone City* by Mitchell Smith, yeah, he liked the hero in that, felt he might take that road himself. Same deal with *Green River Rising*, Tim Willocks; an innocent guy, caught in a prison riot and, against all the odds, coming out on top. Max could see himself, with true *cojones*, and of course, total modesty, saving captured hostages, offing the really serious psychos and leading the saved out of the burning prison with CNN capturing it all on live TV.

There was also G.M. Ford's novel where Frank Corso had to go into the joint and go up against the meanest muthahs this side of the Mississippi. And, of course, the one by that Keith Ablow dude. Yeah, all the Grey Goose he'd been drinking had put Max at the center of all these novels and somewhere in there he'd realized, prison was *part of his karma*, just one more step in the whole, ok, let's not be shy, messianic road of Max Fisher.

He'd watched Ed Norton in *The 25th Hour* and man, he'd wept buckets. They were like spiritual brothers. But fuck, he wasn't letting anyone beat the shit out of his face, no way Jose. The M.A.X. knew his face was his real ace. *The Birdman Of Alcatraz*? Didn't get it. Never once occurred to him he might be, um, *sharing*. Max had been *El Hombre*, had like over thirty people working for him—okay, only three, including his chef and live-in ho, but who's counting?—and he'd tell his employees not brashly, "Let's get one thing straight. The boss distributes, but share, uh–uh, that don't happen." Feeling like Alec Baldwin in *Glengarry Glen Ross*.

When he'd finished all this reading, he'd been flushed with elation. Whoever played Max in the movie, he'd be a shoo-in for an Oscar. Slam dunk. And, fuck, these books didn't look like they were so hard to write. You could probably just hire some schmuck to write them for you. Isn't that what that guy Patterson did? But it wouldn't be James Patterson "with" Max Fisher—no way that asshole was getting top bill—it would be Fisher *with* fucking Patterson.

Finally Max had had just forty-eight hours left to, like, get his shit together, put his affairs in order and, fuck, get ready to spend the next half of his life behind bars. *Behind bars*. The M.A.X. *caged*? Another book Max had read: *I Know Why the Caged Bird Sings*. He got halfway through that one before he realized it wasn't a fucking prison novel.

Max had been renting his penthouse—and he was behind on the rent—no problem there—when you go away, go away *owing*. He had the phone cut off and all the utilities, but arranged that they be shut down the day he went to the slammer, so he could have his last forty-eight hours in comfort. He was drinking, not like he used to, but putting it away, Grey Goose, a decent brand, Max still had his taste and sensibility. He was also doing some rock, to keep the party balanced. Probably in the nick, as the Brits called it, he'd have a hard time scoring coke or even crack and he'd have to make do with that homemade hooch they brewed from potatoes. Or, get this, he might attend A.A. in the joint, run those meetings on a proper business footing, give them a little of the Max Fisher class. He tried to imagine himself in the actual joint, saw himself sitting on the floor like some suffering monk. Hell, maybe they'd start calling him The M.O.N.K. Yeah, spending his days in quiet meditation, giving out little pearls of Zen, nuggets of compassionate wisdom to the other inmates. Maybe he'd shave his head, look more spiritual. Fuck, why hadn't he thought of that sooner? Thanks, rock.

On the morning of his last full day of freedom, while taking a morning dump, he stared at his monogrammed towels. He hated to leave them behind but maybe the new tenants, they'd realize they were literally being given a slice of infamy. His reflection, drug induced, showed the eyes of a real caring man, sad but, like, knowing. His face had changed, even he could see that. It was an almost Thomas Merton look, if he could remember who the fuck Merton was. He remembered reading something about Merton living in a sparse cell, writing his seven-story some-shit-or-other. Wasn't he a monk who'd been, like, hotwired in Bangkok? The fuck was he doing there and messing round with electric fires, wasn't it, like, hot enough there?

Max took out the electric razor, raised it, the buzz of it making him jump. Fuck, how loud was the freaking thing? But, nope, couldn't do it. He looked at that gorgeous hair—actually just some thin gray strands surrounding a widening bald spot, but the rock was now seriously lying to him.

With resignation, he said, "It would be a desecration."

He was getting some good wood going and figured he better get that taken care of; wasn't likely to be much, um, nookie in the joint, definitely not of the female kind. A tear trickled down Max's cheek. Fuck, The M.A.X. had been hurt enough, thank you very much. He was going to have a ball during these forty-eight hours and not let them negative waves come at him.

He called an escort service, arranged for two black ladies to come round. He still had about two thousand bucks in bills that not even his shyster lawyer knew about.

So he drank off the Goose, said, "Let's go for bust, baby. Bring it on."

To prepare for the hookers, Max had popped five Viagras and used a pump to enlarge his dick to its maximum three and a half inches.

Then his doorman buzzed, said, "A lady's here to see you."

Lady, in a knowing way, like he was suddenly Mr. Noble. Once Max had asked him for a movie recommendation and the bollix had suggested *Big Wet Asses 2*.

Max knew how to deal with the *help*, and he said, no *ordered*, "Send the fucking lady up and now, and you better watch your attitude 'cause there are, like, you know how many spics crossing the border right now who'd kill for your job? So you know, fella, *get with the game*."

Slammed the receiver, let him know, you fuck with The M.A.X. you better be packing, and it sent him into a flashback of the wild ride of his drug baron days, and him shooting off a whole round at this big black dude who was *shooting at him*, you believe it? The guy had gone down, The M.A.X. had taken him out, taken him *down*, he'd iced that muthafucka, sent him to the big hood in the sky, and the rush! He remembered the kid, Kyle, looking at him, stunned. God, he was so ready now, his wood solid, he'd shoot if the babe didn't get up there in like—what was it that mad mick used to say?—yeah, jig time.

The bell rang and he checked his reflection. The Goose lied large, why you drank the shite, and he saw a suave, ok, debonair, laid-back guy, handsome in the Sean Penn way. You know, dangerous but sensitive too. Splashed on some Paco Rabanne, rapped:

> *"Dude smellin' good*
> *Dude smellin' score."*

Opened the door, but the fuck was this? He'd ordered two, right? And didn't booze like, make you see double? Nope, there was one, count 'em, one babe standing there. And *one not so hot-looking babe*. Let's be up front up, one *middle-aged* babe. Had he been watching too much Nick at Night or did she look just like the housekeeper from *The Jeffersons*?

He stammered, "The fuck is this?"

She brushed past him, yeah, you believe it, walked right in, brash as she liked, looked around, what, checking out the pad and if it wasn't up to expectations? Like she would what, leave?

She turned, said, "Y'all Marc Fisher right?"

Marc?

And before he could throw her old ass right out she said the magic words:

"Y'all wanna do some candy first? Yo' down baby, get high with momma, then let momma take care of yo' major action, you really carrying a pistol there, lover."

For a moment Max was tempted to call the escort service, complain, but fuck, he'd maxed out his credit card; it was either fuck the old broad or not get any for maybe ever.

So they did a couple lines, then got to it. Jesus, couldn't she even have a rack? He'd even take an old saggy rack like his ex-wife's, but this chick didn't even have A cups. It was like they were freakin' A minuses.

Max, lost in the coke high, was trying to blow into one of the hooker's nipples, like it was a balloon.

She looked down at him, went, "The fuck you doin'?"

"Er, um, nothing," Max grumbled, realizing he had bigger problems, major *major* fucking problems. Where was his goddamn hard-on? He'd taken how many Viagras and the sons of bitches wore off already?

"Ah, c'mon, you gotta be kiddin' me, Jesus H."

He popped a few more blues, then hopped back on. Still no liftoff and, shit, his heart was racing. Wasn't there a warning about Viagra for heart patients? Was this how he was gonna check out, on top of a flat-chested hooker who looked like the Jeffersons' maid on his last night before heading to Attica? Would that be fucking humiliating or what? What would people think of him? He had a reputation, shit, a *legacy* to protect.

After about forty minutes, Max was covered in sweat and the hooker said, "Time's up, suga," and less than a minute later she left, and Max's last chance for straight sex had left with her.

Now, in the cell, the giant was saying, "You deaf, white bread?"

Max tried to focus, said, "I'm sorry, I missed that?"

The big dude roared with merriment, like he loved this fat, white, balding, middle-aged white man already, repeated, "I got me the top bunk, you got the bottom. You hip to that, my man?"

Max was hip to it, nodded miserably, and Rufus said, "And y'all being sorry, y'all be even sorrier in the morning after I ream yer fat ass, and don't y'all be getting on my case about them condoms and shit. Y'all get the meat raw, know what I'm sayin'? Y'all ain't Jewish or nuttin."

Actually, Max *was* Jewish, but he worried it was a trick question. If he said he was a Jew maybe that would, like, turn Rufus on.

Then Max thought, Wait, didn't all these black dudes convert to Islam, change their names to Mohammed when they got sent away? Shit, Max would be Muslim if it saved his, well, ass.

"We might as well be on a first name basis," Max said. "You can call me Mohammed. Mohammed Fisher."

Rufus sneered, went, "A Muslim shot my mother."

Shit.

Max needed another way out, tried, "I have herpes."

Rufus brushed past Max, going, "Yo, I been havin' herpes since I was eleven years old." Then he said, "Sweep up this here crib, bitch, that's what you are, you my bitch. You gonna get yo' self all prettied up for yo' Daddy."

The smell of his BO made Max want to throw up but Max's whole body was trembling and little did he know, a miracle was nearly at hand. A miracle that would lead Max on a journey to, yes, enlightenment.

But right there and then, Max resorted to what he did when he was most terrified. He went Brit, muttered, "I'm buggered."

Two

She knew ways to make a man fuck her, even if he hated her.
When the time came, she would decide.
JACK KETCHUM, *Off Season*

Angela Petrakos was one seriously pissed off lady. One more country, one more clusterfuck.

She'd been a New York babe, had hooked up with Max Fisher and a mick-slash-psycho-slash-poet, emphasis on *slash*. No need to dwell on the freaking disaster that had been. She was of Irish-Greek descent, some dynamite blend, and she had the temper of both mixed with what Joyce had called "all the sly cunning of her race," only in her case it was races, plural. Went to Ireland and hello, like, why the hell did nobody tell her those micks had gotten rich and just a tiny bit cute? Not cute in the American sense—no, cute as in manipulative greedy bastards. And she—Jesus on a wobbly bike, would she never learn?—had hooked up with a guy who looked, okay, hot. Dark long hair, cool, though rip-off shades, the dangerous leather jacket, black naturally, and a way with him. He rocked back and forth on his feet, made her feel like she was, yeah, gorgeous.

Cut to the chase and chase it was. They'd had to flee to America and would you believe it, back into a scheme where yet again she tried to make Max Fisher pay for the shite she'd endured.

She sighed at the memory, muttered, "Let it slide."

So she'd grabbed some bucks and gone to Greece. Visited some relatives in Xios, but that got old fast, so she ferried to

Santorini, supposed site of Atlantis. Got to be good karma there, right?

Um, for a start, what was with the fucking donkeys having to carry you up the cliff to the town? She must've missed that in the guidebooks. But being American carried some weight still, especially if you were a hot, stacked blonde.

She rented a small villa and was surprised at how cheap it was. Georgios, who owned the place, also claimed he was mayor of the village and drove a cab at night and was the chef at the local taverna. These Greeks, they knew how to multitask. He was ogling her openly, staring at her bust to the point where she had to hit him with the old "My eyes, they're, like, up here." At the door, he held her arm and reminded her how reasonable that rent was and how, if she was a little cooperative, the rent might disappear completely.

She knew some Greek, about four words but all the vital ones, and said, "Mallakas," i.e. wanker, and he fucked off.

First it was heaven, the balcony overlooking the sea, sipping on some ouzo, her tan coming along nicely, showing off her serious cleavage. The nude beaches were great, but the constant Greeks hitting on her became a drag. She was so desperate she would've settled for a mick.

She was offered a job as a hostess in a club named *"Acribos."* Her second Greek word: "Exactly."

When she wasn't tanning, she was hiking in the dunes, or just hanging out at the local taverna spinning worry beads, drinking ouzo, and playing backgammon. It was relaxing but, let's face it, boring as hell. She was Angela Petrakos. She needed a buzz, she needed action.

She made a friend at the taverna—Alexandra, an American from Berkeley. They decided to hit the clubs one night and a hit they were. It might've helped that they were the only two women in the place without facial hair, but guys were all over them all night. Near closing time they hooked up with a couple of young Italians who claimed they were eighteen but Angela figured that hers, Luca, was sixteen tops. Alexandra and her guy disappeared, and Angela and Luca wandered down to the beach. She had a full moon, crashing waves, and a horny young Italian. What else did a girl need?

And the guy might've been a teenager but, boy, he knew how to screw. They went at it all night till they collapsed in exhaustion. In the morning, Luca was gone and so was Angela's money. The little bastard had gone through her purse and cleaned her out. Good thing Angela wasn't carrying much. The kid got sixteen euro, Angela got six orgasms. Who got the better deal?

Alexandra left town the next day and Angela was back on her own again. People had been getting to know her and generally treated her fine, but this one old woman, must've been a hundred, gave her the heebie-jeebies from day one. When Angela walked along the streets most people would say *yassou*, hello, to her. But this woman would just glare at Angela, giving her the evil eye, as if she knew, but knew what?

Then one evening at the taverna, she was beginning to get that bored, pissed off feeling again—never a good sign—when she heard, "My word, what a vision of true beauty."

Turned to see this tall guy, looked like that writer Lee Child, whom she hadn't actually read but from the photos on the back of his books she nearly believed there might be a reason to read those mystery novels. She had a Barry Eisler book cause of his jacket photo and one by C.J. Box—hey, she'd always been a sucker for guys in cowboy hats. Who cared if these guys could write, they looked hot. No wonder the micks had to actually write books, mangy-looking bastards they were.

The Lee Child guy was wearing, oh saints above, a safari

jacket, and he had that young Roger Moore look. The best part: *a British accent.*

She muttered, "Thank you, God."

Finally, her luck had changed, a Brit, was there an American gal on the planet didn't want to hear that *Brideshead Revisited* tone?

He asked, oh those fucking make-you-moist manners, "May I join you?"

She would've let him do a lot more than that. But she figured, British guy, he was probably reserved and well-mannered. She didn't want to turn him off and be, like, too forward.

"Oh, yes, please do," she said, trying to sound British, but the American was coming through loud and clear.

He held her hand, kissed it, said, "I'm Sebastian."

God, that accent! She was tempted to shout "I'm available!" but went with, "I'm Angela."

He told her all about himself. Said he was living off a trust fund, traveling the world, and he was, naturally, writing a novel. The writing part she could've guessed. For some reason, she was a magnet for those literary types—maybe it was a misery-loves-company kind of thing.

When it was her turn she knew honesty was the worst policy. She said she'd lived in New York for a while but things hadn't worked out with her fiancé, then she'd moved to Ireland for a while, tried New York again, and now she was giving Greece a shot. She, er, forgot to mention all the violence.

He looked her in the eyes, held her gaze, and said, "I must say, in all my travels, I've never encountered anyone quite as stunning as you."

An all-too-familiar voice in Angela's head was screaming, *Run! Get the fook out while you still can!* How many times had she been down this road, meeting a guy who seemed like "the one," only to wind up screwed, and not in the good way? She didn't have baggage, she had freakin' cargo. Or, as they say in the south, she'd been *ridden hard and hung up wet*.

Translation: She didn't trust nobody.

Later, when Sebastian asked if he could give her a lift home, Angela said politely, "No, thank you."

She hardly believed it herself. Had she really turned down an easy lay with James Bond's twin?

"I must see you again," he said.

His eyes looked so vulnerable, like Colin Firth's. She was tempted to say, screw it, and drag him back to her place and fuck him stupid. But she remained strong, said, "Well my schedule's pretty full."

"Surely you can squeeze me in somewhere," he said, punning like ol' Roger Moore himself.

But she remained strong— when had she ever had the discipline to do that?—and told him, "Maybe we'll run into each other again sometime."

But he insisted on seeing her and she said she "might" be able to meet him for a drink at a taverna near the beach the next afternoon.

Of course she showed. The following night they went out to dinner. At the end of the night he gave her a peck on the cheek goodnight and asked her when he might have the pleasure of seeing her again. She didn't sleep with him until the fourth date—okay, the third, but who's counting? Still, it had to be some kind of record.

And then one night, not long after, he uttered the lure, the never-fail, hook-'em-every-time words and, even more damning, in Greek: "*Sagapoh.*" I love you.

In any language and especially in that British accent, she was signed, sealed and *kebabed*. It was beautiful, lyrical, her beau had finally arrived. He was even talking about taking her to England for a weekend to meet his Mum and Dad. Yeah, she was seriously getting into the idea of marrying Sebastian, settling down, becoming British. Her grandfather, the Brit-hating bastard, would probably turn in his grave, but who gave a shite? She'd be like Madonna. She was already refining her accent and when they got married maybe she'd adopt an African child or, hell, steal one.

She felt like her life was finally starting to get on track. She was still young, just thirty-three. Maybe twenty or thirty years from now she'd be happily married to Sebastian, their kids off at University, and she'd laugh at some of the "mistakes" she'd made early on in her life.

One tiny little glitch hardly worth mentioning, but one night, they were dining at a posh restaurant overlooking the seas when the waiter returned with Seb's Visa card, saying it had been refused. But it was no biggie. As he put it, "Nothing to get your knickers in a twist about, love."

Angela paid in cash, tried to pretend she hadn't noticed a glint in Seb's eyes, no, surely a trick of the Greek light. And okay, so she seemed to be picking up the tab more often, and Seb, the handsome rogue, holding his cig exactly like she'd seen in all those movies, saying, "Darling, slight hitch with the old trust fund, they want to increase my allowance but I damn well refused, I'm writing an opus to make Lawrence Durrell want to weep, so I say damn their impertinence, I'll pay my own way or go down like Khartoum, blazing but bloody defiant."

The fuck was he talking about? She didn't care, she loved it because of the accent. And she loved he was an artist, a real writer, not like her old boyfriends, Dillon with his poetry and Slide with the fucking screenplay he kept talking about. So what if she never actually saw Sebastian, um, write? Once she wondered, Wouldn't, like, a laptop have helped? But she refused to give in to those negative waves. She figured he was literary, kept it all in his head. This was love, the real thing; so what if there were a few inconsistencies? As her mick exes used to say, "Damn the begrudgers."

Then one evening she was at her villa, showering, when she heard a noise in the other room. She figured it was Sebastian, as she'd given him a key to her place.

"Come in, Sebs, darling, I'm feeling quite horny at the moment and a bit of a screw in the shower would be lovely indeed."

Yeah, the Madonna accent was coming along well.

She parted the curtain, smiling, expecting to see Sebs, and then gasped when she saw Georgios, her landlord. His squat body, the clumps of hair from out of his dirty wife-beater, that scowling look—he was like some kind of deranged animal. And, fookin A, was that a *meat cleaver* in his hand?

He growled in Greek, spraying saliva, ending with, "you dirty cunt," and came after her. She managed to duck to her left just in time, the cleaver slicing through the curtain. Naked and wet, she darted out of the bathroom, screaming, but he tackled her from behind. He had the cleaver to her throat.

She closed her eyes, waiting to die and to be with her mother and father again—she just hoped to God there wouldn't be spoons and bodhrans in heaven.

But he wasn't going to kill her, not yet anyway. She should've known.

When he was through, his sweat was dripping, no *pouring*, off his body, onto the back of her neck, and he leaned closer to her, said, "You be my wife, okay? You drive taxi, okay?"

Then she heard, "By God, love, are you all right?"

Sebastian, the useless bastard. He sees her lying on the floor underneath a mad Greek rapist and he asks if she's *all right*? She was tempted to say, Yes, I'm doing wonderful, darling. Why don't you put the kettle on and come join us?

But she noticed that Georgios was momentarily distracted and she seized the opportunity and went for the cleaver. The bastard wouldn't let go of it, so she had to bite on his ear, as hard as she could, tasting the sweat and blood. Meanwhile, out of the corner of her eye, she noticed that Sebastian was just standing there with a curious expression, like he was watching a fookin' snooker match. These Brits, unless they were shooting boyos they were feckin' useless.

Angela didn't stop biting on the Greek's ear. Finally, after she'd kneed him in the balls a couple of times, the cleaver clanged to the floor and she grabbed it. She started hacking into his chest, slashing and swiping. It seemed like all of the past few years were welling up, fueled by the smell of this fooking animal. And she let him have it, all right. Never fook with a woman who has the Greek-Irish gene.

She was kneeling over her victim, gasping, her hands covered in blood. Then she raised the cleaver again and Sebastian went, "Darling, it's not necessary, the bugger's already done for."

Through her pain and rage, the Brit accent gave her a moment of joy. Then she heard the word *bugger*. By fuck, *bugger*.

Georgios, somehow still alive, was coming round, muttering, "Mallakas, menu...?"

She'd give him mallakas, thinking of all the ferocity she'd learned from the micks in her bedraggled life, all the shite from one Max Fisher who'd once said, "Gonna put the meat to you, bitch."

She'd let the bitch part slide, but *meat*? All three inches of his top sirloin?

She raised the cleaver and Sebastian, in that beautiful accent pleaded, "Darling...don't."

She grabbed Georgios by his hair, gave him one ferocious slash across the neck, nearly decapitating the bastard, then said, "Word to the wise, *darling*, don't ever fuck with me."

Then she and Sebastian were on the floor, going at it like animals. The power surge, as she saw the majestic Brit underneath her, her *using* him, and saw—was it fear?—in his eyes. Probably had a little to do with the cleaver still grasped in her right hand. What you might term a power ride.

He whimpered, "Darling, this is all quite nice, but is the, um, weapon necessary?"

And she began to laugh, laugh and come, swung the cleaver across the room and it landed with a pleasing thump against the wall.

Later, when she came round, Sebastian had cleaned up, the Brits, a tidy race. Georgios was neatly wrapped in a roll of plastic sheeting and the blood splatter had been washed clean. She wrapped a flokati rug around her and Sebastian, looking like death warmed up, gave her a cup of the thick sweet Greek coffee, and said, "Precious, we might be, um, in a spot of, um, bother."

She nearly started laughing again, said, "Bother. Trust me, lover, bother is my forte."

She drank the coffee, handed him the cup, demanded, not asked, "More." Then ordered, "Put some of that Metaxi in it, I need to focus."

Making it very clear who had the balls in this relationship.

By dawn's early light, they'd used Sebastian's tiny scooter and driven precariously to the cliff on the other side of the island. All the time, Sebastian expecting the cops to stop them at any moment, and them carrying a literal dead weight between them, on a *bicycle built for two*, as that awful song goes. Angela behind, a new Angela to him, urging, "Get a fooking move on, people will be moving soon."

Lord above, she scared the daylights out of him. He'd thought he'd scored himself a rich American dumb blonde and instead had the Greek version of *Fatal Attraction*, with a cleaver no less. Oh lordy, how had he gotten it so wrong?

She was screaming, "What kind of bike is this for a man? You ever hear of a Harley? Like, a *man's* machinery?"

He was too scared to answer, the demented creature had probably still got the cleaver somewhere. She had seemed awfully attached to it and if he lived to be a hundred, scratch that, if he got to see noon, he'd never forget the way she'd hacked the poor Greek bastard to ribbons. And yes, he hadn't been the most useful person in her predicament, seeing the randy chap, um, *having his way with her*. Gosh, it had been almost exciting. And to say she'd overreacted, I mean *really*. Didn't she know those Med types were hot blooded? It wasn't like the gell (pronounced thus) hadn't been down the M1 before. And then, oh lordy, the cleaver. She was like some bloody Irish guttersnipe.

He'd been in some scrapes, a chap doesn't get to his late twenties, alright, mid-thirties, without the odd ruction, but this, this was like, what was that awful Hollywood tripe? *Texas Chainsaw Massacre?* This was like living a gosh-awful B-movie he and the chaps might rent after a night on the tiles in Cambridge.

Oh, he swore, by all that Cambridge held sacred, if he got free of this mad cow, he was legging it back to Blighty and scoring some dosh however he might and heading straight for Italy, some civilized European country where being British still counted for something. Naturally Sebastian had never actually been to Cambridge. He'd flunked out of a third-rate technical college but come on, isn't a chap allowed a little *leeway*?

And weak—no one knew better than he how lily-livered he

was. As a child, he'd seen the movie *The Four Feathers*; that was him without the end heroics and redemption. He got by on his diminishing trust fund, wonderful manners, sheer culture and, dammit, his boyish good looks. No one, he knew this, no one could do that toss of the black lustrous hair, the vulnerable little-boy-lost look better than he. He had nothing else going for him, he knew that, but with a little luck he'd been hoping it would, at the bloody least, net him one of those rich dumb Americans of which the States seemed to produce a never-ending supply.

She was hammering his back. Damn it all, his back was fragile, old rugger injury. Okay, he never played, but he did follow the game all right.

She was screeching, "Here, you dumb fook."

Crikey, her language was simply appalling.

They dropped ol' Georgios off the cliff and Sebastian, nigh hysterical now, wanted to shout, as the body hit the ocean, *Beware of Greeks bearing cellophane*. And he thought, dammit, he might just yet write the great Brit novel. Evelyn Waugh, eat your bitter heart out.

Three

Hell hath no fury like a mystery writer...dropped.

Paula Segal was nervous, not a feeling she liked having. She laughed to herself, thinking, *Feeling Nervous*, she might use that for a title. Or *Twisted Feelings*? Or maybe *Hard Feelings*—someone else had probably already used that but fuck him, you couldn't copyright a title. Then she sighed and said out loud, "Bad joke." Like she was ever going to have a shot at titling another book.

She was meeting her agent for lunch, not dinner. You knew when they moved you from dinner to lunch, you were semi-fucked, only one unearned-out advance away from a fast latte in Starbucks. Just ask that poor Irish bastard who'd been hot for all of ten minutes. Jesus, he'd had more agents than lattes and look at him now. He couldn't even make a panel at the U.K. Festivals.

She checked her rankings on Amazon—nothing better than 500,000. And worse, she'd gotten yet another shitty review from *Booklist*.

The thing was, she knew she was good. She had three good mysteries under her belt, one nomination for the Barry—she'd lost to Tess Gerritsen, but that was no biggie, everyone lost to Tess—and Laura Lippman had promised her a blurb. Even Val McDermid had smiled at her that time in Toronto.

But she'd been termed "midlist" when she'd started out and more recently had slipped to "cult." Cult equaled nada, sorry, hon. She just didn't get it. She thought only those creepy noir guys got demoted to cult. She'd never even written a short story for Akashic.

She seriously didn't understand why her books hadn't done better. She wrote what she thought was a nice blend of cozy and medium-boiled. Nothing too dark or too scary. Her heroine, McKenna Ford, was a lovely combination of sensitivity and street smarts.

But not according to *Kirkus*, which called her last book, "Tired, unoriginal and pointless. Read Megan Abbott for the real deal."

Jesus, she hated Megan Abbott and Alison Gaylin. Not only did the guys love them but they got rave reviews. Don't get her started on female mystery writers, except for Laura of course. Hey, that blurb might still happen.

Her agent ran her rapidly through lunch, then said, with no gentle breaking in, "You're screwed."

Lunch that.

He added, "SMP's dropping you." Then asked, "You ever try true crime?"

What? She was an artist. She couldn't slum and write nonfiction. She was going to just say, fuck it, it wasn't for her. If she couldn't write mystery fiction she'd rather go back to the telemarketing cubicle.

But then her agent told her about the Max Fisher story and something sparked. She thought, *Hello?* This could be a goldmine; it was like the book was already written. She couldn't believe Sebastian Junger hadn't beaten her to it. Could The M.A.X. be her ticket all the way to the top? Or, well, at least back to the middle.

As usual, she got ahead of herself. She imagined winning next year's Edgar Award for best true crime book, with her old editor sitting in the audience watching, thinking about the one that got away. Maybe Laura herself would present the award. Though they'd only spoken that one time, at the bar at the Left Coast Crime convention in El Paso, and let's face it, Paula had been so nervous she barely spoke. She just did a lot of smiling, nodding, and blushing. Still, she felt like Laura actually liked her, that they'd, dare she even think it, made a connection that went way beyond mystery writing. The encounter had ignited something in Paula, gotten her off the fence, so to speak. She'd experimented in college—who hadn't?—and a bit after college, too, and yeah, once or twice in recent years, but basically she'd thought of herself as straight. But that smile Laura gave her had pushed her over the edge. Hell, over the cliff. Yep, Paula was playing for the other team now. She was on the lookout for a pretty, intelligent, mature, successful lover and Laura Lippman fit the bill. She imagined them living in Baltimore, their Edgars side by side on the mantel, traveling the festival circuit in Europe together...

Okay, okay, it was time to focus, buckle down, get this damn book written.

She attended the trial of The M.A.X. She sat in the back, taking lots of notes. This Max Fisher, he was some character all right. She'd never seen anyone so caught up in his own delusion. He was on trial for major drug charges, and it was like he was gleefully oblivious to it all. Even when the judge sentenced him, Fisher didn't seem to get the gravity of the situation. As he was led out of the courtroom, he chanted, "Attica, Attica, Attica..."

Paula knew she'd have to dig deep, really make readers understand the psychology of Fisher, but deep wasn't her strong suit. Her writing was surfacey, superficial. She often told friends that this was purposeful, that she could write with more depth any time she wanted, that she consciously tried to "dumb it down for the masses." As if the masses had ever seen one of her books.

She had a better chance of bedding Laura Lippman than of getting a book into Wal-Mart.

But a superficial take just wouldn't work for a guy like Fisher, and neither would her usual cozy-to-medium-boiled style. This guy made *In Cold Blood* seem like chick lit. The things the man had done, the unsavory people he'd been involved with, especially that woman he'd been engaged to, Angela Petrakos—she sounded like she could be the subject of her own true crime book. Paula was already thinking, sequel? But telling the Fisher story properly would require some serious hardboiled, noir writing. She didn't know if she had the chops to pull it off.

But the telemarketing cubicle loomed large and made her refocus. She Googled like a banshee and by the time she was done she was thinking, *Edgar? Just the beginning. Why not a National Book Award? Or, hell, maybe even a Quill...*

She had to sit back and try to take it all in. The Fisher story had it all. There were, get this, Irish hit men who even had, whisper, *IRA connections*. There was also some odd stuff about Down Syndrome and gold pins that she didn't quite get but hey, if there was a handicapped theme, hello *Oprah*, right? What would she wear on the show? Would Oprah cry when Paula talked about her long personal journey from unknown cult writer to literary goddess? Yeah, probably.

She snapped herself back into focus, thinking, And, wait, there was even more handicapped stuff, some guy in a wheelchair who photographed women in, let's say, compromising positions. Hello *Playboy* serialization. And there was also

A hero cop: Hello Hollywood. At worst, a TV series.

Boyz in the hood: Hello Spike Lee.

Southern crackers: Hello *National Enquirer*.

And above it all, loomed The M.A.X. There was no doubt that was the book's title: *The Max*. She'd thought about *Hot Blood*,

Tough City, toyed with *Songs of Innocence*. But, nope, it had to be *The Max*.

She was so excited. She went and made herself a dry martini; no one, she knew it, no one, made them drier. It was good, just the right amount of martini, and gave her the boost of confidence she needed as she wrote the following to Mr. Max Fisher, c/o Attica State Penitentiary:

> *Dear Mr. Fisher,*
>
> *I am a mystery writer of high standing in my genre, a friend of Laura Lippman, Tess Gerritsen, etc. I have been commissioned by a very high profile publisher to write a true crime book and I truly feel you are the subject most deserving of my time. I believe you have been the most appalling victim of our Justice System and I would like to set the record straight and I must confess, as a woman, I find you hugely appealing. I enclose a photo.*
>
> *Yours sincerely*
> *Paula Segal (MWA, IACW, ITW, PWA)*

She had the perfect photo for this schmuck—her, bursting out of a bikini, nearly topless. And her favorite part about the photo, she looked demure. Demure was a word you got to use when you were a writer of her caliber. Recalling the photos of Petrakos from the trial, she knew this asshole loved big busts, and was he ever getting the max with this shot. Her previous lover, an Annie Lebowitz wannabe, had taken it. The girl was a lousy lay but she sure could take good photo.

Delighted with herself, she practically skipped down to the post office and sent the letter. Attica, just the thought of it made her shudder.

Four

I think you should get on my body now.
DAVID MAMET, *Edmond*

It wasn't like Max had never been raped before. During a drinking binge in the south he somehow wound up in a motel room in Robertsdale, Alabama with a Chinese guy named Bruce. Maybe it wasn't technically rape because Max might've gone up to the room willingly, but really the saving grace was that he'd been so bombed he couldn't remember any of it.

Man, what he would have given for some hard liquor right now.

The worst part, it was only around noon, and he had nine hours till Rufus and lights out. First, lunch in the mess hall. Jesus Christ, eighty percent of the prisoners were goddamn black. He felt like it was that time in the city he was so absorbed reading a copy of *Screw* that he missed his stop on the 6 train and got out at fucking 125th Street. Walking through the mess hall he was thinking, *Be Richard Pryor in* Stir Crazy. He was even whispering to himself, "That's right, I'm bad, I'm bad." But he must've been shaking his ass too much because the walk didn't get him any respect—it had the opposite effect, getting him catcalls from all the guys. They were whistling at him, calling him "sweety" and "honey," and Max, shaking, thought, Jesus Christ there was gonna be a goddamn gangbang.

He knew he had to do something to get some respect. Maybe he should make a shank and cut somebody. Isn't that what that Eddie Bunker said you were supposed to do? Yeah, but how the fuck was he supposed to get a shank his first day in the joint. Eddie, couldn't you've given us a goddamn instruction manual?

Later, in the yard, more guys were eye-fucking him, saying things like, "Gimme some a dat" and "I wanna tap that big ol' ass, gran'pa."

Gran'pa?

That was the part that stung the most. Yeah, Max was in his fifties, but he'd always seen himself as a hip, happening dude. It hit Max that not only was he a lot whiter than these guys, he was a lot older. It seemed like every guy was a goddamn twenty-two-year-old. What, was he the only guy in the world over fifty who was into drugs and shooting people? He had thirty plus years on all these guys, so how come they weren't treating him like the wise elder statesman? How come he wasn't getting respect, like Morgan Freeman in *Shawshank*? Speaking of *Shawshank*, Max wasn't going into the prison laundry room any time soon. Not until he made that shank, anyway.

As much as he feared the inevitable sexual assault, Max had to admit, on some level, all the attention was kind of, well, flattering. He couldn't get women to look at him the way these guys were unless he was paying them good money, and even then Max never felt *liked*. Jesus, it was bringing tears to his eyes. The M.A.X. crying? At *Attica*? Jesus, that had to be the absolute wrong thing to do—show your weakness. But he couldn't help it. Maybe he was channeling his inner sissy, but what could he say? It felt good to be wanted.

A guy in the yard was bench-pressing—he looked Mexican, Puerto Rican, Dominican, something Spanish Harlemy. And the son of a bitch was huge, looked like he could be a linebacker for the fucking Jets.

Benching what looked like at least three hundred pounds he said, *"Hola, jovensita,"* and blew Max a kiss.

The M.A.X. knew his Spanish, the guy was calling him "young lady." *Jesus H.*

Max turned away and the guy said, "Hey, I finish talkin' to you, *mi puta*?"

Max tried, *"No hablo español."*

"Don't worry," the guy said, "you don't gotta talk *español*. When you got my dick in your mouth all day I ain't gonna hear nothin' you sayin' anyway."

The guy laughed then let the weight fall onto the brackets so hard the whole bench shook.

"Look," Max said. *"No necesito* trouble." Then, hearing the hillbilly in *Deliverance* saying, *You in trouble now, boy*, he said desperately, "I mean, I've got *nada* against Puerto Ricans."

"Puerto Rican?" The guy sounded offended. "I look PR to you? Man, I should cut you just for saying that shit. I'm fuckin' Panamanian."

Jesus, weren't Panamanians supposed to be, like, midgets? The only fucking Panamanian giant on the planet and Max had to run into him. Was that shit luck or what?

Then the guy said, "I should introduce myself properly, if you're gonna be my little *puta*. *Me nombre es* Sino."

Sino? What was that, fucking Chinese? The guy wasn't fucking part Chinese, was he, some kind of ChinoManian? Max had had enough Chinamen visit his ass for one lifetime, thank you very much.

"Sino's what they call me in the Bronx, shit's short for *asesino*. You know why I got that name? 'Cause I like to kill people, that's why. I killed sixteen people and you gimme your ass you won't be number *diecisiete*. Most people in here, they don't like to talk about people they took out, think it's gonna fuck up their parole. But Sino got Life, No Parole hangin' over his ass. Sino ain't goin nowhere so Sino don't give a shit."

Max was about to give a shit—in his pants. But out of nowhere Rufus appeared and said, "Yo, lay off my bitch, *bitch*, 'fore I beat yo' ass."

Sino stood face to face with Rufus, both mad bastards about the same height, and a crowd formed around them to watch the confrontation. Max felt like he was in high school—well, not like he *himself* had felt in high school, but like he might've felt if he'd been a popular girl in high school. It was like Max was head cheerleader and the two jocks were fighting over him. Max had to admit—it felt pretty damn good.

But the good feeling passed quickly. Max was thinking maybe he should've taken the Ed Norton in *The 25th Hour* route after all, gotten somebody to beat the crap out of him before he went away. He was just too damn pretty. A face like his, naturally guys couldn't resist it. Maybe if he hadn't been so interested in getting laid during his last forty-eight hours, and hadn't wasted all his time reading books and watching movies, he could've thought of this practical shit.

Rufus was yelling into Sino's face, "Mohammed Fisher's my bitch. Stay off my bitch, know what I'm sayin', bitch?"

And Sino was screaming back: "I don't see no sign on his ass say he your bitch. I don't see your dick in his ass neither."

Rufus said, "There don't gotta be no dick in his ass. Just 'cause there ain't no dick in his ass don't mean the bitch ain't mine."

Max was tempted to yell, *You're both fucking morons!* but had a feeling that wouldn't go over well. Maybe the guys would decide to share him, holy fuckin' shit.

A guard came over and told the guys to break it up. Rufus grabbed Max by the hand and led him away.

Later on, back in their cell, Rufus said to Max, "You clean yo' ass out good tonight, know what I'm sayin'? I don't want no brown on my dick. My dick got enough brown on it, don't need no more, know what I'm sayin'?"

There was nothing for Max to do now but lie in his bunk and wait for the inevitable. He was thinking about, of all people, Elvis. Max, in those last forty-eight hours of freedom, had watched so many movies, his fucking eyes hurt and how he ended up with *Jailhouse Rock* in his DVD player was anyone's guess. The King, singing on the tiers, had brought tears to his eyes. He'd never really given Elvis a whole lotta time. Let's face it, The M.A.X. was a classical music kinda guy, could pronounce Tchaikovsky without a single moment of hesitation. *Fucking hum that, yah morons.*

Shit, he realized he'd been talking aloud again.

"Well, fucking excuse me!" he shouted. "I'm under a little goddamn pressure here!"

Inmates in the other cells starting laughing and Max blocked it out, thinking about Elvis again. The El was one good looking *hombre* and Max wondered if that's what he should do later when Rufus was, er, visiting him—pretend he was getting screwed by The King. Yeah, he'd pretend to be Priscilla. Max pledged that if he ever got out of this hole, he'd go straight to Graceland, give his thanks for help in a tight spot. Maybe hang with Priscilla. The babe had mileage but serious bucks—he could use some of that.

He was weeping now, and he knew, dammit, only a real man could allow himself that freedom.

After the slop they called dinner it was lights out. Jesus Christ, Max was sobbing again, begging for his mommy. He wished he'd read more of that fucking Genet book so at least he'd know what to expect. He would've paid a fortune for some Vaseline so at least it wouldn't hurt. But he knew, worse than the pain would be all the fucking humiliation tomorrow, all the guys knowing that Rufus had done the deed. He just hoped that Rufus didn't make him walk around the prison wearing lipstick and fucking skirts, like that queen in *Animal Factory*.

But then something weird happened.

He was waiting for the brute to climb down and deliver the meat, but the bunk was still. Maybe Rufus was just playing head games with him, making him think he wasn't gonna get fucked tonight, then…kaboom.

But another ten, fifteen minutes went by and still no Rufus. And what was that noise? Was he actually *snoring*? The fuck was going on?

Max wanted to feel happy, but he didn't dare let himself. It had to be part of some plan or something. A guard would unlock a bunch of inmates' cells and let them into Max's and the goddamn gangbang would begin.

He waited. At some point, he fell asleep.

In the morning, he woke up and wriggled his ass around a little. No pain. Was it possible he'd slept through being anally raped? It wouldn't have been the first time but, nope, his ass was its good ol' self.

Then another surprise: Rufus hung down from the top bunk, smiled, asked, "Yo, what up? Sleep good, Mohammed?"

What the fuck? Was this some kinda fuckin' joke? Was this how the guy turned himself on, let his victims think they were off the hook, then, when their guard was fully down…

"Yes," Max said hesitantly.

"That's good," Rufus said. "If there's anythin' you want me to do today, yo, you just let me know, hear, and I get that shit done for you fast, know what I'm sayin'?"

Max had no idea what to make of Rufus's sudden turnaround, but he wasn't complaining. His ass wasn't complaining either.

Then the biggest surprise of all: At breakfast, there was no whistling, no catcalls, no nothing. Shit, people wouldn't even make eye contact with him. The fuck was going on? Yeah, he was glad he hadn't gotten raped, but the insecure Max Fisher was coming out, asking, *Have I, like, lost my appeal?* Other guys in the room were getting the old come-hither looks, guys younger than Max, and he found himself actually feeling jealous.

In the yard, Max went up to one of the guards, Malis, and asked, "The fuck's going on? How come nobody'll fuckin' look at me anymore?"

Malis, chomping on gum, didn't look at Max, said, "The fuck do I know?"

"Come on, give me a fuckin' break," Max whined. "If this silent treatment is just a set-up, if I'm gonna get ambushed tonight, the least you could do is let me know about it. I'm a well-connected guy, if you get my drift."

Yeah, let the asshole think he was in store for a hefty bribe. Like that was gonna happen.

"You're not gonna get ambushed," Malis said.

"Yeah? How the fuck do you know that?"

Malis continued looking away, chewing his gum, then shook his head as if, thinking, *I give up*, and said, "Look, your story got around, all right?"

"Story? What story?"

"The story about what you got sent away for."

Max was confused, said, "I'm confused."

"All the guys," Malis said, "they know what you did."

"You talking about the drug dealing charges?"

"No, I'm talking about how you cut off that guy's dick down in the city."

The severed dick was a, well, issue that had come up in Max's trial. Max had had nothing to do with it, but apparently the prisoners thought he had. Actually, Angela's latest psycho boyfriend had cut off the dick, delivered it to Max in a shoebox.

"You mean they think I—"

"Everybody's scared shitless," Malis said. "They don't want

to come near you. Hey, and just in case you get any ideas, you come anywhere near my dick, I even see you looking at my dick, I'm gonna fuckin' shoot you. Got that?"

It took a while—okay, less than a minute—for it to sink in. He wasn't a target anymore. He was—get this—a feared man.

He took a little spin around the yard, a *victory lap*, soaking it up, letting all the suckers know who the new King was. Wasn't there a movie like that already? *The Fisher King?*

Yeah, he could learn to like this joint.

Five

I knew I'd never get enough of her.
She was straight out of hell.
GIL BREWER, *The Vengeful Virgin*

When Angela and Sebastian got back to the villa, he was seriously spooked. This was a crazy woman and, lordy, if he ever got the hell away from her, he might well write her as a character in his book. The book he'd never written a line of but he would, he was literary, like Amis and Burroughs. He'd just sit down one day and *voila*, masterpiece. You either had it or you didn't and he bloody well had it.

One literary effort that he actually did produce was a poem in the technical college entitled:

Lenin and Your Letter

He just flat out loved that title. It had politics, love and, to be totally honest, true resonance. And, okay, he'd been a little wiped when he wrote it, but excuse me, look at all the greats— Scott Fitz, Hem, Behan, Bukowski, Berryman, Jerry Rodriguez. Hadn't they all been a little, well, spiffed when they wrote their finest work? You wanted pain, compassion, suffering, Sebastian knew you had to fucking live it.

He just wished he could remember the bloody poem. Only one line had remained with him:

Lenin, you Jewish hack

Ah, the thrill. Did he actually write that? He did. Oh, Booker Prize be praised. And God bless Salman Rushdie. Sebastian had his very brief moment of fame as the student union, all five of them, had accused him of anti-Zionism. Lordy, it was what every real literary lion endured.

Whoops, the deranged bitch was shaking him, not with the cleaver, least not yet, saying, "Hello, shite-face, time to like, you know, clean up?"

And he did, but her language! Was that really necessary? She should go to the U.K. where they mightn't like you but, by golly, they always had manners.

They scrubbed the place down, every last drop of blood, etcetera, gone. Would they bring in forensics of the Greek variety? Hello, let's be honest. The Greek variety of forensics was probably one greasy inspector with his hand out, dropping cigar ash all over the crime scene and trampling on bloodstains. They were clear, and if he could now just get clear of the mad cow he could get his show on the road.

She gave him the golden opportunity, snapped, "Where are my fookin cigs?"

And he jumped on it, said, "Hon, I'll jump on the scooter, get you a fresh pack."

Then, distracted, she said, "And buy some booze, too. Jesus wept."

There was a ferry to Athens—he checked his fake Rolex—in two hours. He put the pedal to the metal and he was out of there. He had a tiny villa rented as close to the port as he could find. He'd learned the hard way, always have your getaway planned. All he needed was his passport, his Cambridge tie, borrowed (so to speak) from a chap—damn tie opened more doors than his wonderful polished BBC accent—his trusty Gladstone bag, one of the few genuine items he owned—and one of those Moleskine diaries, nicely weathered and one of these days, he might actually jot something down in it. He believed he looked suitably battered, had that *climbed the Himalayas and crossed the damn Ganges* look. Made him seem like a Bruce Chatwin traveler type. He hadn't actually read Chatwin, but that hardly mattered. Most of all, he had his stash, the vital element, *the get-out-of-town-and-fucking-fast-old-bean* dosh.

He wouldn't have time to get the deposit back on his little scooter, but as he'd paid with a bum credit card, it was kind of poetic justice; and if he did take the time the psycho bitch would be starting to wonder was he making the bloody cigarettes and come looking.

He shivered, seeing her with that cleaver. God he was sweaty, from fear and stress, the golly goshed heat. He liked to be always, in every sense, cool, but a cleaver can change a lot of habits. He'd had to forego taking a shower in his haste to get out, and he promised himself now that he'd book into the King Kronos in Athens, get the penthouse, use his Platinum Visa, only ever taken out for real occasions and Jolly Hockey Sticks, this was one of those times.

He threw his Jermyn Street bespoke shirts, his beloved linen suit and Panama hat (his nod to Somerset Maugham—and, truly, he must read the crusty old bugger someday), and splashed some cologne on. Not too much, a hint darlings, not like the mad Paddy he'd met who seemed to climb into the bottle, not only of Jameson but cologne. He sighed, thinking, The Irish. They had not one ounce of restraint.

He went to get his stash, carefully hidden under the loose tile in the shower. *Tipota*, Greek for all gone. Not a bean. The bloody hell was this? And a note. A note?

Darling,

    Lest you ever think of running out on me, I'm, shall we say, holding this in trust for you.

                      Xxxxxx
                      Love you loads

Only one time he'd been a little the worse for wear on the old retsina and allowed her to come back to his place and the cunt, she'd cleaned him out.

He checked his wallet. He had his vital credit cards, his return ticket to Athens, and about 200 Euro.

Move, the voice in his head urged.

He did, and fast.

Angela, waiting for Sebastian to return with the cigs and booze, was on her hands and knees, scrubbing Georgios' blood, getting a bad case of déjà vu. Yes, somehow it felt like she'd been through this before, but the worst part was this time she'd seen it coming. She was driving along the tunnel, the headlights coming right for her, and the idea that maybe she should, like, *slow down* or, even better, *turn around*, hadn't occurred to her. Falling for a British accent of all things. Couldn't it at least have been an athletic Brit, a David Beckham type? She knew she was posh enough to get any British guy she wanted, but she wound up with fookin' Sebastian. Honestly, she'd never met a bigger wuss, as you'd call it in America. He was so fooking polite, she was just dying to take him to a few bars she knew in Ireland, introduce him to a few guys she knew, they'd make a man out of him all right.

And what about the way he said "lordy" all the time and wore that God-forsaken safari jacket? He looked like an early victim in an Agatha Christie film, the first annoying bastard who gets bumped off. In bed the other night, he'd started reciting some god awful poem, something about a fookin Zionist. Pluck any drunk off the street in Dublin, he could write a better poem than that shite.

Another thing: Would he open his jaw when he talked? Sometimes she'd have sworn his mouth must be wired shut.

Sebastian was useless, no doubt about it, but right now she needed him, to get out of this mess. After they'd dumped the Greek's body off the cliff she'd decided they had to clean up every drop of blood from the villa, then take off *pronto*. One thing Angela knew how to do was run like hell. They both agreed there was no way they could stick around and explain what had happened. The "he raped me and I killed him in self defense" story wouldn't go over well with Greek cops—after all, nearly chopping off a guy's head wasn't exactly like spraying him with mace. She'd taken it a little too far, yeah, so, what else was new?

And where was Sebastian already? She needed ouzo, a whole bottle of it, and how long had he been gone, a half hour already?

The doorbell rang. Finally! What would his excuse be, that he'd soiled his knickers along the way and what a bloody inconvenience it was?

This was the last time she was dating a Brit.

But when she opened the door she saw a woman—dark with almost a full mustache and a unibrow.

"Where is my Georgios?" the woman demanded.

Angela was tempted to say, Atlantis, but went with, "Haven't seen him in a few days." She was very calm, but no surprise there. She was used to this, her experiences in New York and Dublin, lying to the cops, were coming in handy.

The woman's eyes were trying to look past Angela, into the house. Jesus, why had she gone and opened the door without checking first? It was that fecking Sebastian, screwing with her brain.

But one slip-up—shit, she was still holding the rag, the rag with Georgios' blood. She managed to hide it behind her back and didn't think the woman had noticed.

The woman said, "If you're fucking my husband, I kill you."

Husband? It surprised Angela, but only for a second. These Greeks, they always had wives.

Angela checked to make sure the woman wasn't holding a meat cleaver, then said, "I beg your pardon. I mean, I never..."

Sounding seriously miffed.

"Yesterday, he tell me he go here to fix sink," the woman said, "then he don't come home. I know he like you, blondie. Every day he talk about the sexy girl from Ireland."

Squeezing the rag tightly behind her back, Angela said, "First of all, I have a boyfriend, Sebastian, he looks exactly like Lee Child."

The woman was lost.

Angela added, "Secondly, I have no idea where your husband is, but if you want some advice, you should seriously think about divorcing that guy. I've heard stories about him."

She let it hang there.

The woman glared, said, "Stories? What stories?"

Angela exhaled, as if it were killing her to have to say this, then said, "At the taverna. They're saying your husband's with a new woman every night. He cruises the clubs for American girls or some shite. I was appalled, if you want to know the truth. I don't want to put any ideas in your head, but maybe your husband only *told* you he was coming to fix my sink. Maybe he was really out picking up a girl at a club. You ever think about that?"

The woman was thinking about it now.

Angela continued, "I don't know if you Greeks do divorce, but you should seriously think about ditching that guy. You're a beautiful woman, you can do so much better."

Actually the woman was as fugly as they come, but the compliment seemed to have an effect, at least momentarily. She stood a little straighter, her chin up, said proudly, "Do you really think so?"

"I know so," Angela said, suddenly sounding like a life coach. "Get your hair done, sweetie, buy some new clothes, get a makeover, and start doing things for *you*. You've been doing things for *him* for way too long."

Good thing Angela had watched so much *Oprah* over the years. Finally that shite was coming in handy.

But either the woman wasn't an *Oprah* fan or she suddenly remembered what she'd come here for, because her dark eyes narrowed again and she said, "If you see Georgios, tell him when he comes home his wife is going to kill him."

Tempted to say, Mission accomplished, Angela went with, "I'll do that."

The woman left and the door slammed shut.

Whew, that was close. Angela watched through the window, making sure the woman was gone, then got back to work, scrubbing the floor. Where the hell was Sebastian, that fuck-up? The useless fool been gone at least an hour. The stores were less than five minutes away by moped, was it possible he had gotten lost?

When another hour went by and there was still no sign of him it set in that the stuffy Brit had ditched her. It wasn't exactly unexpected; she knew the wimp wouldn't be able to stand up to the heat, which was why she'd cleaned him out. The spineless bastard! She hoped he drove off a cliff, was feeding the fish like Georgios.

She got the room as clean as it was going to get. She didn't see any blood and even if she'd left some she figured they probably didn't know their DNA from their drachmas on this backward fucking island. She packed her suitcase and hit the road.

Walking to the village, she passed the old woman, and of course got the evil eye. Jeez, the woman was creepy, like some kind of witch. It occurred to Angela that she should have waited until night and left when she couldn't be seen. So, okay, she'd panicked, made one slip-up, what did you expect? She hadn't had a drink in, what, twelve hours? How was a girl supposed to think straight without a little ouzo flowing through her system?

She took a cab to the port on the other, flatter side of the island. She didn't want to have to ride the fecking donkeys down to the docks, but she also wanted to get as far away from the villa and Giorgios' wife as possible. See, her thinking wasn't entirely clouded.

During the ride, the cab driver—he was bald, overweight, with a thick mustache; reminded her of the uncle who'd once molested her—was staring at her in the rearview, literally licking his lips. What was it with these men? At a deserted area where there were lots of dunes and nothing else he pulled over, leaned back, and seemed to be unbuckling his belt.

Angela went Irish, said, "Drive this car right now, or you'll get what yeh deserve, yah fookin' bastard."

The guy had probably never met a woman like Angela before. He recognized that this was the voice of a woman who did not fuck around and with a look of sheer terror he buckled his belt and put the car back in drive.

Then he got a call on his cell, and started looking at Angela in the rearview again. Later, she'd realize that this was another mistake, that she should've gotten out of that car and run like hell.

At the port, Angela found out there was a ferry to Lesbos leaving in a few minutes. She chuckled, thinking, after her recent experiences with men, maybe Lesbos wasn't such a bad idea.

At dusk, the ferry arrived at the Lesbos port and she beelined for the closest taverna, right across from the docks. Finally, ouzo. Jaysus wept, she downed two shots, asked for a third. When the bartender gave her the drink she noticed the two cops. They were standing near the door, looking right at her. She was going to make a run for it, but knew it was pointless.

She chugged the last shot, figuring, Might as well go out with a bang.

Six

*He turned on the TV but he lay on his bed with his
back to it because it was a liar. It held up pictures
and said you could be like them but it didn't
tell you how easily everything fell to pieces.*
MATTHEW STOKOE, *Cows*

Sino wasn't buying Max Fisher's bullshit, everybody sayin' he'd cut off a man's dick. Sino knew the only thing that white *puta* businessman ever cut into was his goddamn steak at Smith & Wollensky. Lying *maricon*.

Yeah, Sino knew lots of *bandajo*s like Max Fisher. He grew up in the South Bronx, by Yankee Stadium. Shit, this was eighties and early nineties, bro, the glory days when crack was king and the Bronx wasn't burning, the shit was already burned. You were growing up in the Bronx then, you needed some money to get high, the Stadium was the place to go. Scalping tickets, man, Sino didn't waste his time with that *mierda*. Serious pesos was in protection. All those suit-and-tie bitches would come up to the games in the summer, be in their Mercedes and BMWs and shit, parking in the cheap lots, like five blocks away from the stadium. Now come on, man, what's up with that *loco* shit? Man has millions of dollars, lives in some damn mansion somewhere, down on Fifth Avenue, and he can't even pay for stadium parking? *Puta* deserve to get his pesos taken.

Sino and his boy would be hanging out in the lots, going up to the cheap motherfuckers saying, "Want me to watch your car for you during the game? Cost fifty dollars."

Yeah, see what the stingy *bandajo*'s gonna do then. They

wanna go to Stadium parking and pay twenty dollars and miss part the game or they wanna pay Sino to not get their car fucked up? Most gringos paid the man, no *problema*, *jefe*, but sometimes a man got cheap, wouldn't pay, or said they were gonna call a cop. Wrong answer, my man. Yeah, if motherfuckers got cheap, they didn't wanna pay, they were gonna pay anyway. Sino and his boy would fuck up the windshield, pop the tires, shit like that. But if they said they was gonna call a cop, shit, that was when the real fun started. Then they got to fuck the guy up, break some bones, see some blood.

This one time, a rich *maricon* from Manhattan, kinda looked like Max Fisher, said he wouldn't pay the money. The *puta* just walked away, laughing, the *maricon* was fuckin' laughing, disrespecting Sino's whole crew and shit. So Sino and his boy took their bats and played some ball, Bronx style. They fucked up that car so bad the junkyard wouldn't even take it.

Later that night, Sino and his boys were doing some reefer, chilling, corner 153rd and Gerard. Somehow the *maricon* found him out there, was probably going around the neighborhood, looking. He went up to Sino and said, "You're paying to get my car fixed, motherfucker."

Motherfucker. Saying that shit through his nose, sounding like the rich Park Avenue motherfucker he was. And the way he was standing, with his hands on his hips, like he was trying to be badass, calling him out and shit in front of his crew. The stupid *maricon* was in Sino's face, like didn't he know who he was messing with.

Sino's boys, man, they started laughing, tears coming out their eyes. Sino knew they were laughing at the *maricon*, not him, but he didn't like it. Then his boy Paco said, still laughing, "Man, you gonna take that shit?"

Sino wasn't.

First he shot Paco in the head, send a message to the rest of his crew, you laugh at Sino, you gonna get popped. Didn't matter that he and Paco knew each other eighteen years, their *madres* came over from Panama together. Had to set the shit straight with somebody and Sino was sending the message, *I pop my best friend, I can pop all you, so,* chingate, *you better watch your laughin' asses.*

Shooting Paco shut up the rest his crew real quick. Then the *bandajo* that started it all, the white guy, turned, tried to run. Sino put four in the *maricon*'s back. He had one shot left, went up to the guy. He was still on the ground, trying to move, but he couldn't. He was still alive though. He was making noises in his throat and blood was coming out of his mouth. Now *that* shit was funny.

Sino laughed, said to the *maricon*, "Say you sorry, *papi*. Say you sorry and I won't pop you no more."

The *maricon* was trying to talk, making sounds like, "S…sah…sah…sar…sar…sah."

"Can't hear you," Sino said and popped him in the head and walked away.

Yeah, Sino, wished he was on the street right now, had a nine on him. He'd put six in Fisher's back real quick. Listen to him beg and shit first, then put one in his head. Or, nah, would be more fun to kill Fisher with his *manos*, squeeze that little-ass neck till he die. He wouldn't mind fucking Fisher too. *Maricon* got a big flabby ass, just the kind Sino liked. Maybe he'd fuck him first then kill him, or kill him then fuck him. Depends what kinda mood he was in.

Max was settling in all right. Already he had *the rep*, a priceless commodity, and he had fresh-pressed denims every day and it looked like the library gig was as good as his. And they'd be stupid not to give it to him—come on, who knew more about books than The M.A.X.? He'd taken a little spin around the library the other day, told one of the guys working there he was "unimpressed" with the selection. Lots of Grisham and Danielle Steele, but where was the beef? No Eddie Bunker, no Genet, shit, not even any Tim fucking Willocks. The fuck? They did have the book about the caged bird by that Maya Angelou broad. Max liked the author photo in the back of that one. Maya was a hot-looking older chick all right, but the picture was a head shot, and Max wondered what her body looked like, if she was in shape. He figured an African chick, her hair in braids, wearing some big baggy blousy African thing, she must have a big set in there somewhere.

Max was also learning the pecking order, the *food chain* of life in the joint. Like there was a sissy on Tier 2 who washed and ironed Max's demins every damn day, and Max, learning fast, treated him like shit. You're in the game, you gotta play it, right? He had his sleeves rolled up and a pack of Marlboro Red tucked in there, like Jimmy Dean. Yeah, he even had the white T inside his shirt, shining in its whiteness, that sissy sure could starch.

He managed to pick up the yard swagger, the one that strolled slowly, aggression leaking from every pore. Yep, he was living it up, living in the moment like a true Buddhist monk. Just being in the prison, day in and day out, seeing the respect, no, *fear,* in all these fuckers' faces gave him a bigger rush than smoking crack ever had. If anybody even looked at The M.A.X. the wrong way, Max would get into the guy's face, go, "You got a fuckin' problem, motherfucker?" Glaring like Denzel in *Training Day*.

Yeah, no doubt about it, The M.A.X. was The King of fucking Attica. His favorite thing was just to walk around and soak up all the respect and admiration he was getting from everybody. Sometimes Max would have some extra fun with it, suddenly rushing up to some fuck's crotch and making a snip-snip motion with his fingers. Man, the assholes looked like they were gonna shit their pants and Max would start laughing his ass off.

In the yard, when The M.A.X. came by people stopped whatever they were doing and they'd say, "Yo, Max," and "What up, Max, man?" It seemed like the whole prison was in awe of him. Well, except for one little hitch.

The population had to be eighty percent black, but there were pockets of other ethnic groups. There were the Crips, Sino's crew of, what're you supposed to call them this week, Latinos, Hispanics, Latin Americans? What the fuck ever. There were also some white people, mostly sissies, but also The Aryan Brotherhood, led by a massive cracker with a whole crew of mutants straight out of *The Hills Have Eyes*, their mouths drooling and always giggling and cussing among themselves.

Jeez, was that English?

He knew these guys didn't give a shit if he once cut off a man's dick or not. These freaks probably chopped off dicks on a regular basis.

The cracker's name was Arma—short for Armageddon. What was up with these deranged assholes shortening their names? Max wondered if she should shorten his name, start calling himself "The Ma." Maybe that would get him even more respect. Nah, it would probably have the opposite effect. Didn't Freud say all guys wanted to fuck their mothers?

If anything he should start calling himself The Ax. Had a menacing vibe to it.

Nah, had to be The M.A.X.

Arma fronted Max in the yard, his Aryan brothers all around him, went, "You-all's the dick cutter, right?"

Max didn't feel the time was right to say, Grammatically speaking, there is only one of me. The guy didn't exactly look like he had a sense of humor.

He nodded, his throat choked from fear. This guy had the dead-eyed stare of a fucking serial killer.

The guy said, "Y'all shacked up with the big dumb nigger, what's with that boy?"

And Max, to his amazement, lied. "I'm working on the inside, we gonna bring them apes into line, we gotta know what they're planning, you cool with that?"

The guy stared at him and it was up for grabs. He'd either gut Max right there or…

He laughed, exposing a whole row of yellowed teeth and many, many gaps. All that moonshine, no doubt. All around him, the brothers laughed along.

Arma slapped Max on the shoulder, said, "You-all's one bright fellah. You was one of them high flyers, m'I right?'

Max, so relieved he nearly wet himself, said, "I made my moola off the niggers. We gonna go up against Zog, we need serious bucks."

Zog? He had no idea really what this meant but on the Discovery Channel he'd heard a Klansman say it.

But, shit, it fuckin' worked.

And then Max on a roll, tried, "The crips, they're gonna move against you, soon."

The riot that was to come down the pike got its seeds right there with Max spouting off crap he'd no idea about.

The cracker frowned, asked, "Them Mex gangs, Sino and 'em, they got weapons?"

Max nodded, as if he couldn't take the risk on verbalizing the lethal threat.

The cracker handed him a leather band, said, "You wear

that, you're part of my crew, ain't no one gonna fuck with you."

Max, learning, improvising all the time, took the pack of Reds, handed them over, said, "On me, bro."

Smokes were the currency of the yard. A pack could get you a sissy for a night, a carton would get you anyone wasted.

Arma and his Nazis moved off, the cracker saying, Them Crips come gunning, you're gonna be my right hand guy.

Max thought, Like fuck, but just wanted to get away.

He said, "You can count on me, bro."

Later, at lunch, Sino sat down next to Max, smiled, went, "Man, I gotta give you props, yo. Cuttin' off a man's dick? That shit's cold. Even Sino never done shit like that."

Max glared at him, the look he'd been practicing, the one that said, *I'm a cold detached psycho motherfucker, a fuckin Aryan, and y'all better not fuck with me*. Then he gave him a sudden smile, throwing him a bone, and said, "Yeah, what can I tell you? I was havin' a bad day."

Sino smiled, said, "Yeah, tell me all about it, cuz. Like how'd you do it? You use a blade, scissors, hedge clipper, what?"

Max, unprepared for the questioning, said, "Saw."

"Saw? Fuck, man, how'd you work that shit out? You say to the *puta*, put your dick out on the table, I wanna saw it off, and the *bandajo* go, 'Yeah, all right, cut my dick off,' and took down his *pantalones*?"

"Yeah," Max said. "Something like that."

"Oh, it was somethin' like that, huh?" He was still smiling. "So now you don't know for sure? Yeah, guess that makes sense. Scary motherfucker like you, goin' 'round, cuttin' dicks off with saws all the time, you might start to forget some shit, right?"

Max was thinking, *Don't give in. He's just toying with you. Truth is he's scared shitless and he's trying not to show it.*

Glaring hard, Max said, "I cut off his dick with a saw because I didn't like the way he was looking at me, and I don't like the way you're looking at me right now, *hombre*."

That was the way—throw the Spanish shit right back at him. Man, he felt like John Wayne, Eastwood, The Rock—somebody badass.

Sino laughed, still trying not to show his weakness, said, "Yeah, you're a scary motherfucker all right, Fisher. Just sittin' here next to you, I'm starting to piss up my pants and shit." Then he touched the leather band on Max's wrist and said, "I see you make some friends today. So now you're what, a motherfuckin' Nazi?"

If cigarettes were the currency of prison, then desserts were the icing on the cake. Max had heard about guys being shanked for a rice pudding. You wanted a favor, you slid your dessert across the table to the guy you wanted the favor from. Today's delicacy was some kind of treacle pie, and Sino's and Max's were lined up in front of them. It was a sign of real juice to just let it sit there, as if just any old con could stroll up and grab it. Yeah, dream on.

Like two fortresses waiting to be attacked, a type of lethal jailhouse chess, Max and Sino stared at each other. Who'd move first? Sino, who didn't exactly seem like the patient type, made a move for one and Max, said, "You don't want to do that, *hombre*."

He was as amazed as Sino was. Did he just, like, call Sino out?

Sino, his spoon almost ready to dip, hesitated. Bad move. You start a move in the joint, you have to make the play, no turning back. Sino cursed, then went, "Don't call me *hombre*. You ain't my *hombre*. *Entiendes*?"

Max, exhilarated at his sheer *cojones*, said, "I'm thinking I might bring that pie to my main guy, Rufus."

And with that, he stood up, took both pies, *winked* at Sino, said, "Y'all keep it in your pants now, hear, pilgrim."

Sino was too stunned to move. Meanwhile, Max went on his way, clueless that he'd just fanned the flames of an inferno that would rage with biblical ferocity.

Max placed the pies on Rufus's bunk and the huge black man, who'd never seen two desserts in one place, was seriously impressed, asked, "How the fuck you get two?"

Max, adopting his lotus position, grabbing some of that inner peace, said, "Took 'em off that little punk, Sino."

Rufus, adopting the lotus position now, though his bulk made it somewhat difficult, wonderingly asked, "We talkin' the same Sino? Leader of the Crips?"

Max, closing his eyes, said, in total indifference, "That who he is? I bitch slapped him for giving me mouth."

Max had already scared Rufus shitless with the dick-cutting rumor, but now Rufus stared at Max like he was looking at a mini-Manson, obvious admiration leaking from every inch of his massive frame.

Yeah, he was a believer.

Seven

Lord Byron once said of Polidori that he was the sort of man to whom, if he fell overboard, one would offer a straw, to see if the adage was true that drowning men clutch at straws.
PERCY BYSSHE SHELLEY,
IN A LETTER TO HIS PUBLISHER, JOHN MURRAY (1819)

Sebastian was at Athens airport. He'd been in a bit of a panic until he arrived in Athens, all his rat instincts shouting, Get to the bloody airport.

Finally did and, oh lordy, British Airways, God bless them, took his dodgy Platinum card without a murmur.

The woman at the counter asked, "Business class?"

He gave his best old-school smile, asked, "Is there any other way to fly?"

They had a good Brit chuckle about this.

He was whistling *Rule, Britannia* as he headed for the First Class Lounge, throwing a look of contempt to the, well, sorry, but let's call them what they were, peasants, as they scuttled along for their economy seats.

He sat in the plush armchair, thought, *C'est la vie*.

This was the extent of his French and he tended to ration it. Though, come to think of it, perhaps Paris might be worth a gander. They still loved the Brits, though it was a shame the buggers had banned British beef, as if there was a better meat in the whole world.

He ordered a Campari and soda, didn't say please. A true gent never said please to the help. He was just about to have a large sip when a very attractive blond girl in her twenties approached, asked, "I'm so sorry to bother you, Mr. Child?"

Child? The bloody hell was this? Then he spotted the paperback book in her hand. A thriller of some sort, written by that Lee Child fellow whom Sebastian had been mistaken for on several occasions. He was about to tell the woman to bugger off when she held out the book and said, "I'd be so honored to have your autograph, Mr. Child."

He gave her his most radiant smile, said, "Call me Lee. And the honor is mine, I assure you."

She handed over the book and a pen. It was a Mont Blanc and he thought, *Money*. Then he thought, *Mile-High Club*.

Seeing as how the blushing woman was obviously convinced he was this writer fellow and just as obviously idolized him, he didn't think a little joint trip to the loo would be hard to pull off at all. He scribbled an illegible scrawl on the book's title page like a real pro, and added a little heart. Touch of class. You couldn't teach that, either it came naturally or it didn't come at all.

He handed her back the book, holding the pen as if he'd forgotten it, asked, "Dare I be so bold as to offer you a refreshment?"

She blushed an even deeper shade of crimson and he thought, *Gotcha*.

She was so flustered, flattered, she never even saw him slip the pen into his jacket. He had one tricky moment after she'd had her second vodka tonic when she asked, "What's next for Reacher?" But he rallied, gave the enigmatic smile that had lured more quail than he could count into the sack, and said, "Now my dear, that would be telling."

They had champagne cocktails after takeoff and he looked out at the cloud of pollution over Athens and thought about the American psycho bitch back on the island. She was probably still wondering where her cigs were.

He had to stifle a laugh, turned to the girl, asked, "What say you, my sweet, to another champers before dinner?"

Her glassy eyes as she nodded yes told him he was about to join the Club.

Later, after he'd rogered her, they crept back to their seats and he got a knowing look from the stewardess. Or was she giving him the *come on*? Sorry, gell, but he was shagged out. A chap had only so much to go round.

The girl snuggled up in her seat and was out in minutes. He waited till they dimmed the lights then went through her handbag. Ah, let's have a look, shall we? Lots of crisp 50 sterling notes and a batch of credit cards. He took only two, a chap wasn't greedy. He ordered a brandy, and some snacks, sat back to watch the movie, something starring Will Ferrell. This chap was in every movie, it seemed.

He started to nod off and had the familiar dream, the one about the student he'd killed. Sweat was rolling down his face as he relived the awful events.

Richard had been one of those upper-class pillow biters, the real deal, descended from one of the families related to the Royals. Well, who wasn't? But he was about 1,000 in line to the throne, meaning only 999 buggers had to croak before Richard got a shot at it.

And, lordy, the chap was loaded, had buckets of dosh. And generous with it, too, spent it like it was water. Sebastian hated him, damn scoundrel had it all. But Richard fell in love with Sebastian, who encouraged him in the belief that buggery was definitely in the cards. Meanwhile, pay the freight you bloody homo.

Richard, like all blue bloods, had access to the best drugs, clubs, people; all of which was damn hunky fucking dory with Sebby. Yeah, what Richard called him. He'd pick out a suit from his closet, a beautiful Jermyn Street made-to-measure beauty and say, "I'm tired of this, Sebby, you have it," and throw it across the room to him.

Time came to pay the freight, Sebastian was almost ready to let it happen. It was a Brit tradition, how else could you explain the whole Public School system?

They'd been partying hard, lots of the old champers, a little nose candy to chill out. They ended up back in Richard's lovely flat.

First false note, Richard had ordered, not asked, "Pour me a Gordon's."

It was the imperious tone that irritated Sebastian to no end.

Sebastian, a little the worse for wear, snapped, "What am I? Your servant?"

And Richard, in that totally dismissive accent, said, "You're the help, darling, a leech. So once you get the drinkie-poos, hop over here, Sebby, and service my Lancelot."

He had a name for his dick? Well, all right, who didn't. But he also had a name for Sebastian, and it was the more demeaning of the two.

Sebastian lost it, strangled the upper class twit with his Eton tie, screaming,

"Don't you dare call me Sebby!"

And then horrified, strung him up from the light fixture, took all the available cash and yes, a few suits and ties, and prayed to everything unholy that he'd get away, that he'd, dare one say, *swing it*.

The family hushed it all up. Sebastian even read the eulogy at the very private mass, quoted a passage from Wilfred Owen.

Later, when he saw the movie *The Talented Mr. Ripley*, he so identified with Matt Damon, he almost shouted: *I'm with you, old chap!*

Eight

*Cuccia was angry that he would have to renegotiate
the price of a hit gone wrong, he would be dealing
from a very weak hand.*
CHARLIE STELLA, *Charlie Opera*

After that shit in the mess hall, with the *bandajo* Max Fisher takin' all his pies, and his whole crew sittin' there, watching like, You gonna take that shit? Sino knew he had to make a move. Shit, not only was he dissed, but he got *called* by that white pudgy middle-aged white motherfucker.

His face burned, man, rage. He swore on his *abuela*'s life, he'd gut this white trash from his balding head to his tiny dick. He knew he'd have to act and fast, to be crewless was to be chowder. Yeah, he'd love to do Fisher himself, but that wasn't the way it was done. When you were the main man in charge of a whole crew, you told people to do shit, you never did it yourself. White people had a name for that shit. Out saucering? Yeah, he was gonna out saucer this shit.

In the yard, he spotted a new fish, kid named Carlito. *Puta*'s first day, looked like somebody'd already cut him a new asshole. The *bandajo*'d been caught driving a stolen car, first time. Man was Mex and got the max, five and change.

Yeah, was time to make the man earn his way in.

Carlito stood with his back to the wall. He'd been told about the train and couldn't get Tom Hanks in that goddamn movie, going *All aboard the train*, out of his mind. He'd been told his only hope was to join a gang in, like, Speedy Gonzales time. But how the fuck did you join? He'd seen the Crips, and the other gangs, all giving him the dead eye, not like he could wander up, go, "What's shakin', dudes? And, oh, I wanna join the gang."

Then he saw a dangerous-looking one heading his way. The guy was smiling, like a Great White, put out his hand, said, "*Muchacho*, how's it hanging, boss?"

As Carlito took it and felt the man squeeze real tight, Carlito tried to figure out where it had all gone down the shitter. He'd had a nice lady, girl named Maria, and she'd been making marriage sounds. She was such a sweet *senorita*, they grew up together in Guadalajara. He was making seven bucks an hour from his job in the garage. Yeah, the garage—he knew cars, and that was how the shit hit the fan.

Maria had gone to see her Mama and Carlito had decided to let off a little steam. He'd been pulling twelve-hour shifts, getting the down payment ready on a little apartment, and Dios Mio, he was wound up awful tight, so he got together with a few *amigos*, they were downing some Dos Equis, nice and cold and going down so easy, till one of the *hombres* ordered up shots of Tequila. Carlito was basically a beer and chips kinda guy, but he didn't want to look bad, like some *maricon*, so he had the shot and then, Madre Mio, a whole lot more and he didn't know, they were falling out of the bar, laughing and high fiving, when one of the *hombres* spotted the Firebird, red and with the keys in the ignition. The owner gone to the ATM. Next thing, Carlito was driving the baby, like he owned the highway. State Trooper chased him for half an hour before the bird ran outa gas and Carlito ran shit out of luck.

He'd paid all of their savings to a slimy lawyer who promised, "Probation, no problem, first offense, *no problema*."

He got five years and change. *No problema?*

The lawyer shrugged, said, "You got any more of that there green, I'll lodge an appeal."

Maria had taken off with the few remaining dollars and Carlito got to ride the bus.

Scared, chained, out of it. A guy sitting beside him asked, "First time, *chiquito*?"

He nodded in total misery.

The guy, covered in prison tats, said, "You're a real pretty boy, they gonna ream you good, *compadre*."

The guy was staring at Carlito's solid gold Miraculous Medal. Carlito, with difficulty, using his manacled hands, tried to button the prison-issue shirt and the guy laughed, a laugh born of pure nastiness and worse, deep malevolent knowing, said, "First day in the joint, it's like, every worst nightmare you ever had and bro, it's worse, 'cause it's true and it ain't gonna git no better, so you do what you can, you get wasted, you hear me, fish, you gotta get some serious dope going in your system—then it don't, like, hurt. Me, I got my main running buddy up there, he'll hook me up right after orientation, and you wanna, you want some of that good stuff, help you *get focused*, you come see me, I fix you right up but it costs, you know what I'm sayin'?"

He shut up for a bit then said, "Speed. The ol' reliable, amphetamines, they set you right up and Bennies, ain't nuttin on God's good earth like those beauties."

He laughed, obviously feeling the effect of some of the above, began to sing, "Benny and the Jets." Was it horrible, man, or what? Even worse than having to hear Elt himself do it.

The guy added, "That there medal, always wanted me one of those babes. You want some *recreational drugs*? That there is the freight, *muchacho*."

Carlito snapped himself out of his reverie, tried to pay attention to the guy holding onto his hand. Leader of the Crips. His mouth went dry and he smiled like some wetback fresh from the border.

Sino swept his arm round the yard, said, "Who you with?"

Then in a mocking tone, continued. "I tell you, fish, you with nobody. You got, like, *de nada*, you hear me, fish?"

Carlito did.

Sino said, "See those *hombres* over there? Yeah, the ones lookin' at you, like you a big juicy *empanada*. They gonna run a line through yo skinny ass, you don't be with somebody."

Carlito was already crying, bawling like a damn baby.

Sino moved in close, said, "Yo, you join my crew, you be safe, know what I'm talkin' about?"

Carlito nodded. He'd have joined the army at this stage. Anything. Sino palmed him a toothbrush, handmade blade embedded on the top, said, "Yo, you wanna make some bones, you show yo' got *cojones*. Know what I talkin' about, *jefe*?"

Carlito wanted to run, but where?

Sino looked at his watch, a shiny TAG Heuer knockoff, said, "Twelve noon, fat middle-aged white dude, takes his shower on C…you go rip him a new one, *comprende*?"

Sino sauntered off and Carlito began a whole new set of tremors.

At twelve noon Carlito headed to the showers. He'd managed to score some bennies from the guy he'd rode the bus up with. Cost him his gold Miraculous Medal he'd always worn. In a haze of drug-induced adrenaline and outright fear, he saw the fat white dude and launched himself. The phrase *It got away from him* might be appropriate here. He was still slashing and chopping when the guards clubbed him senseless. One of them, who'd seen most all a prison could offer, muttered, "Holy Mother of Christ."

And too bad for Sino, what remained of the fat dude on the shower floor was the armaments guy for the Aryan Brotherhood.

Carlito heard another guard say, "*Hombre*, you just fucked yourself good," and everything faded out.

Nine

A caged woman is a beast of ferocious instinct.
SEÑOR RODRIGUEZ

When they brought Angela to the prison in Lesbos her first thought was, Jaysus, this place lives up to its name. She was brought to a holding cell with eight other women. Each was hotter than the last and most of them were in micro-minis, skimpy tube tops, a couple even in bikinis. Most were talking in Greek, and a couple of blondes were talking in some other language, maybe Swedish.

Angela went up to one of the blondes and asked for a smoke. Jaysus, with the day she'd had, she could've used a whole carton.

The woman's friend, the other Swede, slid one out of a pack.

Angela took it, held it out for a light, said, "I'm Angela."

"Inga," the woman with the cigarettes said. "This is Katina."

Angela asked, "So is this a prison or a nightclub?"

Thought she was making a joke, but Katina said, "Both."

"There was a raid at Niko's last night," Inga explained. "Heroin or something."

"But we have nothing to do with it," Katina said.

She sounded a little too defensive. Angela glanced down, noticed the track marks on her skinny arms.

"Yes, we were just there, you know, partying, when the police come," Inga said. "How do you say, the wrong places at the wrong times?"

Thinking, *The story of me life*, Angela asked, "So what did they charge you with?"

"We do not know what's going on," Inga said. "They told us nothing. They just bring us here, that's it."

"We are, how do you say," Katina said, "in the dark."

"What about you?" Inga asked. "What did you do?"

"Oh, nothing," Angela said. "I was just having a drink, minding my own business, and next thing I knew two cops were taking me away."

"It's crazy in Greece," Katina said. "They arrest everybody, no?"

The prison wasn't like any prison Angela had ever heard of. The officers who'd arrested Angela hadn't notified her of any charges, or at least she didn't think they had. During the ride over they were talking in Greek and the only parts Angela picked up were when they were commenting on her *oreo megala vizia*—big, beautiful tits—no surprise there. But, of course, Angela knew why she was being taken away. The cab driver on Santorini must've told the authorities that she'd boarded a boat for Lesbos and then the Lesbos police—Lesbian police? Jaysus, it sounded like something out of Greenwich Village, but that was probably what they called themselves—had been notified. They were probably just waiting now to coordinate with the Santorini cops. She didn't know if they'd found some evidence that could hang her or if she was just a suspect by default. Not that it mattered. She'd heard enough stories over the years from her father about the Greek justice system. It was your classic, old-world, eye-for-an-eye, guilty-until-proven-innocent mentality. She figured she'd never be formally charged with anything. She'd be handed over to Georgios' relatives and quietly killed, case closed.

Fookin' Sebastian. If he hadn't run off like the coward he was, she never would've had to take that cab to the other end of Santorini. They would've ridden together on the moped and she wouldn't be in this shithole right now. They hadn't even let her make a phone call. Not that there was anyone to call. A lawyer would be useless and her family was even more so. Her mother's side was all ex-IRA and her father's side was as backward as Georgios' family.

"Do any of the guards here speak English?" Angela asked.

"There was a young guy here last night," Inga said, "maybe nineteen years old. He was hitting on all the women."

"He told one girl, if she give him blowjob she can get out," Katina said as she casually reached out and held Inga's hand. "He is like a teenage boy, his eyes jumping out of his head with so many beautiful women. He even offered to pay, fifty euro, keeps showing it, pulls money out of this belt tied round his waist. Keeps zipping and unzipping the belt, saying 'Want what's in here?' Pig."

Angela thought, *Bingo*.

Angela asked Katina, "When does his shift start?"

The girl shrugged, said, "Night."

Angela looked around the cell, which was getting hotter and less comfortable as the sun rose. She said, "How do you pass the time in here?" and then got strange looks from the girls and thought, Uh-oh.

Sure enough, by the time the scorching midday heat hit top level, the sun blasting through the bars, the other women, who hadn't been wearing all that much to begin with, began unbuttoning their shirts, rolling up their sleeves, pulling off sweat-stained clothes. Angela watched one woman roll her tube top down to her waist and lie down on one of the cell's two metal bunks. It was like a signal to the others—in minutes, all eight women had stripped down. The two girls who'd been in bikinis tossed their tops in a corner of the cell and sat down side by side in a patch of sunlight, one with her arm around the other's waist. A very large Russian woman took off her blouse, revealing a skimpy bra through which Angela could make out a tattoo in the shape of an eagle across the woman's breasts. Jaysus, this fookin' Lesbos more than lived up to its name. Too bad Angela was straight or she wouldn't've been in such a hurry to get out of this place.

Inga lit another cigarette, inhaled deeply, then passed it to Katina. The Russian woman came over, started stroking Katina's arm, kissing her neck. She looked at Angela, and purred, "You like?"

Angela shrugged, moved to the water bucket, thinking, Whatever turns you on, lady. As Angela used a dirty towel to wipe off her face, she could see the women pairing off on the floor, the bunks, standing against the wall.

She found an empty corner and sat down, closed her eyes, but it didn't stop her hearing the sounds around her. She bit down on her lower lip and focused on two things: the young guard and, especially, the money belt.

At midnight, the kid arrived and, Jaysus, the Swedes were right, he seemed like a child let loose in a candy shop. He had an overall deranged look about him, as if someone had hit him in the head with a baseball bat and he was wandering around, permanently dazed. But when it came to men sometimes Angela wasn't exactly picky. Hell, she'd been engaged to Max Fisher, hadn't she?

The important thing was that the kid was the only guard on duty at night and sure enough, he was wearing the money belt.

Angela knew she had to work fast. She was surprised no one from Georgios' family had shown up yet, but it was only a matter of time. She figured she had till morning, tops.

When the kid came by all the women spoke at once, complaining, demanding to be released. But Angela caught his attention, pursing her lips and batting her eyelashes, doing her best

Marilyn Monroe come-hither look. Okay, so maybe she was overdoing it, but it worked, didn't it?

The kid came right over and Angela whispered, "So what does a girl have to do to get out of this place?"

The kid smiled. Jaysus, panted, "Come with me." He opened and closed the cell door with a giant skeleton key.

They went into what you'd call the office. There was a desk, a chair, and not much else. The walls were corroded and a fan was spinning haltingly overhead.

"Get naked," the kid said.

Usually it was a turn-on for Angela when the guy ordered her around, but not this time.

"I thought you'd want a little…" she looked at his crotch "…lip service."

"You kill somebody," the kid said. "If you steal, blowjob, okay, but you kill, you have to fuck."

Angela had a feeling arguing this logic would be pointless. Besides, it wasn't like she had a lot of bargaining power.

They went at it—or rather he went at it—for what seemed like three or four hours. He wasn't the worst she'd ever had, but that was only thanks to Max Fisher. The kid was lost in his own world; she could've died and he wouldn't have noticed. At one point she had a flashback to Georgios and she had the temptation to reach up, grab the kid's head, and snap his neck. Thank God she resisted. She was in enough trouble, and killing a fookin' prison guard wouldn't exactly improve her situation.

Finally it ended, and the kid, like every goddamn man Angela had ever known, fell asleep. She took his money belt, got his keys and then on impulse, picked up one of his heavy boots from where he'd tossed it before climbing on top of her, walloped him upside the head with it, said, "We call that cold cocked."

She had to move fast. Did she think of releasing the other women? Did she fuck. It was every bitch for their own selves.

She was exhausted, and as she headed toward the docks she thought about how she'd gotten here, to this low point in her life. A few years ago, things had been going so well for her. It seemed like just yesterday she was living in New York, working as an executive assistant, dating guys, living in a studio apartment in Gramercy Park. Yeah, she'd made a few bad decisions —a few spectacularly bad decisions—but did she really deserve *this*?

She boarded a ferry to Naples. As the boat pulled away, she yelled, "Greece, you can kiss my Irish arse goodbye!"

She remained in the back of the ferry staring half-dazed, watching until the lighthouse at the tip of Lesbos faded to nothing. Good fookin' riddance.

She counted the money from the kid's belt, was surprised to find nearly two thousand euro. It'd be enough for a new outfit and a plane ticket, so sayonara you bastards, she was getting the first flight out of this shitehole and back to the States.

Of course then she'd be nearly broke again. But she knew that Max, the little bollix, he'd have money stashed and if she was in that place of total desperation she could do whatever it took to get hold of it. Then, just maybe she could use the stake she got to set up something to sustain her till she could come up with a longer-term plan.

Right there and then, she'd have killed for some lip gloss and perfume. She could still smell the guard. She was tempted to jump into the sea and wash herself clean.

Say what you want about Greek ferries, they have one great feature—a bar.

She headed down there, ignored various suggestions from the motley crew and ordered a large Metaxa. The barman leered at her and she gave him a look that no doubt withered his coming hard-on.

He muttered, *"Mallakismeni."*

Yeah, like she gave a shit.

Over in a corner, she saw a girl in her very early twenties, sobbing quietly. She looked pale—maybe English, maybe a fucking albino—and broken.

Angela thought, *Welcome to my world, honey.* Had one motherfooker, like, ever helped her out? Was there one cocksucker on the whole planet who hadn't fooked her over in some way? Nope, not one lousy decent human on the planet. She thought, You paddle your own frigging canoe, no time like the present to learn that life sucks and if you were a single woman, guess who gets to do the sucking?

Still, there was a good heart in Angela once upon a time and it still flickered—dimly, but there.

She approached, asked, "Join you, girl?"

The girl looked up, looking relieved to see not only a woman, but an American. She began to weep profusely, said, "Oh, please do."

The British accent reminded her of Sebastian, but Angela was still sympathetic. She drank off half her brandy and Christ, it burned, bitter and with a kick like a Santorini mule. Which was why she was drinking the shite.

She offered the remainder to the girl, who protested, "Isn't it a little early?"

Such a Brit.

Angela said, "Darlin', it's been too late for you and me since we landed in this fooking country."

For a moment the girl seemed startled at the profanity and then they both began to laugh, prompting the Greek men at the bar to throw the evil eye at them. Nothing scarier for a macho type than the sound of women's laughter. They fear it's directed at them and they're mostly right.

The girl told Angela the usual tired story, boyfriend fooked off with their cash. Same sad song, same sad result, and all she had was her return ticket on the ferry.

Angela would never quite know why she asked, "How much is the airfare home?"

Stunned, the girl said she could get a cheap flight for maybe three hundred euro.

Angela gave her four hundred, gripped her hand tightly and said, "Buy yourself a nice dress, have a meal and get home as if the devil was chasing you."

Ten

*Riots generally had no causes, or the causes were pretty small,
like a particularly bad meal in the mess hall.*
PATRICIA HIGHSMITH, *The Glass Cell*

Violence was in the air in Attica, you could practically smell it. After the Aryan was found dead in the shower, rumor spread that Sino's crew was behind it. Two days later Carlito, the Mexican kid, was found dead in the shower—his throat slashed after he'd been gang raped. Max felt sorry for him, but, come on, what did the moron expect, going up against the Brotherhood with nothing but a sharpened toothbrush? Hadn't he boned up on prison literature before he got sent away? Eh, not everybody could be as savvy and as street smart as The M.A.X.

Rumors were spreading that when Sino got out of the hole the Aryans were gonna make their big move. Rufus and his boys were planning to get in on the fun, and the spic gangs and the Bloods were going to get their licks in, too. Max could hardly contain himself—a major prison uprising was brewing! Riots at Attica, it was so fuckin' Pacino. Someday, when they filmed the story of his life, the riots would be the fucking set piece. It was going to be biblical, historical, and Max Fisher was going to be in the middle of it all.

One morning, when Sino had been away in the hole for about a week, the mail guy came by Max's cell, held out an envelope, and said, "Fisher."

Max was surprised to hear his name called. Rufus got letters all the time from God knows who, but so far Max had gotten *nada*. After all, who was there to write him? He didn't expect to hear from his relatives, that was for sure. They all said he'd disgraced the family, they never wanted anything to do with him again, yadda yadda yadda. As far as Max was concerned, that was fine with him. His brother called him a loser and a lowlife. Jesus Christ, the guy was a fucking teacher and he was calling *Max* a loser? Come on.

Max was a big-time criminal, a fucking celebrity. He figured there had to be, like, dozens of websites devoted to him, and blogs, and, hell, fan clubs. Maybe the letter was from one of his fan club members.

Max looked at the return address: Paula Segal.

His first thought: *Somebody I banged?*

Yeah, probably. He'd had so many conquests over the years, how could he keep track? Now that he was famous, now that he'd made it, she probably wanted to weasel in, score some of his dough for herself. Yeah, like that was gonna happen. His ex-wife had taught him all about pre-nups.

He opened the envelope—there was a note and, oh yeah, baby, a picture. And, whoa, hold the phones, this chick was hot! After nearly three weeks in lockup, Rufus was looking better to him every night—but this girl, fuck, she was a serious knockout. Okay, Max hadn't looked at her face yet, but those huge gazongas, had to be 36-C's at least, maybe D's. They were high, too, and he liked the way they were squished together in that little swimsuit, and so tight you could bounce a quarter off 'em.

Finally, after maybe a minute or two, he looked at her face. Nah, she didn't look like an ex, but that didn't mean anything. Would Hef recognize all of his conquests? When you were a big-time player like Max Fisher, women tended to blur.

He skimmed the note, something how she was a writer, knew some other chicks—Laura Lippman, Tess Gerritsen, hopefully they were stacked too—and, holy shit, she wanted to write his life story. See, Hollywood was calling, and sooner than he'd expected. Yeah, it was all coming together, just at its own pace, that's all. He was already the most feared man at Attica, and now some hot babe from Manhattan, a big-time writer, was all over him. Obviously she'd want to fuck him. She had to get to know her subject as well as she could, didn't she?

As soon as he could get his hands on some paper and a pen, Max wrote:

Dear Paula,

 Love the picture!!!!

 As you can imagine I get A LOT of requests like this. James Patterson wanted to write my story, but I said, No, thanks, Jimmy, way too busy.

 That said, drop by and I'll squeeze you in. Just make sure you wear something like in the picture.

  Love,

  The M.A.X.

 P.S. Bring Laura and Tess. The more the merrier.

A few days later, Max was called down to the visitor's room. He had his hair slicked and a rolled-up sock in his crotch—yeah he was ready to rock 'n' roll.

There was only one chick there, Paula, but, man, she looked even hotter in person. For the last couple of nights, Max had been jerking off, imagining this moment, and talk about living up to a fantasy. She was in a low-cut top, loose enough that you could almost see her nipples. Man, if the glass wasn't there he wouldn't've been able to resist. He would've just reached out and grabbed 'em.

He stared at her tits for a while longer, then realized she was talking to him. He put on a headset, heard:

"Mr. Fisher, I can't tell you what a pleasure it is to meet you. I've read everything about you I could get my hands on. I was at your trial, but I didn't have the opportunity to introduce myself. Thank you so much for agreeing to meet me here, and fit me into your tight schedule. I can't tell you how much I appreciate it."

Jesus, Max thought, she was like a bad date—she never shuts up.

But he smiled, had to keep up his celebrity persona, and said, "You have great tits, but you've probably heard that dozens of times before, right?"

She smiled. What, she thought he was joking? Then she said, "I've booked a motel room in the area. I was hoping we could talk once a day over the course of the next several weeks. I'm trying to arrange with the warden a better place to meet, face-to-face, in private. He said it requires some arrangement, but hopefully it's something that could happen soon. I'm just so…"

Max was looking at her rack again. Fuck, they were so close yet so far away.

"You single?" he asked.

She hesitated, then said, "Yes. Yes, I am."

"Me, too," Max said. "See? We already have something in common." He laughed then added, "I want to proposition you." He realized that didn't come out right and said, "I mean, I want to make a proposition *to* you. Me and you, we seem to get along, right? We have a lot in common, make each other laugh. I was thinking, how about we, you know, get married?"

Why was she laughing? Eh, she was probably just so happy she couldn't contain herself. That had to be it.

"Hey, don't get too excited," he said. "There'll be a pre-nup—a *serious* pre-nup. If you think I'm gonna give you half the Fisher fortune, think again, *muchacha*. I made that mistake once and I'm sure as shit not gonna make it again. But, yeah, it'll be great to be married to you because me and you, we could have those, what do they call them, congenital visits? No, that's not it. Conjugal visits. Yeah, we'll have those."

Max had been thinking about his herpes, but she didn't have to know about that. Things were going so well, there was no reason to ruin the mood.

"I don't know what to say," Paula said.

God, were her tits, like, growing?

"Say yes," Max said.

"I'm very flattered, obviously," she said. "I mean, you're a very attractive man, and I'm so honored that you're taking the time to—"

"Look, honey, you want me to write this book with you, don't you?"

He liked that—let the not-so-subtle threat hang there. That was the way to play hardball with the literary bitch. After all, not only had he cut off a man's dick—yeah, he was starting to believe it himself—he was the king of Attica, a feared man, and he might as well start fucking acting like it, right? You want The M.A.X. to give something, you gotta give him something in return.

Like that.

"I'll think it over," she said. "In the meantime, I was hoping we could—"

"I look like Chris Rock?" Max asked.

Paula looked confused, said, "I'm confused."

"I look like Chris Rock?" Max repeated. "I look like a goddamn comedian?"

"No, but—"

"Then pay me some respect, okay? I'm an important man, I'm a big man. I need you, but you don't need me. So you're gonna give me what I need or you're not gonna get what you need. You know that and I know that, so let's not pussyfoot around. Let's just keep the action going, the ball in play, all right?"

He had no idea what half this shit meant but, hell, he was on a roll. Yeah, you better believe it.

Her voice starting to weaken, she said, "Mr. Fisher, I can't—"

Max dropped the headphones, got up and walked away. He went all the way to the other end of the room, making it seem like he was leaving for real, then, at the door, he stopped and turned back. Sure enough the book bitch was calling to him, trying to get his attention.

Max had her!

But he took his time walking back, milking the moment, then put the phones on and she practically screamed, "If I say yes, will you do the book with me?"

Ah, desperation. He loved it.

Max, waited, said, "Sweetheart, I'm gonna do a lot more with you than write a fucking book."

Max Fisher had to be the smarmiest, sleaziest, most self-deluded guy Paula had ever met—a goldmine all right. She'd been worried, on the way up to Attica, that maybe Fisher would be a disappointment. After all, how could a guy be so far out there, so far gone? But, no, this guy lived up to his rep and surpassed it.

Just arriving at Attica had been such a fucking blast. The walls of the prison seemed to reek of testosterone and she'd laughed, said to herself, "Wanna talk about sperm count?"

She had to put that in the book. But first, Jesus, first, she needed to do another line. Yeah, just to get into the full Max Fisher mindset she'd started doing coke, and the sheer rush of snorting a line outside Attica was incredible. So she did one line, okay four, but c'mon, this is the toughest joint in the whole country and she was about to meet the craziest bastard any writer could dream of.

What was that book called, *The Journalist and the Murderer*? Yeah, something like that, Joe McGinnis, hottest true crime writer in the biz, two movies made till his subject, the killer doctor—McDonald?—sued him and sayonara Joe. Dealing with these guys was like juggling grenades. But if you could handle it…and she could, she knew she could. Now it was Paula Segal's turn in the spotlight, on center stage.

The coke kicking in, she took a sip of her stone-cold vanilla latte. (Decaf. She wasn't reckless. That caffeine was, like, addictive.)

She reached in her glove compartment, the nose candy giving her that icy drip that was pure heaven, and yup, there were her Virginia Slims. A cigarette, even a girly one, and she was so ready to rock and roll.

Oh, she loved Fisher. Who could invent a guy like that? She already had the chapter written in her head where he proposed marriage. Perfect, fucking perfect.

He hadn't been able to take his eyes off her tits. His obsession with busty women had come up during his trial and, okay, she'd expected him to respond more or less the way he had. It's why she'd worn what she'd worn. But he'd gone further. Three weeks in jail and he was ready to propose marriage to a complete stranger. One with nice tits, but still. Couldn't this asshole tell she was a dyke now? But if he couldn't, he couldn't. Not her fault. It was her right as a journalist to milk it for all it was worth. She decided to string him along, let him think she wanted to marry him. Jesus, how far would a man go just to get laid? But if that's what it took to get him to open up in a few private sessions, give her some juicy quotes no one else had, baby, let him eye the twins all he wanted. About time they gave her something other than a backache.

Leaving the prison, Paula was shaking, not from fear but sheer hot exhilaration. Well, exhilaration and cocaine.

She did another line then, looking up at the gun turrets, realized she'd better get the car and her ass in gear.

As she pulled out of there, she was debating, Should she reveal in the book that she was gay? Then she thought, *How big is the pink dollar?* and laughed again, that damn coke. *How much did dykes spend on true crime books?*

But no, pulling an Ellen might alienate the great white majority. The hell with it, she'd ask her agent what to do, her *new* agent, not this fucking loser she had now.

Getting back to the motel, she found the coke high, like a sad dick, was wilting and she needed to stay up, stay on top of her game. She thought, *Nice cold dry Martini would do the biz, maybe a bit of hot sex. She'd check her trick book—*

But, shit, she wasn't in the city. Her trick book was back home, and anyone listed in it was three hundred miles away. She needed some rough trade right here, right now. There had to some hot bull dykes somewhere in Attica, New York, right? Every prison these days had a diversity hiring requirement, and those butch female guards had to hang out somewhere.

Her thoughts skipped back, from sex to her book. She could see the dust jacket, had to be black and white, maybe they'd use Fisher's mugshot. Or maybe she'd just take one herself, how difficult could it be? She had a digital camera.

Then the blurbs! Maybe she could get Dominick Dunne or Sebastian Junger or, better yet, Bill Clinton. He liked to read and, God, he was going to love to read about Max Fisher. Ah, and then, once word of her book got around, people would start asking *her* for blurbs, Even Connelly and King would be calling her. But she'd adopt a policy of *no blurbing* herself. Sorry, not even for Laura L.

She said aloud as she was putting on her leather gear, primed for a night on the prowl, something that would have gotten her thrown out of the very bars she was about to visit: "Max Fisher, I love you."

Eleven

*Ehi, chi ha fascino puo permettersi
di camminare impettito, no?*
KEN BRUEN AND JASON STARR, *Doppio Complotta*

Sebastian was so bloody happy to be back in old Blighty. Gosh, it was good to speak English with English people. He'd noticed the girl on the plane had spare keys in her bag and stupid cow, her address in Hampstead written right on the fob. Who knows, he might do a little reconnaissance there. He always kept his ears open for useful details. She'd mentioned she worked as a paralegal; perhaps while she was paralegalizing, he could stroll through her gaff, see what other goodies he might liberate.

The prospect of rifling her place tickled his fancy. Nothing like a touch of B-and-E to whet the appetites. He had for the past few years rented a one-room apartment in Earls Court. His parents paid the freight, mainly to keep him out of their home. Patrick Hamilton had written, "Those whom the gods have abandoned are left an electric fire in Earls Court." It was indeed, depending on your vocabulary,

A kip

A hovel

A dive

A shithole

But it was a bolt hole, and it was useful to have an address. It had one wardrobe that held his prized Armani suit, his three pair of Italian-made brogues and, of course, the mandatory striped shirts, all bespoke. And, naturally, an assortment of ties, from Police Federation to Cambridge, Eton and Oxford to the Masons. Vital items for a con man on his uppers.

He needed an infusion of cash, a rather large one. He took out his remaining bottle of Gordon's Gin—was there any other?—and drat, no tonic or bitters, really, he'd have to take stock. There was a miniature mountain of bills that had accumulated in his absence, and he threw them in the garbage. The upper classes didn't actually *pay* for stuff. Really, did anyone ever see Prince Charles worry about the light bill?

He tossed back the gin, said, "Hits the spot, ye gads."

And went to the bathroom. It was about the size of his cupboard. Shame about the hot water. There is a slight downside to not paying the utilities. He'd have to ring ol' Mum, get her to post some cheques to these various chappies. He splashed on some Hugo Boss, a fellow had to smell right, and then as he peed, he went, "The bloody hell is that?"

Couldn't be. But it looked like...were those *blisters*?

He stood stock still, thinking, Herpes? Him?

"The bitch," he said, and he slammed his fist into the wall, hurting his knuckles. Then he shouted, "This is just too *bloody rich!*"

And in his rage, he made a decision that, by day's end, would in fact lead to his killing somebody.

He went back to the tiny front room, drank off rather a large measure of neat gin and in a lightbulb moment thought, Hampstead, by golly. Somebody is going to pay for this injustice, this travesty of life.

He went to the pub first, see if any of the chaps were around, maybe hit them for a rapid fifty for cab fare. You didn't think he was going to ride the tube, now did you? Come on, really, get with the cricket, old bean.

The usual suspects were lined up along the bar and greeted

him less with warmth than expectation, expecting that for once he might be flush and stand a round of drinks, they admired his tan, and when he shouted to the bartender, "Pint of your best bitter, my good fellow," they shrugged, collectively, same old, same old.

It was the kind of pub where everything was for sale, even your mother, well, your mother's pension, anyway. There was a quite a brisk trade in old age pensioners' pension books, and of course there was always someone cashing some unfortunate Australian backpacker's travelers cheques. You recommended a good cheap hostel to them, clean and friendly, and while they went off to make the call, you relieved them of their belongings.

Doing the chaps and gells a favour, actually. Now they'd really have an adventure, see how friendly London was when you were skint. Which is why all the bar staff in Earls Court had Aussie accents, the trips to Italy, etc., shall we say, um, deferred.

Sebastian managed to bum a twenty from an Irish guy who was three sheets to the wind and got the hell out of there. The black cab to Hampstead cost most of the borrowed dosh but ah, glorious Hampstead, where Sebastian felt he belonged—that, or of course, Windsor.

He paid the driver and gazed in wonder at the address. It was a semi-detached in a nice leafy lane. Whistling a few bars from *Bridge on the River Kwai*, he let himself in, hoping to fuck she didn't have a dog.

Cash, the house reeked of it. Flokati shag rugs on the floor and paintings, dammit all, one of them looked like a, golly gosh, *a Constable*. And the decoration, even to his untrained eye, had obviously cost a bundle, all that posh leather furniture that creaked when you sat in it but looked good in the glossy mags. First things first, he found the drinks cabinet, found, ah yes,

Gordon's and mixers. Then he found a nice large Gucci holdall and began to fill it with swag.

Then upstairs and women, ha, so predictable. Under her rather dainty lingerie he found nigh on five large in notes and nearly had a coronary when he found, in a leather pouch, a roll of Krugerrands, with a note:

Love from Daddykins
  Xxxxxx

He was toasting Daddykins when a voice asked, "Who the hell are you?"

Turned to see a woman in her fifties, with a cleaning brush and apron. He was startled, then tried, "Golly, one wasn't expecting the char to arrive."

For the life of him, he couldn't remember the name of the bloody cow who lived here. Meanwhile, the cleaning woman was like all her class, suspicious, and accused, "You're a burglar."

In his agitation, he thought she called him a *bugger*. Now I mean, steady on, a chap had some horseplay with the rugger boys in boarding school, it was part of being English, but to be actually called a homo…

She picked up the phone near the bed, said, "I'm calling the coppers."

A combination of herpes shock, bugger accusation, gin, and *Ripley's Game* meshed and he had the phone cord round her neck in no time. She fought like a demon, they fell over the bed, but he held on for grim life and even began to laugh hysterically, shouting, "Ride 'em, cowboy!"

Took a time and she managed to scrape his face, hurt like a…a bugger? The cord was near embedded in her throat when she finally gave out and went limp.

He was shaking, rose off her. He got all his loot together, too drunk to realize his prints were all over the place. He didn't dare call a cab, so he legged it down the leafy lane, found a tube station and, loath as he was to use that service, he did. On the train, a wino asked him for a contribution and he answered, "Bugger off."

When he finally got to Earls Court, he was seriously knackered, the adrenaline long gone, and his hangover had kicked in with a serious intent. Probably explains why he didn't notice his door had been forced. He just wanted to have a shower and count the loot and oh, have a large gin. Killing people was harder work than they led you to believe. He'd done it twice, and you know, it didn't get easier.

He was reaching for the light switch when he got a massive wallop to the head that sent him sprawling across his tiny living room, the bag of swag spilling every which way, a rainbow of miniature paintings, jewelry, Krugerrands, cash, a few pair of the girl's lace panties he'd grabbed, even one of the flokati rugs.

He turned to see Georgios standing over him. Georgios, how the fuck could that be? The guy was fish meat off the cliffs of Santorini. Jesus, how rough was his hangover? Hallucinating already?

Georgios hissed, "I'm going to cut your balls off, mallakas, for the death of my cousin."

Good to his word, he had a very lethal looking knife in his right hand. Sebastian held up a hand, asked, "You're his cousin?"

He didn't know whether to feel relief or fear. He ranted, "I tried to *save* Georgios. It was that crazy American bitch killed him. Why do you think I left her behind? She's completely mad."

The knife was raised, and Sebastian had an inspiration that saved his balls and his life.

He said, "See all this treasure, we can use it to track her down, extract proper vengeance for your noble cousin."

Noble certainly stopped the mad bastard in his knife tracks. He asked, "Why should I believe you, mallakas?"

Sebastian was on his feet now, grabbed the gin bottle, poured two large measures and, with a shaking hand, offered it to the guy, who grabbed it, tried it, made a face. Sebastian knocked his back like a drowning man, said, "I was living on Santorini for months, I never even heard of your noble cousin, why would I kill him? But this crazy woman, she owed him rent, she stole from me, she is truly demented."

The guy had put the knife down, thank God, and was looking at all the cash and goodies lying on the floor.

Sebastian quickly added, the gin urging him on, "My parents are rich and this is my inheritance."

Why they would have given him some rather delicate items of lingerie was tricky but the Greeks knew all about the, um, peccadillos of the Brits.

The guy said, "I found your credit card in Georgios' home."

Dammit, must've fallen out of his pocket while he was bending over, wrapping the body in plastic. Fucking credit cards, always came back to bite you in the bum.

The Greek pushed his glass towards Sebastian, grunted, "More."

Sebastian thought, the scoundrel might have tried *please*. But this was probably not the best moment to mention it.

The man said, "My name is Yanni."

Would *Damn jolly good to meet you* be overdoing it? Sebastian settled for, "Glad to meet you. Alas, I wish it were under happier circumstances, but be assured, I will track this lady down and wreak revenge for you and your family."

He was thinking, give the bastard five hundred for his trouble and get shot of him. Well, let's not be rash, two hundred was probably a fortune to a chappie like this.

The guy had rock-hard eyes, said, "We."

Sebastian echoed, "We?...I'm not sure I follow you, old chap."

Yanni was looking at the knife again, said, "I don't trust you English, we stay together till this is avenged, okay?"

With a sinking heart, Sebastian mustered his best grin, said, "Splendid, rather chuffed to have you on board."

Yanni grabbed a pile of cash and Sebastian thought, *Steady on*.

The Greek was heading for the door, said, "Now we eat, drink some ouzo, and plan how we find this she-devil."

Sebastian wanted a shower and more gin and to be rid of this lunatic.

"Capital," he said.

Twelve

Dyke City

If there was a dyke scene in Attica, New York, Paula Segal sure as hell was going to find it. She did a couple of lines of coke on the dashboard, made sure her push-up bra was doing its necessary pushing up, and was ready to roll.

She drove to downtown Attica and a good thing she didn't blink too long or she would've missed it. It was the typical small upstate New York town that had been thriving during the time they filmed *It's a Wonderful Life* but now it looked like a ghost town, probably the casualty of a nearby Wal-Mart. But the lesbians had to hang out somewhere, right? She drove by a few dilapidated blocks, past the mostly abandoned shops. There were a few bars, but only one getting any business. As she entered, Kiss' "Rock And Roll All Night" was blasting. She had a feeling this wasn't a good sign.

The place was crowded, that was the good news. The bad news was the ratio was bad, i.e. there were practically all men. Standing in the doorway, Paula felt the sets of male eyes leering at her desperately, as if she was the first woman they'd seen in years. Jeez, was the whole town of Attica a freaking prison? Did they release them right into the goddamn bars?

One guy grabbed her arm—he looked frighteningly like Sean Penn in *Dead Man Walking*—and said, "Hey, how about a little dance, honey?"

Like you could dance to Kiss.

She yanked her arm free, hissed, "Fuck you, townie."

God, men were so fucking gross. Had she actually used to like them or had she gone through the eighteen years of her sexually active life faking it? Eh, whatever, she was just so glad she was through with all of that crap.

The woman working the bar—she wasn't bad looking. Blond, a little heavy but, hey, Paula liked big girls. The woman looked briefly in Paula's direction and half-smiled, but Paula couldn't tell if there was more to it, if it was a come-on or not. As a newbie lesbian, Paula's gaydar wasn't fully developed yet. Since she'd, well, *turned*, she'd accidentally hit on several straight women and she was sure she'd let some hardcore dykes, easy lays, slip through her fingers. She hoped it all averaged out in the end.

Paula sat at the bar and decided to go native, ordered a bottle of Schlitz.

Watching the woman get the drink, Paula eyeballed her ass. Nice. She liked her shoulders, too—they were big and meaty. She had at least a few tattoos, wasn't wearing makeup, and her hair was cut short, boyish. Looked like a dyke all right.

"Hey, I'm Paula."

"Bonny," the woman said.

Paula smiled, said, "Shake your bon-bon, shake your bon-bon."

Bonny was deadpan. Maybe she didn't like Ricky Martin?

Trying to loosen her up, Paula said, "It's kinda guy-heavy here tonight, huh?"

"Yeah," Bonny said, "but this is the clientele. What're you gonna do, you know?"

"I know what *I'm* gonna do," Paula said.

She smiled, letting the implication linger, as if there was any doubt what she had in mind.

"Excuse me, are you hitting on me?" Bonny asked.

She seemed if not disgusted, seriously annoyed.

Before Paula could respond a fat guy with a scraggly red beard appeared.

He said, "What's the problem, honey?"

"This lady's hitting on me," Bonny said.

Paula said, "Um, I think there's a, um, misunder—"

"You tryin' to pick up my wife?" Bearded Guy asked.

Somebody in the bar yelled, "She's a fuckin' dyke!" and then everybody started yelling.

Paula hightailed it out of there, back to her car. As she was getting in, Bearded Guy came running over, saying, "Hey, if you're lookin' to have one of 'em threesomes, maybe I can talk Bonny into it!"

Back in her motel room, Paula got undressed and into bed, thinking, So much for hooking up in this hick town. She read a few chapters of Lippman's *What the Dead Know*, then on pay-per-view she found a good all-girl porno movie—*Horny College Chicks Get Dirty*. As the girls went at it, wrestling and clawing at each other in the mud, she moved her hand over her crotch, whispering, "That'll do, pig. That'll do."

In the morning, Paula left bright and early for her first session with Max.

The warden had come through, and she found herself sitting face-to-face next to Fisher, a guard near the door. Fisher was, naturally, staring at her bust.

After last night the last thing she was in the mood for was a predatory man. But she reminded herself that her career was at stake and she had to put on her game face.

Fisher asked, "So you wanna set a date?"

She stared at him. She didn't know what he was talking about, said, "What're you talking about?"

"Tomorrow my morning's full," he said, "but how about the afternoon?"

Talk about gaydar malfunctioning, what was wrong with this guy?

"I'm sorry, a date for what?"

"Our fucking wedding," he said. "The M.A.X. needs to get his pipes cleaned. I already got permission from my counselor and last night I wrote out a pre-nup. It basically says, You don't get shit. Sorry to be so blunt about it but, hey, I learned from the Donald. I know it's probably not legally binding, but it'll give me something to fall back on when our marriage goes to pieces and, let's face it, I know it's gonna feel like a honeymoon now, but it's only a matter of time before it all goes to shit. Trust me, when it comes to shit relationships I've been there, done that."

Trying not to laugh, she said, "This is all so sudden. I need some more time to think about it."

Fisher wouldn't crack. He said, "I need an answer pronto. No marry, no talkie. You have ten seconds to decide."

He started the countdown and she was thinking how she couldn't lose this book deal. But marry Fisher? God, he made Ron Jeremy look like a catch. But if she had to do it, she had to do it. This was her last shot and she wasn't giving it up for anything.

He was at "two" when she blurted, "Yes, yes, I'll marry you, I'll marry you."

Fisher leaned over and, Jesus Christ, he kissed her. Cringing, she was thinking of that line from *Planet of the Apes* when Dr. Zira kisses Charlton Heston: *You're so damn ugly.*

She couldn't wait to get out of there, to take a shower, but she reminded herself of her ultimate goal, to write the best damn true crime book ever, and she tried to keep her disgust from showing.

Max was talking about the marriage license and setting a

date for sometime next week. Hopefully she'd have all the material she needed by then and wouldn't have to go through with it.

Speaking of which. She said, "Tell more about this hit man you and Angela Petrakos allegedly hired to kill your wife. Did he really call himself Popeye?"

It spread like wildfire that The M.A.X. had had a *hot* visitor.

One guy asked, "That, like, your wife?"

Max gave him a withering look, sneered, "Ain't you heard, peckerhead? My first bitch wife got chopped to pieces." Let the other cons hear this as he paused. Added a wink, then said, "By person or persons unknown."

They could check this out and see indeed it was true. It should further enhance his violent rep.

The guy took off, muttering, "No offense, bro."

Man, Max was having the time of his freaking life. Did he own this joint or what? Even the guards were looking at him with fresh respect. And the writer babe, the bust on that chick! He was hard just replaying the scene and the way he'd laid down the rules to her. He could see she was panting for him, he knew all about how those crazy dames married guys in the joint. Soon he'd have a stack of letters from women wanting to be his penpal. The M.A.X. might allow one of the queens to do his letter writing, they were good at all that romance shit.

Another con stopped, asked, "Mr. Max, you need me to run any errands, stuff like that?"

Max gave him his imperial look, said, "I seem to be running low on decent booze."

Let it hover.

The guy, some variety of spic, licked his lips, said, "There's the prison hooch, I can get you a bottle of that." Trailed off as

The M.A.X. gave him the silent treatment then said, "There's a bottle of Chivas going for like five cartons."

Max gave him a tiny pat on the shoulder, said, "Now you're talking, *hermano*, deliver it to my cell in say, ten minutes?"

When Max finally got back to the cell, Rufus was standing there, gazing in wonder at a bottle of Chivas, said, "You the man, yo, how the hell you get this shit? How much it gonna cost?"

Rufus, who knew how the system worked, had never even seen real booze in all his years in lockup. Max smiled, took the bottle, said, "I let him live."

Max clinked his prison-issue tin cup again Rufus's. Chivas in a tin cup. Thought to himself, Hmmmm, maybe a good title for the book of poetry he'd been thinking he might write someday. He was just so on fire. Then he laughed to himself and said out loud, "I'm a fucking riot." Later, he'd remember saying this, after he'd become the cause of one of the bloodiest fucking riots to come down the pike. Wouldn't seem so funny then, but for now he couldn't stop chuckling.

He had another shot of the Chivas, man, that was good shit, he didn't know if the big guy appreciated the finer things in life but hey, hang in there, The M.A.X. would bring him right along. He reminded Max of the giant in *The Green Mile*, and he made a mental note, tell the writer babe to put ol' Rufus in there.

Then he realized the big guy was...*sobbing?* The fuck was that? How good was this booze?

Max, allowing his sensitive side to show, asked, "Hey, *amigo mio*, whassup?"

Then to keep his Spanish in trim, added, *"Que pasa, compadre?"*

Rufus, massive tears rolling down those cheeks, said, "Yo, Max, man, I just been feeling so bad and shit, know what I'm sayin'? When you came in here, me wantin' to ram a rod up yo' pretty ass and shit? That shit was wrong, know what I'm sayin'? That shit wasn't me talkin', man, you gotta know that shit's true." He sobbed some more, then said, "Outside, man, I never even been lookin' at another man's ass, know what I'm sayin'? But inside here, shit, it fucks with a man's mind and shit. You see the sissies walkin' 'round shakin' they pretty asses and you start wantin' some of that shit yourself, know what I'm sayin'? You start sayin', 'Gimme some a dat shit,' 'I want some a dat shit.' 'I wanna fuck that shit.' Know what I'm sayin'?" He wiped his eyes on the back of his hand. "And, Max, yo, if I been knowin' you was some hot shit gangsta an' shit, I woulda been cleanin' yo' ass fer you every day 'stead a wantin' to fuck it, know what I'm sayin'? Why would I wanna fuck some big time gangsta's ass for? That's shit's crazy, man, shit makes no sense and shit. And some a the shit I been sayin' to you, man, like how I been hatin' Muslims and shit, I didn't mean none of that shit. I don't know why I said that 'cept I was crazy cause I been in this jail too long and I been gettin' too much sissy ass. It fucks with a man's brain and shit, know what I'm sayin'? And now, every night, I been afraid. Yeah, I been afraid that I wake up my dick won' be on my body no more. Every night, 'fore I go to sleep I pray to Jesus you won't take off my dick. And every mornin' when I wake up, first thing I do is I check to make sure my dick's still there. So that's what I'm sayin' to you is thank you, man. Thank you for not takin' my dick off, and I hope you forgive me for disrespectin' you and shit. I didn't mean none of that shit. That was just bullshit talkin', that wasn't me."

Man, Max was soaking all this up, he didn't want it to stop. He knew moments like this, they didn't come along too often in life and he had to milk it for all it was worth. He had this huge terrifying black cellmate, a serious gangsta who could crush him with one hand, and not only was the man living his life in total fear of Max, he was also begging for his forgiveness. He glared at Rufus hard for a long time, as if he were weighing all his options.

Then, expansive and like the Mahatma, forgiving like Gandhi but with a shitload of Chivas on board, Max finally said, "*De nada, señor.* Ain't no big thang."

Whoops, how did he go Texan? Eh, what the fuck ever. He was forgiving the mutherfucka, not forgetting, or as Dr. Phil might say, *Moving on and moving up.*

But Rufus kept talking and truth to tell, it was grating just a tiny tad on Max's nerves. He was about to snap when Rufus blurted out, "I got a secret, man."

Max, in his most humble, quiet voice, said, "Pray tell?"

Which reminded him, he better get that preacher validation on the web, 100 bucks and you were like, *An ordained preacher of the church of outreach saints.* Two fags on the upper tier wanted to get hitched and he'd told them for four hundred bucks he would perform the ceremony. Was there truly no end to his talents? Prison was ripe, fucking abundant in business opportunities. Ask that Watergate guy, Colson.

He had to refocus. Rufus was spilling, "We got a break comin'."

Max, muddled by the Chivas and his myriad schemes and languages, thought first he meant someone was, like, going to cut them a bit of slack, then he realized, *prison break.* Sweet Jesus, like the TV series. This would put the book up there with Dan Brown. Wait till Paula heard about this. It would have to at least get him a great blowjob, right?

Rufus was saying, "Yo, I only trustin you cause you a gangsta and I got respect for you an' shit. I ain't even tol' the rest of my crew, but you the man, Max Fisher, know what I'm sayin'? We been plannin' this shit for three years. And we ain't stupid and shit neither. We're gonna do this shit up right, know what I'm sayin'? Now we got a gangsta like you on our side, shit, we're gonna be all set up. So you wanna be in, you just say the word and you in, know what I'm sayin'?"

Max waited, trying his hardest to stay stone-faced, to put the fear of God in his cellmate, then asked, "When y'all gonna make your move?"

"When them riots come down," Rufus said, "know what I'm sayin'? Everybody be fightin' and shit and we be sneakin' our asses outta this jail. Damn, I can't wait to get outside an jam my dick into some real pussy, know what I'm sayin'? Man, I been fuckin' so many sissies' asses I don't even 'member what real pussy feel like."

Max was thinking: Riots, a prison break, Hollywood, fame. Was he the luckiest guy on the planet or what?

"Count me in, baby," he nearly shouted.

Thirteen

*All day long I experienced infinite sadness amid grey
surroundings. I collected one by one my sullied hopes,
and I cried over each of them.*
ANDRE GIDE, *The White Notebook*

Manhattan used to give Angela a big buzz, but not anymore. The city had disappointed her so many times that arriving in midtown and being in the center of it all once again left her feeling depressed more than anything else. It reminded her of all the failures, all her disappointments, all her dreams gone to shite. She couldn't even muster up a fantasy that this time around things would work out differently. Why should they?

Her cash was running so low—maybe that gift to the British girl on the ferry hadn't been the smartest move in the world— that she couldn't afford a cab and had to take a bus into the city. A hotel was out of the question, so it was either Max Fisher or bust. She had no idea if he'd take her back, but she was out of options. If this didn't work she might have to sleep on the street tonight, or on the subway.

She took the 6 train uptown and headed over to the apartment building on the Upper East Side where she'd spotted him briefly the last time she was in the city. In a strange way she was looking forward to seeing him again. Yeah, he was bonkers and sleazy, but she wasn't exactly the portrait of mental health and fidelity her own self. Maybe they were destined to be together —two tortured souls who'd been around the block more than a few times and who, in the end, realize they're perfect for each other. You could even see something romantic about it, if you squinted.

She went to the concierge desk. The guy was on the phone and Angela looked around, impressed with the décor in the lobby. Jaysus, Max was probably rolling in it. Before she'd left for Greece, she'd read in the paper how he'd become a drug dealer, and she knew he must have been doing well at it, to live in a swank building on the Upper East Side. But she'd had no idea he'd been doing *this* well. Too bad she didn't look her best after the long flight, the ferry ride to Athens and the, well, encounter in the Greek prison. She knew a first impression was everything and she wanted Max to see her in her best light. But then she expanded her chest and looked down proudly, remembering that with Max these babies were all she'd ever needed.

The concierge finished the call and Angela said, "I'm here to see Max Fisher."

The guy nearly laughed, said, "He doesn't live here anymore."

"Oh, okay, do you know where he's living now?"

"Yeah, Attica."

Angela was still lost in her daydream, imagining living off of Max's millions, straightening out her life once and for all. She figured, Attica, that must be the name of some luxury condo: The Attica. Yeah, it was probably right next door to Trump Tower or something.

"Is that on the Upper East Side, too?" she asked hopefully.

The guy laughed again, said, "It's a jail, honey. You know in upstate New York? He got sent away. You didn't hear about it? He left owing three months rent. Cheap son of a bitch never tipped me, not once...You're not a relative, are you?"

She didn't answer, just walked away.

She should've known. Wasn't it always the way? Whenever

she had the slightest hope that things might work out for her after all, fate always snuck up on her and kicked her in the ass.

She went outside and naturally it had started to rain. Pushing her suitcase ahead of her, the rain pouring down on her, she walked across town to the Port Authority bus terminal and spent the last of her money on a one-way ticket to Attica.

The bus didn't leave till five A.M. so Angela had to spend the night in the terminal. The saddest thing was no one even tried to pick her up.

When she was a teenager, living with her parents in Weehawken, New Jersey, she took buses into the city all the time and guys at the Port Authority always hit on her. Once, when she was seventeen a guy in a leather vest with a handlebar mustache approached her and asked her if she was interested in becoming a model. She was so naïve then she actually thought it was a good career opportunity, that she'd been discovered. So they went to his "studio"—it didn't ever occur to her to ask why a photographer would have his studio in a practically condemned S.R.O. in Hell's Kitchen—and after a few minutes of general-type questions he asked her to take her clothes off. She thought this was a little, well, unusual, but he explained that all the girls did it and if she wanted to make a thousand bucks a week she'd have to take nude modeling gigs.

She knew where this was leading and asked, "Wait, so are you, like, a porno director?"

"I make adult films, yes," he said.

She couldn't figure out if she was offended or flattered. She knew she should be offended, but it was kind of exciting, the thought of getting into the adult entertainment business. And, hey, she could be the next Jenna Jameson.

So she took off her shirt and undid her bra, waiting for the admiration to begin. But when the guy got a look at her barely A-cup breasts he said, "Sorry, no thanks," and practically kicked her out of the place.

She hadn't thought much of it at the time, she'd just been pissed off; but if there was a life-changing moment in Angela's life, that had been it. The rejection by the porno director had led to a downward spiral. Several years later she took the Pam Anderson/Anna Nicole Smith route and got her boobs done and went blonde and even started wearing the blue contacts. She barely looked like her old self. But had her new look made her any happier? Had it fuck. For years her body had sent out the wrong signals, attracted the worst possible men, and what was it doing for her now? Men were walking by her, ignoring her, like she was fooking invisible. If you couldn't get a guy to notice you at the Port Authority you knew you were way past your sell-by date.

Finally, she got on the bus and, unable to sleep, stared blankly out the window. If she'd been in a less hopeless state she might have realized that there wasn't much point in spending the last of her money to go visit Max. After all, how would a guy serving a stiff jail sentence, who was apparently broke when he got sent up and whose life had clearly gone down the shitter, be able to help her? In her desperation, she was hoping that Max had stashed some money away and would help her out for old time's sake. Yeah, okay, their relationship hadn't always been great and she'd nearly gotten him killed a couple of times, but it hadn't been all bad. There had been times when she felt close to him, when she'd actually enjoyed his company. Okay, maybe she was just imagining this, but he was certainly the wisest man she'd ever known. All right, maybe that wasn't saying much given her dating history. But despite all his shortcomings, there was no doubt that he was a sharp guy, right? He'd built a business and become a self-made millionaire. You can't pull that off and be a total idiot, can you? He also seemed to have made quite a splash as a drug dealer, showed that the first time wasn't just a stroke of luck. He was also in touch with himself, always meditating and talking about Buddhist shite. Maybe at the very least he could advise her, tell her what to do to straighten her life out.

When she arrived in Attica, she was exhausted, had barely slept in forty-eight hours. Still, she was focused and went right to a drugstore. Her checkered history had taught her some things like check out for CCTV. Nope, nothing she could see, so she helped herself to some Chanel. Max had always been partial to his lady smelling fine. Then she went down the block to a thrift shop. The owner was absorbed, reading a copy of the local pennysaver, so she went to the back and boosted a dress, low cut to let that cleavage show, and though hardly cutting-edge fashion, it was clean and bright. She already had her heels, never left home without them.

Good to go, she left the store, her mood slightly elevated. It was a rush to shoplift right under the shadow of one of the country's most notorious prisons. It lifted her confidence, showed she still had some moves, and she felt she was going to need them.

She hitched a ride to the prison. Wasn't hard—seemed like everyone was heading in that direction. It was apparently the big attraction in town, like freaking Disneyland.

She hadn't inquired about visiting hours and she found out she needed to arrange her visit in advance. No problem there though—a little flirting with the guard got her through, the stolen dress already paying some dividends.

She was in the visitor's room, waiting for Max to appear. She expected Max to shuffle in looking beaten, defeated and lost. Older guy like him, not exactly athletic, they'd have eaten him alive by now. She figured she'd give him a dose of sympathy, a little TLC, and that might shake the bucks loose from him.

Her first surprise was when he was led into the room, was she imagining it or was the guard acting all deferential? And Max, glowing with well-being and satisfaction, a smile of utter confidence on his face. He looked like he'd been on a health farm for months. Even looked like he'd lost a few pounds.

He motioned to the guard, and Angela could read his lips: *I'll call you if I need you, Bob*.

Dismissing him? The fook was this?

He sat, stared at her deadpan for a while, then said, "So what's shaking, babe?"

Total strut, acting like he didn't miss her at all, like he might've even forgotten she existed.

She said, "I heard you were here and I was concerned and thought I better come and see if you needed anything."

He gave his high-pitched laugh, the one that had always grated on her nerves. But she hid her distaste, knowing pissing him off wouldn't accomplish anything. Naturally he was staring at her tits.

"Them the same babies I paid serious green for?"

Actually, she'd paid for her own boob job, but if he wanted to believe they were his, why bust his bubble?

She tried to look coy, been a long time since she'd had to use that gig, said, "All yours, hon."

Jesus, she could tell it was killing him, he was dying to come around, cop a feel. Instead, he sat back, yawned. Fucking yawned. Was she, like, boring him?

He asked, "So, my treacherous bitch, what's the real reason you're here? Last time I saw you, you were putting it to me big time—and not your first shafting of The M.A.X. either."

The M.A.X.?

She tried to stay coy, not easy, said, "We all got bent a little out of shape back in those crazy days but I realize now, I'll never meet a man like you again."

Prick bought it. Always did.

He said, "You got The M.A.X., you don't need nothin' else, dig?"

Christ, how could she have forgotten what a dumb arrogant bollix he was?

Poverty will do that, make you stupid. But here she was and all out of options. She said, "I thought we might start over."

He stared at her, said, "You're broke."

Not so dumb.

She said, "Well, I won't lie to you. Things have been a little tight."

"And you coming to The M.A.X., cause he like yo' fixer and shit, right?"

God, was he for real? There'd never been a white man whiter than Max Fisher, and here he was talking like some kind of rapper.

He spread his arm out, said, "See that yard out there, with the most dangerous dudes on the planet? I run 'em, run 'em like the fuckin' losers they are."

How, she asked herself, had someone not gutted the little bastard already? And how on earth did he manage to become top rooster in such a place?

"You always were extraordinary," she said, and wanted to throw up.

He leaned over, said, "Gonna share a secret with you babe, the joint ain't been built that can hold The M.A.X."

Jaysus, he was completely mad.

He continued, "We're busting outa here, me and my crew."

She didn't know how to respond, tried lamely, "That's wonderful."

He smiled, accepting the praise as his due, said, "You want back with The M.A.X., you gonna have to prove your loyalty."

She said, getting the faint whiff of money, and remembering how if she didn't hook up with somebody tonight she'd be sleeping on the street.

"You name it darling, it's done."

He scribbled something onto a piece of paper, then slid it across and said, "Get it done."

She looked down. He'd written two words:

GUNS

CAR

She didn't have bus fare back to the city and he wanted her to get him guns? Never mind a *car*.

She nearly laughed till he reached in his denim shirt, took out a roll of bills, said. "To get you started. And oh, get some decent clothes, that dress looks like it came from fucking Goodwill."

Then he was standing and did cop a feel, a long one. She moaned. He mistook it for a sound of pleasure.

He said, "Go get your pretty ass in gear. Sooner you get me out of here, the sooner The M.A.X. will be putting the meat to you."

Then he shouted for Bob, winked at her, said, "Don't fuck up this time, bee-atch, you know what I'm sayin'?"

Fourteen

Hop smiled. "Nice, could you run my life, baby?"
"Some challenges are too great, my friend."
MEGAN ABBOTT, *The Song is You*

Max couldn't believe it—Angela was fucking back! He'd had to contain himself because, hey, that's the way you had to play it in the joint. Max had done his DD, studying the bros in yard, and almost all of them had the dead-eye glare. Not a lot of smiling faces in a maximum security prison and he knew if you wanted to survive you had to look hard, be hard, always have your game face on. Besides, it was part of Max's hip-hop persona. Look at Eminem. If Slim Shady didn't smile, Max sure as fuck wasn't going to.

But Jesus Christ, Angela looked fucking hot! Her bust, shit, it brought back so many great memories. Fuck, even her stretch marks looked hot. But what was up with that cheap dress? You wouldn't see a crack whore on the West Side Highway in something like that. And she was nervous, too, not the confident, cocky Angela who'd screwed him over so many times before. She looked a little shocked—scratch that, way shocked. Hell, she looked defeated. Angela, down and out? The fuck did that happen? The Angela he knew never stopped fighting. No matter what shit came down the road, she was there, scratching and biting like an alley cat, mouthing like a fishwife on steroids, and screwing the world. She'd ripped him off and just about every other dumb bastard whose path she'd crossed, but she'd never *caved*, no siree.

Suddenly Max found himself feeling like he was wasting his time with Paula. Yeah, the girl had a nice rack, and there was her book—but come on, there was no way he was gonna marry that cow if he could have Angela, the real deal. He and Angela were, like, *destined* to be together. Okay, yeah, so she'd tried to kill him a few times, but doesn't all true love go through rough patches? He'd bet there were times when Cleopatra had been more than a bit pissed off with Tony. And Romeo and Juliet probably wanted to scratch each other's fucking eyes out. Him and Angela, they were like Bonnie and Clyde—maybe occasionally too fast on the trigger, but still, together for life.

Yeah, Max wanted Angela, he wanted her bad. He wanted to cop a real good feel of that rack, too, but he had to see what she wanted first. Naturally it was money but, hey, he couldn't exactly blame her for that. Max had always been her Mr. Moneybags, her go-to guy for the green. And, he had to admit, her desperation was more than a bit of a turn-on for him. He didn't know what she'd done to fuck up her life this time but it must have been something big, maybe the biggest yet, because she was clearly at the end of her tether. Man, Max loved playing this role—Max Fisher the hero, Supermax swooping down to save the day.

But he wasn't going to bail out the psycho bitch just for the hell of it. His mind was working double-time—when wasn't it, right?—and he was thinking, How could he use this? Yeah, Rufus had invited him in on the break, but Max always liked to have a Plan B. Come on, let's face it, Rufus didn't have all the seeds in his apple. He probably had one-tenth or, hell, one hundredth the intellect of The M.A.X. Rufus had claimed some friend of his, some fucking gangbanger, would be waiting in a getaway car after the break, but did Max want to gamble his life on that? Fuck, Max had always been the Big Boss; he wasn't exactly comfortable letting some street thug he hadn't even met call the shots.

Which was why he'd slipped Angela a note to get weapons and a car. Knew he could trust the bitch as long as he was the one paying her. He figured he'd hit her with more instructions the next time he saw her. And, oh yeah, he knew she'd be back. Show Angela some moolah with the promise of more to come and you'd hooked her for life. It was what he loved about her. That, of course, and her tits.

Leaving the visitor's room, Max headed back to his cell. Sino was due to return from the hole tonight and, for the first time, Max caught a whiff of the riot in the air. It was a certain tension you could almost reach out and touch. Everyone was being ultra-careful, keeping their faces down and avoiding eye contact. The gangs were huddled together and the guards, the bulls, were way nervous. Tooling up, yeah, that was it. The gangs were stockpiling, shivs, crowbars, acid in bottles, you get that shit thrown in your face, that's all she wrote. Plywood was disappearing from the woodshop and clubs were being honed for maximum damage.

Max was getting a little concerned. All the talk about riots was cool and everything when it was all talk, but now it was getting a little too real, too imminent. But he psyched himself back up, telling himself he had the white supremacists all in his corner, plus Rufus. No one was gonna let The M.A.X. get hurt.

Straddling both sides, playing the middle, that was the way to go.

Rufus told him their homies had some serious armament ready to roll and even though some of them muttered about the white boy being part of the crew, Rufus slapped them down.

To sweeten the pie, Max had told him, "My main man, we get out of here, I'm going to set you up in a penthouse, lots of white meat and all the white powder you could stuff up that massive nose."

But the Crips, that was a different story.

Rufus said, "That Sino, he got a hard-on for yo' ass, boss. He get out, he gonna try to waste yo' ass in the craziness and shit."

That worried Max a little till Rufus said, "No worries my man, they let him out, Sino gonna be washing his brown ass in de shower and, shit, I settle his jones right there."

Meanwhile, Rufus finally filled him in on the escape plan. It was so shot full of holes, Max couldn't believe it. In the smoke and mayhem of the riot, Rufus and crew were gonna hijack a laundry van and just mosey on out the main gate before full lockdown happened. They already had the uniforms, hidden away in a corner of the laundry room.

Could work, maybe, but Max was amazed. This was the plan they'd be working on for years? Max had figured they'd have a tunnel, a guy working on the inside, *something*. But he didn't want to ruin the party by bringing up any, like, doubts. Besides, he figured sometimes you did better going with something so basic, so crude, no one would ever imagine you'd try it.

When Rufus asked, "Boss, can you handle hardware, yo?" Max nearly sneered. He was the guy who'd emptied a full clip into the meanest muthahs you'd ever meet. Yeah, he could handle hardware, yo. He told Rufus all about the Colombians he'd smoked that time in Queens. Actually, he'd only shot one guy, and it had been a wild lucky shot, but like a fish story it got bigger with each telling. In the latest incarnation he'd smoked three sick-asses all packing serious heat.

Max went, "Get me a Mach 10, it's like my weapon of choice."

Rufus stared again at this stone cold killer, said, "Sound like you good to go, boss."

The Crips started the first step in what would be an out-and-out conflagration, burning their mattresses, taking a bull hostage. Later, the white supremacists cornered Max in the canteen. The leader, Arma, sitting Max down at his table, asked, "What's the deal, dude?"

Max, delighted to be called dude, said, "Ready to rumble."

"Ready? Man, it's already started. The Crips are burning mattresses, getting everything riled up, and they're coming for you first."

Max, terrified but not showing it, said, "I guess we'll just have to go medieval on their inferior asses."

Arma asked, "Their top guy, that Sino, how good is he?"

Max gave his superior laugh, made a show of looking at his watch, said, "About now, he's having the last shower of his life, he's going *clean* down the drain. One of my boys is helping him soap up as we speak."

Arma was impressed, said, "I'm impressed." Then he said, "But speaking of your boys...the niggers...*my* boys are a little concerned how much you're hanging with them."

Max leaned over, whispered, "They're gonna burn, and you my man, you're gonna own this joint."

He stifled a chuckle, thinking, *What's left of the fucking place*.

Arma said, "You're one cold cracker."

Max, standing, said, "You ain't seen nothing yet, dude."

Left him with his mouth hanging open.

Fifteen

There's an armor the city makes you wear and look at him defenseless,
helmet dropped back blocks ago, no arm among enemies strong enough
to string the arrow that could pierce his skin, rendering all cowards.
Let us bow. No one bows.
COLSON WHITEHEAD, *The Colossus of New York*

Sebastian was in New York. He did not want to be in fucking New York and he certainly did not want to be in New York with a homicidal Greek who smelled of olive oil all the time.

Yanni had never once let him out of his sight and two days after their first meeting had bought tickets to America, saying, "We get this done now."

Sebastian was seriously afraid of the maniac. If he had demurred, he was sure the crazy bugger would have slit his throat. He tried to look on the bright side, maybe they would score some serious dosh off Angela. Assuming they could ever find her.

What did irritate Sebastian a tad—well, ok, a lot—was that Sebastian was paying the freight. Yanni had disappeared with the biggest of the paintings; it had turned out to be the real deal, a bloody *Constable*, and he'd promptly fenced it. He'd flung ten large at Sebastian and said, "Your share."

Was he going to argue that the scoundrel had probably gotten a damn fortune for it, hell of a lot more than twenty K? He took the cash, and talk about damn cheek, Yanni made Sebastian pay for the tickets, in business class no less. Put a hell of a dent in the ten.

Yanni carried on scandalously on the plane, drinking champagne like it was water, leering at the hostesses and, when the in-flight movie came on, something starring Nicole Kidman, he kept nudging Sebastian and making lewd comments. Sebastian tried to act like he wasn't with Yanni, knocking back gin and tonics like a good un and trying to make sympathetic eyes at the stewardesses, as if to say *I've nothing to do with this cretin.*

In New York the heat and humidity was fierce and as Sebastian wiped his brow, Yanni scoffed, "This is *tipota*, in Santorini we see this as mild spring day."

Sebastian, his lined suit creased beyond repair, felt a hatred for this bounder like he'd never felt in his whole shallow life and resolved, soon as this business was concluded, he was going to kill the fucker slowly and whisper as he died, "That's not heat, brother, it's just a mild slashing of your olive stinking throat."

Ah, the things to look forward to.

Then they were in a cab and heading for Queens. Who'd said anything about staying in Queens? Didn't the fellow have the decency to consult him about their travel arrangements? He was planning on getting a couple of rooms at the Mansfield, a small hotel he'd read about in a cheap mystery novel once; it sounded classy and was right across the road from The Algonquin. Couldn't ask for a better pedigree than that. But Yanni, lighting up a Karelia in the cab, didn't care about pedigree. So off to Queens they went.

Blowing smoke in Sebastian's face, Yanni said, "We stay with my family in Astoria, they help us track the she-devil. She has Greek blood, they will track her down."

Sebastian finally found his voice, said, "Actually, old chap, I'd rather stay in midtown and we can meet up later, let you reunite with your family in peace."

Yanni, his eyes as black as hell, squeezed Sebastian's thigh, hard—the animal had a grip like a vise—and said, "You don't make decisions. I tell you how it is, you say *epaharisto poli*. You get to leave when this is done, you understand, *mallakas*?"

He did.

The family were a nightmare and, lordy, how many of them were they, enough to storm Manhattan by themselves...and noisy, radios blaring, everybody roaring in Greek, tons of kissing and hugging, only not for Sebastian, whom they looked at with derision. No one said a word to him. It was like *My Big Fat Greek Wedding* without the one-liners.

At dinner, more talk in Greek. It sounded like six arguments were going on at once. Sebastian couldn't understand a thing, just wandered around, trying not to get in the way.

One of the uncles, he noticed, had his wallet sticking out of his back pocket, just begging to be snatched. Sebastian often wondered why people were careless with their valuables. Were they trying to give their money away? Out of sheer boredom, Sebastian snatched it, not expecting to find much. The guy's hair was a mess and he was wearing a horrendous shirt open to his belly button, proudly displaying a chunky wooden necklace—not exactly the look of a man of wealth.

When the fellow discovered his wallet was missing there was the usual fuss with everyone talking at once, helping him look around for it. During the commotion, Sebastian managed to slip out of the apartment without Yanni seeing. He sprinted around the corner and then two more blocks, hopped a turnstile. A subway was at the station, ready to depart, and Sebastian yelled, "Hold the doors!"

A homeless guy put his hand in front of one of the doors, delaying the close, and Sebastian managed to slip inside in the nick of time.

"Thank you, squire," he said. If he'd had some American coins he would've tipped the kind fellow, but he didn't. He settled for shaking the man's hand, a gesture neither of them enjoyed very much.

He rode the subway into Manhattan, proud of his ingenuity. He was a cunning ol' chappie, wasn't he?

It had been ages since he'd been to the city and he was planning to check into his usual room at his usual hotel—those kind fellows always gave him the top floor suite—and then take in some of the sights. He could do with some good food as well. There was a Brazilian restaurant in midtown he quite liked where the maitre d' was a good sport and always gave him the best table in the place and, oh yes, free drinks. He didn't know what they put in those bloody drinks but the last time he'd gone there he'd left so drunk he'd fallen over a pile of garbage on the curb and not gotten up for the better part of an hour.

At the Fifty-ninth Street stop, Sebastian disembarked and was about to climb the stairs when he heard, "Where you think you going, Brit boy?"

He thought he must be hallucinating but he turned around and sure enough Yanni was there. The bloody hell?

Covering his anguish with a sarcastic grin, Sebastian said, "I was just going for a bit of a stroll, care to join me?"

Back in captivity, or Queens, Sebastian spent days watching reruns of *The Odd Couple* and drinking that thick treacle they called coffee. The only thing that made it at all palatable was if you put a nip of Metaxa in it. And Heavens to Betsy, the Greeks might be a pain in the arse, no slur on their homoerotic heritage, but they sure did keep an awful lot of booze in the house.

Another saving grace: One of the women of the house, Irini, had that dark sultry look, the doe-brown eyes and one of those lush Greek figures that so quickly ran to fat but until then was simmering hot. Her English was almost American, with only a slight Greek inflection. She was forever cleaning and each time he got a buzz building, giggling away at Oscar and Felix, there she'd be, telling—not asking, mind, telling—him to move his big English legs out of the way. The drinks, the reruns, and Irina helped him keep his mind off his situation.

Which was looking worse each day. The men were pulling

out all the stops to find Angela, but so far had found nothing, zilch, *tipota*. Like she'd vanished off the island of Manhattan, assuming she'd actually made it there in the first place. And Yanni's brood were seriously pissed. The Greek network was good and they prided themselves on tracking any Greek, anywhere, but it wasn't happening. And Sebastian was worried all that anger would wind up being let out in his direction someday soon.

Irini, hands on her hips, her wedding band shining, asked Sebastian, "Why you no help the men, you sit here all day, doing nothing?"

But he spotted a slight sheen of moisture above her lip and realized, this filly wanted rogering, a tad of the old Billy Bunter. And by golly, he was the chap to do it.

He said, "I could find her in five minutes."

Her eyes widened, and she asked, looking a bit like a mare in heat, "How?"

He gestured around the cramped living room, said, "They keep me a virtual prisoner, if I had access to a laptop, I'd have her tracked in no time."

She said, "I have a laptop. For my studies."

He wondered if there was a course in sweeping.

She lowered her eyes demurely, said, "It is in my bedroom."

He rose languidly. Sebastian tried never to do anything in a hurry unless it was...flee.

He said, "Show me what you've got."

Her room was filled with talismans—the evil eye, a mega statue of Makarios—and lo and fucking behold, in the middle of all this devotion, a poster of Guns N' Roses.

That was all she wrote. He rode her on the flokati rug and get this, the bitch bit him, twice, till he asked in his best Brit tone, "Try not to bite the merchandise."

Afterwards, still sweaty and naked, he opened the laptop

and got Google to work its dark magic. His one idea was to find an address for Angela's ex, that Max Fisher bloke she'd complained about so much. Instead, he read about Fisher's bloody arrest. He was simply appalled to discover that Fisher had been a drug dealer. What sort of man had Angela been associating herself with? As if there had been any doubt, he was certain now he'd been the classiest lay she'd ever had.

But arrested, this wasn't good at all. He'd been hoping Fisher could help them find Angela. How could he help them from a jail cell in Attica?

But then he thought, who knows. That Hannibal Lecter chap had been able to help Jodie Foster from his jail cell in that movie, the *Lambs* one. Maybe this Fisher could be of at least *some* use.

When you've only got one straw, you grasp at it.

One article from the *New York Post* gave the address where Fisher was serving his sentence; that not only meant Sebastian knew where to find him, it also meant Angela knew. He'd have laid stiff odds that she had paid him at least one visit there, and who knows, maybe she'd come more than once. Maybe he'd know where she was and could steer them to her.

Sebastian was downright proud of his ingenuity. A bloody Sherlock Holmes, he was. It would have taken the Greeks, what, five years to come up with this angle?

Irini gave him a cold Amstel and, by golly, it was good. She said, "You must be quick."

He winked at her, said, "You sang a different tune on the rug."

She said, "If Marko comes home, he will cut your balls off."

He got right on it.

Sixteen

*The man who shoots people in the legs for effect,
thinks that I might have been unnecessarily violent?*
ALLAN GUTHRIE, *Two-Way Split*

First thing Sino was gonna do when he got out—come at that *bandajo* Max Fisher hard. His two weeks in the hole, he been thinking about that shit all the time, thinking of different ways to make the man feel pain.

Fuckin' Fisher. Sino shoulda taken his *gorda* ass out himself, made a mistake out saucering that shit to that *puta* Carlito. You can't trust a Mexican to do nothing 'cept make burritos and even then, check out all the PR's they hire at Taco Bell.

Fourteen *dias* in the hole and it didn't break Sino at all. Made him stronger, more *duro*. He spent the time workin' out down there, doin' a thousand push-ups a day, and thinkin' maybe he do Fisher with his hands. Take his time with it, maybe start in on his face, to hear some bones breakin', that was always a lot of fun. Fisher, the *bandajo*, would be screamin' and beggin', and that'd only get Sino goin' more. Maybe he'd break his arms, then his legs, all the bones in his body one by one, till he was one big pile of *maricon* bones. But he'd still be alive 'cause, yeah, that's what Sino wanted, to make the man stay alive, to keep feeling pain.

Or, maybe he should burn Fisher's ass? Yeah, seeing a man die in *fuera* was like a fuckin' fiesta.

Wait, hold up, Sino had a better way to do it. He'd get a shank and cut him up real good. Name's Fisher, right? So Sino gonna cut him up like a fish. Do it nice and slow too. Little cuts first, make the man see some blood, then get in deeper, make him see some *real* blood. He'd cut his whole body up but save the best part for last. Man say he cut a man's dick off, like to talk about it all the time? Maybe Sino gonna cut off Fisher's dick, feed it to him, *then* kill him.

Make that *bandajo* wish he never took that pie from Sino.

Angela had the cash, now all she had to do was trade it for the weapons and the car Max wanted. Way back, her boyfriend Dillon, that wannabe boyo—and what a piece of work he'd been—had introduced her to Sean, a genuine boyo, as lethal as they came. She'd seen him roll a dead cop in a blanket and dump him like an old carpet. Sean was from that fierce and ferocious school of old paramilitaries, the sort that'd never surrender, they'd sooner go down in a blaze of armalites and were always tooled to the max.

Sean, whose only claim to an income came from irregular shifts as a taxi driver, had a stammer and an atrocious record with women. He'd get seriously drunk, approach the most attractive woman in a room, and with his stammer go, "I'm Se…a…n… I've…n-n-n-n-n-o…job……will you let me r-r-r-r-r-ride you?"

Subtle, right? It was certainly clear and direct communication, but he was batting zero.

Angela knew he had the hots for her, due to the drool that leaked from his lips any time he looked at her. Time to make it sing.

He lived in an abandoned warehouse on the Lower East Side. He didn't bother too much with security. His rep was well known—you rip off the boyos, dig a deep hole.

Angela knew how to visit a murderous mick: Bring a seven course feast—six bottles of the black and a liter of Jameson.

She climbed the shabby, worn stairs to his apartment on the second floor, seeing rats scurrying in the stairwell corners. They didn't trouble her. After Greece, four-legged rodents were the least of her fears.

She knocked on his door, which had a massive Green Harp on it. He pulled it open and she thought, *Jesus, he's gone downhill*.

Never an oil painting, he was dressed in a Galway Hurling T-shirt and baggy combats. He was barefoot and his face, under the red beard…it looked like someone had taken a blowtorch to it. Probably someone had—though Sean was still here, so whoever did it was surely now feeding whatever still swam in the East River. She noticed the SIG in his left hand, held casually.

Took him a moment to register who she was, then he went, "A…n…g-g-g-g-g-gela?"

Nothing wrong with his memory.

She smiled, said, *"Conas ata tu?" How are you?*

You want to lure a boyo, talk Irish.

He smiled. Most of his front teeth missing, and his gums, burned because he'd forgotten to close his mouth when they used the blowtorch. She did the real smart thing, the sort of move that kept her, if only precariously, in the game. She hugged him tight. He was an Irish man, and with that bust up against him, he was already signed, sealed and fooked.

Then Angela said, "I'll be needing some weapons and a car," and Sean went, "I d-d-d-dri-v-ve a c-c-c-c-c-c-c-c-cab."

She oh so accidently brushed his cock. The bastard was rock hard. She wondered how long it had been since he'd gotten laid. Yeah, how long since the Pope gave a shite?

She said, "Let's have a jar. You still drink, Sean, darling?"

Let sensuality leak all over his name. He'd come before the next teardrop fell.

He said, "I…I…t-t-t-t-t-ta…k-k-k-ke……the od-d-d-d-d-d jar, right……e…n-n-n-nough."

She went into his tiny kitchen and surprise, it was spotless. Bachelors, they went one of two ways, became total slobs—i.e., Max—or became obsessive-compulsive. He was the latter.

She found some Galway Crystal Glasses, those babies went for a fortune, weighed serious tonnage and were no doubt an heirloom from his beloved mother. The micks loved their Mums; no doubt there was some fookin' Irish lace tablecloth neatly folded and lovingly stored somewhere in the place. She made the working stiff's version of *The Black and Tan*, always amused the boyos, and they were one hard fooking act to amuse. Ask the Brits.

A large shot of the Jay and add just the right amount of Guinness, it was an acquired taste but it got you there, fast.

She brought the glasses in and, indicating the immaculate sofa, cooed, "Join me *a gra*."

Nervously, he did, his combats showing a massive tent. She handed him the glass, said, *"Slainte amach."*

The very personal version of cheers.

His hand shook as he took it and they clinked the precious glasses and drank deep. Well, Sean drained his, and she hopped up, said, "Let me freshen that, *amach*, and we'll talk guns and why you're going to help me."

She added three fingers of the Jay and not so much of the black.

He half finished that, a dribble coming from his lips, tried, "A-a-a-a-ngela……I……d-d-d-d-dr…iv-v-v-ve… …a……cab."

She put her hand on his dick, said, "I always had a thing for you, Sean."

The continued use of his name and with such tenderness, plus the booze, was really screwing with his head. Not that it looked like it took much, since the blowtorch incident; looked like his mind was mostly scrambled eggs anyway.

She unzipped him, asked, "Would you like me to take care of that stallion you have rearing up there?"

Would he fooking ever. He'd have sold the mother's linen, glasses and grave for it.

She said, "I'm going to be your woman, okay, darling?"

He nodded, too weak to speak, and she asked, "The guns?"

He stuttered, "How......m-m-m-m-m-man...y......d-d-d-d-o......y-y-y-y-you, you...y-y-you......w-w-w-w-w- want?"

Seventeen

He had to hit him, but only him and only once.
After that it was sadism.
JIM FUSILLI, *Closing Time*

In the morning before the night when all hell broke loose, Max met Paula for an interview session for the book. She'd arranged to have another private meeting, wearing something super low-cut, but this time the view didn't give Max any liftoff.

"Sorry, babe, the wedding's cancelled, kaput, finito."

Said it stone-faced, no emotion, figured, Why sugarcoat it? Gotta hit hard, hit low, and hit early. And, man, he loved delivering bad news—what a fuckin' rush! It reminded him of the days when he was a CEO and he got to fire people. That was the best part of his job—crushing the assholes' dreams, watching them fucking melt.

"Oh," she asked, "and why's that?"

He could tell she wasn't taking it well. She'd probably been planning for the big day, telling all her friends. Fuck, she'd probably had the band picked out.

"No offense, baby, but something bigger and better came along. A lot bigger and a lot better."

Still hurting she asked, "This won't affect the book, will it?"

"No, my motto is, Always do what you say you're gonna do."

"All right, then," she said.

Was she stifling tears? Yeah, probably.

But she was a pro and managed to put it behind her. She started in with her questions:

Do you remember your first meeting with Angela Petrakos?

Was it love at first sight?

What are your impressions of her boyfriend at the time, Thomas Dillon, AKA Popeye?

It was rough for Max, having to relive that dark period in his life. Well, it wasn't really, but he acted like it was, knowing that sounding like it had been painful and traumatic was what sold books. Wasn't that how Oprah did it?

Then Paula started asking the harder questions like: Did you want to kill your wife? Did you plot with Angela and Dillon to kill your wife? And—the most potentially incriminating of all— did you hire Dillon to kill your wife?

If Max hadn't been flying so high, if he hadn't been in the midst of the power trip to end all power trips, he might've thought it over first and realized that confessing to his wife's murder, and admitting involvement in other murders and crimes he'd never been charged for, wasn't exactly in his best interest. But, hell, he let it fly. It was the equivalent of an outright confession, details that could get him the death penalty.

But right then Max wasn't thinking penalty, he was thinking publicity, he was thinking celebrity. That was what it was all about, right? Why hold back on the meat? You're gonna open the door, open it all the way.

And Paula, yeah, she was eating it up, telling him how excited she was about the project, and how the biggest challenge would be to fit all this amazing material into one book.

"I might have to make it into a trilogy," she said, and Max suddenly had a vision of the great Hollywood trilogies. *Star Wars, The Godfather, Shrek, Revenge of the Nerds.*

Imagining billions of dollars in DVD sales, merchandising, box office receipts, imagining walking onstage to accept his Oscar, Max made another impulsive decision.

He said, "You wanna get a first-hand look at The M.A.X. in action? What're you doing tonight at, say, midnight?"

"I don't have plans," Paula said. "Why?"

"How'd you like to ride in a getaway car with The M.A.X. and the rest of his crew?"

Yep, he told her all about the whole prison break, down to the last detail. Probably not a good idea to share this info with a woman he hardly knew—and, worse, a woman he'd just fucking *dumped*—but the escape was going to climax the greatest moment in his life, and he wanted his biographer there to witness it.

Later, heading back to his cell, Max was still pumped, thinking how lucky a thing it was to be Max Fisher, when he saw Sino. He'd probably just been released from the hole—he was in cuffs, being walked along by a guard. When Sino saw Max he stopped and the guard stopped with him. Sino gave Max the dead-eye glare, and his nostrils flared and his jaw shifted as he grinded his teeth. Max didn't back down. He shot back with his own mean-ass look, feeling like he was in a Western, two *hombres* staring each other down before the big shootout.

Then, suddenly, Max smiled widely. He made his thumb and forefinger into the shape of a gun, pointed it at Sino, and bent his thumb, pulling the trigger.

Man, the look on the big lump of meat's face was fucking priceless.

Paula went back to the motel, real disappointed. She wouldn't be the next Mrs. Max Fisher—how would she ever get over it? She laughed, thinking, *Was the guy for real or what?* Sometimes she thought he was fucking with her, with all the weird accents, the tough talk, the outrageous stories. It had to be some kind of schtick, a put-on. She was always waiting for him to crack up and say, Got you good there, huh? But it had never happened. And now he claimed he was staging a prison break? Probably a delusion like the rest of it. But hey, if it happened, she was going to be there to chronicle it. A first-person account of her subject escaping from Attica? It would be like Junger getting a chance to ride the boat into the perfect storm.

After she parked her car, she walked to the soda machine near the motel's office and bought a Tab—had to watch the figure if she was going to attract maximum babe-age. She figured she'd find some girl-girl porn on TV, rub one out, then try to find some decent food for lunch, not an easy task in this shithole town. After the incident at the bar, she was trying to keep a low profile. For all she knew it was legal to shoot dykes up here. Jesus, up here you wouldn't even know you were in New York. It was like a fucking red state.

As she headed back toward her room she stopped and did a double-take when she saw Lee Child walking toward her with another guy. What the hell was Lee Child doing up here? Was he on an author tour? Was the guy his media escort? Was there a mystery bookstore in Attica? Were there any bookstores in Attica? Were there any *books* in Attica? Hard to imagine that they even knew how to read up here.

Back in her straight days she'd had a big thing for Lee—who didn't, right?—and now she was so flustered, so starstruck, she couldn't even say hello or call out his name. She just watched with a dumb expression as he and the guy he was with went into their room.

She wondered: Why was he staying at this crummy motel? Wasn't he loaded?

Then she had a thought that terrified her—was he up here to try to steal the story out from under her? She knew he was doing well these days, at the top of the *Times* list and all, but every writer was always on the lookout for the next big thing. Hell, Paula herself had gotten most of her ideas for books at the bar at one mystery convention or another. Piss-drunk authors would tell her their best ideas, then forget the conversations in the morning. Maybe Lee saw The M.A.X. as his next blockbuster, his big move into true crime. The more she thought about it, the more sense it made.

She marched over to room 16, started banging on the door.

If Sebastian thought riding in an airplane with Yanni had been a dreadful experience, and spending time with his family in Astoria had been painful, then riding in a car with him was a full-blown nightmare. Had the fellow heard that there'd been an invention—a true breakthrough—called deodorant? Lordy, the smell of the man! And he didn't even have the decency to open the passenger-side window. He had all the controls on his side of the car, and he insisted on riding with the windows closed and no air conditioning. He mentioned something about allergies or whatnot, but Sebastian knew it was only to inflict maximum torture on him.

They passed a rest area and Sebastian had never been so excited to see a McDonald's in his entire life. Naturally the mad Greek wouldn't let them stop, though. He said something about "making good time" and "saving gas," but Sebastian figured he was just being an ass.

They'd left at the crack of dawn and arrived in Attica at around noon. Oh, lucky them! Talk about a party town! Sebastian honestly didn't know how his life had descended to this horrid state. A few weeks ago he'd been living it up on Santorini and now he was in a place that made those Western ghost towns you saw in the movies seem lively, being dragged around by the Greek from hell.

Their room wasn't ready. That's correct—room, singular. Yanni insisted on sharing a room, even sharing a king-size bed, so Sebastian couldn't slip away.

"Oh, come on now, you can trust me," Sebastian said as they

stood at the front desk. The sarcasm couldn't have been thicker.

"We sleep in same bed," Yanni insisted, "and you wear handcuffs."

The clerk heard this and with a concerned look said, "Uh, sir, this is a family motel."

"*Please*," Sebastian said. "I'll treat myself to a nice-looking chappie every once in a while like any good un, but I'd rather die than be a bottom for this cretin."

"*Cretan?*" Yanni said, deeply insulted. "Yanni is not from Crete, my family live on Santorini nine hundred years." Sebastian apologized for misremembering.

They waited in—where else?—the car until the room had been serviced. As soon as they got in, there was a hammering at the door. Sebastian answered it, saw a woman there, full figured, longish brown hair—attractive enough, but something about her made him think, *lesbian*.

She was saying, "Son of a bitch. You think you can steal The M.A.X. from me, you fucking British bastard."

Sebastian replied with an ultra polite, "Sorry, have we met?"

"Yeah, at last year's ThrillerFest. I told you how much I loved Jack Fucking Reacher, remember?"

Going along he said, "Oh, of course, silly me. How could I forget?" He had, of course, no idea who she was, but he said, "I'd invite you in, my sweet, but alas, I'm otherwise occupied."

Then Yanni was behind him, naturally, never more than Karelia spit away, and he asked angrily, "Who is this cunt?"

Sebastian said, "I say, old chap, steady on."

The woman looked at the Greek and said, "What did you call me?"

Sebastian, if not always ready, was most definitely nearly always prepared, had taken some hooch from the Greek's home, and said, "Now let's all calm down. Come in, gell, have a drink, and dammit, we'll thrash this out between us like civilized human beings."

"Where you get booze in this shithole?" Yanni asked, and the woman asked, "The fuck is a *gell*?"

But they took it inside, neither of them the sort to turn down a drink.

Sebastian got the two plastic toothbrushing cups from the bathroom and produced a battered tin cup he still carried from his Chatwin days, he really believed he'd lived like ol' Bruce. Then, with a flourish, out of the Gladstone bag came a bottle of scotch. Sebastian murmured, "Alas, we're all out of ice, the maid has the day off."

He poured lethal measures and nobody complained. He toasted, "To jolly good company, what?"

No one answered him.

They drank in silence, getting the good stuff to ignite in their system. When they'd killed the scotch and the contents of the room's minibar, the woman said, "You're not fucking Lee Child."

Sebastian nearly laughed at the double entendre.

"Child?" Yanni asked. "Where child?"

Then Sebastian, scotch calm, said, "Ah, you've rumbled me, the game is up as old Sherlock used to say, or was that afoot? I'm actually Lee's half brother. We don't get on, and truly, I'm chuffed with his success."

Yanni, tired of a conversation he was having trouble following, pointed his finger at the woman, asked, "Why are you here?"

She'd drunk the scotch way too fast and it loosened her tongue.

"I thought he was stealing my book," she said, wagging a finger in Sebastian's direction.

"Your book? What are you talking about?" Sebastian asked.

She told them all about some bloody awful book she was writing about Max Fisher and Angela, and about the murders

Fisher had committed, and how he'd apparently become a feared man in prison. Sounded like a real winner all right. The punters would surely be rushing to the stores to buy that one.

Then she told them about a prison break at midnight.

Sebastian had a lightbulb moment, said, "Prison break?"

"Yeah, there're going to be riots, big riots. I'm a big riot!" She looked at her glass. "What's in this shit anyway?"

Sebastian egged her on, going, "So about the prison break…"

"Oh, yeah, it's at midnight tonight, at least that's what The M.A.X. said. The M.A.X.!" She laughed. "You believe that's what he calls himself now? He put a 'the' in front of his name and he has initials. Initials! Is he a character or what? I'm gonna make a fortune on this book and Pulitzer, look out. Oh, and Angela, I'm dying to meet that crazy bitch. She's going to be in the getaway car with some IRA guy. Is this gonna be a trip or what?"

Yanni put a switchblade to the woman's throat said, "Shut up, cunt, and take us to this she-devil who killed my cousin. *Now*."

The woman continued to smile drunkenly until her eyes focused on the knife and she started to scream. Yanni backhanded her in the face and knocked her to the floor.

Sebastian upended his tin cup and, patting its bottom, drained the last trickle of scotch. "Oh, lordy," he said, "was that really necessary?"

Eighteen

Let the riots begin...

Max was dozing when the riot began. He was gently stirred by Rufus who said, "It's on, boss."

Max, still groggy, heard what sounded like the seventh circle of hell and smelled smoke, lots of smoke. He asked, "The riot?"

A click sounded and their cell door slid open.

Rufus said, "They already got in the control room, yo. The man, he gonna come down hard, we got to move, know what I'm sayin', make it to the laundry truck. Once they bring in the troops, we gonna be fried meat."

He handed Max a bandana, said, "Rap the rag round your mouth, breathe through your nose, and stay real close, yo. Gonna be biblical out there."

Max was terrified and exhilarated all at once, and the bandana, shit, he felt like The Boss. He grabbed the bottle of Chivas, swallowed a fiery amount and handed it to Rufus who drained the rest. Then Max picked up a broomstick they'd stowed under the bottom bunk, broke it in half, said, "Rock 'n' roll."

The tier was chaotic, cons running everywhere, and Max saw one of the guards being held by a Crip, broken bottle to his neck. The Crip looked at Max, winked, then slashed the guard's throat.

Max felt the Chivas rebel and he let Rufus get ahead as he bent over, gagging. Then, out of the smoke, came Sino, his face streaked with blood like war paint, like a deranged angel of death. He hissed, "Hey, *bandajo*, where you goin'? I'm gonna cut yo' ass in a hundred pieces and then I'm gonna burn yo' *puta* ass, bitch."

Max was unable to move and as Sino closed in on him he thought, *After everything, this is it.* He felt his bowels loosen and then Sino's eyes went wide, his mouth made a silent *O* and he looked down at the shaft of wood that had been driven through his chest. He fell forward.

Arma, leader of the white supremacists, bent down, put his boot on Sino's back, pulled out the shaft, said, "I'll be needing that, spic."

Max was trying to form words that would express his thanks when a crew of Crips appeared, armed with homemade clubs, knives, even a frying pan.

Arma turned to face them, then said to Max, "We'll go down like white men, right, boy?"

Max thought, *Like fuck we will*, and took off, looking back to see Arma disappear beneath a sea of Crips.

Then Rufus grabbed Max's arm, pulled him through the inferno.

Before Rufus could drag Max to the next tier, a guard came running. It was the guy, Malis, who'd once been nice to Max in the yard. He stopped, begged, "Save me."

A tiny con grabbed the guard and said, "Your face is dirty," and threw a jarful of acid at him. Max watched in disbelief as Malis' face began to literally melt, peel off in layers. The con dropped the empty jar and ran, a knife coming loose from his belt and clattering to the floor as he went. Max whipped it up almost by reflex, grateful to have something deadly he could hold in his hand rather than just a broken broomstick.

Rufus was pulling Max along again, going, "Gotta get yo' ass in gear now, boss."

As Rufus dragged Max through the smoke and chaos, it hit Max hard that he hadn't killed anybody yet. What the fuck? He was The M.A.X., the alpha dog, the Big Boss, the Springsteen of the Big House, and he was what, getting yanked along like he was some kind of fucking sissy? He had to take somebody out, that's what he had to do. His rep was on the line. He had to show Rufus that The M.A.X. was one sick-ass muthafucka. Also, he knew that this was a moment he'd look back on his entire life. This moment would define him, make him proud. Didn't all the World War II vets go on and on about all the nips they took out? Didn't the Vietnam dudes reminisce about the gooks they'd blown away? This was Max's war, the high point of his life, and if he choked now, didn't come through with at least one killing, he'd never forgive himself.

They went down a flight of stairs, stepping over bodies, then headed toward the delivery entrance. Up ahead in the smoke Max spotted a guy. He had a flashback to the time he'd killed all those drug dealers, blew 'em to smithereens, and that gave him the confidence boost he needed.

Holding the knife, he broke free from Rufus and charged the guy. He was roaring as he ran, making crazed animal noises like Mel Gibson in *Braveheart*. He plunged the blade into the guy's back, and it was fucking harder than it looked in the movies. It wouldn't go in more than an inch at first and he had to use both his hands to work the blade in there. The whole time he was screaming his ass off, drooling like a rabid dog.

When he was through he let go of the body, letting it fall to the floor. The guy looked dead all right. Fucking wasted.

He wiped the blade of the knife on the dead man's pants, then looked back at Rufus, expecting to see a terrified, respectful look from his soldier.

Instead he got, "Fuck you do that for, boss?"

Max, still pumped, said, "Didn't like the way fuckin' Crip was lookin' at me. Bro had to go."

Rufus said, "Man, that wasn't no motherfuckin' Crip. That was our ride, yo."

Max didn't know what the fuck he was talking about, said, "The fuck're you talkin' about?"

"That was K, man. He was with us an' shit. He was gonna ride our asses out in the truck."

Max felt like, well, like a fucking moron, but he had to cover and went, "Your *man* was planning to double-cross us. Soon as we cleared the gates he would've wasted us both."

Rufus wasn't buying it, went, "K wasn't gonna double-cross nobody, yo. K was my boy an' shit. Man, I been with the nigga since I got inside, knew the bitch on the outside, too. I been plannin' this breakout with him, shit, since my first day in lockup."

It was starting to hit Max just how badly he'd fucked up.

He said, "I know you don't wanna believe your own man would fuck you over, but I got spies working for me, okay? And this guy, J—"

"K," Rufus said.

"K, L, M, N, O, P," Max said. "Who gives a shit what his name was? The guy was a fuckin' rat, all right? So forget about him. He's better off dead."

Max reached into K's pocket, found a set of keys, then Rufus said, "Yo, K got the uniforms too. Gotta put that shit on."

Max found the uniforms, tucked under K's shirt. They were bloody, but what the hell were you gonna do?

They put the uniforms on as fast as they could, then they made it all the way down and the laundry truck was right there. Shit, this stupid plan might work.

They were about to get in when Max heard, "Hey, dude."

He turned and saw Arma, battered, covered in blood. Shit,

he looked like Bruce Willis at the end of the first *Die Hard*. He was still holding the bloody wooden shaft, going, "You ain't turnin' nigger on me, are you, dude?"

Angela and Sean were in the sedan at the meeting point, about a mile away from the prison. They could hear the alarms sounding and knew the riot was on. Angela had taken time over her appearance, thinking, What does a girl wear to a riot besides a fookin' Kevlar vest? She'd decided on basic black. Not only was it appropriate but it made you look thin, she hoped. Sean, well fashion was not his gig. He was wearing the green army jacket beloved of the boyos, they practically slept in them, along with his *de rigeur* combat pants and Doc Martens with steel toe cap. On his knee, he had a pump shotgun, and there was a mess of other weapons in the back. Angela had selected the SIG, she was familiar with that baby and you know, it sort of accessorized her outfit. Sean reached in his jacket, took out a flask, drank deep, offered it to her, and she took it, swallowed, raw Jay and by Jaysus, it burned.

Sean said, "A...a...a......d-d-d-d-d-drop......of...of the...c-c-c-c-creature."

He reached in his other pocket. If he produced snacks, she'd shoot him.

He didn't, but he did take out a grenade.

Catching her eye, he said, "Been sav-v-v-ing it f-f-f-f-f-f-for...a...s-s-s-spec...ial...occ-c-c-c-c-c-asion."

Even from where they were, they could see the smoke rising from the prison and the wail of sirens had started, like a hurt banshee. The copters would be there soon. She looked down to check out the SIG in her lap and saw a tent in Sean's pants. She muttered, "Like, *now?*"

Not far from them but out of their line of vision were Sebastian and Yanni. They were watching Angela's car.

Yanni was slugging from a goatskin bag—where the hell had he got that?—and Sebastian knew it was ouzo. Sebastian was taking the traditional route, gin and tonic, in a plastic bottle. It was whispering to him, "Nothing to worry about."

Right.

In the distance, Attica was burning, but here things were calm. For now anyway. Sebastian had begged Yanni not to just rush over to Angela's car and blast away, and for once Yanni had listened to him. It was the possibility there might be money to be had if they waited for Fisher to show up that had convinced him. They were here to wreak vengeance—but a little profit would be nice, too.

Yanni had a Ruger and the metal glinted as he turned it this way and that, waiting. He handled it like someone who had long experience with weapons. Sebastian was carrying a Walther PPK, for the love of Bond and Britain. He'd once gone pheasant hunting and managed to hit the gamekeeper, to the delight and hoots of his fellow drunken shooters. He'd give a lot to be back there now.

Paula was lying across the back seat, still sleeping off her booze and the clout to the head.

Yanni shifted suddenly and they saw a laundry truck pull up. An old guy—Fisher—and a huge black man jumped out. They piled into Angela's car and the car pulled slowly away, no massive getaway, just a cautious stealing pace.

Yanni hit the ignition and smiled grimly, said, *"Poli mallakas."*

Sebastian took a long swig from the gin and hoped he wouldn't bloody castrate himself during the ride.

Max knew he needed to think of something quick, went with, "I was just here gettin' set to kill this here nigger."

Rufus, the fucking idiot, said, "You was doin' *what*, boss?"

Still calling him boss, just what Arma needed to hear.

But it didn't matter because Arma wasn't buying the crap anyway. He said, "What y'all wearin' laundry clothes for? Y'all tryin' to run out and leave your Aryan brothers to burn? I save yer sorry ass back there and you turn coyote and leave me?"

Max's mouth sagged open, but he couldn't think of anything to say. He couldn't figure out how Arma had survived the heap of Crips who'd descended on him.

"I shoulda known," Arma said. "Shackin' up with the dirtiest nigger in this here prison. He probably put so much a his black meat in you all them nights, he been gettin' to you, made you black yerself. Ain't that right, Fisher? You don't know what color you are no more, do you?"

The sirens were blaring. Lockdown was going to happen any second. If they were going to do this, they had to do it now.

"I told you," Max said, "I'm gonna kill the guy, but I want to do it in private. I just want it to be me and him, *hombre a hombre.*"

Arma said, "I'll show you how it's done," and the next second he was attacking Rufus, trying to stick his shaft into the big man's neck. Rufus was fighting back, but Arma was quicker and the wood gave him a longer reach.

Knowing this would be another defining moment in his life, Max went over and drove the knife into Arma's back. This time he knew how do it, getting it in the first time, through all the bone and muscle and stuff.

"Fisher, you fuckin' nigger," Arma said.

He tried to turn, bring his shaft up to use on Max, but he crumpled to the ground.

Holy shit, killing people was fun! Max felt like a hunter, like a real fucking man.

Max left the knife in Arma's back and said to Rufus, "You okay?"

Rufus said, "Yeah, just some blood, ain't no nothin'. But, yo, boss, you got some moves, yo."

They got in the truck and headed out of the prison. There was so much chaos at the gate, the guard took a cursory look at Max and Rufus and waved them through.

"We did it, boss," Rufus said. "We really fuckin' did it."

Max was still lost in his own world, high from killing Arma. No wonder crackheads killed people, it was fucking addicting. Max couldn't wait to kill again. He wanted more. More, more, more.

Rufus gave Max directions and he followed them. About a mile away from the prison on a dirt road they approached a dark sedan. Max drove the laundry truck off the side of the road, out of view, and then he and Rufus ditched the truck and jogged over to the sedan.

Angela and her IRA friend were in the front. Max and Rufus got in the back and Max said, "Where the fuck is Paula?"

"Who?" Angela asked.

"The big-chested girl? My biographer," Max said, like it was obvious.

"The fook're you talking about?" Angela asked.

He didn't have time to explain, or to wait.

"Drive," he said, and the IRA guy drove away.

Max leaned over the seat, gave Angela a big fat one on her full lips. Man, she smelled good, like fucking Irish Spring. He remembered how much he loved fucking Irish chicks and he couldn't wait to give Angela the meat tonight. He said, "Man, I can't wait to give you the meat tonight, bitch."

"Who're you callin' bitch, you fookin' cunt."

Ah, the mouth on her. He loved it.

Rufus was still babbling, "We did it, boss, we did it, yo. We really done an' did it."

Then Max looked back and noticed the car behind them. It wasn't directly behind them—it might've been thirty or forty yards back—but it was still unsettling to see it there, tagging along.

"I think that car's following us," Max said.

Angela looked back and said, "What car?"

"There's one car on the fucking road," Max said. "Pick one."

Angela was built, but he'd forgotten how dumb she was.

Then the IRA guy spoke his first words. Well, if you call it speaking.

"I'm p-p-p-p-p-positive…the c-c-c-car isn't…f-f-f-f-f-f-fah-fah-fah-fah…"

"The fuck is he saying?" Max asked.

"I haven't a clue," Angela said.

"He saying ain't nobody back there, yo," Rufus said.

Figured, two idiots could understand each other.

Max looked back again, but the headlights were gone.

"Just sit back and start celebratin', boss," Rufus said. "We did it. We really motherfuckin' did it."

Nineteen

I wanted more. Give me more.
MEGAN ABBOTT, *Queenpin*

Angela needed a shower, a drink, to get laid and to get—of course, as always—rich.

The drive to the Canadian border had been bizarre. Sean, muttering stuff in his stammer that nobody could follow and Max insisting they were being followed. She'd forgotten how paranoid he'd always been, long before anyone got hurt. And she was still seething about him "putting the meat to her."

He would, like fook.

Angela was plain dumbfounded by the huge black man. With one hand he could have strangled them all and instead, he was brown-nosing Max, gazing at him with, there was no other word for it, total admiration. Was it some kind of gay thing? Prison does weird shite to people.

They reached the border just before dusk and Sean pulled into a trailer park, said as he checked his notes and found a key, "W-w-w-we're......nu-nu-num-b-b-b-b-ber...t-t-t-t-twenty s-s-s-six."

Nobody was saying much as they trudged their way to the trailer.

Angela couldn't believe it, she had finally hit bottom: trailer trash. She'd be here for life, wearing denim shorts, her hair permanently in rollers, no AC, and three snot-nosed brats wailing at her for sodas. And she'd have no man, of course.

She shuddered.

In the car, Max had reached over, asked, "Cold? Wait till I get in you, you'll be so hot."

She'd nearly gut shot the bollix then and there.

Someone had made slight preparations for their arrival. There was coffee, a thermos, three bunk beds and, sitting in the middle of the trailer, a bottle of Jay and about twenty beers.

No food.

Angela heard Max whine, "No food?"

Then he grabbed the bottle of Jay, said, no, *ordered*, "Y'all grab some glass or other, The M.A.X. has a toast to make."

Jameson out of Styrofoam is a travesty but Angela figured it was one of the least of the sins on her conscience.

Max said, "I toast our valiant rescuers, Angela and..." He paused, getting ready for his renowned wit, continued, "Sh-sh-sh-sh-sh-sh-sh...Sean."

No laughter, and the Irish guy was giving him a look that said, "You're dead."

Angela could see Max was confused by how badly his humor had backfired.

He added lamely, "The joint hasn't been built that could hold The M.A.X."

Later, Rufus was making hungry noises and Max was famished too. Since Sean had already passed out drunk, it was decided Rufus and Angela would head for the nearest grocery store—a 7-Eleven off the highway—and stock up. Rufus would drive, stay out of view, and Angela would do the shopping.

At first, Angela was a little, well, concerned about being alone with Rufus. After all, he was a big, scary-looking guy and he'd been locked up so long, he probably couldn't wait to get his big mitts all over a woman. But after what she'd been through in Greece, Angela wasn't about to let a man get the best of her, no matter how menacing he was. She had a gun with her, in her handbag, and God knows she wasn't afraid to use it.

In the car, Rufus was going on, telling her how great it was to be in the "outside" again and how the first thing he wanted to do was go see his mama in Syracuse. Angela was starting to zone out when she heard the word money.

Rabbit ears up, she echoed, "Money?"

"Yeah," Rufus said, "from the job I pulled 'fore they sent my ass to Attica. Me an' my crew we robbed a bank and shit. Got two hundred somethin' thousand dollars, but they never found it 'cause I buried it in my mama's backyard, that's why. So when I get home, first thing I'm gonna do after I kiss my mama hello and eat some a her fine apple pie is I'm gonna dig up that money, then I'm gonna go off, live in Mexico."

Suddenly Angela saw Rufus in a new light. He was no longer a scary, dangerous escaped convict who might rape and kill her. Now he was the sweet mama's boy with two hundred grand in his backyard who was going to be her ticket to her new life. And, besides, she'd always liked black guys. Okay, not more than any other type, but not less either, and he was a big strong guy, he could protect her; and despite whatever awful things he might have done to wind up in prison, compared to some of the other men she'd dated he was practically a saint.

She wanted to make sure he knew she was available and interested. So she said, "Just so you know, I'm just here, helping Max out, for old time's sake. We're not together or anything like that."

She could tell Rufus wanted her badly. Jaysus, it looked like his dick was about to burst through his pants.

He said, "Yo, that's good, cause I like you and shit, yo. I think you fine. I never seen a set a titties on a white woman before like the ones you got. You got big ol' black titties, know what I'm sayin'? They kinda like my gran'mas. Yo, I don't mean I been lookin' at my gran'ma's titties an' shit, but you know what I'm sayin'."

Angela knew there had to be a compliment in there somewhere and said, "Thank you, I'm so flattered."

Rufus continued, "But the way it is, yo', I don' wanna move in on the boss's action, know what I'm sayin'? I know how much the boss love your titties too. 'Fore we broke out, every night he was goin' on 'bout your titties, goin', Wait till you see my bitch's titties. I ain't callin' you bitch, that what The M.A.X. be callin' you. He be goin', You're gonna love my bitch's titties, they so big, they're the best titties you ever seen. An' wanna know somethin'? Muthafucka was right."

Angela, thinking about that money, how it could change her fucking life, said, "Don't worry about Max. If you want my titties they're all yours."

They pulled into the lot next to the 7-Eleven.

Rufus cut the engine, said, "Mind if I kiss you? Been a long time since I kissed a woman. Talkin' about a natural-born woman, know what I'm sayin'?"

Angela batted her eyelashes, went, "I thought you'd never ask."

Wow, Rufus knew how to kiss! He was tender and slow and he really knew how to use that big, long tongue of his. Was Angela imagining it or was she feeling a serious spark between them? She couldn't remember the last time she'd enjoyed something as simple as a kiss with a man.

There was no doubt what she had to do: Ditch Max and go with Rufus. Max was broke anyway, so what use was he? And she had a feeling this Rufus thing had legs, it was the real deal.

Rufus waited in the car. Before Angela left he said, "I'll be missin' yo ass, baby." He was such a sweet man, so thoughtful.

Angela stocked up on all the food Max had instructed her to buy: Yodels, Ring Dings, Fritos, Pop Tarts, lots of Slim Jims, etc. As she was paying at the register, she noticed a dark blue car pull up in the parking lot out front and just idle there. She didn't think much of it, though, just collected her change from the guy at the counter and wished him a good night.

She was imagining life in Mexico, as Mrs. Rufus, when she stepped outside and noticed the guy walking toward her through the shadowy lot. She couldn't see his face well but, fuck, there was no doubt he was Greek, and he looked familiar somehow. Then he passed under a lamppost and she saw why he looked familiar. He was a dead ringer for Georgios. She remembered the woman back in Santorini, vowing vengeance for Georgios' murder, and she knew this had to be connected. A voice inside her head was saying, Oh, come on, stop with the paranoia, you're starting to sound like Max. The Greek network for tracking people down is good, but it couldn't be this fookin' good.

But she knew that little voice was fooking wrong as soon as she saw the knife in the guy's hand. He was coming at her, baring his teeth, and somewhere in the distance she heard a woman shriek. The man was almost on her, and he was saying something—it sounded like *"she-devil."*

She managed to reach into her handbag, grab the gun. Before the guy could reach her she whipped the gun out and fired a shot, hitting him right in his goddamn face.

Then she ran, past the guy's idling car, trying to get to Rufus. She didn't make it. She had her hand on the door when she felt an intense pain ripping through her chest. The next moment she was on the ground, lying on her stomach with her cheek on the pavement. She saw a blurry image of a guy leaning out the open door of the idling car, holding a gun. It was Sebastian, that bastard.

Her last vision was of Sebastian, smiling, blowing smoke away from the barrel of the gun. She couldn't believe it. Of all the guys who could've done her in, it had to be that useless fookin' wuss? Talk about last laughs. That God, he had some fucking sense of humor.

Twenty

*Because the way things turned out, hearing what
he heard, seeing what he saw, knowing what he knew,
it was no way to live.*
JOE R. LANSDALE, *Lost Echoes*

Sebastian was getting a tad cranky, just how long were they going to follow this bloody car? They'd dropped back when Yanni had realized they'd been spotted, but then had caught up with Angela again a few miles further on, and as far as they could tell, no one in Angela's car had noticed them since.

He had another shot of gin and realized he needed a piss and bad. Paula, awake now in the back seat, was scribbling notes—didn't that make her sick, writing in a moving car like that? He hefted the Walther in his hands and by golly it was true, the gun maketh the man. That and a Savile Row suit, carnation in the buttonhole, of course. The car in front finally showed brake lights and Yanni stopped, cut the engine. They could see a trailer park, and Sebastian thought, A rather shabby one, my dear.

Darkness was coming but they could see Angela, the Fisher chappie, some brooding-looking white guy in a combat jacket, and the mammoth black guy. Yanni raised his gun and hissed, "Now you die, you whore."

Sebastian could hear Paula take a deep breath and he put his hand on Yanni's arm, a very risky gesture, and said, "Steady on, old bean, you do it now, it's too quick, she doesn't get to *feel* it —and most importantly we don't get any money."

Yanni withdrew the gun, muttering a string of obscenities. Sebastian could swear his own beloved Mummy was in there.

Paula said, "I didn't know there was going to be, like, you know, shooting and stuff."

Yanni turned to her, spat on the seat, said, "Shut your mouth, you harlot."

Sebastian thought that was more than a little rude and really, wasn't it crossing the line? He began to wonder if ol' Yanni had just the *tiniest* issue with women.

The trailer door opened and Angela and the black chappie came out, got in the car and took off.

Yanni, putting the car in gear, asked, "What is this?"

Paula said, "Probably going to get supplies. There's gotta be a 7-Eleven close by. You got a trailer park, you got a 7-Eleven."

Sure enough they pulled up outside said establishment and, lordy, was Angela *necking* with the black fellow?

Sebastian muttered, "Get a room. And herpes."

Finally, she got out and went into the store.

"Herpes," Paula said. "That's funny, Max was just telling me the story today, how Angela gave him herpes and how she said she got it from her ex-boyfriend, the Irish hit man."

Just what Sebastian needed to hear—the bloody history of his condition.

"I kill the she-devil right now," Yanni said, leaving the gun on the seat and pulling out a long-bladed knife he'd brought along.

"Let's be sensible, shall we?" Sebastian said. "I wouldn't mind doing away with the cow myself, but I don't think you want to be committing a murder on CCTV now, do you?"

Paula, from the back seat, said, "Wait, you guys aren't serious, are you? You're not really going through with this, right?"

Then Angela was leaving the store, smiling blissfully, carrying an overstuffed bag of junk food, and Yanni was out of the car, charging her like a madman.

Paula shrieked, "Oh my God!" and then Angela pulled out a gun and shot Yanni right in the face. Sebastian had to give the ol' gell credit, she had some tricks up her sleeve. Or, rather, in her purse.

But Sebastian couldn't let her get any ideas and try to shoot him as well, could he? Beating her to the shot, so to speak, he aimed the Walther and fired at her back as she passed, hitting her spot on. Not bad at all. Rather like shooting pheasants.

Sebastian was still feeling right proud of his accomplishment when he remembered the black guy waiting in the car. He was going to walk over, do away with him as well, but, dammit, the car was already speeding out of the car park.

Watching Angela get killed had been sad and horrifying, of course, and the image of the puddle of blood pooling around her on the asphalt would stay with her forever, but Paula wouldn't have traded the experience for anything. What true crime author gets a ringside seat for a homicide? A double homicide if you included the crazed Greek. After *The Max* was written and published and beloved by millions, the demand would be huge for a book solely about Angela Petrakos. She was the ultimate femme fatale—hey, that wouldn't make a bad subtitle, got to write that down—and who would be more qualified than Paula to tell her story? The ideas were vivid, so fresh in Paula's head, she started scribbling them down in her pad, afraid she'd forget them.

She'd written maybe three pages when she snapped out of her writer's high and realized she was in the back seat of a car with Lee Child's homicidal half-brother driving.

Suddenly terrified, Paula asked, "What're you going to do to me?"

Sebastian said, "Nothing much. No offense, gell, but I don't really fancy lesbians, I'm afraid. And least when it's not a *ménage*."

He pulled over on to the shoulder, took all her cash and jewelry, and ordered her to get out of the car. She shut her eyes and cringed, afraid he'd shoot her, but he just said, *"Ciao, mi amore,"* and left her in the dust.

Twenty-One

*Shit, he thought, as his eyes glazed over
and the roaring in his ears slowly receded.
I can't believe I'm dying in a goddamn trailer.*
MICHELLE GAGNON, *The Tunnels*

When Rufus returned alone, Max instinctively got his piece and put it in the waistband of his jeans, like the cool guys did in the movies. Rufus entered the trailer, fell to his knees, sobbing like a baby, and began to spill out a story of some white guy offing Angela.

Max felt his heart lurch, Angela gone? He couldn't fucking believe it.

He shouted at Rufus, "Yeah, and how come you're still alive? And where's her body—you just left her lying there? I treat you like my son and this is what I get?"

He had his gun in his hand and could feel grief and rage engulfing him.

Rufus was pleading and crying and then Max heard him say he loved her. *Loved* her? His Angela? And, worse, Rufus was going on now about how they'd been kissing just before she got wasted, how she was the best damn kisser he'd ever met. *It was so tender, yo, so sweet.*

Kissing?

He put the first round in Rufus's belly—weren't gut shots supposed to be agony?—and Rufus stared up at him with shock in his eyes. Max jammed the barrel in Rufus's mouth, went, "Fucking kiss this."

Emptied the clip.

Sean had been in a drunken stupor but the gunfire woke him—you want a mick's attention, let off a few rounds. He staggered out of the back room, the pump shotgun in his hands and saw the black man's almost headless torso lying at Max's feet.

Sean looked stunned, like he was in awe of Max, and why wouldn't he be? Guy from Ireland, IRA connections, he must've seen a lot of crazies in his bedraggled life, but there was crazy and there was Max crazy. Max knew he took insanity to a whole new level. Nobody was as crazy as he was, nobody.

Sean carefully lowered the shotgun, then asked, "W-w-w-w-w-w-w-where's A-A-A-A-A-Ang-g-g-g-gel-l-l-la?"

Max said, "She's dead. The love of my life, mon cherie, mon amour, mon Juliette."

Sean said, "Sh-sh-sh-she...w-w-w-w-was...m-m-m-m-mine."

"Well she's no one's now," Max said. "Saddle up pilgrim, time to hit the trail."

They packed fast and burned rubber out of there like the very Hound of Heaven was after them.

Max, sipping from the remains of the Jay while Sean drove, began a long monologue about Angela and busts and dickless cracker kids. Then he punched Sean on the shoulder, a tear in his eye, and said, "Last of the *campaneros*."

Twenty-Two

Words are not as adequate as teeth.
TOM PICCIRILLI, *The Dead Letters*

Paula Segal was stunned. She had written what she felt was a very compelling proposal for *The Max*, which included a synopsis of the entire book, and pretty soon expected to be living the literary high life—author tours, press conferences, award ceremonies. One thing she wasn't expecting—rejection.

Her agent broke the news to her over—yep—lattes at Starbucks.

He said, "There was a fairly strong consensus among the editors I went out to. The material's simply too dark."

Paula was in shock. This had to be a bad dream, or at least a bad joke. Her agent would crack a smile at any moment, say, Had you going there, huh? And then unveil the real news, that there was currently a bidding war going on for the book. All the major houses wanted it, and it was only a matter of whose eight-figure deal to accept: Knopf's or Harper Collins'. Or maybe there was only one major player, Sonny Mehta from Knopf, and on a signal from her agent Sonny would come through the door, ear-to-ear smile, and give her a big welcoming hug and say, "Welcome aboard, hon."

But, nope, her agent was still looking at her with that helpless expression that she'd gotten to know all too well over the years as her fiction-writing career had descended farther and farther into the toilet. But this wasn't fiction, this was non-fiction, true crime. This was supposed to be where all the bucks were, and she had the inside track on the hottest crime story of the year.

"What the hell do you mean, too dark? It's crime, it's murder, it's drugs, it's a riot, it's a prison break, it's IRA hit men, it's cold-blooded murder. It's *supposed* to be fucking dark."

Paula was yelling. A few customers and the baristas were looking over.

"Believe me, I understand where you're coming from." Her agent was looking around, smiling apologetically. "But there's dark and there's dark. As Ken Wishnia says, there're twenty-three shades of black."

She didn't want to hear about fucking Wishnia, she wanted to hear about a fucking book deal.

"Okay, so we got some rejections," she said. "Big whoopty shit. What's the next move?"

Her agent looked discouraged again, said, "Well, there's the second tier, but if I'm being completely honest I think it's unlikely the second tier will be interested. I went out with this fairly wide and, just to be completely up front, we didn't hear anything very encouraging from anybody. They all said the same thing: subject matter too dark, characters too unlikable."

"Wait," Paula said, knowing what was coming next. "What do you want me to do? You're saying you want me to—"

"How about writing a young adult novel?"

"You've gotta be kidding. You want me to give up *The Max*, my baby?"

"It's not a matter of what I want," he said. "It's what the market wants. And the market doesn't want Max Fisher."

"Bullshit," Paula said. "Bull fucking shit."

She stormed out of the Starbucks, deciding, Fuck agents, she'll sell it herself. How hard could it be to sell a hot property, the next *In Cold Blood*?

She sent the proposal out with a well-thought-out cover letter to practically every editor in New York and they all had the same response—story too dark, characters too unlikable. It had to be collusion, some kind of conspiracy. Or maybe her agent was bad-mouthing her all over town? Something like that. Years as a telemarketer had primed her well for rejection, but hearing all the negativity about *The Max* was tough to take. She was doubting herself, starting to lose hope.

She was almost ready to give up, head back to the call center, when she opened a copy of *Time Out New York* and saw that Laura—yes, *her* Laura—was reading tonight from her latest book at the Barnes & Noble on Union Square. She thought, *Has to be a sign.*

She rushed to her salon, demanded an appointment even though her hairdresser's schedule was full for the day. When Sergio asked her what she wanted done she took out a copy of *Mystery Scene* with Laura on the cover and said. "I want to look like *her*."

Sergio gave her the Lippman do, a short bob, flirty and sexy but not too showy about it. Afterward she couldn't have been more pleased. She looked as classy as Laura herself. When Laura saw her she'd have to realize they were meant to be together. Drinks would follow, maybe dinner, another meeting or two. Maybe she'd eventually move in with Laura in Baltimore, or they could just travel around the world together, two hot literary goddesses on the road...

And in the meantime Laura would help her get *The Max* into the hands of an editor who didn't have his head so far up his ass he couldn't see Pulitzer Prize material when it was handed to him.

A few minutes after Paula arrived at Barnes & Noble, Laura entered, rushing in, taking off her coat as she went, elegant and graceful as always, smiling, saying hello to all her adoring fans. Paula, in the front row, was staring at her, trying desperately to make eye contact. Surely Laura would remember her from the bar in El Paso and from their Internet exchanges. But after apologizing breathlessly for being late—traffic, her cab couldn't *budge*—and telling an effortlessly witty story about her signing the night before at the Mystery One bookstore in Milwaukee, Laura went right into her talk, and then read from her latest Tess Monaghan mystery. The book was another winner, no surprise there. A line of about thirty people formed, and Paula got on it at the end. Her heart was racing. She was worried that she might actually pass out. How embarrassing would that be? Fainting at her future lover's book signing.

Finally it was Paula's turn. She handed over a copy of Laura's book and Laura, smiling, said, "Thank you so much for coming. Who should I make it out to?"

Paula thought, *It's not possible. She's looking right at me.*

Then she thought, Come on, cut the poor woman some slack. After all, she was a best-selling novelist in the midst of a major book tour. She was probably burnt out, that's all.

"You can make it out to me. Paula Segal."

Still no recognition.

"So how've you been?" Paula asked.

Now Laura looked at her, the first prolonged eye contact. She was squinting, trying to get it to click.

"You know, Paula Segal. We met at Left Coast Crime in El Paso a few years ago?"

Still nothing.

Trying to jar her memory, Paula said, "You know, Paula *Segal*. I was a Barry Award finalist. I write the McKenna Ford mysteries?"

After a few seconds Laura's face suddenly brightened and she said, "Oh, right. It's great seeing you again. How are you?"

"I'm fine, thank you."

Paula was trying to hold Laura's gaze, to let her know she was interested in a lot more than just getting a stupid book signed.

Then Laura said, "Should I make it out to you, McKenna?"

"No, my name's Paula."

"Oh, that's right, I'm sorry, Paula," Laura said. "It's been a crazy day. How do you spell your last name?"

"S-E-G-A-L."

Was it possible that Laura actually didn't remember her?

Nah, Laura had to remember.

"Yeah, so, I'm writing the Max Fisher story," Paula said. Then she couldn't help adding, "For Knopf."

Paula was proud of the way she'd just casually dropped that little lie, and prouder of how she'd been so modest about it. Like, Yeah, I've written the biggest true crime story of the new millennium, but it was no biggie, just another day in the life of a future Pulitzer winner.

Laura finished writing, handed her back the book, said, "I'm sorry, Fishman?"

"Fisher," Paula said. "You know, *Max Fisher*? The infamous businessman-slash-drug dealer who escaped from Attica last month?"

Laura looked lost then smiled and said, "I'm sorry, I've been touring for three weeks straight and I'm a little behind on the news lately. But that's great, congratulations. I wish you lots of luck with it."

The next guy in line was holding a stack of books and was inching closer. Laura was already smiling in his direction, making eye contact with him. But there was no way Paula was moving along—not yet anyway. She didn't want to blow her one opportunity. After all, when would she get a chance like this again?

"I was thinking," Paula said, "maybe we could go out for a drink after you finish up here. You know, just to catch up."

"Oh, I'm sorry," Laura said. "I'd love to, really, but I have plans."

"Just one drink," Paula said.

Shit, was she being too insistent? No, just eager, that's all, and there was nothing wrong with eagerness. Eagerness was the way she'd made it as far as she had. If she weren't an eager beaver she never would've landed the Fisher project in the first place.

But did Laura just say "I can't"?

Nah, must've heard her wrong.

"So what time's good?" Paula asked. "Maybe around eight o'clock, eight thirty?"

"I said I can't make it."

Paula was stunned, went, "Please, it'll be so great. We have so much in common we can probably go on and on, talking all night long."

"I'm sorry, but I'm actually having dinner with Dennis Lehane tonight."

Den, it figured. Paula knew Lehane from the convention circuit. Nice guy, he'd bought her a couple of beers at Bouchercon in Chicago. For an hour she'd gushed to him about how much she loved *Mystic River*—the book, not the film—but did he ask for her room key or even her phone number? Um, no. God, Paula was so glad she was through with men. But there was no way Paula was going to let fucking Dennis Lehane or anyone else get in the way of her and Laura. She decided to take a chance.

"But I love you," she nearly shouted.

Paula knew she'd rushed it, that she should've at least waited till they'd had a chance to talk a little. But desperate times and all that.

Laura seemed totally confused and maybe a little shocked. She said, "I'm sorry?"

"I've known it since we met in El Paso, Laura. We're soul mates, we have everything in common, we should be spending the rest of our lives together."

A bookstore employee came over and said, "You're going to have to step away, ma'am. Other people want to get their books signed too."

How had this happened? How had it all gone to shit so quickly?

"We have to be together," Paula pleaded. "I've read *Charm City* twelve times. I nominate you for the Anthony every year. I even read your fucking short story in *Bloodlines*."

"Ma'am," the bookstore employee said.

"Shut up, you skinny little bitch," Paula said.

Shit, did she really just say that? Why was Laura getting up, backing away? Why was someone yelling for security?

"Laura, wait, come back here!"

Paula tried to go after her but a security guard grabbed her and hauled her toward the escalator. Laura was receding into the distance and Paula found herself screaming, "We were meant to be together! You were going to give me a fucking blurb!"

But Paula couldn't even see Laura anymore.

"You're off my top friends on MySpace, bitch!" she yelled, her voice carrying as she was led out to the shameful street.

Twenty-Three

*We would all end up in an explosion of colliding bodies,
clogging the cosmos with flying shit.*
JIM THOMPSON, *Child of Rage*

Somewhere in North Dakota, Max and Sean crossed the border into Canada. Max didn't mind getting into the trunk, his only worry was that the dumb mick would forget to let him out.

Turned out his concerns were justified.

Over an hour after the border crossing Max was still screaming, banging, trying to get the fucker's attention. Good thing he had his piece with him and could shoot a couple of holes in the trunk or he would've suffocated. Still, for a while he thought he might die back there, trapped in a trunk. What a way to go. The gunfire had set up a whole range of odd sounds in his head and it was almost like music. He laughed out loud, thinking, Now there's a title for a book, *Trunk Music*.

See, The M.A.X. was always working the angles, never stopped with his sheer genius. You put some other bollix—and using the word, he shed yet again another tear for his beloved Angela —in the trunk of a car, he'd be screaming in panic. But The M.A.X., he was thinking up book titles.

Finally the idiot pulled over, opened the trunk, babbling, "S-s-s-s-s-s-sorry...M-M-M-Max. I fuh-fuh-fuh-fuh...gah-gah-gah..."

Max slapped him around a little, nothing too heavy. After all, he needed the kid, he was stupid but a good driver, another fucking Rain Man, and a big-time prison escapee like Max Fisher couldn't be driving himself around, now, could he? Yeah, the guy had been some kind of legendary paramilitary, but all the fight had gone out of him ever since Angela died.

It was starting to sink in for Max, just what he'd accomplished. He turned on the radio, listened to reports of the Attica riots on NPR as they drove. Forty-two people had been killed, including six guards and, of course, there was also Angela and Rufus and the crazy Greek, though the authorities hadn't put it all together yet. But who was left standing? That's right, the only legend in these here parts was The M.A.X.

And get this—the reports were calling him "armed and dangerous." Man, did that sound good! Meanwhile, he was a free man, in fucking Canada. It made Max want to weep. Maybe there was justice in the world after all.

Later, they stopped off at a shopping mall and Sean went to feed his face. There was a small bookstore and Max went in, looked at the bestsellers to see if *The Max* was number one yet. Nope. Zilch. Nada. The fuck was up with that? Some guy named Richard Aleas was selling well but no Paula Segal.

The clerk was eying him and Max, afraid he'd get recognized, figured he'd better buy something. He spotted the Will and Ian Ferguson book, *How To Be a Canadian*.

Bought that, the clerk asking, "On vacation?"

Max answered him in an Irish brogue, another little tribute to Angela, saying, "Ary, no, I'm over here to see me cousins."

Boy, he thought that was pitch perfect. The tiny germ of an idea was taking shape in his head.

While he was waiting for Sean to return he flicked through the book and found this:

There is nothing you can't discuss in Canada when it comes to sex. Do not talk about love, however. That makes Canadians uncomfortable.

Then, from behind him he heard, "T-t-t-tis me."

Here was Sean, ketchup on his upper lip.

Max muttered, "Fuck on a bike."

Across the mall from them were two Mounties and, seeing them, Sean said, "Th-th-th-th-they...a-a-a-a-a-always......g-g-g-g-get...their m-m-m-m-man."

Max, trying out some more Irish, hissed, "Don't you be drawing bad luck down on us, laddie."

Then he thought, Wait, was that more like Scottish?

They got back in the car, more of fucking Canada. Was this country, like, endless? They were in the middle of nowhere and Max saw a sign saying *Grand Prairie, 479 Kilometers*. Gee, now that was something to look forward to, a grand prairie. Jesus Christ, a guy could get fucking bored in this place. Where were all the goddamn people?

Meanwhile, Sean—Jesus, Mary and Joseph, the guy was getting on Max's fucking nerves. The constant stuttering, not understanding a goddamn word he was saying. They checked into a motel and Sean in the bathroom started going, "T-t-t-t-t...f-f-f-f-f-fah...l-l-l-l-lo-lo-lah..." Max screamed, "The fuck're you saying? Lolita? What the fuck about Lolita?" and Sean continued, "L-l-l-l...g-g-g-g-g-g-ga..." Max didn't know if the guy had a speech impediment or he was just a fucking moron, but there was a limit to how much more of this shit he could take. He was a patient guy but this was fucking ridiculous.

The next day, they were driving, continuing north and west. They bought burgers and were eating them on the side of the road, and Sean started going, "You want some k-k-k-k-k-k-ketch-ketch-ketch," and Max suddenly lost it and said, "I'll give you ketchup, you stuttering fuck," and shot the asshole in the head, in mid-stammer.

Max shot him again, and that shut him up for good.

He took Sean's wallet and passport and then pushed him out of the car, onto the side of the road, where there was a bit of scrub to cover the body. Then he wiped up the car as much as he could using the paper napkins from the burgers and took off on his own.

He kept the radio turned off, didn't want to hear about *armed and dangerous* or *hot pursuit*. Man, it was nice to have Sean off the board. In the silence, though, he could hear Sean's voice, going, *Th-th-th-th-they…a-a-a-a-always……g-g-g-g-get…their m-m-m-m-man*, and he almost wished the fuck was still alive, just so he could shoot him again.

He wouldn't have thought it possible, but Canada was even more boring when you were driving through it all by yourself. He was missing Angela like hell. He knew it was crazy to miss a bitch who'd fucked up his life twice and probably would have fucked it up again, but he felt like he'd lost a, well, a part of himself. Things just wouldn't be the same without her around. Even when he was locked up in jail, thinking he'd never see her again, it was nice knowing she was out there somewhere.

In Edmonton, he checked into a hotel under Sean's name, using the cash from Sean's wallet to pay. But this couldn't go on for long. The money would run out and then what?

He was drinking again—what else was there to do in Canada? It was too goddamn *calm* here, everyone was too goddamn nice. He needed edge, he needed assholes, he needed America. Besides, he was certain that while he was up here freezing his nuts off he was missing out on all his fame back home. That dame's book was probably exploding right now, it was probably bigger than *Da Vinci* and *Potter*, and Scorsese was probably filming the movie, or maybe Spielberg. God, Max loved that. Spielberg knew how to yank the heartstrings and when Max got sent away to Attica the whole audience would be fucking bawling.

If he was in New York right now he'd probably be mobbed by adoring fans, signing autographs. Instead he was holed up in a motel in Saskatchewan, or wherever the hell he was, living under the name Sean Mullan.

Then the idea hit him—a way to get back in the game, to get back on top. It was so obvious, he didn't know why he hadn't thought of it sooner.

A few days later, he drove to the Washington border, at the Pacific Crossing on Route 15. He did his DD of course, found out from some locals at the pub that the best time to cross the border was early morning, and that of all the border inspectors the young blond guy in the leftmost lane was the most lax. Max waited another couple of weeks for his beard to come in a little thicker, then he dyed it red.

The morning he was going to attempt to cross the border, Max checked himself out in the mirror, compared his appearance to Sean's passport photo. It wasn't too bad. Yeah, Max looked a lot older, but if Sean had put on some weight and started losing his hair since having the photo taken, it wasn't so far off.

All right, so maybe the resemblance wasn't there at all but, fuckit, Max had to give it a shot.

He drove to the border, stayed in the left lane. Sure enough, a young blond guy took his passport, asked, "Enjoy your time in Canada?"

"Yes, had me a great time," Max said.

Bingo, the brogue was working in full force. So far, so good.

The guy was looking at the passport, said, "I have an aunt from Ireland."

"Is that right, is it?" Max asked.

Who gave a fuck, but he had to keep the BS going.

"Yeah, from Limerick. That near where you're from?"

"No, me from Belfast," Max said.

Shit, that sounded more Tarzan than Irish. At least the lilt was okay. He had to stay with it.

"Oh, yeah?" the guy said. "It's rough over there, I imagine. Bombs going off all the time, right?"

Would the asshole let him through already?

"Oh, a few wee bombs," Max said. " 'Tis nothing."

The guy squinted, "You got anything on you? Any weapons?"

Max had unloaded all the hardware. Only had one piece, a SIG, tucked away just in case.

"No, no weapons, me afraid. Me left me weapons back in Belfast."

The guy looked at Max closely, squinted, said, "Why do I feel like I've seen you before?"

"Maybe 'tis an Irish thing," Max said. "Don't the Brits say we all look alike?"

He thought this would at least get a laugh.

"No, that's not it," the guy said. "You come through here before?"

Max, sweating through his shirt, said, "Sometimes. I have me family in Seattle and I visit them every wee while."

Fuck, he was losing it. The whole plan was going to shite.

"Irish family in Seattle, huh? How'd they wind up there?"

Max couldn't think of anything, said, "Gold rush."

"Gold rush?"

"Yes, 'tis an old wing of me family. 'Tis a rich wing, too."

"I thought the gold rush was California?"

"Aye, 'tis true, but they weren't the smartest people, me relatives."

The guy squinted at Max again, as if studying him, then smiled and said, "Well, welcome to America, Mr. Mullan. It's a pleasure to have you back."

Driving away slowly Max could barely contain himself. He was back on his home turf—America, the land of freedom. Yeah, okay, there was a downside, he had to be fucking Irish, maybe for the rest of his life, but hey, he could pull it off. After all, how hard could it be to be Irish? He already liked to drink and kill people, he'd be a goddamn natural.

Humming that anthem Angela used to sing, *The Soldier's Song*, he drove at a nice easy pace till he hit the open road. Then, thinking he better start getting used to his new identity, he shouted "Bollix to ye all!" and fucking floored it.

Don't Let the Mystery End Here.
Try More Great Books From
HARD CASE CRIME!

Hard Case Crime brings you gripping, award-winning crime fiction by best-selling authors and the hottest new writers in the field:

PIMP
by KEN BRUEN & JASON STARR

Former drug kingpin Max Fisher is back, with a new drug to sell, while a certain femme fatale from his past tries to persuade Hollywood that her and Max's life story could be the next big thing on reality television.

The Cocktail Waitress
by JAMES M. CAIN
"AN ENDING YOU'LL NEVER FORGET"—STEPHEN KING

The day Joan Medford buried her first husband, she met two men: the older man whose touch repelled her but whose money was an irresistible temptation, and the young schemer she'd come to crave like life itself...

Five Decembers
by JAMES KESTREL
EDGAR AWARD WINNER FOR BEST NOVEL OF THE YEAR

A shocking double homicide in 1941 Hawaii leads police investigator Joe McGrady overseas as the world begins to burn around him. "A crime epic for the ages," says Dennis Lehane.

The LOST Detective Novel
From the Creator of PERRY MASON

The KNIFE SLIPPED

by ERLE STANLEY GARDNER

Lost for more than 75 years, *The Knife Slipped* was meant to be the second book in the Cool & Lam series but got shelved when Gardner's publisher objected to (among other things) Bertha Cool's tendency to "talk tough, swear, smoke cigarettes, and try to gyp people." But this tale of adultery and corruption, of double-crosses and triple identities—however shocking for 1939—shines today as a glorious present from the past, a return to the heyday of private eyes and shady dames, of powerful criminals, crooked cops, blazing dialogue and wild plot twists.

RAVES FOR THE KNIFE SLIPPED:

"A remarkable discovery…fans will rejoice at another dose of Gardner's unexcelled mastery of pace and an unexpected new taste of his duo's cyanide chemistry."
— Kirkus Reviews

"A treasure that's not to be missed."
— Book Reporter

"A gift to aficionados of the Cool and Lam series."
— New York Journal of Books

"A time machine back to an exuberant era of snappy patter, stakeouts and double-crosses."
— Publishers Weekly

**Available now from your favorite bookseller.
For more information, visit
www.HardCaseCrime.com**